Love
Is Blind

Love Is Blind

Parry "EbonySatin" Brown
Pat Simmons
Lisa Watson

URBAN BOOKS LLC
www.urbanbooks.net

Urban Books, LLC
10 Brennan Place
Deer Park, NY 11729

ISBN 1-893196-63-1

First Printing February 2004

10 9 8 7 6 5 4 3 2

*This is a work of fiction. Any references or similarities to ac-
tual events, real people, living, or dead, or to real locales are
intended to give the novel a sense of reality. Any similarity in
other names, characters, places, and incidents is entirely coin-
cidental.*

Submit Wholesale Orders to:
Kensington Publishing Corp.
C/O Penguin Group (USA) Inc.
Attention: Order Processing
405 Murray Hill Parkway
East Rutherford, NJ 07073-2316
Phone: 1-800-526-0275
Fax: 1-800-227-9604

Just a Click Away

By
Parry "EbonySatin" Brown

DEDICATION

To all my girls: Nicolle, Michelle, Shanelle, Krystal, Krysten, Symoni and Nierah

ACKNOWLEDGMENT

First and always I must give thanks to my heavenly Father for the gifts He has bestowed upon me. For without Him I truly am nothing.

Very special thanks to Carl Weber for his vision and enthusiasm about this project. As always to my agent and friend, Portia Ophelia Cannon, who has done a superb job with negotiations and running interference; I must say a very heartfelt thank you.

When my heart beats, the rhythm it plays is Neville Abraham and I love you for what you bring to and out in me. For the part of heaven God has put here on earth, my gurls Glynda Ard, RaMona Williams, Wanda Wilson, and Twania Hayes; thank you for keeping me sane and knowing that time and space will in no way separate us. I could never do what I do without the very capable assistance of Chanté Sims. Your skill and dedication have turned *my* dream into *our* reality.

I'm sending a very special shout out to my author family who encourages and keeps a sistah forever on her toes: Victoria Christopher Murray, Travis Hunter, Pat G'Orge Walker, Blair Walker, Pat Simmons, Lisa Watson, Victor McGlothin and the scores of others in this literary struggle.

Lastly, but most assuredly not least, to the book sellers, readers and book clubs around the country who have embraced me since the beginning and have consistently supported me in all I've done; I humbly say thank you and hope to never disappoint you.

Chapter One

"RaMona's on line one for you, Ms. Ellington. Kamesha's cheerful voice startled Mysti as she sat with her finger perched on the left button of the state-of-the-art rollerball mouse staring at the word *personals* on Yahoo.com.

"Thank you, Kamesha." Mysti regained her composure. "Mona, my sistah. How are you? And before you ask, yes, I did get your invite to the pool party. You never give up, do you? And what is up with your boojetto friends giving pool parties in the middle of winter?"

"Gurl, why do my friends have to be all that? Besides, winter is not officially here for another week. It is eighty-one degrees outside! This is a party with at least twenty-five eligible, employed, benefited brothas, and you think I'm not going to invite my *boojie*, workaholic best friend? Besides, once you finally get out you always have a great time. Keith will be there." RaMona finally came up for air.

Mysti ignored the plug for RaMona's choice du jour. "Well, the jury could come back at any time. Be it tonight or next Thursday. I have to be available. But I will take it under advisement."

"I'm not taking no for an answer. This party is on a Sunday afternoon. There is no way you would have to work. You'd betta get out that black two-piece we bought last year on Paradise Island. You know if my thighs didn't fight for position, folks would be calling me KFC."

Mysti could hardly contain her laughter. "KFC?"

"Two piece and a biscuit, gurl!" RaMona laughed at herself.

"You're such a fool. But I *will* think about the party. I'm just not sure if I want to go to another one." Mysti kicked off her shoes and propped her feet on top of her desk, crossing her long, shapely legs at the ankle. "They make me feel like I'm a prime cut of beef in the Bristol Farms showcase." Mysti sighed. "But I sure could use a good time. I realized walking in from the trial today I've been consumed with this case and the three before that for so long,. I don't even have anyone to call to celebrate a victory."

"Oh? So what am I?"

"You're my oldest and dearest friend, but gurl, sometimes I just want to celebrate with someone I can roll over to the next morning and ask what's for breakfast. And I know you're feeling me. So don't even try to guilt me out here."

"Well, whose fault is that? All you do is work. I work harder at getting you a man than I did for my damn self." Mysti could feel RaMona snapping her neck. "If you don't stop taking legal briefs instead of a brotha in Calvin Klein briefs to bed you're going to be fifty, and I'll still be looking for a date for you."

"You know we have this conversation way too often." Mysti wanted to get RaMona onto a different subject and out of her Kool-Aid. "Do you know anyone who's ever placed or answered a personal?"

"A personal ad? You mean like love at loser dot com?" RaMona laughed hysterically.

"What makes you say that people who place and answer ads are losers?" Mysti was defensive.

"Because they are. People need to meet in the grocery store, at church, or at a pool party. Speaking of which, are you coming with me or not?"

"Let's say not. And I think I'm going to hang up while I still like you. I'll talk to you later." Mysti broke the connection before RaMona had a chance to object.

Mysti smiled to herself as she thought of how absolutely insane she was for even thinking she should read personal ads in hopes of meeting a Mr. Right or even Mr. Right Now.

Kamesha stuck her head through the small opening in the doorway. "Ms. Ellington, would you like to review your calendar with me before I leave for my dental appointment?"

Kamesha Franklin had been Mysti's assistant since Mysti had become a senior associate more than five years before. The firm had hired Kamesha within two weeks of graduation from the University of California at Los Angeles where she'd majored in football jocks, with a minor in theatre arts. However, Kamesha's father was a sports agent to many of the top athletes in the country and was the top-billed client in the entertainment law division of Haynes, Wilson, McCarthy, and Stith. So guess where daddy's little girl started when he wanted his precious princess to have a career in law to fall back on if Hollywood was too blind to see she was the next Halle Berry?

In the infinite wisdom of the *some of my best friends are black* office manager, Kamesha was placed with the only black associate in the firm, senior or otherwise. On their first day together, Mysti took Kamesha to lunch and explained her goal to make partner in five years. She wanted Kamesha to help her accomplish this and would teach her as much as she could absorb about law and a good work ethic. And if she were a good student, no matter how high Mysti went in this firm or another, Kamesha would be with her until she no longer wanted to be.

Kamesha watched in wide-eyed amazement, and the best administrative assistant, now paralegal, in the firm's four divisions housed in three offices, was born.

"Sure, come on in. I forgot you're having the dreaded dental surgery today. I can't even imagine having four wisdom teeth removed at one time. Before we get to the calendar and case status, may I ask you a personal question?" Mysti leaned forward over the blotter with the kente cloth border toward Kamesha.

"Sure, Ms. E." Kamesha's crystal-clear green eyes lit up like a Christmas tree in Rockefeller Center at the possibility of getting a rare peek into Mysti's personal life.

"Do you know anyone who's placed or answered a personal ad?" As the whispered utterance quietly filled the air, Mysti knew she'd made a mistake.

"Sure, Ms. E! All of my friends have at one time or another. It's the way to date in the new millennium," Kamesha boasted proudly. "I've had at least three boyfriends from one cyber love connection or another."

Mysti sat up straight and adjusted her jacket, clearing her throat. "Okay. Thank you, Kamesha."

"Why do you ask?" Kamesha was disappointed the personal conversation would end so abruptly.

"I was just curious. I'm sorry, I shouldn't have been prying." Mysti averted her eyes.

Kamesha sat on the edge of her seat smiling. "You're thinking of placing an ad, aren't you?"

"Absolutely not!"

"Well, if you must know, my mother met my stepfather on Yahoo, and you were at their wedding last year."

Mysti couldn't mask her enthusiasm. "Really?"

"I knew it! You *are* going to place an ad! Or have you done it already?" Kamesha bounced her four-foot-eleven self up and down like a five-year-old.

"Your mother met Marv on the Internet? You're kidding me?"

"Yep, like six years ago, after her and Daddy broke up. She got into the chat thing, going to offline parties—the whole nine yards. She and Marv had been chatting back and forth and finally met in New Orleans at one of those parties. Love at first sight, and the rest is in the rice tossing."

"What's an offline party?" Mysti was far more interested than she wanted to divulge.

"It's where people who've met in chat rooms get together in person and have a weekend of activities. And it's nothing weird or perverted about it. Just regular folks like you and me. So you should do it, Ms. E. All you do is work. You are *foine* and a man would be lucky to meet a successful, smart, sexy sistah like you."

Mysti didn't know how to respond, but Kamesha had given her a nudge hard enough to at least make her want to read a couple of the ads that had been placed. "Well, we'd better get to work so that you can get to the dentist."

As much as Kamesha wanted to continue she knew the subject was closed—at least for the moment. They spent the next several minutes going through Mysti's calendar for Monday and Tuesday while Kamesha was at home recuperating. Mysti wished her well and told her not to worry at all about work while she was gone. She promised to have it all waiting for her return.

Kamesha dug her three-inch heel into the high-grade industrial blue carpet. She stopped abruptly and turned to face her boss and friend. "Ms E, please don't think I'm overstepping my bounds, but I think you need to get a life outside this office. That's what I told my mom after the divorce, and look at her now. I know you want to be partner, and I want it for you, but not at the sacrifice of all else. Have a great weekend."

Mysti stared transfixed at the ten-foot mahogany door long after it closed. *Out of the mouths of babes*, was that how the saying went? With nothing substantial on her calendar in light of the pending trial verdict, Mysti sat back and relaxed in the mid-back, blue cloth chair. What would it feel like to lean back in her own custom-made blue high-back leather chair as partner? But with no one to share the small or enormous victories with, was it all worth it? Well, yes. Hell, yes! But it sure would be nice to have a good significant date every now and again.

Mysti began fingering the maroon ball on the mouse. The blackened flat monitor gave way to the Yahoo.com screen with the slightest tap. My *mom met my stepdad on the Internet* rang in her ears as she watched the pointer dance across the screen. She purposely avoided the area with the link to the personals.

"What am I doing?" Mysti spoke to the Annie Lee *8 1/2 Narrow* art piece on her desk. "Would you place an ad? Of course you wouldn't! But maybe if I just read a few. What would you think about that?"

As Mysti sat waiting for the woman leaning against the pole rubbing her feet to answer, she *accidentally* clicked the link to the personals. Suddenly there was a picture of a seemingly loving couple inches from each other's lips. The caption above their heads read *Make a Connection.* Just below them was another picture under the Success Story heading. A couple clad in wedding regalia smiled and boasted of meeting quality people online. After e-mails, then phone calls, followed by dates, they had strolled down the aisle before God and man to proclaim their cyber-found love.

Mysti's palms began to sweat as her eyes scanned the screen. She could place an ad for free. She could read ads for free. But it cost twenty dollars a month to connect with someone. Well, that did it. There was no way she was paying one dime to meet a serial killer.

As though someone had taken possession of her hands, Mysti found her fingertips touching the keys causing the letters to fill in the blanks on the screen. She clicked the Find Match button. Four hundred and forty-two ads were listed for men between the ages of thirty-five and forty-five who sought women within fifty miles of her front door. The sheer number shocked her. Could there be four hundred forty-two desperate losers in her neighborhood or was Kamesha right?

Narrow Your Search headed a section where she could be more specific about what she sought. *Location: hmmm, Los Angeles is a big place. Let's change that to twenty-five miles. Ethnicity: Well he's got to be a brotha. Body type: I'm five foot eleven. Can't have no five-foot man. Age: A few years younger might be interesting, and surely not too many years older—thirty-five to forty-five. Smoker: Yuck! Have kids: Do I care? Let's say no preference.*

Mysti felt the muscles in her shoulders relax as she was really getting into making the selections. She stood and removed her black Jones New York custom-tailored jacket, slipped on her Ferragamos and made her way to the kitchen for a cup of tea. She ran into Mike Alexander, her direct competition for the coveted partnership.

"I thought you'd be off celebrating your victory. Word is you've won the case. Congratulations," Mike said.

"Well, you and I both know it's not over until it's over. The longer the jury takes, the less likely we've won. But you know that better than anyone, don't you, Mike?" Mysti couldn't resist taking a dig at her nemesis since the last case he'd lost had cost him a bid for partner. "But I'm working on something a little different this afternoon. Taking some time for Ms. Ellington. Ciao."

Mysti smiled all the way back to her office. Suddenly she felt a little giddy. Kicking her shoes off again she spoke to no one in particular. "Where was I?" *Education: Well if I say anything less than a college grad, he will have an issue with me being a successful lawyer. Religion: Christian for sure. Relationship type.*

"Wow. How do I answer this one?" Mysti said aloud. "Two hours ago I didn't even know I wanted any type of relationship. I know I don't want just sex. Been there, done that!" Mysti contemplated several minutes, weighing her options. She dismissed Friend and Pen Pal, which only left Committed and Just Dating. *What's a sistah to do?* She wasn't looking for marriage, but she *was* looking for stability. If she ordered him a sweater for his birthday she wanted him to be around to receive it. *Relationship Type: Committed.* Before she could think about it, she hit the Find My Match button. There before her were twenty-six choices.

Mysti simply said, "Damn!"

Chapter Two

Why on Earth would I want to do this? There is nothing wrong with me. I don't have to go these extremes to get a date. The thoughts crowded Mysti's mind to the point she didn't hear the faint knock at her office door. As the door slowly began to open, Mysti sat up straight and hoped she didn't look as guilty as she felt.

"Come in, Mr. McCarthy." Mysti spoke with mixed emotions as she stood, grabbing her jacket from the back of her chair.

"Please, Ms. Ellington, relax. And how many times do I have to tell you to call me Jerry? Come sit with me on the couch. And I know you don't have on any shoes under that desk. Keep them off." The five-foot-three-inch founding partner of the firm smiled warmly showing his browning teeth, the by-product of many years of cigarette smoking.

"Well, if I'm to call you Jerry, Mr. McCarthy, you surely must call me Mysti. And I think I'll just slip my shoes back on, if that's okay with you." Mysti moved with the grace of a gazelle around her desk to the blue couch that matched her junior executive chair.

Jerome McCarthy patted the cushion for Mysti to take a seat next to him. In her many years with the firm he had never been quite this friendly. The mild-mannered man who sat in her office was soft spoken and left the tirades to the managing partner Alexander Samuel Stith III. His initials described him more than perfectly.

"Ms. Ellington . . . I mean, Mysti, I wanted to come in and personally congratulate you on the extraordinary job you did with Cruz versus Bullocks Industries. And win or lose, you should be very proud. Your closing summation alone was nothing less than brilliant."

"I know that information flows through the grapevine rather freely, Mister . . ."

Jerome McCarthy held up his finger, moving it back and forth as though he were chastising her.

"Okay, but Jerry, that is going to take some getting used to."

"Well, at least you all don't call me *Stiff the Ass.*" He laughed loudly at his own attempt at humor.

Mysti looked at him, stunned.

"There is nothing that happens on the forty-sixth floor of the Arco Towers that I don't know, Ms. Ellington." Jerry winked.

"As I was saying, I know information flows as freely as rain water in the L.A. River through the legal grapevine, but how do you know so quickly about what happened in court today?"

"I assure you, I know these things. You've worked long and hard since you joined us. I knew when we first interviewed you, you'd make a difference. I'm seldom wrong. I want to be the first to tell you, I will be voting for you for the available partner position." Jerry made eye contact without intimidating her.

"Jerry, I don't know what to say. I'd be lying if I said this isn't what I've worked my tail off for, but to know that all of my efforts haven't gone unnoticed makes me feel appreciated and yes, even proud." Mysti felt her heart beating in her temples. "And someone once said that's better than money. I'm not so sure about that, but it is surely a close second. But I still don't think we should jump the gun. The jury is still out, and who knows what will happen with them. Others have been the perfect candidates only to have a jury change not only our client's fate, but the lawyer's fate as well."

"I assure you, Mysti, you have a very bright future with this firm. We want you to be happy. I'm a man who shoots straight from the hip. I think you appreciate honesty. You make us look good. Many firms want a top-notch black woman who's a bulldog when it comes to litigation, who has not only the respect of her colleagues, but the bench. They covet our position."

His words stung Mysti between the eyes like an angry wasp. Was this about race? Her grandmother told her all the time: *everything* is about race. Why couldn't she just be a top-notch female attorney who was known as a bulldog?

As though Mr. McCarthy could read her mind he spoke slowly. "Listen, Mysti, don't get all caught up on me saying you're a black attorney. But the fact remains, you are, and if you were green with purple hair that wouldn't change a thing."

But would I be making partner if I were a white woman? "I understand, Jerry. I appreciate your candor," Mysti lied because she didn't understand at all.

"I want you to enjoy your vacation. You've worked very hard this year and you deserve to celebrate. I wanted you to know where I stood before you left. I believe you'll be picking out new furniture when you return."

"Jerry, I don't know what to say. But thank you comes to mind. I want to be sure Kamesha will make the move down the hall with me." Mysti could feel her blood flowing through her body.

"I would think you'd have it no other way. We have a pretty high-profile case we want you to take a look at while you're away. Tell us what you think and if it's something you think you can handle. I'll have Stith's assistant bring it to you on Monday. Your verdict should be in by then. You leave a week from today if I have my facts right."

Stunned the unofficial owner of the firm knew or even cared so much about her personal goings-on, Mysti managed, "Yes, and I'll be gone until the first full week in January."

"Good, good. Are you spending time with family and that someone special?"

"I will be spending time with family. I plan to maybe go skiing for a week."

"Well, just remember all work and no play . . ." Mr. McCarthy began to rise and a frown found its way to the old man's face. The rumor was he was going to be eighty-five on his birthday in February and was going to semi-retire.

"Are you alright, Mr. McCarthy—I mean, Jerry?"

"Just an old man, Mysti. I'd like to say something a little personal, if that is okay with you."

"Sure," Mysti replied nervously. For the first time in the five years she had worked at the firm, she took in the full view of the firm's patriarch who barely came to her shoulders.

"I'm a very rich man by anyone's standards, but the

reality is I'm a pauper. For as long as I can remember, there was nothing more important to me than the law and building this firm. I've lost everything of value because of it. Today, I grow old alone because my lovely Miriam would no longer tolerate my neglect. My children barely send me Christmas cards. I have three great-grandchildren I've never seen. Don't let the law take the harmony out of your life, my dear."

"I'm really sorry to hear that. I'll remember your advice, Jerry." Mysti smiled, wondering if Mr. McCarthy had put emphasis on the word *harmony* because he knew it was her middle name. "But you know it is not too late. The holiday season is right around the corner, and its the perfect time to mend fences and build new bridges. It takes a strong man to make the first move. Go see your great-grandchildren. Don't wait for them to come to you."

Seconds passed like hours as Mysti held her breath thinking she'd said too much. Mr. McCarthy stared at the black faux marble table and began speaking slowly. "You're probably correct. Perhaps I'll start with a phone call. You're a very lovely young woman who is wise beyond her years. Very wise indeed."

Mr. McCarthy measured his movements as he turned to leave. "Don't let these walls become your prison," he said as he patted her left shoulder. And with that he was gone.

Mysti fell back on the couch. "What just happened here?"

Chapter Three

As Mysti sat contemplating the pros and cons of the Internet matchmaker game, she didn't know how long she'd been in a daze when the phone rang. She remembered Kamesha had forwarded the phones to her direct line and quickly moved from the couch to the desk.

"This is Mysti Ellington."

"Okay, this is the skinny. There will be seven worthy brothas coming to this pool party." Of course, Mysti didn't have to ask who was calling.

"I'm not even going to ask how you found this out."

"Just listen up, gurlie. Two firefighters. Talk about having your flames fanned! One is a captain in charge of terrorism response. Honey, the other a paramedic . . . be still my heart. One lawyer—not a candidate for partner, but worthy to have his briefs reviewed. Three engineers—civil, mechanical, and chemical. You know precision is a wonderful thing. And last but most certainly not least, an electrician. I bet he can turn you on! All are single or divorced. Some have children, some don't. So now you *cannot* say no to a sistah after she has gone to all of this trouble to get the resumes of the prospective applicants." RaMona had to laugh at her antics.

"You know you've been in HR too long. How did you find out all of this information? I know you didn't call them up individually and ask them." Mysti paused momentarily. "Please tell me you didn't!"

"Not exactly," her friend responded slyly.

"What exactly?" Mysti faked anger.

"I called my boy, Gregory. He's the one giving the party. I asked which of his homeboys would he want his sister to date, and this was the list he gave me. Pretty awesome, huh?"

"Please tell me you didn't let him know this inquiry was on my behalf."

"Well, of course not. But what if I did? The shame of it is not in looking, but in a got-it-going-on sistah not having."

Mysti was silent.

"Uh-huh, I thought you'd get quiet on that one."

"Well, if I do agree to go with you—and that's a big if—I want you to do me a favor."

"Gurl, you know I would be a contestant on *Fear Factor* for you."

"Promise you're not going to pass judgment either." Mysti weighed the potential backlash of sharing her desire with RaMona.

"Out with it! You know judgment passing is thrown in for free."

"I really want to look on the Internet for some potential candidates."

"No, you don't," RaMona screamed into the phone.

"I knew I shouldn't have mentioned this to you. I'll call you tomorrow and let you know my decision. I'm going to be here about another half hour and then I'm going to try to get ahead of the traffic. I didn't realize how tired I am."

"You need some vitamin D, I'm trying to tell you."

"Good-bye, Mona. Love you." Mysti smiled as she hung up the phone.

RaMona had been in her life since they were in fifth grade. RaMona, the very plump little girl with thick glasses, sat on the school steps at recess with her chin in her hands. Mysti tripped on her shoelaces just as she ran past RaMona who appeared to be crying.

RaMona jumped up to help her and ask if she was okay.

"Why are you sitting here all by yourself?" Mysti had asked.

"They say I'm too fat to play ball with them. I just don't want to be teased again today."

"Who said you're too fat to play tether ball?"

"Everybody." RaMona was looking at the ground.

"Well, you come play hopscotch with me then. Don't nobody want to play ball with them no how."

That day on the playground had been the beginning of the dynamic duo. Throughout school they'd always taken the same magnet classes, almost always making straight A's. When RaMona couldn't make the cheer-leading squad, Mysti never tried out. They joined the swim team and went to the city finals, but when Mysti was cut, RaMona resigned. Double dating was their safety net. If they were always with boys together, neither one could get into any *serious* trouble. The proudest day for both of them and their parents was when they boarded the plane to New Orleans to begin college life at Xavier University at the ripe old age of sixteen.

When RaMona got to Louisiana and discovered there was a whole population of young men who loved a woman of size with deep chocolate brown skin, she lost her mind. She was dating three or four nights out of the week and almost flunked out of school twice. But as a true friend, Mysti tried to convince her that no boy was worth facing her parents if she didn't graduate.

During their junior year RaMona met a United States Navy lieutenant who swept her off her feet and into his bed. She emerged with child and her life drastically changed. Her father reported the young officer to his commander and he was forced to marry her. For the first time in more than ten years the friends were separated. Of course, wedded bliss was short lived and RaMona got a divorce.

With her educational dream deferred, RaMona returned to Los Angeles and began working for a large foreign car manufacturer in the human resources department. She'd found what she was born to do. She was all up in everybody's business and it was legal. When little Roderick started kindergarten RaMona decided to return to college part time. As Roderick graduated from fifth grade, his mother graduated with honors from Loyola Marymount University with a degree in business. Three years later she was the regional director of human resources and responsible for hiring and firing more than ten thousand people while following every letter of the law.

After Lieutenant Roderick Johnston had sufficiently crushed any remaining self-esteem, RaMona dove into the quagmire of lousy choices. She'd manage to select one loser after another because she believed he had potential. Nothing Mysti said could convince her that the only thing she needed to be fixing was a sandwich. RaMona continued on the road to destruction until she hired a motivational speaker for International Women's Health month who changed her life. The speaker proclaimed sexy doesn't have a dress size and if you're receiving bad treatment, guess whose fault it is. She left the seminar with a totally new attitude and began fixing herself.

She listened to the woman's tapes and read her book over and over, all the while refusing to even consider dating. She repeatedly said, "Not until I *know* I deserve only the very best." She realized she didn't have to show cleavage to her navel or skirts slit to her waist to be considered attractive. She wore less makeup and just relaxed around men because she finally realized she held all the cards. She was the one who had what they wanted, not the other way around.

During a semi-annual regional managers meeting, RaMona made eye contact with a sharply dressed brotha. His stare made the hair stand up on the back of her neck, and she had trouble focusing. She called a break a half hour before its scheduled time. During the break Maxwell Cooper made his way to the front to introduce himself. He was the plant manager for the upholstery unit. In seven minutes of the ten-minute break she learned he was divorced, had a two-year-old son who lived with him, sang in the choir, and had a shepherd named Mini. He wanted very much to have coffee with her over the weekend because it was his ex-wife's time with his son. She accepted.

Now that RaMona was on the primrose path to the altar, she wanted nothing more than to bring her best friend along, even if it was kicking and screaming.

Chapter Four

Mysti could no longer concentrate and found it fruitless to remain in the office. On her way in from court she'd felt the sun on her face and she wanted that feeling again at this very moment. While most of the country was shoveling snow, Los Angeles was enjoying a typical December, and she wanted to be a part of it. She grabbed the Coach briefcase her mother had given her when she'd been made senior associate. The beautiful but very thin case carried little more than her PDA, checkbook, wallet, and car keys, but it looked good. She tried rarely to carry a purse. She had all of her jackets custom tailored to include an inside pocket, like a man's suit coat. It somehow leveled the playing field just a little.

As an afterthought she began closing the programs on her computer. She hesitated as she saw the Internet browser page still on the Yahoo Personals. What a silly notion she'd had. Perhaps her friend was right. RaMona had met Maxwell the traditional way.

Successful men surrounded her. Though she would never date anyone in her firm, there were at least one hundred law firms, accountancy corporations, investment entities and other businesses in the towers. Maybe she just needed to open her eyes.

As she quickly passed through the glass doors, she managed to escape with only a few "have a nice weekend" and felt free. She was reasonably certain the jury would be out until at least Monday afternoon. They, like her, needed to feel the wind on their faces. On the elevator at the thirty-second floor three very handsome designer-suit-wearing, briefcase-carrying black men entered. They smiled and she looked away. *Girl, what is wrong with you? Smile back at them!*

The elevator went express to the lobby level and they stepped aside to let her off first. To amend for her more-than-rude behavior before she turned and said, "Thank you and you gentlemen have a nice weekend."

As she swiftly moved across the marbled lobby floor she could feel their eyes on her ample behind. Her hips involuntarily swayed just a little harder. She'd have to chastise them later. She wondered how many times a brotha had made eye contact with her and smiled and she had looked away. Lord, no wonder she didn't get asked out!

Waiting for the elevator to the parking garage a very pleasant scent tickled her nose. Without any forethought she turned to see who stood behind her. It was the men from the thirty-second floor. She smiled again, pointedly making eye contact with each.

"Getting out a little early for the weekend too, I see," the shortest of the three said.

"Yes, they already got a pound and half of flesh today."

"Well, you sure can't tell by the looks of you," the one with the perfect smile added. His buddies all agreed.

"I'm going to take that as a compliment," she said as the elevator doors opened and she entered.

"It was meant as one. My name is Curtis Barr." The one with the perfect smile extended his hand.

She took it and appreciated the good strong handshake. "My name is Mysti Ellington. I work on forty-six."

"I'm Bert Williamson. Are you an attorney?" the short one quickly asked.

"That's what they tell me."

"Forgive my boy. He doesn't get out much. I'm Anderson McPherson."

"It's very nice to meet you. This is my floor. I hope to see you all again."

"What do you know, I'm parked on this level, too," Bert said, catching the closing doors.

"Fool, you rode with me," Curtis teased.

They all laughed. "Have a great weekend, fellas." Mysti's hips did that swaying thing again. Oh, she was really going to talk to them when she got home!

She paid top dollar for a reserved spot near the elevator. The firm gave her a parking allowance and she paid the extra one hundred dollars per month just to be able to have a spot that read M. Ellington. She liked seeing her name in print.

She opened the small trunk and tossed in the briefcase. She slipped her jacket off and laid it neatly on top of the briefcase. With the push of a button the doors unlocked to the immaculate black Mustang GT convertible. As she slid her firm, well-exercised body into the leather seat, the cushion seemed to hug her. She turned the key and the eight cylinders roared to life. Brian McKnight proclaimed he loved someone with every beat of his heart. She leaned over to the glove box to retrieve a hair clip, unlatching the convertible top before she sat upright. As the electronic roof lowered itself at the push of a button she twisted her shoulder-length warm brown hair and clipped it into place. She planned to put the two hundred and sixty horses to the test this afternoon.

She eased the car out of the space and headed for the exit. Just ahead of her on the upward winding corridor to the street were Bert, Anderson, and Curtis. Anderson was driving a late-model, money-green Avalon. She smiled to herself. Was it as easy as changing one's perspective to meet decent men? How long had she worked in the same building with them? Maybe she should leave early on Fridays more often.

Chapter Five

As she maneuvered through the streets of downtown Los Angeles toward the Harbor Freeway, which would lead her to the ever-crowded California Route 101 she thought of throwing caution to the wind. Just not take the Winnetka exit. Continue north until she was in Santa Barbara.

The sun had begun to move to the west, which caused the left side of Mysti's cinnamon colored face to tingle. She loved her convertible, but she would never be able to get used to the direct sunlight.

As she inched along through traffic she wondered what was stopping her from going to Santa Barbara for the weekend. RaMona was correct; there would be nothing happening with the jury before Monday, yet she was hesitant. Money certainly wasn't the issue. Did she just not want to go alone?

When had she become so unbearably dull? In college she had focused on her studies, but she definitely knew how to get her party on. She wasn't quite as wild as RaMona, never letting anything or anyone interfere with her goals, but she knew how to relax and have fun. She had graduated from Xavier and began her first semester at Stanford Law School by her twenty-first birthday. Even with the demands of law school she managed to have a social life. Then came the practicing of her craft. For as long as she could remember she had to be the best. The second of three daughters, she seemed to always go unnoticed. Her oldest sister, Lyric, was the prettiest. Taking features from their Creole mother, she more than passed the brown bag test with long wavy hair, gray eyes, and perfect teeth. Lyric inherited their father's musical talent. Their father, Earl Ellington, was rumored to be a distant cousin of the great Duke. Mysti had never seen any family tree tying the two together, however. The youngest by seven years, Symphony was a spoiled brat who to this day could manipulate her parents into purchasing oceanfront property in Wyoming.

Mysti seemed to always be lost as her parents fussed over Lyric's attempts at modeling and Symphony's incessant whining. Being different in any way as a child was never a desirable thing, but Mysti couldn't help but feel that she was. She was always taller than any girl—or boy for that matter—in her age group, and her name was Mystique. She found refuge in reading and was known by her first name at the library by the time she was ten. Her constant need to excel went unnoticed until her parents were called to the school when she was eleven. The principal explained to Mr. and Mrs. Ellington, that their second oldest daughter was a very gifted student, and her teachers wanted to recommend her for the magnet program, which would require her to travel to the San Fernando Valley to attend school.

But by enrolling in this program not only would she be greatly challenged, she'd also move from the sixth to the eighth grade.

Although they allowed her to enroll, her parents' lack of faith in her ability to handle the standards of the new program and enter high school at such a young age disappointed Mysti to say the least. She made it her mission every second of every day to prove them wrong.

Meeting challenges became a way of life as she grew older, and to this day she was driven by competition. She volunteered for the most difficult cases and looked for ways to get the attention of the partners.

Now here she sat on a Friday night in pre-rush-hour traffic that inched along, trying to get to the freeway where it was *really* congested. There was nothing exciting waiting for her at 6969 Hoping Circle. Her exotic fish never seemed excited to see her. Muffin, her cat, was self-centered and thought it was all about her.

You need to get a life outside of this office, Ms. E. Kamesha's words ran through her head over and over. What life did she have outside of the forty-sixth floor of Arco Towers? Of course, there was always RaMona. She was a friend who cared genuinely about her well-being. Relentless meddling withstanding, she was closer to her best friend than her family. She loved her parents and had gotten over what she had considered emotional neglect. But she had very little to do with her sisters. Lyric was a prima donna who believed the universe began and ended with her. She had the perfect little life with two perfect little gifted children and the perfect cheating husband. Symphony was still the whining, her-way-or-no-way little girl she'd always been who believed Mysti should write her a check whenever the need arose. She loved her family, but Mysti didn't like them a whole lot.

RaMona never wanted more from her than love and

acceptance, which she'd had since that day on the playground. Mysti was never lonely because she enjoyed her own company, but tonight she felt alone. My *mother met my stepdad on Yahoo*. Kamesha's voice continued to haunt Mysti as she finally reached the Harbor Freeway.

She toyed with the idea of going to Santa Barbara and finally dismissed the notion. She'd protested, but knew in her heart she would attend the pool party with RaMona, but that was on Sunday. She needed something beside depositions and court transcripts to occupy her time tonight. To drown out her own thoughts she hit the FM1 button on the car stereo. The sweet tenor sound of Phil Perry's voice filled the air around her. He crooned many words but she only heard *love don't love nobody*. She felt like she couldn't breathe. She needed more air but the top was already down. Truth—or was it deprivation?—seemed to be suffocating her.

She had chosen to put all else above a personal life. Did she even want a family of her own? Her childhood had been filled with struggles to get attention. Would her children be faced with the same thing?

Mysti shook her again. "Gurlfriend, what is wrong with you? Snap out of it. You haven't had a date in a few weeks. Or is it months?" No matter, she needed to straighten up her attitude and show plenty of gratitude because God had richly blessed her, and she was now going to take charge of her personal life. There was that word again . . . *personal*.

Traffic finally broke free after the merge from the Harbor to the Hollywood Freeway. Mysti felt the wind in her hair, and with it came a true sense of relief. She didn't quite know what had come over her, but she did know she wasn't going to go back to that kind of thinking. She cranked the stereo a little higher as she let the sounds of KTWV 94.7 FM take her away. She recognized the soulful sound of Najee as he made beautiful music on his saxophone.

The temperature rose by ten degrees as she entered the San Fernando Valley. The evening had the makings of a great night, and she planned to enjoy it fully. Her attitude adjustment was beginning to take hold, and she felt much better. She *may* even call her sisters just to say hello.

She arrived at the Winnetka exit as the five o'clock traffic report was beginning. She had just missed a six-car pileup that had traffic backed up for three miles. This had truly been a lucky Friday for her. First the big boss came in to congratulate her on a job well done, she met three foine brothas in her very own elevator, and she'd gotten out of Los Angeles just in the nick of time.

Chapter Six

Turning left onto Hoping Circle brought a smile to Mysti's face. At the graduation party, given by RaMona when Mysti finished law school, Mysti's parents had given her a twenty-five-thousand-dollar check. Her mother had announced to all who were in attendance how generous they had been to their daughter and suggested that now maybe she could trade in her ten-year-old Honda Accord for a nice luxury car befitting an attorney. Her father had helped as she put the many gifts in the car to leave.

Holding the trunk opened he began, "You know, Mysti, I know we were not so good as parents. Oh, you had a nice home, clothes, books, and a few special things, but the thing you needed from us—me in particular—was time and attention. I was so caught up in my music and your sister's talent I missed out on that which I can never get back: seeing you grow into a fine young woman. Your mother's priorities get kinda mixed up sometimes. You may want a new car and if that's the case you do just that, but if you want to invest in your future, buy yourself a condo. Nothing fancy, just something that can pay you in the future. You've proven that you didn't need your dear ol' dad to make a success of yourself, and there is no way to make up to you that which I didn't give. But I sure wish you the best of everything life has to offer and just ask that you give me a chance to be a real dad now."

"Daddy, I love you and thank you for the advice. You were a great father, and Mommy was a good mother. Sometimes I would just get lost in the shuffle, but I always knew you loved me."

"Kinda like the little fella in that movie *Home Alone?*" They both laughed as they had watched that movie together countless times and always found it hilariously funny.

She had taken her father's advice that day and found a very comfortable one-bedroom condo in Long Beach. With her first bonus as a senior associate and the thirty thousand she cleared from the sale of the condo she moved to the nice cul de sac in the Valley.

She had fallen in love with the house the moment she turned onto the street. It had a warm family feel, a place where children could play and their parents feel safe. Pressing the garage door opener as she turned into the driveway, a sense of peace washed over her. She gathered her briefcase and jacket from the trunk, deciding to leave the top down. She might decide to go for a drive later. She removed her pumps and placed them meticulously on the five-level shoe rack that lined half the wall of the two-car garage. Shoes were arranged by purpose, then color. There were eight pairs of navy blue pumps. She slipped her more-than-tired feet into her waiting animal-print slippers. She pressed the button that lowered the garage door. She slipped the key into the lock that led into the spacious kitchen. Muffin nibbled at the kitty chow she'd left that morning, never even acknowledging her entrance. She really needed to get a dog.

Throwing the briefcase and keys on the black granite-covered center island, Mysti hung her jacket over the back of one of the two bar-height chairs. She took three steps to the cabinet to retrieve a wineglass. The five steps to the black refrigerator took a little more energy than she expected, which made her realize she was coming down off the closing argument adrenaline high.

She removed the cork from the bottle of Kendall Jackson Chardonnay with her teeth, poured a half glass and drank it down in two gulps. She then poured the remaining golden liquid into the glass and tossed the bottle in the trashcan under the sink.

She took a sip and moved to the pantry to get a new bottle of wine to chill. It was going to be that kind of night.

With her jacket thrown over her shoulder, glass of wine and briefcase in hand, she headed toward the master bedroom at the far end of the house. Passing the front door, setting the briefcase on the floor, she stooped to pick up the mail—cable, electric and three credit card bills. No need to look for a love note or sweet card. How did the California lottery commercial go? You *gotta be in it to win it.* Picking up the briefcase she continued her trek.

She stopped by the third bedroom turned office and dropped her briefcase on the daybed that doubled as a couch, flinging the bills into the in basket. The first of the month would arrive soon enough to worry about American Express, et al.

She moved on to the open French doors that led to her sanctum. Stepping into the master suite, various

shades of purple greeted her. A six-by-nine rug at the
foot of the king-sized, maple four-poster bed accented
the ivory carpet. With her energy leaving her at an
alarming rate she felt like tossing all eight of the laven-
der and white throw pillows onto the floor and climbing between the feather-top mattress and the white
down comforter. She resisted the temptation and went
into the walk-in closet. First hanging her jacket, she
then removed her skirt and blouse placing each on its
designated hanger. From the chest of drawers positioned in the middle of the spacious closet she pulled a
sweatshirt and matching pants. Despite the warm temperatures during the day, it was almost guaranteed to
become breezy by dark. She returned to her room and
took another sip of wine. She removed her diamond
stud earrings that had been a gift from Symphony for
graduation—a gift she reminded her of often.

She grabbed the new novel by Victoria Christopher
Murray from her bedside table and headed toward her
office. She would quickly check e-mail before she ad-
journed to the patio. She decided she would order
Chinese take-out later.

It felt good to be home and in her loungewear well
before six o'clock. She sat in the high-back leather
chair and let the comfort envelop her. It wouldn't be
long before she'd be perched upon a chair much like
this one in her own partner's office. She looked at the
expensive banker's desk that had come at a really nice
price from a furniture auction courtesy of some now de-
funct savings and loan. She swiveled to the left and
moved her fingers across the keys.

Miraculously the URL to Yahoo.com appeared instead of the intended hotmail.com. *Personals* loomed in
front of her and she quickly entered the criteria of the
man she sought. She didn't pretend this time. Who was

she trying to fool? She waited impatiently to read the ads of the twenty-six men who fit the bill. Much to her astonishment the number had grown to twenty-nine in just a few short hours.

"Wow, this is amazing," Mysti mumbled to herself.

Chapter Seven

For what seemed like minutes but was actually hours, Mysti read ads and profiles and looked at pictures. There were those who only were looking for a "discreet friend." They were discarded without even a second thought. But for the most part the ads sounded like reasonably intelligent men with their heads and hearts in the right place. When she reached for her almost empty wineglass she glanced at the digital clock—8:31 P.M. She couldn't believe so much time had passed. She now realized she was starving.

She downed the remaining wine and walked to the kitchen to open the new bottle. When she went to reach for the corkscrew she remembered she needed to order food. From her junk drawer she retrieved a menu from her favorite Chinese take-out and ordered the house fried rice and orange chicken. They were busy and delivery would take an hour. She was starving. She removed the stubborn cork from the new bottle of Mr. Jackson as she liked to call it. He was her date for the evening. She poured a full glass and started to place it back in the refrigerator when she decided she would take it to her office with her. From the cupboard above the refrigerator she retrieved an insulated bucket. Filling it half full of ice, she placed the wine bottle in it, grabbed a handful of Ritz crackers, two wrapped slices of American cheese and some grapes. With her bounty she returned to the office.

She was back at the computer within five minutes with all tasks accomplished. She was now ready to make a second pass through the ads. Out of the eighteen that remained she wanted to narrow her search to five, no more than seven choices.

They all seemed to have promise, but what would make five stand out above the rest? The first semifinalist was forty-one with a son. He was divorced, a teacher in the San Fernando Valley and loved snow sports. The six-foot physically fit Christian sounded like the perfect match, and definitely geographically desirable. Print.

Moving on to the next candidate, the six-foot six-inch former professional basketball player gave little information but included a picture. The brotha was foine! He desired a physically fit, financially independent sistah for strolls in the park and moonlit walks on the beach. Something in the back of her neck twitched when she read the ad, but she ignored it. Print.

The next three didn't make the cut. Seemed too needy. But then she found another that looked interesting.

Loves home-cooked meals, long drives on Highway 101, playing Scrabble, rainy Saturdays with a remote control and surround sound, mental sparring. Professional seeks same. You need only be happy with the way you look. Need someone to help me learn to not work so hard. Print.

The doorbell chimed. There was no way another hour had passed. The clock proved her wrong: 9:25 P.M. She ran to the door and the familiar face of Chang Li smiled back at her.

"Good evening, Ms. Ellington. I got here as soon as I could. We are very busy tonight," Mr. Li said in perfectly spoken English.

"That's no problem." Mysti signed the charge slip as she spoke. "I've been so busy in my office I never noticed how much time passed."

"Good night and don't work too late," Mr. Li said as he moved swiftly back to his car. "It's Friday night."

Mysti was famished. She flipped the switch and the overhead fluorescent lights brought the room to life. From somewhere else in the house Muffin appeared purring.

"Oh, so I guess you can speak to me now that you want something. Well, if you think you're getting a shrimp after snubbing me all evening, think again!" Mysti pulled a white plate from the glass-front cabinet.

She quickly fixed her a plate and accidentally dropped a shrimp from the house fried rice, knowing Muffin would catch it before it hit the floor. Leaving the containers on the counter she returned to her office with plate, chopsticks and napkin in hand.

"Now where was I? Three down, only two more to go." The next four had less appeal than the first time through, then she read one that caught her eye.

> *Soul provider seeks soul mate. Only the serious need apply, no head games, baby daddy drama. I'm a shoot-straight-from-the-hip guy who wants to settle down with the right sistah—and yes, only sistahs need apply. You must be fit and trim, employed, drug, tobacco, and disease free.*

"Brutally honest, but I can respect that," Mysti said. Print.

Either she was getting tired, drunk, or a combination of the two. She couldn't figure out why she even chose the others. As the clock displayed 11:41 P.M. she read the last one.

Pilot with major carrier seeks spontaneous, adventuresome life partner to share the skies and beaches in far-away lands.

According to his statistics he was tall, dark, and handsome. Print.

"Whew, this is harder than preparing for court. How in the world do people do this all the time? I need to prepare a response. Should I do a different one to each or just a generic one I can use for anyone?" Mysti debated out loud.

Hi there,

I was perusing the ads and found yours to be of interest. About me: professional African-American physically fit female, single, no children, no drama. I am alcohol, drug, and disease free. Looking for stable relationship with a physically, emotionally, and financially available professional African-American man who knows who he is and what he wants. Must have a great sense of humor and like the simple things in life. If our interests are mutual, I look forward to hearing from you.

Mysti read and reread her response before she copied and pasted it into the message to each of the five that she'd chosen. As she hit the last send button, it was one-thirty on Saturday morning. She had just invested eight nonbillable hours.

When she got up from her desk she was stiff from sitting in one place for so long. She took her glass and plate along with the empty wine bottle to the kitchen. She quickly closed the containers and placed them in the side-by-side refrigerator. She rinsed the dishes and left them in the sink. She needed to unload the dishwasher, and there was not an ounce of energy to accomplish that task.

She turned off the kitchen light and walked slowly to the bedroom. Walking past the bed and into the bathroom she stepped onto the cool marble floor with her bare feet. She switched on the vanity mirror and looked over at the oversized Jacuzzi tub and quickly dismissed the thought. She brushed her teeth, unclipped her hair, and removed her sweats. She pulled a nightshirt from behind the door and moved to the bed. She threw back the covers and slipped between the sheets.

"Lord, I thank You for another perfect day . . ." Sleep crept over Mysti before she could finish her prayers. Dreams came and went throughout the night. She was surrounded by men of all sizes, shapes, hues, and occupations based on their uniforms. They stood in line waiting to be interviewed by her. Those who didn't make the grade fell through a trap door. Others were taken to a holding area. She had a royal court of maidens who seemed to serve her every need. One of them handed her a clipboard with five names. They were the chosen few. Now the choice was hers.

Chapter Eight

With a start Mysti awakened to a room lighted only by the moonbeams shining through the arched paned window above the patio door. Green numbers read 4:04 on the Bose CD player/radio. After only a little more than two hours of sleep she was wide awake. She rolled over and moved to the sitting position in one smooth motion.

"Boy, that Chinese food has made me thirsty." Mysti dug her well-groomed toes into the plush carpet. While stretching, her mind quickly went to Yahoo.com. She felt foolish as she thought back to the evening before. *What in the hell was I doing?*

Without putting on her slippers, she slowly moved toward the bedroom door, heading for the kitchen. There was only one catch: The office stood between her and the place she needed to go to quench her thirst. As she moved down the hallway past the guest bedroom she slowed her steps as though the office held some monster waiting to pounce. Could she actually move past the room without checking her e-mail? Had any of the men responded yet?

"You are just being silly! Get some water and take your butt back to bed." Mysti laughed at herself in the antique framed mirror above a small table overrun by a huge philodendron. She squared her shoulders and moved quickly past the office. In the kitchen she filled a sixteen-ounce glass with water from the dispenser in the refrigerator door. She drank it down without stopping to take a breath. Not giving the water a chance to quench her thirst she retrieved the large jug of cran-apple juice and filled the glass halfway. With two gulps the juice disappeared. As she placed the glass in the sink, she decided to empty the dishwasher. She hit the power button on the under-the-counter CD player, and Anita Baker's voice filled the spacious kitchen. *Giving You the Best That I've Got* made her wonder what would happen if she gave a man the best she had to offer.

In all of her relationships the man had taken second, third, or even fourth place behind the law. Why should anyone be content being fourth? Surely she wouldn't have tolerated such neglect. Why was she so afraid to put forward so much of herself?

Placing the last plate in the cupboard, the song changed to the sexy voice of Tyrese, begging for some-one to be his lady. She'd had enough. *Off.* Within sec-onds she had loaded the few dishes and was turning the light off to return to bed.

Almost on the other side of the opening of her office she felt a magnetic force pulling her toward the com-puter. Resistance seemed futile. Looking over her shoul-der as though someone would be there to chastise her, Mysti slipped into the chair as her fingers glided across the keys. With two clicks she was into her mailbox. There it was, a response! With trembling hands she lightly tapped the mouse to open the e-mail from PROBLK-MAN69 and her breath caught in her throat, unable to escape.

Hey Sexy Lady,
   Liked what I read so far. Send me a pic and let me what you look like.
PBM69

How does he know if I'm sexy or not? Does he equate fit with being sexy? That is a rather rude way to ask for a picture.

"Picture? Oh, dang. I never thought I would need a picture, but I guess that makes sense." Mysti began to think of what kind of picture she was willing to put on the Internet since it could end up anywhere in the galaxy. She thought of a picture with RaMona she really liked from the office Christmas party at the beginning of December.

With no effort she found the picture in her in basket waiting to be moved to the box where she put all the pictures she planned to put into albums. Someday.

She placed the picture facedown on the combination flatbed scanner, printer, and copier. Within seconds her image clad in a clinging black dress and her best friend in a custom-designed African outfit filled her screen. It didn't take a genius to see that they were having a great time in that picture. Of course, RaMona was trying to match Mysti with every single man in the hotel ballroom, waitstaff not withstanding after a few chocolate martinis.

"This should do quite nicely." Mysti smiled to herself.

With a little cropping and resizing the picture was ready to be sent off to Mr. PROBLKMAN69.

Dear PBM69,

 Thank you for the prompt response. I've attached a photo per your request. I'd appreciate a picture from you as well. Looking forward to opening meaningful dialogue.
The Mystique One

Mysti quickly attached the picture to the e-mail, but before she hit send she realized that it was four-thirty in the morning. How desperate would she seem to be up in the middle of the night waiting for an e-mail response from a stranger? She decided to send the e-mail in the morning after her workout class. With that she closed the e-mail account and headed for the door. Turning to look at the computer she wondered one more time if she could possibly be doing the right thing. She flipped the switch and the room went dark.

My mother met my stepfather online. As she climbed back into bed Kamesha's words rang in her ears yet again. She picked up the remote control from the bedside table and with a touch the screen on the twenty-seven-inch television illuminated. Surfing through countless infomercials she stumbled upon her favorite love story: *Sleepless in Seattle.* She'd seen it at least a half-dozen times so she set the sleep timer for an hour. Hopefully, she wouldn't need more than fifteen minutes.

Lawnmowers and birds chirping awakened Mysti from a dreamless sleep. As she peeped at the clock she knew she'd missed her Saturday morning spinning class. Ten-twelve. "Wow, I slept really good. Thank You, Lord, for a new day and a grand opportunity to praise You once again." Mysti threw back the covers and energetically arose.

After a brief stop for morning relief, she padded her way to the kitchen to make coffee. But first she made a quick detour at the office.

Mysti quickly logged into her e-mail account. "Well, Mr. PROBLKMAN69, we'll just see what develops." She found the draft of the e-mail she'd composed earlier and with only a hint of hesitation she clicked send.

Suddenly she felt as if she had plunged from a diving board only to find there was no water in the pool, and it was too late to do anything about it. Craving a steamy cup of coffee she decided to check her inbox after she'd set the pot to brewing.

As she approached the kitchen the phone rang. Quickening her steps she reached the black cordless phone mounted near the entrance by the third ring. Looking at the Caller ID before she answered she smiled. "Good morning, my sistah."

"Hey, hey, hey!" RaMona's cheery voiced greeted her.

"Oh, aren't we cheerful this morning? You must have seen Max last night or are you making him breakfast as we speak?"

"Gurl, this song in my heart has nothing to do with that man. Well, perhaps a little to do with him. I just love life. Now you know why I'm calling. I want to know if you're going to the pool party tomorrow."

Mysti fidgeted nervously. "I swear you are so persistent. I still haven't decided. How about I decide after church?"

"Why is it so hard for you to make up your mind? You know you want to go. You are a barracuda in the courtroom, but put you in an arena of your peers and you get so bizarre."

"Whatever. What are you doing today? More wedding stuff?"

There was nothing RaMona liked better than talking about her wedding to Max, which was still fifteen months away. "No. And besides, as my maid of honor if I'm planning, you're planning." RaMona laughed.

"You do have a point, I guess."

"What are you not telling me?"

Mysti smiled at her inability to fool her best friend. "I don't know what you're talking about."

"You're wasting precious moments. There isn't even any need for you to pretend you don't know what I'm talking about. Just dish the dirt."

"I answered ads online last night." Mysti held her breath waiting for the descent of her friend's wrath.

"Lord, Jesus. Say it ain't so! I can't leave you alone for one evening."

"It's done. I'm grown."

"Grown? Who said anything about you not being grown? It's a whole cemetery full of stupid-ass grown folks."

Mysti felt foolish. She wasn't sure if it was because she had answered the ads or because she had told RaMona. "You know I don't have to take this abuse from you."

"Oh hell yes you do! As your oldest and dearest friend, it is my responsibility to make sure you don't do something suicidal."

"I haven't gone out with anyone or told them where I live or work. I'll get to know them online and on the phone first. People have been meeting this way for years. Many are married with children."

"And many are dead!"

"How many people for sure do you know are dead as a result of Internet dating?"

"One is too many."

Mysti didn't have a comeback. "I promise I won't meet anyone alone, and I won't meet them at all until I feel comfortable with them. Please just support me on this. I want what you have, Mona. And this just seems the best way to get to the prize. It's fast, efficient, and safe. Now suppose I went to this pool party tomorrow, hooked up with one of the brothas who you think is Mr. Right, and he turns out to be a woman beater. Now you see no one is going to know that in advance, will they?"

"Touché. "RaMona almost sounded defeated. "Just promise me you'll be careful. You're my only sister."

"I promise." A smile found its way to Mysti's heart.

RaMona felt she needed to change the subject. "Are we going to seven-thirty or nine-thirty?"

"Definitely seven-thirty. I'm going to work out after church. I didn't go this morning. You want to join me?"

"Gurl, I don't do no work, especially work out, on the Lord's day." RaMona laughed at her own lie.

"Just say you too triflin'. I've seen you replace the shingles on your house on a Sunday." Mysti was laughing so hard it was difficult to talk. "Talkin' about you don't work on the Lord's day. You need to fall where you are and ask for forgiveness."

"Whoa, look at the time. Gotta go, gotta run!"

"I just bet you do. Kiss my nephew for me and tell Max I said hey. Love you."

"I love you, too." RaMona spoke in an affectionate whisper. "And Mysti, just promise me you'll be careful."

Hesitating for only a moment, Mysti smiled and said, "You can bank on it!"

Mysti hit the talk button and the connection was broken. She turned the oven to three hundred fifty degrees. She quickly made coffee and mixed some batter for muffins. She put the batter in a pan and placed it at the top of the double oven and set the timer for fifteen minutes. She pulled a peacock-blue juice glass from the cabinet and filled it with orange juice. From the small cabinet above the sink she dished out her daily vitamin regimen and downed the eight pills with one swallow of juice.

With juice in hand she headed for the office. Now it was time to see if anyone else had responded. Today was going to be interesting to say the least.

Chapter Nine

After sifting through forty-one junk e-mails and sorting the remaining messages by sender, Mysti had two more responses. Somewhere between four-thirty and eleven she'd found new confidence. She quickly opened the first one.

Dear Mystique One,

Just your screen name is intriguing. I'm sort of new at this and don't know what is proper etiquette. I just know that I am not into games. I want a lady (a real lady) to call my own. So here goes.

I try to be exciting, but the truth be told I'd rather be at home watching Star Trek than in a club. I read extensively and enjoy movies, good and the not-so-good. I'm a bit of a car enthusiast, but I don't drive a fancy one. I love my work and give it my all on every shift. My passport has a few stamps, but Hawaii is my favorite place, and I plan to move there someday.

I got out of a really bad marriage five years ago, but I

*brought with me a really wonderful daughter. She lives
with me, but my mom takes care of her for me when I
work. I'm a decent enough looking guy, athletic (basketball) with no bad habits.*

*Well, I hope this is enough information to pique your
interest, but not so much that you don't still have meaningful questions to motivate stimulating conversation.*
Stephan

"Wow." Mysti reread the e-mail to make sure her eyes
hadn't deceived her. Stephan sounded wonderful. What
in heaven's name was wrong with him that someone
hadn't scooped him up? He sounded more than perfect. He wrote so well that she couldn't imagine what
verbal communication would be like.

There was something about the sincerity in his words
that made the hair stand up on her arms. But could this
be a game he was running? Again, why was he available?

To break the spell she decided to open the next response.

Hey you,
*If you're rooking for Mr. Right, your wait is over! You
are the woman I've been looking for all my life. Give me
your digits and let's get this party started.*
DocLove12

Mysti straightened her back and cleared her throat.
The third response had snapped her out of the fog
caused by the second. "That's certainly a contrast."

Dear DocLove12,
*With knowing so little about me I find it difficult to
believe that I could be your Ms. Right. I'm willing to*

*continuing talking via e-mail, but I'm moving slowly
and don't want to speak on the phone just yet.*

*Please send me five questions you'd like for me to an-
swer, and I will do the same once I receive yours.*
The Mystique One

*Why do men assume we are so desperate that we will fall for
any line they are laying down? I'm so sure I'm the woman he's
been looking for all of his life. I'm willing to bet he has said
that in every response.* The buzz of the oven timer broke
into Mysti's rambling thoughts.

As she pushed away from the desk she thought again
of Stephan. What a nice letter that was. She knew she
had to take her time and answer him. He was so far the
front-runner. She warned herself against getting too excited. She knew he, too, could be running game, but
was more sophisticated than the others or was just better at the game.

Her banana-nut muffins had baked to a perfect
golden brown. She grabbed a container of low-fat yogurt from the refrigerator and poured a cup of coffee.
She sweetened the coffee with chocolate raspberry
creamer and four teaspoons of sugar. The quiet in the
house suddenly became deafening. She abandoned her
breakfast and crossed the kitchen to the family room
where the big-screen television and state-of-the-art surround sound stereo system sat idly. With the digital remote control she pushed one button, and the stereo
and television sprang to life. The digital cable was already tuned to station 908. The smooth R&B sounds of
Prince—or was it the Artist Formerly Known As?—filled
the house.

With that minor interruption she returned to her
breakfast. In a bowl she crumbled the muffin and poured

the yogurt over it. She grabbed a spoon from the drawer, picked up the coffee and bowl, heading for the office.

In the steps required to take her back to the gateway to her fantasy, Mysti thought only of Stephan. She wanted to be sure to answer him appropriately. She didn't want to expose her enthusiasm too soon. Placing the breakfast next to her she reopened his e-mail, reading it again before responding.

> *Dear Stephan,*
>
> *My interest is indeed piqued. I'm a professional and have dedicated all of my attention to my career to the point I have almost no social life. A date consists of Kendall Jackson or my favorite twins, Ben and Jerry.*
>
> *I've never been married and have not been blessed with any children. I enjoy a good book and any movie that requires me to have a box of Puffs on standby. I love to dance, but can't remember the last time I worked up a sweat while shaking my groove thang.*
>
> *I appreciate your candor and look forward to hearing from you again soon. I'd like for you to send me five questions, and when I receive yours l will do the same.*
> *The Mystique One*

For the first time since she'd started this madness less than twenty-four hours before Mysti felt like she was doing the right thing.

"Gurl, did that sister preach this morning or what? I feel like just getting my praise on again out here in the parking lot." RaMona faked feeling the Spirit.

"It was pretty incredible how she seemed to be talking directly to me. Abundant living, and it has nothing to do with money." Mysti stood next to the Mustang with keys in hand.

RaMona began digging in the abyss called her purse. "I've never even thought about some of the things she talked about enhancing our quality of life. I'm definitely buying the tapes for this one. I sure wish they made CDs."

"Wouldn't that be great? Are you sure you don't want to go work out with me? Then we can have breakfast and talk about the wedding," Mysti said, trying to appeal to her friend's most vulnerable side.

"I sure need to be on a StairMaster, but I promised Mama I'd meet her at her church at eleven. It's family and friends day, and she begged Junior and me to come be her guests. I wonder how long it'll take before Junior causes me to cuss his sorry, triflin', no-good ass out. Forgive me, Lord. I just left the church house and here I'm acting out before I leave the parking lot. Did I say how triflin' his won't-work-nowhere, no-how butt is?"

"You may have mentioned it once or twice before. Well, have fun, and I'll see you at the pool party say at three-thirty?"

With astonishment RaMona paused with mouth agape. "You're going to the party? I don't believe it. Why didn't you say anything before?"

"I'm saying something now. I just decided. What else am I doing? I'd love to go meet some eligible benefited brothers as you put it. So see you there?" Mysti smiled sheepishly, loving to catch RaMona off guard. "I spent last night in front of the computer, and I just need to be among living and breathing folks."

"On that you can bet your last money, 'cause it's going to be a stone gas, honey! Love you. I'm out. Wear the black two-piece." RaMona darted off in the direction of her Porsche Cayenne, an engagement gift to herself.

Energy always seemed to create a cloud around RaMona. Mysti smiled broadly as she cranked up the

ponies. She loved everything about her friend and wanted
to be as confident and self-assured. As she backed out of
the parking space, she paused to let fellow churchgoers
pass. One was a tall, handsome young man. It made her
think of Stephan. As she'd checked before church for a
response to her e-mail she was disappointed to find he
hadn't answered. It was then she decided she would not
sit at home and wonder every thirty-seven seconds
when he was going to answer, and decided that she
would attend the December pool party.

For reasons unknown to her, she had become more
cognizant of the men she'd seen for years. Everywhere
she looked there were foine brothas. Where had her
head been before that she hadn't noticed the bald, tall
one with a diamond stud and the million-dollar smile,
or the stocky brotha with the eyes that sparkled when
he smiled?

She shook her head to replace the pleasant images
with the traffic on Manchester Boulevard as she headed
toward the San Diego Freeway. She'd spend a couple of
hours at the Spectrum Club before she headed home.
She didn't want to be solely focused on the computer
and the lack of e-mail from Stephan.

As she made the right turn to enter the northbound
entrance of the freeway she regretted not lowering the
car top. The morning was clear and clean, just warm
enough to promise a hot December day. The drive to the
club was uninhibited by typical L.A. traffic and within
five minutes Mysti was pulling into the crowded health
facility parking lot.

As she parked next to an immaculate BMW, she wondered what the owner looked like. "Gurl, you are out of
control. Get it together. You are bordering on obsession."
Mysti laughed as she spoke to herself aloud. Gathering
her bag from the trunk, her curiosity was satisfied as the

medium-built, honey-brown, tailored-blue-suit-wearing brotha approached the BMW just as she heard the double chirp and saw the lights flash.

"Good morning, my sistah. Looks like we did just the opposite. I did the gym first and now am headed to give God some praise. You look really nice."

Mysti smiled as the polite gentleman tantalized three of her five senses. "Why, thank you. You're looking rather dapper yourself. Yes, I went to the seven-thirty and now I'm guilt free to do whatever I want."

"Same here, except I'm doing the nine-thirty and will be done just in time to see my Raiders at the kick-off."

"Ah, a man with a plan. I like that. You have a great day."

"You do the same, my sistah."

The gentleman tossed his bag into the trunk and was slipping into the leather seat in what seemed to be one smooth motion. Mysti could feel his eyes on her behind, and her hips started to sway involuntarily again. She really had to get them under control.

How long had she ignored beautiful black men because she was so caught up in her own world? And sistahs wondered why black men were crossing to the other side in alarming numbers. She read somewhere, why be tolerated when celebration feels so much better?

After a one-hour workout and a twenty-minute swim, Mysti decided to take a little time for a sauna and steam. Wrapped in a towel she stepped into the room filled with white air and heat that took her breath away. She found a space on the lowest bench, stretched out her towel and lay naked. She couldn't see the other women in the room, but heard varied conversations. She wanted time to think, so she tuned out their voices.

She was lost in thought about the possibility of meeting Stephan. Her mind then went to the pool party and that she would attend with a new attitude. She would make eye contact and smile more. Her thoughts were interrupted by what could only be described as ghetto-fabulous sistahs, speaking way too loud and with an embarrassingly Ebonic dialogue.

"I played his ass like the fool he was," said the one seated on level two.

"You know how they is. Show 'em a little tit, rub up on 'em and they think they gettin' the snatch. Ain't spent but five dollars for a watered-down drink. Spend five, get five," said the one seated on Mysti's level.

"Yeah, his own five fingers!" The two women slapped hands and laughed.

Mysti hated to hear her sistahs act out and decided to cut her steam treatment short, and gathered her towel, wrapped it around her and left. She decided to forgo the sauna and headed for the shower.

Thoughts began vying for position: *Have I had the same attitude only on a professional level. That brotha can't have any of my time because he doesn't have a degree. I won't go out with him because I make more money.* "Lord, don't ever let me feel like my sistahs. This is not a game. I'm not up for bid to the candidate with the best credentials."

Mysti quickly showered and dressed in khaki shorts with a white tank top. Looking in the mirror, she decided she needed only a little color on her cheeks. She felt invigorated both in mind and body. Within forty-eight hours she had transformed her thinking, truly a testament to the power of the mind.

Chapter Ten

"I didn't think you'd ever get here." RaMona greeted Mysti at the gate leading to the backyard where the guests were gathered.

There were beautiful black people as far as the eye could see. Though no one was in the pool, more than half the women wore bikinis—the thong seemed to be the garment of the hour. *Damn, what am I doing here?* "You know I didn't want to be too early. I wanted things to be in full swing when I arrived, and I see I timed it just right.

"Gurl, you need to get in here and rescue these brothas from this harem of hoochies," RaMona whispered.

Mysti surveyed before speaking. "What can I do? They look pretty content to me."

Grabbing her arm, RaMona dragged Mysti toward the bar where three brothas in varied arrays of foine stood talking to the bartender who was no offense to the eyes either. "I want to introduce you to our host."

RaMona was moving so fast that Mysti tripped just as they arrived at their destination. *Nice going, Mona.*

"Are you okay?" The brotha wearing a Hard Rock Café shirt from Paris quickly moved to assist Mysti as she regained her composure.

"Yes, thank you very much. My friend here is in a bit of a hurry." Mysti felt her face flush.

"Aiding damsels in distress is my favorite pastime." He took her hand and brought it to his lips. "My name is Keith."

"My name is Mysti. Again thank you, Keith."

"I'm not mad at RaMona. She told us her best friend was arriving shortly and that you were quite something. I'm going to take a huge leap of faith here and make the assumption that you are the friend, because you are truly something to behold." The tallest of the three stepped forward. "My name is Kenneth. Friends, and I hope to soon have you in that category, call me Ken."

As Mysti looked into Ken's eyes she noticed something that made her uncomfortable. "Hi, Kenneth."

"And this is Michael." RaMona moved the three steps to the remaining of the trio and pulled him into their circle. "Say hello, Michael."

"Hello, Michael—I mean Mysti." His complexion flushed a deep shade of crimson as he extended his hand. A shy one.

Mysti extended her hand. "Hi, Michael. It's nice to meet all of you."

Finally taking her hand, Michael only smiled.

His damp hand and weak handshake immediately turned Mysti off. That he refused to make eye contact with her didn't help his cause in the least.

"Let me introduce you to Greg, our host and bartender." RaMona took Mysti's elbow gently this time.

"Mysti Ellington, this is Gregory Birmingham. He mixes a mean Long Island Iced Tea."

"I've heard a lot about you, Mysti. Welcome to our home. Please feel free to relax and enjoy yourself. What can I get you to start? I have a pitcher of Long Island tea just waiting for some ice, a straw, and your lovely lips."

Damn, this brotha is foine and charming and obviously doing quite well for himself, Mysti thought, but said, "Well, since I'm driving let's start with a glass of Chardonnay."

"Will Kendall Jackson be acceptable?" Greg asked, showing her the bottle of wine she recognized so well.

Oh Lord, I'm on a first-name basis with him. "Yes, that will do quite nicely."

"You have a really good friend in RaMona. She's good people. I've known her since I first started at Toyota. I'm glad she convinced you to come. We do this the same weekend every year, so be sure to put it on your calendar for next year," Greg said, passing her a perfectly filled wineglass.

"You and your wife have a lovely home. And this backyard is very impressive." Mysti took in the Olympic-size pool, Jacuzzi, pool house, built-in barbecue, and professional landscaping. She'd looked for a house in View Park when she was ready to make the move from her condo, but the price tag for entrance into the black Beverly Hills was way beyond the means of an associate, even senior. Now as a partner . . .

"Oh, I'm not married. My brother, sister, and I share the place. My brother is in Japan on business and my sister is running around here somewhere being the perfect hostess."

Two women approached the bar waving empty glasses. "Gregory, my little ol' glass is empty. What can you do about that?" the one in the animal-print thong asked, obviously already above the legal limit.

"Ladies, your wish is my command. Two iced teas coming up!"

Mysti seized the moment to break away from the bar. This time she grabbed RaMona's arm and dragged her out of earshot of the bartender. "Gurl, why haven't I met Gregory before? You always trying to hook me up with somebody, why not him?"

"Sorry to disappoint you, but Gregory is looking for the same thing as you are," RaMona said very matter of fact.

"Please say it ain't so! Not that foine-ass brotha behind the bar," Mysti said in astonishment. "He's so manly."

"A manly man who likes effeminate men." His boyfriend is running around being the other perfect little hostess with Grace, Greg's sister," RaMona dished the dirt.

"Now, as far as I know, Keith, Ken, and Michael are as straight as the crease in some jeans from a Chinese laundry. What do you think of them?"

"Michael is the most appealing physically, but that shyness is a bit annoying. There is something not quite right about Kenneth. But now Keith seems to fit the bill. What does he do?"

"What do you care what he does? This is a party." RaMona's right eye twitched. A sure sign she was trying to hide or avoid.

"Monaaaa?"

"Well, remember when he said his pastime was rescuing damsels? Well, it's not exactly a pastime. He's a paramedic."

"So what's wrong with that? Why didn't you want me to know that?"

"He hasn't finished college, don't think he even goes

anymore. And I know you don't date men who don't have a degree. But he's a good brotha."

"Am I that shallow?" Mysti's body seemed to slump as she saw her own reflection in her friend's eyes.

"The truth?"

"Of course."

"Yes, ma'am, you are. I've been trying to get you to see that good men come in all kinds of packages and that college may not be for everyone."

Mysti stood stunned and wondered why her friend had never said those words to her before. Or perhaps RaMona had and she'd turned a deaf ear to her. Mysti realized she had much work to do on herself.

"You okay?"

"Yeah, I think I need another glass of wine. I want to talk to Keith."

"Now that's what I'm talkin' 'bout. You are a quick study. No wonder you are bound for a corner office!" RaMona laughed and turned to follow her friend.

Returning to the bar area, Mysti had a newfound determination to have a meaningful conversation with Keith. He appealed to her and seemed genuinely nice, but time would tell. After refilling her wineglass, RaMona left her to talk to Keith.

Mysti walked up behind the three friends as Kenneth made a not-so-kind comment about a sistah who had a little more on the outside of her bikini than in it. "Hi, Keith."

Startled by her presence the three men turned. Michael flushed red, obviously embarrassed by his friend's comments. Kenneth smiled slyly and Keith's eyes sparkled slightly as he smiled. "Yes, my damsel?"

"I was just wondering if I could join you for a moment. RaMona is off on a peacekeeping mission of some sort. So how do you all know RaMona?"

"I just met her today, but if she's a friend of Greg, she's a'ight with me," Michael said, showing a little more confidence.

"I met her last year when I did a emergency preparedness workshop. Now I do the CPR training every three months. She invited me to the party, quite honestly to meet you. She's told me a lot about you. I brought these knuckleheads along because they don't get out much."

"I didn't even know if I was coming until this morning. What would you have done if I hadn't shown up?"

"Been terribly disappointed. But I would have waited for the next opportunity. She had convinced me you were worth the effort." Keith's words warmed her from the inside out.

"I don't know what to say. I hope you aren't disappointed after that kind of buildup. That's a lot of hype to live up to." Now Mysti felt her face getting warm.

"There is no way I could be disappointed. Would you like to go sit on the side of the pool? It's heated. You look very cute by the way." Keith stepped to the side to let her move in front of him. She tried desperately to telepathically communicate to her hips, but she failed. They did their own thing.

For what seemed like only minutes she sat and talked to Keith about politics, sports, law, wholesome versus hoesome women, great movies, lousy movies, good wine, and great times.

When the dinner bell rang Mysti realized the sun had set. Her feet had shriveled to beige prunes and her wineglass had been refilled a few times. She had learned he was a diehard Clippers fan, no matter what the rest of L.A. thought. He had been with the Los Angeles County Fire Department for ten years, divorced with a daughter of whom he had joint custody. He was only able to make the party because it was her mother's weekend. He believed in God, but didn't attend church regularly. He was extremely easy to talk to and made her laugh—a really nice combination.

"Shall we?" Keith stood and extended his strong hand.

"Why, but of course." Mysti felt giddy, and she had almost forgotten she hadn't received a response from Stephan when she checked the e-mail just before she left for the party.

The food was exquisite. With virtually every conceivable meat made for the grill presented, garnished with fresh vegetables and fruit for color and consumption, it was hard to decide where to start. The wine had gone to Mysti's head, and she knew she had to eat heavy food and cease alcohol consumption. She chose chicken, pork ribs, and a hot link. To give her feast balance she added potato salad, corn on the cob, and greens.

"I like that," Keith commented as they found a table near the pool.

"What?"

"A woman who is not afraid to eat on the first date."

With a look of surprise Mysti turned abruptly. "Is this a date?"

"I sure hope it is. I like your style and would love to see you again. What do you think of that?"

"That would be nice, I guess. I'm just surprised you considered this a date is all." Mysti bowed her head to say grace.

After a few seconds Keith lowered his head, more out of respect for Mysti than to bless his own food. When she raised her head, he said, "You know this is a blind date. Your friend orchestrated the whole thing. She's good. You didn't even know."

Mysti began laughing as she realized she'd been played and didn't even know she was in the game.

"Yeah, she's the best. Her heart is in the right place though, that's for sure."

"You're very lucky to have someone who loves you that way."

"You don't know how right you are."

As if on cue, RaMona appeared with a woman who bore a striking resemblance to Gregory—her bathing suit cover-up matched his shirt. Mysti assumed this was Grace, their hostess.

"So are you kids getting to know each other?" RaMona began with a devious smile. "I want you both to meet Grace, Greg's sister and our hostess. Grace owns a catering company and is responsible for this decadent food. Wait until you try her German chocolate cake and peach cobbler. Grace, this is Mysti and Keith."

"Hi, Grace. It's a pleasure to meet you. I'm having an absolutely wonderful time, and this food is unbelievable," Keith volunteered, eyeing Mysti.

"I have to echo Keith's sentiments. Everything is quite nice. I'm glad RaMona dragged me kicking and screaming."

"I'm sorry it has taken me so long to get around to greeting one of the handsomest couples here. Even when I'm not supposed to be working I just don't know how to shut it off." Grace oozed charm much like her brother.

"Oh, we're not a couple," Mysti blurted, not realizing how it must have sounded.

"Oh, forgive my error, but perhaps you should consider becoming one. If you will excuse me, I want to make sure everyone has what they need. It was so nice meeting you, and I hope you join us again. We do this semi-annually at Christmas and the fourth of July."

"Thank you. I surely will be back." Mysti smiled.

"Well, if this lovely lady is returning, you can mark me down now." Keith winked at Mysti.

Turning to leave, Grace smiled and simply said, "Enjoy the rest of your evening."

Despite the heat lamps, Mysti caught a sudden chill. No matter how warm the December days, the nights were biting. Keith noticed her shiver and immediately offered his jacket. Placing it around her shoulders his scent tickled her nose. *Man, he smells good.*

They finished the meal in silence. As the uniformed servers moved about the area clearing dishes, the deejay changed the tempo of the music and many of the guests made their way to the dance floor to show their cha-cha slide skills. Most of the women had put on cover-ups after the sun had slipped into the western sky, but a couple of the sistahs still worked only a thong and as they took two steps up and two steps back, all their mama gave them jiggled.

Keith watched in amusement before turning to Mysti. "I'm really glad you came dressed like this. Don't get me wrong, that," he said, pointing in the direction of the hoochie harem, "is nice eye candy, but how much candy can a brotha consume before he gets tooth decay?"

"Thank you for noticing," Mysti managed to say between laughter. "I honestly couldn't wear that under any circumstances."

"That's nice to know. Do you dance?"

"I thought you'd never ask." Mysti followed Keith to the dance floor.

Keith was as smooth on the dance floor as he was in conversation. They went from the cha-cha slide to the electric slide to dancing together for five consecutive songs. Mysti was out of breath and sweating by the time she returned to their table. She couldn't believe the good time she was having. She'd thank RaMona in the morning.

"You know I hate to say this, but I need to get going. I have a little bit of a drive and I have to be in the office early tomorrow. I've had a great evening."

"I should get going, too. I have a shift tomorrow. May I call you?"

Mysti pulled a card from her purse. "I was hoping you'd ask. Here's my card. I work traditional hours on most days. I'd like to see you again. Call me, and I'm sure we can work something out. Will you walk me to my car?"

"Now would I let a damsel brave this forest alone?"

"I'd like to say good night to our hosts and find RaMona. You know I'll hear I told you so until Jesus comes." Mysti willed her hips not to sway as she walked toward the bar. Failure.

"Gregory, I just want to thank you again for a wonderful time. I've had an absolute blast. I'm looking forward to July fourth." As Mysti extended her hand, Greg came from behind the bar and hugged her.

"We're so glad you graced our home with your charm and beauty. And seems like you made a new friend, too." He winked at her.

"It does seem to be that way. Please tell Grace good night for me if I don't find her before I leave."

"I surely will. And you take good care of her, Keith. She's special."

"I will if she lets me. You ready? I see RaMona over at the card table." Keith gently guided Mysti in her friend's direction.

"Come on, play it if you dare. I'm gonna cut you like you stole my last good pair of J. Renees." RaMona had full command of the bid whist table.

Mysti waited for a break in the action. "Mona, I'm leaving. You know what I have going on tomorrow. Call me later."

"Gurl, why are you leaving so . . ." RaMona stopped abruptly as she saw Keith standing behind Mysti. "Ooohhh! Handle your business, gurlfriend. I'll call you tomorrow."

"Call me tonight. Keith is only walking me to the car. You're such a mess. Love you." She bent to kiss RaMona.

As Keith walked Mysti out she could feel daggers at her back as the women envious of her obvious connection with one of the most eligible men in attendance stared. The walk was quiet. As they exited through the gate he took her hand. It felt so natural.

As they reached the car he turned to face her. "I haven't had this much fun in a very long time. I'll call you on Tuesday if that's okay. I'd say tomorrow, but one never knows what it'll be like on shift, and I'm a man of my word."

In her head she wondered why he hadn't offered his number. "That's fine. I'll be tied up most of tomorrow as well. I had a great time, too, and I do want to hear from you again."

As though he was reading her mind, he said, "May I give you my number? You know a brotha wouldn't be mad if he had a voice mail waiting when he finished twenty-four hours of damsel rescuing." Keith pulled a pen from his pocket.

She unlocked the car with the remote control and pulled her PDA from the console positioned between the seats. "If I write it on a piece of paper it's as good as lost."

"Ahhh, a woman in tune with modern technology. I like that. My number is 323-555-9985. Until Tuesday." He kissed her lightly on the cheek.

The touch of his lips shot flashes of heat throughout her limbs. As he helped her into the car and closed the door she lowered the window. They only smiled knowingly.

He backed away from the car as she pulled away from the curb. She watched in her rearview mirror until his image disappeared.

Chapter Eleven

"Alright, alright! I concede, you were correct. I had the time of my life. Keith seems really nice." Mysti twirled her hair as she spoke to her best friend. "I could've talked to him all night. Why haven't you ever told me about him before?"

"I've tried. I never gave you any specifics, but you wouldn't hear it." RaMona worked her neck as she yelled.

"Dang, you don't have to scream on a sistah just because she is slow on the uptake."

"See, you make it almost impossible to be mad at you. How you gonna argue by yourself?" They both began laughing.

"Gurl, I'm going to take a bath and crawl my wide butt into bed. I'm so tired. Greg and Grace throw a hell of party, don't they?" Fatigue weighed heavily in RaMona's voice. "Just one more thing: Will you abandon this craziness with looking for a man on the Internet?"

"The one I was interested in meeting hasn't responded to my last e-mail, so we'll see. I'm not putting all my eggs in Keith's basket. I just met him. I'll be keeping my options open. I'm going to bed, too. But thanks again. I had a really great time."

As Mysti hit the talk button she had the urge to check the e-mail, just one more time. Despite the obvious chemistry between her and Keith, she couldn't get Stephan out of her mind. She didn't understand it. She dealt strictly in logic and this defied it. Throwing the cover back, she headed barefoot to the office. She was far past pretending to be going elsewhere. In just two days she had become obsessed with the intrigue of it all.

Opening the browser her pulse quickened. Junk, junk, junk . . . DocLove12.

> *Hey Mystique One,*
> > *Got spunk. I like that.*
> > *Questions:*
> > *Your favorite position?*
> > *Your freakiest fantasy?*
> > *Ever done it with another woman?*
> > *Willing to try?*
> > *Are you scared of twelve inches?*
> > *Hit a brotha back.*
> *DocLove12*

Mysti stared at the screen speechless. She quickly returned to the mail she had sent him originally to see if there was any indication in what she'd written that would make him think she was looking for this kind of relationship. Convinced she hadn't she sent his mail to the trash.

Anger burned in her throat at the very thought that he would approach her in such a disrespectful manner.

She began to wonder if RaMona was right after all; the men seeking love on the Internet were maniacs.

Her hand trembled so hard it was difficult to control her index finger to click the mouse. She continued to scan her inbox for mail from Stephan. At the very bottom she spotted it. BlacKnight. The trembling increased as she feared what bizarre response waited just a click away. The previous anticipation was replaced with trepidation as she double-clicked.

Dear Mystique One,

I see that you wrote me early yesterday. I was at work and then today had a full day. I'm just getting a chance to check e-mail. I'm really tired and since I only get to ask you five questions, I want to choose them wisely. I promise to send them to you before I go off to work tomorrow.

From the lateness of the hour, you may receive them both at the same time. My wish for you this beautiful night is a restful sleep with dreams that make you smile.
Stephan

"Now that is nice." Mysti decided she would check her other mail in the morning. She was suddenly beyond exhausted. She craved the comfort of feathers.

Turning off the light, she smiled to herself thinking of the eventful weekend she'd had. When she'd left downtown Los Angeles on Friday she didn't have the slightest inkling that by the time she returned to work on Monday she would have not one, but two prospects.

She climbed into bed and set the television sleep timer for thirty minutes. She never saw the first commercial.

Chapter Twelve

"Traffic has sped up to a crawl on the 101 south-bound as Cal-Trans has reopened two lanes after an overnight tanker spill." The familiar voice on the radio bolted Mysti awake.

"It's seven thirty-one, seven o'clock thirty-one." Steve Harvey declared the time in his unique way.

"Oh my God! I haven't overslept on a workday in five years. I won't get to work before ten with the traffic." Mysti leapt from the bed and headed for the shower, dropping her nightshirt en route. She was showered and in her underwear applying makeup in four minutes, in her suit and fumbling for her keys in thirteen minutes. At 7:57 she was backing the Mustang out of the garage.

As she pulled onto Winnetka she realized she hadn't checked her e-mail. She swore to herself for oversleeping, but she'd had the most peaceful night's sleep in months. She would check as soon as she got to her office.

She crawled along for an hour and forty minutes on the freeway before she arrived downtown. She finally was able to accelerate to thirty miles per hour when she made the transition to the Harbor Freeway and was taking the exit in five minutes. She maneuvered easily through traffic and was pulling into her parking spot at ten o'clock on the dot. She walked through the glass doors of her office at 10:10. Much to her amazement Kamesha sat at her desk.

Mysti stopped at her desk. "What in the world are you doing here? I didn't expect you back until Wednesday."

"Other than a little swelling, I'm fine. I'd rather use two days on the Mexican Riviera than watching *Jerry Springer.*" Kamesha's eyes and cheeks were puffy and she talked like she had a mouth full of cotton.

"Believe me, I'm glad to see you, but don't overdo it. If you start to feel bad, go home. I mean that." Mysti headed for her office.

She logged on to her computer, ignoring the flashing voice mail indicator. She felt terribly irresponsible, but at this moment she had no control over her actions. Her computer had never loaded so slowly before. She impatiently tapped the gold tone letter opener on the edge of the blotter. She quickly brought up her personal e-mail account and skimmed the in box.

"I really need to do something about all of this junk mail." She highlighted the top seventeen mails and clicked delete. The next nine she skipped. PROBLKMAN69—double click.

Got the picture. I hope you're the thin one. If not, don't bother to answer this. I'm tired of you sistahs claiming to be a sports car when you are really a van.

Delete.

The e-mail didn't upset Mysti. She filed him under stupid with DocLove12. She jumped, looking incredibly guilty as Kamesha walked into her office.

"You okay, Ms. E?" Kamesha laughed. "You look like you saw Tupac walk through the door."

"Oh, I guess I'm a little nervous about the judgment," Mysti lied. The fact was she hadn't once thought of the jury since she walked through the door. What was happening to her?

"So how was your weekend? Please tell me you had some fun." Kamesha was placing several documents in Mysti's in basket.

Mysti didn't want to give up too much information or seem too excited. "RaMona invited me to a pool party and I went. And to answer your next question, yes I had fun. So you see, I took your advice."

"Now that wasn't so hard, was it?" The ringing phone interrupted Kamesha. "Ms. Ellington's office. Thank you, I'll let her know. The jury's back. They want you there at one."

"Whoa, that didn't take long. What do we think that means?" Mysti's rhetorical question made Kamesha laugh.

"That I'll be working for a partner!"

"Don't get too excited. I don't want any of us to be disappointed. Although the big boss came by to see me on Friday after you left."

Kamesha sat on the edge of the blue guest chair in front of Mysti's desk. "Really? What did he say?"

"Just came by to congratulate me on a job well done."

"Oh, I'll order the moving boxes!" Kamesha jumped up from the chair and ran around to hug Mysti. "I knew you would do it. I'm so proud of you."

"If it is in fact done, we did it together. You'd better

call the client. And Kamesha . . ." Mysti hesitated for a moment, suppressing emotion.

"Yes, Mysti?" Kamesha rarely called her by her first name, by her own choosing.

"I can never thank you enough for all that you did to make this happen."

"Cash works nicely." She laughed and hugged her again. "I'll make that call to Mr. Bullock. Congrats again. I'm really proud of you."

Smiling warmly Mysti simply said, "Thank you."

Kamesha returned to her work area and Mysti suddenly felt a potpourri of emotions. She was happy, scared, sad, and grateful all at the same time.

She got up from her desk and closed the door. "Lord, I just want to thank You. Not for winning, but for helping me believe I can do this. Let me always remember from whence my blessings flow. Let me always grab someone else by the hand and pull them along. And thank You for a wonderful, loving friend." Next she hit speed dial three.

"RaMona Kirby's office." A pleasant, professional voice Mysti didn't recognize answered.

"Is she available? This is Mysti Ellington calling."

"Will she know what this is regarding?"

"Oh yes, she'll know."

The smooth sounds of Kenny G serenaded Mysti as she waited.

"Gurl, did you hear from Keith?"

"No good morning? No hi, Mysti?"

"Good morning, Mysti. How are you, Mysti?" RaMona patronized.

"Good morning, RaMona. I'm just fine and how about you?"

"Cut the crap. Get to the good stuff."

Laughing hysterically, Mysti was finally able to answer. "Gurl, I'm doing great other than oversleeping for the first time in like five years. I haven't heard from Keith, but he said I wouldn't. I do have news though."

"What? Tell me. Tell me."

"The jury is back and my future is in the hands of twelve people. Mr. McCarthy came in and talked to me on Friday and said I'm a cinch for partner. I don't know if it's true or not, but I'm a wreck."

"Gurl, don't even think about it twice. That firm is going to be Haynes, Wilson, McCarthy, Stith, and Ellington on January first."

"They won't change the name. But it'll be an awesome experience. I have to be in court at one."

"I'll pray for you then. I'll set a reminder."

"I know I shouldn't tell you this because you'll probably scream on me again, but I got some really off-the-wall responses from the matchmaking site. I just want you to rest assured I won't be in touch with them anymore."

"Well, I'm really glad you've come to your senses before you're Dr. Jordan Cavanaugh's next patient. Besides I have a good feeling about you and Keith. He's a real good guy. Loves that baby of his."

Mysti felt guilty about not telling RaMona about Stephan. They had promised each other they would never keep secrets. Mysti wasn't convinced RaMona would understand and knew she definitely would not support her decision.

"As much as I'd love to continue to dance at this party, I have a meeting in a few that I'm not ready for. I stayed at the party way too long schooling folks at the whist table. So this morning I'm paying the price. I should be back in the office by the time you come from court. Call me the minute you leave the courtroom."

"I promise I will. And again RaMona, thanks for yesterday."

"Just doing what a sister does. Love you."

"Love you, too."

Mysti picked up the documents from the in basket and began mindlessly thumbing through the papers. Her mind was still on e-mail, and she laid the documents to the side. With a light tap of the mouse the screen saver disappeared and the list of incoming mail reappeared.

Sixteen junk mails, three forwards, an e-mail from her cousin in Japan, and there it was. Double click.

Dear Mystique One,

I realized as I typed this at five A.M. that I don't know your name. If you still aren't comfortable telling me, I understand. I thought of you often last night as I wondered what questions to ask. I have a million questions for you, but it was very difficult to narrow them down to five, but here goes.

1. If you could vacation in any place (price not withstanding) where would you go?

2. It's Sunday morning and you wake up with the sniffles, but not really sick. Do you still go to church?

3. You and I are kicking it. We've decided to rent two movies, one action adventure, one chick flick. Which do we watch first and why?

4. We've both been working overtime, and we haven't been able to see each other for weeks. You get a break. What do you do?

5. You've had plans with your girfriends for months and I get concert tickets as a surprise, not knowing your plans. What do you do?

I hope these meet with your approval and I look for-

*ward to your five. I've got to get to work. You have an
awesome day. I look forward to hearing from you soon.
Stephan*

"Whew." Mysti whistled through her teeth. "This
brotha is deep."

Mysti had five very basic questions: favorite color,
food, movie, etc., but this brotha was serious. His questions were well thought out and looked into her character.

A soft knock startled her. "Ms. E., why are you so
jumpy?"

"Why do you keep sneaking up on me?" Mysti's over-
reaction took both of them aback. "I'm sorry. I didn't
mean to snap at you. I guess I'm a little more nervous
about the Bullock case than I realized. What can I do
for you?"

Eyeing her boss suspiciously, Kamesha answered
slowly. "Mr. Bullock is on his way. He said he'll be here
at the office at eleven and wants to take you to lunch
and then ride over to the courthouse with him. He
would like for you to meet him out front."

"Now that's a first, riding to the courthouse in a
limo."

"Just a preview of things to come, Ms. E. Are you sure
you're okay? You just don't seem to be yourself. You've
had big verdicts before." Kamesha sat on the edge of
the visitor's chair.

"I'm really fine." Mysti pondered the prudence of
sharing her weekend activities with her assistant. "Was
there anything else?"

Clearly disappointed by the lack of information,
Kamesha rose, shaking her head. "I'll have everything
ready."

"Could you close the door on your way out? I just need a minute to collect my courage."

"You got it. And don't worry, you'll do just fine," Kamesha said sympathetically.

Mysti let out a sigh of relief as she heard the door close. She had to put her emotions in check before she met with her client. She felt bewildered and confused. She wanted to answer Stephan before she left, but wasn't sure there was enough time. Her answers needed to be as well thought through as his questions, and she needed to think of equally meaningful questions to pose to him.

Dear Stephan

Your e-mail this morning is most welcomed, and I look forward to responding in depth this evening. My calendar is full today and I would like to devote as much time as necessary without rushing. I wish you, too, a great day.

Mysti started to type her name and then thought better of it. Suppose this was someone who talked a good game yet was a lunatic like the others? She decided to use Ellie. A soft knock on the door signaled her it was time to meet her client. She typed her alias and hit the send button.

Chapter Thirteen

Resounding applause rose throughout the forty-sixth floor as Mysti entered the office. She had done it! She'd won. Over lunch Mr. Bullock had praised her on the brilliant handling of the case and he, too, told her win or lose she had nothing to regret. He was requesting that she handle all of his legal matters in the future. Even with the endorsement of one of the firm's biggest clients, she wasn't sure if she'd pulled it off and could expect her promotion. But now, her feet barely touched the floor. An aisle was formed of well-wishers patting her back or giving her a high-five.

When Mysti finally reached her office Kamesha waited inside. She closed the door and the two professional friends hugged each other and jumped up and down like teenagers at a victorious homecoming game.

"Oh my God. Can you believe it?" Kamesha spoke first.

"I've wanted this for so long and now that it has happened, no I can't believe it." Mysti hugged Kamesha again and screamed.

"RaMona called and wants you to call her the minute you walk in. And I quote 'Does the hussy have a cell phone that works?' She was pretty ticked since she hadn't heard from you. She asked me what happened, but of course I didn't tell her. Mr. Stith has ordered a celebration in the conference room at four-thirty, including champagne. Congratulations again." Kamesha hugged her once more. "I'm going to leave you alone and hold your calls to give you a chance to let it all soak in. I'm so proud of you."

As Kamesha left, Mysti kicked off her shoes and fell back into her junior executive chair. She would only have four more days in this office. When she returned in January, she would be on executive row. Now that she had reached her career goal, what next?

Hitting the speed dial to connect her to RaMona she suddenly felt weary. All of her reserves had been tapped and she really wished her vacation started today. Third ring, voice mail. "Give a sistah a call at the office."

She yearned to tell someone she loved the good news. Congratulations and celebration from those she worked with was one thing but from the people who really mattered was quite another. Her mind easily made the transition from new partner to life partner.

What if Stephan and Keith turned out to be equally wonderful? How would she make a choice? Should she tell one about the other? "Don't be a fool, gurl!" she said aloud.

Her phone buzzed in the middle of her thoughts.

"RaMona for you," Kamesha sang over the speaker.

"Thanks." Mysti did everything she could not to scream into the receiver. "Hello."

"Don't hello me. What happened? I've been pacing like an expectant father." RaMona spoke in her warp speed manner.

"Well . . ." Mysti teased.

"Gurl, I'm going to hurt you!"

Laughing Mysti finally said, "The jury found in favor of my client. We won!"

Both women began screaming. Suddenly tears cascaded down Mysti's cheeks. All of the pent-up stress had found its crack in her dam of strength. She was so grateful to God for giving her the fortitude to make it in a world that was less than kind to women, especially black women.

RaMona could hear Mysti crying. "Gurl, what is wrong with you? This should be the happiest day of your life."

Between sobs Mysti managed, "It is. I guess I've been so stressed about all of this and not realizing it. I'm so relieved to have it behind me."

"So what are we going to do to celebrate?" RaMona wanted to change the mood before she, too, started crying. No self-respecting friend would let her cry alone. "I was thinking dinner at Reign via limo so we can have champagne by the gallons. I know Max will want to come, too, if that's okay. I can call Keith if you like."

"Gurl, I don't know him like that. This celebration should be for those who are near and dear to me. The three of us will be fine. I should call my parents, but my mother will surely say something that'll piss me off, so I'll just save that celebration for a little later. Mona, gurl, thanks for always keepin' it real. I don't know if I could have made it without you."

"Sure you could have. It just wouldn't have been as much fun. So what is Ms. Gonna be Partner doing this afternoon? Please don't tell me you're starting a new case."

Mysti weighed what she was about to say carefully before she began. "I'm sure the minute I open this door there'll be a steady stream of well-wishers. Then I'm going to answer an e-mail from one of the men from the personals online. I asked him to send me five questions and you should hear them. He's a deep brotha. Then we're having an office celebration at four-thirty."

RaMona was silent.

"You there?"

"Of course, I'm here. I just thought Keith would've helped get this nonsense out of your system. You know I only want you to be happy, but I don't think this is the road to bliss. *But, I* did promise to be supportive, so I'll keep an open mind."

"I appreciate that, Mona, and I do promise to be careful. When I signed my last response I didn't even use my real name. Little does he know my screen name *is* my real name. I signed it Ellie."

"So why Ellie?" RaMona seemed subdued.

"You know that's what all my friends always called my mom when we were young."

"Oh, that's right. Gurl, that is taking a sistah waaaaay back. How is Miss Ellie? And why do you think she's going to say something to piss you off if she comes to dinner with us?"

"She just will. She'll harp on what I haven't done instead of focusing on how much I've accomplished. It's just her. I'm sure my parents will write me a nice check and tell me to get a real car. I don't want anything to spoil the good time I know the three of us will have, so if it's okay with you, just us and bring my nephew, too. He'll be my date."

RaMona laughed. "It's your party. Have it your way. I have another meeting and must scoot. I love you and congrats again. We'll set a date and time to go out when I talk to you tonight."

"Sounds like a plan. Love you, too." Mysti hung up first, leaving her hand on the phone for a long moment while she thought of the love she had for her friend.

Contemplating if she should call her mom and dad she decided that she'd probably miss them and leave a voice mail, which suited her just fine.

First ring. Second ring. Third ring. "Hi, Mom and Dad. It's Mysti. I just wanted to let you know that I won the case. Mr. McCarthy came to my office on Friday and told me he was voting in my favor for the partnership, so it looks pretty good. Your little girl has arrived. We'll celebrate during the holidays. Love you."

With a sigh of relief Mysti replaced the handset into the cradle. She had done her duty and had the foresight to combine two visits into one. Oh yeah, this was a great day. She knew she had delayed the inevitable and it was time to open her door. She slipped her shoes on, stood, and squared her shoulders. Ms. Ellington was ready to receive guests.

Chapter Fourteen

Kamesha stood in the doorway looking exhausted. "Do you need anything else from me before I leave?"

"I can't believe you were able to hang in here all this time. If you're feeling less than perfect tomorrow, take the day off. I promise you nothing major will be happening. I must be honest with you though, I'm really glad you were here today. I wouldn't have wanted you to miss the celebration that you contributed so heavily to make possible."

"I just had a feeling today was going to be really special. I'm really tired though. I may come in late if I don't take the day off."

"That sounds like a really great idea. Why don't we say noon at the earliest?"

Kamesha smiled. "You always steer me strong, not wrong, so let's call it a plan. Don't you stay too late. Good night."

"Good night." Mysti had drunk several glasses of champagne and still felt the effects. She felt so wonderful at this moment, yet she craved someone very special to share it with.

With a light touch from her right index finger the computer screen came to life. Her e-mail account had timed itself out. With just a few keystrokes she was searching for the letter from Stephan. She reread his questions twice more, each time amazed at the depth of his interest.

"Hmm, I think I need a cup of tea before I start this." Mysti made her way to the kitchen through the office where only a few junior associates remained nose deep in their assigned cases.

While waiting for the water to heat in the microwave, Mysti wondered what life would be like if she had a steady man. He could be waiting at home with dinner cooked or ordered, wine chilling, and strong hands to rub her chronically aching feet. But could she handle the demands of a relationship and a law partnership? The demands by the firm had been brutal at times, yet she loved every minute of it. But would a man understand her devotion to a job? The ding of the microwave shattered her daze.

Why was she so afraid of a committed relationship? Was she afraid of failure? As she dipped the Lemon Zinger tea bag in the steamy water, she resolved she would work hard to overcome her commitment issues. But how? What were her first steps?

"Start by answering Stephan's questions." She blew on the tea before taking a sip and headed back to her office.

Without the slightest hint of trepidation she began typing.

Dear Stephan,

I've thought about your questions a lot today and must tell you again that I'm quite impressed with the thought that went into them. You've made my questions seem shallow by comparison, and I believe I'm going to have to re-think them. But here goes.

1. In a forwarded e-mail, someone sent me a Power Point presentation from the Hilton in Bali. It is the most magnificently romantic place I've ever seen. I would want not only to vacation, but to spend my honeymoon there.

2. This was probably the hardest of all the questions. I'm ashamed to say I would probably pull the covers up close around my neck and not go to church.

3. It would depend on whose movie we watched first last time. This is an unfair question because I love action adventures.

4. After a long, hot bath, I'd dress in your favorite scent, some really comfortable sweats, stop at Togo's and get us a picnic lunch and bring it to wherever you are. (Oh you didn't think I was cooking, did you? LOL.)

5. I would hate to disappoint you, but my plans have been set first. I would recommend you take a buddy or sell the tickets, but I wouldn't leave my girls hanging.

Well, there you have it, now my turn.

1. We've had what you consider a senseless disagreement, but it is serious to me. How do you handle a resolution?

2. Your favorite team is in the playoffs, but it is our anniversary. What do you do?

3. What is your idea of a perfect date?

4. What's your favorite household chore?

5. How do you keep track of special occasions?

Wow. That was so much harder than I expected. I look forward to hearing from you soon.

Mysti had sobered and was ready to leave when the phone rang. She debated if she should let the voice mail system pick it up. On the third ring she answered. "Mysti Ellington."

"I can't believe you're still in the office." The sexy bass voice on the other end caused Mysti to roll her eyes.

"Hi, Dennis. How are you?" Mysti asked very matter-of-factly.

"Is that any way to greet an old flame?" Dennis chimed.

"The flames, much like a Duraflame log, only lasted a few hours." *Lord, how did I ever get involved with this fool?*

"Look, baby, the word is on the street. You whipped, flipped, and locked it down in the courtroom today. I know you need to have someone to celebrate with. I'm just offering to help a sistah out is all."

Mysti thought of the wanna-be player on the other end of the phone and her sheer stupidity for getting caught up in his mess. Women calling her cell phone all hours of the night accusing her of sleeping with their man. She was smart enough to give him his stepping permit after the third call. Apparently, she was one of five women; two of whom were having his baby. She later heard he was a lousy lawyer who only drew a check from the County of Los Angeles Public Defender's office.

"Dennis, I appreciate the offer, but I think you should spend the time reading to one of your many children and if you time it right, you might be able to make it to see two of them tonight." *Click.*

She smiled smugly as she was reminded she changed her cell phone number after the third woman had phoned her at one-thirty in the morning.

She gathered her briefcase and started to pick up a file, but decided she had no inkling to open anything but a bottle of wine. She was starving, as the finger sandwiches were a distant memory. With keys in hand she made her way through her door and out of the office with one well-pitched good night to cover the few who remained. Down the elevator and across the lobby toward the parking garage she moved swiftly with thoughts of rotisserie chicken and macaroni and cheese from Boston Market.

"Where's the fire?" She turned to see Curtis Barr approaching.

"Hi, Curtis. Looks like we keep the same schedule. What are you doing here so late?" Mysti smiled warmly.

"I'm an accountant and we're in our year-end. We close for the week between Christmas and New Year's, but the deadlines in January remain the same, so I'm always here late in December. We took off early on Friday, just because we'd all had enough. Bert and Andy are still working. I come in early. I'm pretty much spent by six o' clock."

The elevator door opened as Curtis stepped aside to let her pass. "I understand. I'm a morning person, too. Though I do work late into the night more than I care to admit. But not tonight."

"You say that with a lot of conviction. Is tonight special?"

"I had a major victory in court. I'm going to go home and open a bottle of vintage Monday to celebrate."

They arrived on parking level R. Mysti's level. "He's a very lucky man. Beauty and brains."

Mysti held the door opened as she answered. "Not very original, but the answer is there is no he. Good night, Curtis." She stepped off the elevator.

This time Curtis held the door, "You've got to be kidding me. There's no way a brotha can let you celebrate alone."

Mysti raised her right eyebrow.

"How about I take you for a drink at the Bona-venture? The nice lounge at the top?" Curtis quickly added.

"That's a nice offer, but I don't even know you."

The buzzer sounded indicating the elevator door had remained open too long. Curtis stepped off. "And how do you propose we get to know each other? We'll drive our own cars and you know where I work. How much of a threat can I pose? Besides, you shouldn't have to celebrate alone."

"I really shouldn't drink anything else. I haven't eaten and I've had a few glasses of champagne. I do appreci-ate the offer, however. Perhaps another time?"

Not to be dissuaded Curtis countered, "How about dinner? Nothing fancy, just two people who're starving deciding to eat at the same place at the same time."

"You're persistent for an accountant." Mysti laughed.

"Everything has to balance. Hunger is a liability, food's an asset. Know what I mean?"

Shaking her head, Mysti smiled and said, "Nothing fancy? Like a Denny's?"

"Come on, now. How you going to play a brotha? I can hear you now. 'Gurl, can you believe he bought me a Grand Slam?' I don't think so. How about Santa Monica? Which way do you go home?"

"I take the 101 North. But Santa Monica is good." Mysti began laughing at herself. She couldn't believe she'd said yes.

"Fantastic! There's a beautiful hotel with a fabulous café overlooking the ocean. The address is One Pico Boulevard. You take the Fourth Street exit, make a left to Pico, and make a right. The street will end in their valet parking area."

"Whoa this sounds a little fancy. How did we get from Denny's to fine dining?"

"It's casual dining, I promise you, but some of the best you'll ever have."

Mysti had one very pressing question: "Won't she be expecting you at home?"

"How did you put it? Smooth? I'm not married, no steady girlfriend. I do, however, have four fish. I think they're all female." Curtis' smile was captivating. His easy manner and sense of humor drew her in. "I don't know, a jealous fish can be a dangerous thing, ya know!"

"Well then, Mr. Barr, I think we should get going."

"I'll see you there in about twenty minutes?"

Tilting her head slightly to the side with a crooked smile she said, "Twenty minutes it is."

Curtis pressed the down button and began humming as Mysti walked across the parking lot to the Mustang. Her steps seemed lighter. Her heartbeat increased slightly. She wasn't sure if she'd made the right decision, but she did feel safe. And no matter how much mental turmoil she was in, the fact remained she would be enjoying, if not celebrating, the evening with a man who was funny, witty, and seemingly a nice guy. And it was only dinner. She would insist she pick up the check. If he protested, they'd go dutch.

She lowered the top and switched to a Luther Vandross CD. The upbeat tempo made her want to bounce in her seat. She cranked it just a little higher than she normally would have in the garage, but she was entitled. She was going to be partner at one of the leading law firms in Los Angeles.

The evening was cooler than she had anticipated and the top down may not have been a wise decision. She turned up the heat and moved the temperature to the highest setting. The combination of cold and warm air intoxicated her. As she drove, she was again awe-struck by the events of the past four days. She had gone from starvation to the Home Town Buffet in three point six seconds. She laughed and turned up the CD as Luther serenaded her, promising love would be better the second time around.

Had there ever been a first time? She couldn't remember loving someone with reckless abandon. She hadn't had the bring-me-tea-when-I'm-sick, wash-his-dirty-drawers kind of love. At thirty-seven she was more than ready. In the words of the esteemed author E. Lynn Harris, she needed a love of her own.

As she pulled into the parking lot of the hotel, she immediately thought Mr. Barr had good taste. The young man in the denim blue shirt and beige khaki pants greeted her. "Good evening, miss. Will you be dining with us this evening?" His badge read CARLOS.

Mysti emerged from the topless chariot smiling. "Yes, Carlos. I'll be dining with you this evening."

Chapter Fifteen

"So, tell me all about yourself. How long have you been a lawyer?" Curtis asked as soon as they were seated.

"Almost thirteen years. This is my third and hopefully final firm. What about you? How long have you been an accountant?"

"Just starting my fourth year. I was military for eight years, came out, went to college, and now I make sure debits equal credits." Curtis looked at the menu as he spoke. "I bet you make a lot of money up there on the forty-sixth floor. Oh, and by the way I seem to have forgotten my wallet on my desk. I hope that won't be a problem for you."

Taken aback by his comment Mysti finally spoke. "Uh, no. I guess that won't be a problem." She reconciled in her mind that she was going to offer to pay anyhow. "Did you travel much while you were in the military?"

"Oh yeah. I've been practically all over the world. I

love traveling when someone else is paying for it. I took this job because they told me that after five years I would become an international field auditor. So I can order whatever I want?"

This time Mysti was stunned. She had every intention to offer to pay for dinner. How rude of him to ask such a question when he was the one who insisted they have dinner. "I'll gladly pick up the check for both of us. After all this is my celebration." Mysti's throat began to tickle. A sure sign something wasn't right.

"You must make a lot of money." There it was again.

"You seem to be very concerned about my fiscal status, Curtis. We just met. Why is what I make of such interest to you?" Mysti did nothing to hide her annoyance.

"I've just dated some sistahs lately who look at a brotha with dollar signs in their eyes. It's just nice to meet someone who can pick up the check at a nice restaurant like this with no sweat. I'm saving for a C230, peacock blue, so can't be spending all my money on the honies."

"Good evening. I'm Antonio. I will be your server this evening. Our specials are . . ."

"Antonio, I've changed my mind. If the gentleman wants to order you may serve him, but please be aware he left his wallet on his desk. I just remembered I need to wash my hair or was it rotate my shoe trees?" With that Mysti had her purse and was gone. She never looked back to see Curtis' bewildered face as she sashayed out of the restaurant.

As she waited for her car she hoped she didn't have to share her space with Curtis Barr ever again. She was glad, however, he wasted no time in showing his true colors. Now she remembered why she hadn't dated for so long. *Why am I wasting all of the precious time and good energy on trying to date? It never turns out right.*

She silently tipped the valet, never even checking his

nametag. She didn't remember if she even said thank you as he closed her door. Men!

Rush-hour traffic had dissipated, and Mysti maneuvered easily over the Santa Monica Freeway heading for the northbound 405. The cold air and heat that had intoxicated her earlier, aggravated her and she wanted to raise the top. It would require she pull to the shoulder—she didn't want to stop. She pressed the gas pedal just a little harder, moving the speedometer just above eighty. The roar of the eight cylinders gave her a sense of power, the only power she seemed to have. The car hugged the curb as she leaned into it. She just wanted to be at home. How had she let this clown shatter her perfect day? Had there been a warning sign? Of course there hadn't. What was the saying? Unlucky at cards, lucky in love? She needed to head south to the Hollywood Park Casino with a quickness.

The trip to Hoping Circle was a blur. Her conscious mind took charge as she saw the garage door start to rise. Her anger faded to the slow burn of disappointment. She craved food and a good friend.

Muffin lay curled in a ball sleeping as Mysti entered the kitchen. She was going to look for a dog while she was on vacation. Throwing her keys on the counter and briefcase on the barstool, she headed for the refrigerator. Leftover Chinese and eggs. Yuck! Opening the freezer nothing appealed to her, but she was starving. She eyed the low-fat, low-cholesterol, low-taste, and low-content meals in the green package and finally chose the Hawaiian chicken. Seven minutes in the microwave on high.

Pouring a glass of Kendall Jackson, Mysti drank it down without stopping. She then poured a second and tossed the bottle in the trashcan under the sink. She went to the pantry only to find she was out. Damn."

She picked up the glass and made her way to the bedroom. As she passed the office, she decided to fire up the computer. As anger rose in her throat yet again she decided if she hadn't heard from Stephan she would give up this madness. And if Keith didn't call the next day, he could lose her number. She didn't have the energy or the time for games. Leaving the office she decided she'd get the wine when she returned. The steady hum of the microwave told her it was time to dine momentarily. She picked up the pace.

She quickly changed into a purple nightshirt, tossing her suit in the pile of designer wear ready to go to the cleaners. Gathering her underwear she moved to the bathroom where she caught a glimpse of herself in the beveled mirror above the vanity. She stopped momentarily and searched her eyes. She saw a kind, loving, confident woman. "Then why in the hell can't I find a kind, loving, confident man?" Mysti began laughing as she thought this would be really funny if it weren't so sad. She tossed her undergarments in the hamper and proceeded to the kitchen just as the microwave signaled her gourmet selection was ready.

Grabbing a fork and a napkin, she removed the protective film and headed for the office, stirring the chicken and rice. She sipped the wine as she opened the browser for her e-mail. She took a deep breath and began adjusting her thinking. She had given Curtis Barr far more energy than he deserved. As she began to relax, fatigue worked its way upward from her feet. She leaned her head on the back of the chair and closed her eyes. Today had been the single largest victory in her career. She was confident the partnership vote in ten days would yield Mr. and Mrs. Ellington's second oldest a lifelong dream.

The shrill of the phone startled Mysti and she picked

up on the first ring without looking at the Caller ID. "Hello."

"Hi. May I speak to Mysti?" a low, sexy voice inquired.

Hesitantly Mysti answered, "This is Mysti. To whom am I speaking?"

"This is Keith. I got a moment free tonight and thought I'd give you a call to see what happened in court today."

Mysti's pulse quickened. "What a pleasant surprise. I didn't expect to hear from you until tomorrow."

"I hadn't planned to call before tomorrow either, but it's been slow today and I've thought of you often. I just wanted you to know I really enjoyed meeting you yesterday. I would like to see you again. In this stench called the single life you're truly a breath of fresh air."

"What a nice thing to say. I have thought of you a few times today as well. I'd like very much to see you again."

"How's Friday?"

"That would be a nice start to my vacation."

"Then consider it a date. How is seven-thirty?"

"Sounds perfect. What type of date is this? How should I dress?"

Keith hesitated and Mysti immediately tensed up. She surely hoped he didn't think he was going to come to her place and end up in her bed. In the middle of her thoughts he spoke slowly. "You know, I hadn't really considered where I'd take you. I just know I have to see you again. Maybe a movie, but we can decide what you want to do when we speak later this week."

He planned to call her again before Friday. This was a good thing. "Sounds good to me. So you say it's been slow today. Is that unusual?"

"Actually it is very unusual, and I hope it doesn't mean we'll be out all night. But enough about me, what happened in court today? Did you win?"

"Actually I did and I feel really great about it." Mysti went on to explain what happened in detail and into her third sentence she heard a bell and a woman's voice over what sounded like a public address system.

"Sorry, my sweet. I have to run. Will call you tomorrow." He never gave Mysti a chance to answer before he hung up.

Keith's sexy baritone voice still rang in her ears as she took a sip of wine followed by a forkful of Hawaiian chicken with rice, which was not as hot as she'd like. She smiled as she thought of the extra effort he made to let her know how he enjoyed her company. That was nice.

She rose to return her frozen dinner to the microwave to warm her food and the phone rang again. This time she checked the caller ID and smiled as she recognized RaMona's cell phone number. "Hey, gurl!"

"Hey, hey, hey! What are you doing?" RaMona was in a splendid mood.

"About to reheat a microwave dinner." Mysti sounded disappointed.

"See I knew I should've insisted I take you out tonight. You should be out getting your champagne on! Anyway Max and I want to take you out Friday night. How's Crestations?"

"I actually have a date Friday night. How is Saturday?"

"A date? With who?"

"Keith." Mysti quickly changed the subject. "Saturday night is great, and I can stay over at your place and we can go to church Sunday."

"Gurl, he called you already? I thought you were going to talk tomorrow!" The pitch in RaMona's voice would give Mysti a headache if she listened to it much longer.

"He called and said he wanted me to know how much he enjoyed our time together yesterday. He was really sweet. He seemed genuinely interested in what happened in court. Did you tell him I was up for a partnership?"

"Absolutely not. That's not the kind of information you give out before you have some time vested. Don't want a brotha with dollar signs flashing in his eyes from jump street."

Mysti debated whether she should tell RaMona about the encounter from earlier in the evening. "I know exactly what you mean. I went out to dinner with someone from my building tonight, and all he talked about was how much money I must be making. Told me he was glad to be out with a sistah who could afford to pick up a check."

"Who is this and if you went out to dinner why are you having seasoned cardboard now?"

" 'Cuz he made me mad and I left him there without eating." Mysti was glad she'd decided to share with her best friend.

"Gurl, the way you love food, you had to be real mad! No, wait! That's me who loves food like that." RaMona laughed at herself. "Was it someone from your office who took you out to celebrate?"

"Not exactly."

"What exactly?"

"Someone from my building. I saw them on the elevator on Friday. Three foine brothers. Today when I was leaving I saw one of them and he seemed nice enough. Gurl, he picked an expensive restaurant and conveniently forgot his wallet, so I left him there staring at my hips as I switched away. But hindsight is twenty-twenty. I should have ordered a bunch of food and excused myself and gone to the ladies' room and never returned. But that would have made me no better than him. As it was, I just left."

"Besides he works in your building. You'll run into his sorry ass every day if you had done that. Even though Max and I work for the same company, in the unlikely event things don't work out I don't ever have to see him again."

"Yeah, you have the power to just exercise him to Cleveland!" They laughed.

"So how does Crestations sound on Saturday night? Maybe after your date with Keith, you'll want to invite him along."

Mysti shook her head as she weighed her response. "RaMona, slow your roll. I want to take this slow with Keith. I also want to see what develops with Stephan. I was about to check for e-mail from him when you called."

With great exaggeration RaMona said, "Why are you still chasing this fantasy? You've got a great catch in Keith, and you know he's not a serial killer or a pervert."

"And just how do we know for sure he isn't a serial killer? In case you don't know, they don't advertise."

"Gurl, he works for the fire department. That's like being with the CIA."

"And what have we learned about the CIA lately? I'm doing this, RaMona. I've just got a feeling."

"Take two antacids."

"Ha, ha, ha. Don't trivialize my feelings about this."

"And did you have a feeling about the date tonight, or the one three months ago?"

"This is different, I can't explain it. One more time, I'm asking you to support me."

"Okay, okay. I'll hush. But my money is on Keith. I want you to understand that."

"So I'll see you on Saturday night."

"You say that like I'm not going to talk to you twenty-five more times this week."

"I love you. I'm going to reheat my food and check my e-mail then I'm going to bed. I've had a long day."

"Night, night. I love you, too."

As Mysti looked down at the now coagulated chicken and rice, it had lost whatever little appeal it had. She picked it up and proceeded directly to the garbage disposal. She pulled a large bowl from the cabinet, went to the pantry, and retrieved an unopened box of frosted shredded wheat. She poured the bowl half full and garnished it with sliced bananas, added milk, and returned to her office. Nothing would distract her from e-mail this time.

Chapter Sixteen

Dear Ellie,

It was great to log on and find an e-mail from you. I've been working today, but decided to take a little break. Your answers made me smile and told me a lot about your character. I like what I read.

Your first question is a very good one. It's hard for me to answer this without knowing exactly how "senseless" the disagreement was. I believe I would simply listen to what you have to say and we may just resolve it by agreeing to disagree. But I don't argue, and for someone who is dear to me, I never part angry.

Our anniversary will start at 12:01 A.M. with a romantic smorgasbord. It will continue with the opening of your eyes to greet the day. There will be special treats for you throughout the day. Dinner will be served before the tip-off. At tip-off you will be presented with a dessert basket. In the basket will be sweet treats and love coupons. You'll be able to redeem a coupon at each commercial. If *you're not a basketball fan, I promise you will be by the final buzzer.*

Dates vary from the very simple to the romantically sophisticated. I have fun no matter what I do and believe the perfect date is one where both people part smiling.

Mysti took a deep breath and sat back in her chair letting her head rest on the cool leather. Could she dare begin to think this brotha was for real? She leaned forward again and continued reading.

I love a clean kitchen and bathroom. While I wouldn't go so far to say that cleaning anything is my favorite, I'd have to say I like the end result. But washing the car is therapeutic and that I love to do.

Oh, why you gonna call a brotha out? I forget everything I don't write down and then sometimes I forget where I wrote it. But if it is important I remember for my lady, then I write it several places. I plan to get a PDA, but I keep forgetting.

I hope this gives you a little more insight into the heart of a sincere man. I look forward to hearing from you again soon. Your e-mails brighten my day.
Stephan

Mysti read the letter a second time. Stephan's writing skills amazed her. She could feel emotion in his words. She could imagine his smile as he typed. She craved to look into his eyes. Would she be looking into the soul of a man she could love with all that was within her?

Exhaustion oozed from her every pore. She could no longer sit erect and decided she'd answer his e-mail in the morning. She got up from her desk without shutting off the computer, flipped the light switch, and headed to her bedroom.

She picked up the remote as she threw back the covers. "Why am I even going to bother?" Adjusting her pillows, she slid under the comforter and turned off the light. The next sound she heard was birds chirping.

Chapter Seventeen

Tuesday seemed to drag on endlessly. Stith's assistant brought Mysti the next case the partners wanted her to consider. As she read the file she couldn't help but laugh. A thirty-seven-year-old man was suing the Los Angeles County Sheriff's department for shooting him in the buttocks as he climbed over a fence after he allegedly robbed a convenience store. As a result of his wounds he'd lost almost three inches of his penis.

The office buzzed with the news that Ms. Ellington was moving to executive row. Two of her senior associate colleagues took her to a congratulatory lunch. She busied herself with the file and return phone calls proclaiming there was no time to answer Stephan's e-mail.

Kamesha decided she'd take the full day to rest, and Mysti was relieved she didn't have to pretend she was being productive. She decided to leave a half hour before the normal quitting time in hopes of missing Curtis. When the elevator stopped on the thirty-second floor Mysti held her breath as the doors opened. How is it she had done nothing wrong yet she felt guilty?

The sight of the garage door rolling up gave her a sense of relief. Tonight she would finish her novel and maybe turn in early. She needed to definitively decide how she would spend her well-earned vacation.

As she began unloading her bounty from Trader Joe's she heard the phone ring. Her pulse quickened slightly as thoughts of Keith flirted with her conscious mind. On ring two she quickly moved toward the door leading to the kitchen, hoping to catch it before it rolled over to voice mail. Ring three she was impatiently fumbling with the lock that had never before presented a challenge. The half tone of ring four told her she was too late.

She returned to the car, grabbing the three bags, and slammed the trunk closed. She placed the bags on the hood of the car as she removed her shoes, placing them with the blue business pumps. Retrieving her animal-print slippers with her feet, she opened the door, easily picking up the bags. Muffin stretched and meowed as she entered the kitchen.

She quickly put away the groceries and chilled a bottle of wine. Though she was starving she decided she'd check the voice mail first. She had four messages.

"Hi dear. This is your mother. I'm very glad to hear you won the case. We're very proud of you. But perhaps we'd better hold off on that celebration until the promotion is official. We look forward to seeing you Christmas Eve. No need to bring anything. Dad sends love. We'll try to catch you this weekend. Bye, bye."

Mysti shook her head as she pushed three for delete. Negativity hung in the air around her mother like funk in a chicken coop.

The next call was from her realtor advising her this

was a good time to consider upgrading her residence. Dang. Had the word already hit the street that she was headed for the partnership? Delete.

"Okay I know you've had time to reconsider my offer." Delete. Why hadn't Mr. Baby Momma Drama gotten the message when she hung up on him?

"Hi, Mysti. This is Keith. I was hoping to catch you. I'm looking forward to seeing you again, but I was hoping we'd have a chance to speak tonight. I'm taking my baby to see that new Disney flick and should return by eight-thirty. I'll try you back then." Save.

A smile slowly moved up from Mysti's toes, making its way to her lips. There was something in the way he spoke that warmed her. She looked at the keys strewn on the counter and silently cursed them for making her miss his call.

As she made a salad with chunks of grilled chicken she imagined Stephan's voice. He was someone she wanted to get to know better. Keith's conversation had been nice, and he surely seemed like a brotha with his head and heart properly aligned; but she just couldn't shake the feeling there was something very special about Stephan.

After sprinkling her salad with bacon bits, croutons, sunflower seeds, and a smidgen of ranch dressing she grabbed a tumbler from the cabinet, filled it with ice and water, and headed for her office.

She decided she would take her time before she checked e-mail. She didn't want to seem too anxious though no one else would even know. She separated bills from solicitations. There was no stack of personal. She opened the credit card bills to make sure no one had decided to use her credit to finance a vacation to the Orient. She played with the salad, but really wished she had a hot piece of fried chicken from Rosco's

Chicken and Waffles. She tossed away old catalogs and straightened her desk. She finished the salad and returned the bowl to the kitchen.

Grabbing a Red Delicious apple from the fruit bowl, she headed back to the office. She didn't know why she was procrastinating to answer Stephan's e-mail. She fought so hard for professional success, yet was she afraid of a relationship triumph?

The phone once again interrupted her. "I'm never going to get through this." Mysti was slightly irritated. The words BLOCKED ID stared back at her from the small digital device next to the phone. With a deep sigh she picked up the handset. "Hello."

"Hi. May I speak with Mysti, please?" the sultry voice on the other end inquired.

Mysti had been so caught up in her own thoughts and deeds she had forgotten Keith hadn't called as promised. "This is Mysti."

"Good evening. I'm sorry it took me so long to call you after I got in, but Daddy Stupid let Miss Thang have candy and lemonade tonight. Big mistake. I just got her to settle down. How are you?"

"That's quite alright. I was catching up on some e-mail. I just finished dinner." Mysti took a quick guilty glance at Stephan's e-mail.

Turning slightly so her back was to the computer monitor she said, "Sounds like you had a great evening with your little princess." A smile tiptoed across her lips.

"It was pretty awesome, but it's amazing how I can fight fires and rescue folks all night and not be half as tired as just spending a few hours with Alexis."

"What a nice name."

"She's pretty special. I want you to know I've thought of you quite often since Sunday. There's something different about you. You were head and shoulders above the other women at the party."

"That's a very sweet thing to say. I've thought about you a time or two as well. I've been caught up with work, but I'm so ready to start my vacation. Now that the trial is over I seem to have lost some steam."

"You've come down from your adrenaline rush. It happens in my business practically every hour of every day. What do you have planned for the holidays?"

"Believe it or not I haven't decided. I know that's terrible, but my plans don't include anyone else, so I'll just get in where I can fit in. I do plan to spend Christmas Eve and Christmas Day with my parents. I may go skiing the day after Christmas."

"Locally?"

"No, I have a friend in Utah, which always has wonderful powder. It's actually where I learned to ski."

Keith wanted to ask if the friend was female, but felt that it was too obvious. Instead he asked, "There are black folks in Utah?"

Laughing, Mysti said, "Carl Malone and Jeri."

Keith's heart sunk. Well at least she was being honest. He couldn't be mad at her. Besides they had only met two days before. And she did say the F word. "Do you and Jerry ski often?"

"I go at least twice during the season and once in the summer. You haven't seen beauty until you've been to Utah."

Must be a friend. No brotha is going to only see this woman three times a year. "I've driven through from Denver to Vegas during a thunderstorm. It was pretty spectacular. Saw one of the most beautiful rainbows ever in my rearview mirror."

Conversation with Keith was as easy on the phone as

it was in person. "What do you have planned for the holidays?"

"I actually work on Christmas Day so we'll do most of our celebrating on Christmas Eve. I'm covering a couple of extra shifts over the next three weeks; lots of vacations. I was hoping to see you sometime during your vacation if you're in town. Lexi's mom has her for a week. Perhaps we could spend a day together. Have you ever been to Disneyland during the holidays?"

"You know I've lived here my entire life and I've never been to the Magic Kingdom during the holidays. People say it is so romantic. I've had friends go there for New Year's Eve."

"Why Mysti, are you asking me out on New Year's Eve? I accept."

There was a pregnant pause as Mysti search for the right words.

Keith sensed her discomfort and quickly interjected. "I'm sorry, I didn't mean to put you on the spot. I'm sure you already have plans. Please forgive an overzealous brotha."

"No need to apologize. I was just trying to remember the last time I had a date on New Year's Eve. For the past three years I've been in Utah with Jeri. We'd sit in the hot tub and sip champagne and promise not to be in the same spot next year."

Okay, Jerry in hot, bubbling water, sipping champagne with Mysti and it's not a date? Oh, he's gay. "Well, sitting in a hot tub with you sipping vino sure sounds like a date to me."

"Ohhhhhh, you think Jeri's a guy? Silly, she's my girlfriend from college. She's a lawyer for the Jazz."

Laughing, Keith simply said, "Why you gonna call a brotha out?"

"I guess I can see how you would have thought that.

Let's get past this uncomfortable subject with some straightforward, honest answers. I'm not seeing anyone at the present. I haven't had a meaningful date in almost two years. What is very interesting, however, is that I decided last Friday to take control of my destitute personal life and I began perusing the personals, then on Sunday I met you. Things are definitely looking up."

Feeling slightly uncomfortable with her honesty, something that had been quite elusive in his previous relationships, Keith fidgeted in his leather LaZ Boy. Should he tell her he was corresponding with someone online as well? Women were funny creatures and he didn't want to blow this. He took a sip from a banana, coconut, and strawberry smoothie before responding. "Whew, I know I have no right to not want you sittin' in a hot tub with another brotha, but that was exactly what I was thinking. You know how proprietary we men folk can be, lifting our leg and marking everything in sight."

"You're very funny. But I appreciate your candor. I'm very interested to pursue this to see where it takes us. You seem to be what the doctor would prescribe."

Over the next hour Mysti and Keith's conversation went from politics to socialized medicine to fire and rescue to quiet evenings alone to family dinners. As she glanced at the clock she realized they'd been talking for more than an hour.

"You know, Keith, it's been a long time since I felt this comfortable talking to a man. You sure make it seem easy."

"I've had a great time, too. Your conversation is not shallow. I like that. You can learn so much about a person by asking questions that have nothing to do with relationships. I also like that you have an opinion."

Mysti laughed. "Remember you said that. Three months from now you might not feel the same way."

Wow, she must like me. She plans to still be talking to me in three months. Hot damn! "By then I'll be pleading the fifth and saying I have no idea what you're talking about."

"Don't make me hire a court reporter!" Now they were both laughing.

"I hate to do this, but I have to be up at four. I have a shift tomorrow. I know I said we'd go out on Friday, but how's your schedule for Thursday? Would you have dinner with me? I don't want to wait an additional twenty-four hours."

"I'd love to. What time and where?"

"What type of food do you like?"

"I don't eat liver or McDonald's. Everything else is fair game."

"Now I don't want to do the wrong thing here, so guide a brotha in the right direction. Fine, casual, or fast dining."

"That's too funny. I heard about someone having a blind date where the guy took her to the drive-through at Taco Bell and asked her to pay half. And my friend Jeri had a basketball player fly her to Paris for dinner. So let's just say somewhere in the middle of that. Have you ever been to Todai?"

"Actually I have, and I love it. How about I pick you up at seven?"

Mysti vacillated. Did she want him to have her address?

Sensing her hesitation Keith quickly added, "You can meet me there if you're more comfortable that way."

"You're quite perceptive. How about in Woodland Hills on Ventura Boulevard? I can get you the exact address.

"No need, I know exactly where it is. Mysti, I've had fun again tonight, and I look forward to Thursday."

"Me, too. Good night."

"Good night."

With the sound of the click, Mysti smiled and replaced the handset.

She turned her attention once again to the computer monitor. There was something magnetic about Stephan and his e-mails. Why was she so intrigued?

Shaking the mouse, the screen came to life. She began reading again.

Dear Stephan,

I've read your letter more than once, and again I'm very impressed. I'm so new at all of this I don't know where we should go next. The next logical thing seems to be chat online. I have AOL Instant Messenger.

I'm winding down at work, and beginning on Friday I'll be off until the first full week in January. I plan to visit with a friend during the holidays and do some family stuff locally. If we are compatible with live conversation, we will move to the next step.

I think I may have gotten lucky the night I answered your ad. Your philosophies and candor are refreshing. I enjoyed reading the answers to the questions, but must admit my favorite was the answer to the anniversary question. Somehow I believe you're right. I would be a basketball fan for life before the final buzzer.

Let me know when it would be convenient to chat online.

Ellie

Mysti wished somewhere there was an instruction book on what was right and what was just plain stupid when meeting people on the Internet. If such a reference guide existed she was totally unaware.

She felt good just her date with Keith and equally

as comfortable with chatting live with Stephan. A week ago she wasn't talking to anyone, now she had two men who had captured her attention. Was her heart far behind? Who would she choose? Did she have to choose? She wasn't committed to anyone, so she would play the hand to see who held all the trumps.

She answered three other e-mails and generated a new one to her sisters telling them she looked forward to seeing them at Christmas. She requested a wish list from the children and a call to collaborate on a gift for Mom and Dad.

She closed the e-mail window and shut the computer down. She'd read until she fell asleep, have a good workout in the morning before work, and then count the hours all day until she was one day closer to vacation.

Chapter Eighteen

A s Stephan brushed his teeth he felt compelled to check his e-mail just once more. He'd hoped to hear from the Mystique One before he went to bed. There was something so familiar about her, yet he couldn't explain it. He only knew that no matter what else was going on in his life, he had to meet this woman. Her words on the screen made his heart smile.

As he turned off the light in the bathroom he stepped into his neat yet simple bedroom. The British racing green comforter brought a rich feel to the maple furnishing. He went to the chest and pulled clean pajamas from the bottom drawer. The day's activity had worn him weary and he craved sleep. Yet the seventeen-inch flat-screen monitor beckoned.

"This'll only take a minute." He powered up the CPU and opened the door leading to the hallway. He slept with his door open in case his daughter cried out during the night. "I had a feeling she'd written!"

He opened the e-mail and smiled to himself as he

read her words. She wanted to chat live. Yes! He hunted and pecked out his message.

Dear Ellie,

I never thought you'd ask. I have AIM and will be available to chat on Thursday afternoon or anytime on Friday. I look forward to spending time getting to know you from the inside out.

I enjoyed your answers as well. I know that we are onto something special. If nothing else I think we can be great friends. Mental sparring with you would be quite entertaining.
BlacKnight

Chapter Nineteen

Mysti sifted through e-mail as she sipped sweet and spicy tea. Kamesha was back at the helm, looking fit and as sharp as ever. Upon reviewing her calendar Mysti decided she could have stayed in bed on this gloomy Wednesday. She'd decided the penis reduction case was the perfect launch to her partnership and would advise Stith in the afternoon when she'd announce she was taking two mental health days immediately preceding her vacation. She realized as she showered she had nothing left in reserve and she was due the break.

Dressing in designer slacks, turtleneck, and loafers, Mysti almost felt like it was casual Friday. The steam from the tea tickled her nose as she marked mail for deletion. The phone interrupted her.

"Yes, Kamesha?"

"Mr. Stith can see you at one-thirty."

"That'll be fine. When you get a moment could you please come into my office?"

"Be right there."

Within thirty seconds Kamesha stood before Mysti with steno pad in hand. "Close the door and have a seat."

A slight frown creased Kamesha's brow. "Is everything okay?"

"Oh yes, I just want to talk to you about what will be happening, and this is for your ears only. Relax. There's no need to worry."

Her body relaxed slightly as she took a seat in front of her mentor. She stared curiously at Mysti and smiled. "You look different. Kinda glowy. Is there something I should know?"

"I have no idea what you're talking about. I'm probably the most tired I've been since law school."

"No, this is different." Kamesha hit the desk and startled Mysti. "It's a man, isn't it?"

"Absolutely not!"

Throwing her head back with laughter, Kamesha said, "How does the saying go? Thou doth protest just a little too much. That's awesome, Ms. E."

"Kamesha, you're delusional. Anyway, I called you in here to talk to you about what I think will happen when I return from vacation, which by the way I plan to start as soon as I speak with Stith about the new case."

With great interest Kamesha leaned forward. Before Mysti could continue a rapid knock on her door interrupted. "Enter."

Behind a huge arrangement of pink roses, the office mail runner spoke in a formal tone. "Delivery for Ms. Ellington."

"Who in the world is sending me such beautiful flowers?" Mysti stood and walked to meet Dexter halfway across her office. Pulling the card she spoke absentmindedly. "You can place them on the credenza. Thank you, Dexter, and Merry Christmas. I'll be starting my vacation this afternoon."

"Feliz Navidad, Ms. Ellington, and congratulations. The good news has made its way to the mailroom. Looks like I'll be delivering your mail to the west wing."

The well-dressed young man smiled as he left the office, closing the door behind him. Mysti didn't dare make eye contact with Kamesha.

"So now, the prosecution reserves the right to recall the witness. Let me pose this question again: Does that glow have anything to do with a man?"

Mysti never looked up from the card. "And I repeat I have no idea what you're talking about. These are just to congratulate me on a job well done."

"I see." Kamesha smiled to herself.

Mysti stepped to the credenza and bent to smell nature's perfume. The scent tantalized her. She stood, turned, and walked back to her desk. "Now where were we?" She slipped the card back into the envelope and slid it under her blotter.

Kamesha knew not to push her as much as she knew those flowers were from a gentleman suitor. "You were telling me what to expect in the new year."

"Right. Right." It was clear Mysti's thoughts had lost their footing. "Without sounding cocky, I believe I'll—" Mysti pointed to Kamesha then to herself repeatedly— "we'll be moving down the hall and around the corner. You've been the wind beneath my wings for a very long time, and I just want to assure you that the promise I made to you the day I took you to lunch so many years ago is still as solid as the Hope Diamond."

Kamesha smiled and hesitated as though in thought before she spoke slowly. "Thank you, Mysti. That means a lot to me. I was hoping I'd be going with you, but I'd understand if you had to make other decisions."

"No, you wouldn't!" They both laughed.

"Okay, so I wouldn't." Kamesha laughed nervously. "But I love working for you and can't wait to help you pick out new furniture!"

"And neither can I. You'll be working with Baxter while I'm on vacation, but you know how quiet it is around here during the holidays. Just get some rest because we'll hit the ground running in January. The case I'll be handling is high profile and even higher politically. May be a bumpy ride. When the announcement is official, I'll be lobbying for you to get a salary increase, as well. Do you have any questions?"

"Not a one. I love my job, Ms. E., and you're the reason. You've pushed me to my limit, only to have my limit increase. I never knew I could be this good at anything."

"And you're the best. One day I expect you to be sitting on this side of the desk having this conversation with your right hand."

"Now that would be awesome. I'm also glad you're getting your groove back. You've taught me, now it's my turn to teach you."

Mysti didn't answer for a moment. Then she smiled and said, "If there's nothing else, I think we're done."

"I think that covers it for me."

Kamesha seemed to glide out of the office with her naturally auburn hair bouncing. Mysti immediately pulled the card that had accompanied the flowers from under her blotter. She pulled it from the tiny envelope and read the words again.

Hope these help you to anticipate Thursday half as much as I do.
Keith

With the slightest tremble in her hands Mysti picked up her PDA to search for Keith's number. She quickly dialed it and on the third ring listened to the sweet sounds of Keith Washington before she heard Keith's voice.

"You've missed me, but if you leave a message it won't be for long." *Beep*.

"Hi, Keith. I just wanted to thank you for the beautiful flowers and yes, I'm looking forward to seeing you again as well. I'm sure you know to come hungry. The spread is wonderful."

Mysti hung up the phone, staring at the card once more. She smiled. How had he known where she worked? They had never discussed where she worked. She laughed out loud. "RaMona!"

Picking up the phone again she hit the speed dial that would connect her to RaMona's office. Her assistant answered on the first ring. "RaMona Kirby's office."

"Is her highness in?"

"Hi, Ms. Ellington. She is, but on the phone. Do you want to hold for a minute? She shouldn't be long."

Laughing, Mysti said, "You know we lawyers don't hold on long."

"She's finishing up now. Have a great day."

"You, too." Mysti listened to the enthralling voice of Sade and began to hum along when RaMona's voice interrupted the middle-aged temptress.

"Hey, gurl, what's the good word this morning?"

"Don't even try it. You know what's up this morning."

With a snicker, RaMona played innocent. "What are you talking about?"

"Did you give Keith confidential information?"

"How is where you work confidential information

when your name and where you worked was in every local and probably national newspaper yesterday?"

"Aha! So you did know he was sending me flowers?"

"Oh, see that was some slick lawyer stuff you just worked on me. Okay, so what was the harm? You got the brotha feeling like Thumper."

"I'm pretty excited about seeing him, too. We've talked and had a great time. He's really easy to talk to, that's for sure. And I think he's a decent guy."

"I told you I checked him out before I tried to hook you up. Of course as a firefighter, he's not a criminal. I know he doesn't have a bunch of women. Greg gave me the skinny. Mr. Webster must have been looking at that hunk of burning love when he defined foine. So why am I hearing a but?"

She did like Keith, however, there was a but, and the but had a name. BlacKnight aka Stephan. "I just can't explain it. Stephan has me going. Maybe it's the mystery, but I have to meet this man."

"You are working me! It just seems like no matter what I say you're going to pursue this Internet thing. Have you even spoken to him on the phone?"

"No, but we're going to be chatting online this week. I want to take it really slow."

"But if you're taking it slow with him then what about my boy Keith? You just gonna leave him hanging while you figure all this out?"

"He doesn't have to hang as you put it. I haven't made any commitment to him, nor have I asked for one. And you know I believe that which God has for ya, no matter what you do or where you go, you'll come back to it."

"Oooo wee, why you gotta bring God all up in it? So when are you going to know one way or the other what you're going to do? This is making me a wreck!"

"You trippin'. This is my life, but you're a wreck."

"That's 'cuz I'm your regress, gurlfriend. What you do, I feel. So I guess I can wait for you to work all of this out of your system because Keith is the man for you. I can just taste it."

"Take two Tums."

"Hardy, har, har. So how long are you going to chat before you meet him?"

"RaMona, I don't know. I'll have to feel him out. It may end up being never, but I can't get into something serious with Keith forever wondering what if."

"Okay, waving my white drawers. I give up. I promise not to bring it up again. You do what you think you need to do."

"What drawers? And you know you're lyin'. But that's okay by me. I know you love me, and that's all that matters. If you will allow me to change the subject, I'm starting my vacation today. I'm so physically and mentally exhausted. I'm going in to talk to Stith and then I'm outta here."

"Oh, what a great idea. Maybe you and . . ."

"I thought you weren't saying anything else."

"See, you all up in my Kool-Aid and don't know if it even has any sugar in it. I was going to say maybe you and I can go shopping tomorrow."

"Yeah, sure you were. But that sounds great. I'll call you later today. Love you."

As Mysti hung up, she shook her head and smiled to herself at her friend's antics. Actually shopping with RaMona sounded like the perfect plan for her first few days off. A chill tiptoed up both her arms as she thought of Stephan. If his conversation in chats was decent she'd arrange to meet him soon. As much as she hated to admit it RaMona's point was a valid one. She needed to decide if she wanted to pursue a relationship with Keith.

If only she could shake the feeling there was something very special and slightly familiar about Stephan.

Chapter Twenty

Two weeks later

BlacKnight: *You know I've enjoyed our time together here online more than I could ever say.*

MystiqueOne: *Me, too. I can't believe how many hours we've spent talking and learning about each other.*

BlacKnight: *I know tomorrow is New Year's Eve and I wouldn't dare be so presumptuous to think you don't have a date, but I'd hate for this year to end without looking into your eyes. You've made me wait for a picture and now a one-dimensional photograph would be a disappointment. How about a frappuccino at Starbucks say at 11:30 a.m.?*

Mysti stared at the screen. She'd known it would come to this sooner or later. She wanted it as much as she longed for spring rain in April. But now she was afraid. She'd had three dates with Keith, each one more magical than the last. She'd kept him at length, but her arms grew a little shorter each time.

MystiqueOne: *The truth is I do have a date tomorrow night. It's someone I've been seeing just a short while. But I like him very much. But there is something about you that has me so intrigued that I must meet you, and we should just do this. I can't string myself out any longer. Nor can I not see you. If I let this go I will forever wonder what if.*

Now it was Stephan's turn to stare at the monitor. He couldn't believe her words. They echoed everything he wanted to say. His heart caught in his throat. Would she be as understanding as he?

BlacKnight: *I'm really glad to read those words because I'm in the same situation. I've started seeing someone who is wonderful in every sense of the word. We haven't made a commitment yet, and before I do I really want to meet you in person. I, too, don't want to be sitting in my rocking chair watching the ocean wondering what would have happened if I'd just had coffee with the MystiqueOne. So does this mean you'll meet me at Starbucks tomorrow?*

MystiqueOne: *I guess it does. We've spent so much time talking and you seem like such a nice guy. Which one? You know there is one on every other corner.*

BlacKnight: *How about the one in Ladera? Magic's place. Do you know where it is?*

MystiqueOne: *I know exactly where it is. How will I know you?*

BlacKnight: *I'll be the good-looking brotha with a pink carnation in my left hand.*

MystiqueOne: *As opposed to the good-looking brotha holding a pink carnation in his right hand? LOL.*

BlacKnight: *LOL! Touché. I guess I'm a little nervous. I'm hoping you like what you see and at the same time I'm confused about what will happen if you do.*

MystiqueOne: *Now you need to get up out of my head this time. I was thinking the same thing. If I do like you that will further complicate my life.*

BlacKnight: *And if you don't?*

MystiqueOne: *I'll be always wondering what it would have been like to sip a five-dollar cup of cold coffee with coconut and chocolate in it with one of the nicest people I've ever talked to.*

BlacKnight: *Dang, I need to go to the ATM. Only have enough for a four-dollar cup of cold coffee. LOL!*

Laughing with this woman was so easy for him. He didn't want to like her the way he did, but in matters of the heart his grandmomma had told him, trying to make your heart do what your head is telling it is a lot like trying to push mud uphill. Not impossible, but very difficult and could get a little messy.

BlacKnight: *I should probably get going. I need to answer e-mail and get to bed. I have a date before noon tomorrow.*

MystiqueOne: *Yeah, me, too. As always it's been great. I'll be wearing a black turtleneck and black jeans with a short leather jacket. I'll be the nervous-looking sistah with the confused look on her face.*

BlacKnight: *There's no need to be nervous. It is what it is. No more. No less. This falls into the what-God-has-for-ya, nobody-can-take-from-ya category.*

Mysti sat transfixed. Those had been the exact words she'd told RaMona. Tiny prickly fingers tickled the back of her neck. Now she was more than just a little anxious. Why had she been so determined to continue to get to know Stephan despite the wonderful time she had with Keith? Now for him to say her words made her uneasy.

MystiqueOne: *I've been known to say that a time or two myself. Well, until tomorrow, my friend.*

BlacKnight: *I hope after all of this hype you're not disappointed.*

MystiqueOne: *I don't think that's possible. We've said countless times this is so far beyond the physical. You could have one eye in the middle of your forehead, and I wouldn't really care.*

BlacKnight: *Same here. But we need to make a pact. If there is no chemistry and we decide that the other person in our life is more what we want, then we'll still be friends.*

MystiqueOne: *I don't know how that would work, but I will surely try to keep an open mind. I do so enjoy our conversations. I'm really gone this time. I'll see you tomorrow at 11:30 at Starbucks-Ladera.*

BlacKnight: *Ciao, bella.*

Stephan leaned back in his steno chair and smiled to himself. Ellie had captured his attention though his heart almost belonged to another. In all of his years he'd never been in this predicament. His challenge to this point had been finding one woman who had at least half of his top ten requirements. MystiqueOne's words on the computer had him so captivated he'd not even asked for a picture. Her excellent vocabulary and ladylike demeanor intrigued him. Her cyber handle fit her perfectly; indeed she was mystical.

Mysti logged off the computer and headed for the family room. Kenny G played softly and she went to light the gas wood-burning fireplace. The mahogany wood would burn slowly and she'd have time to enjoy the fire while she contemplated the repercussions of her actions. Keith had become important enough in her life that she was spending the most significant of all holidays for a single woman—New Year's Eve—with him.

Their first dinner together had lasted for hours, and they had joked about the restaurant rescinding their all-you-can-eat policy. After leaving the restaurant she'd decided he posed no impairment risk and abandoned her car to take a scenic ride through the Santa Monica mountains. He'd taken her to places she didn't know existed though she'd lived in Los Angeles her entire life.

When they returned to the parking lot to retrieve her car she'd hated to see the evening end, but he had a shift the next morning. They parted with promises of speaking within a few days. Her heart sang a happy tune as she drove back to Hoping Circle.

As she pulled into the garage she heard the phone ringing. Sure that it was RaMona checking in for a reading on the romance-o-meter, she decided to let the voice mail pick it up. She wanted to relish the previous few hours she'd spent with a man who would be very easy to love. Her vibrating purse startled her and she answered the cell phone without thinking. "Yes, Miss Nosy."

"I'm not sure who Miss Nosy would be, but this is Mr. Real Content calling to see if you made it home safely. I can't get you out of my mind. I know we said in a few days, yet it has only been a few minutes."

"I'm glad you called. I was thinking of you, too. I didn't want to seem like a fatal attraction, so I resolved to wait for what I considered a respectable time frame."

"Oh, so you think I'm fatalistic?" Keith had tried to feign hurt.

"No silly, but you know how men think. If she calls too soon or too much, she has desperation issues."

"I'm hoping we are past all of that. I just want to get to know you. I want to slow dance with you."

His words had made her smile. They talked for a short while as she stood in the garage. When they said good night the second time, Mysti could do nothing to dissipate her smile. Every day had become more special than the one before it. Now here she sat anticipating her meeting with Stephan. What was wrong with her? Or maybe it was what was right with her that these two very successful brothas found her irresistible.

She'd learned that Stephan was in public service, a Christian, divorced with one child. They'd purposely steered away from too much personal information based on some of the horror stories each had heard of people on the Internet divulging too much information to con artists. She yearned to know all about Stephan. She wanted to know as much about Stephan as she knew about Keith. How else could an intelligent woman make an informed decision if she didn't have information?

With the aid of natural gas, the mahogany log burned hot within minutes. The fire gave the room an inviting glow as the warmth penetrated Mysti to her soul. She walked through the family room into the kitchen and opened a fresh bottle of Kendall Jackson. She opened the overhead cabinet and retrieved a Waterford crystal wineglass. Tonight was special. She dared take a chance with her personal life.

After filling the glass three quarters, she returned to the black leather sofa in front of the fireplace and took a seat, curling her feet under her. Kenny G soulfully played the Louis Armstrong hit "What a Wonderful World." The fire hypnotized her as she sipped the wine and listened to the beautiful saxophone music. Letting her mind wander, she imagined what it would be like to gaze into Stephan's eyes and to hear his laughter.

Suddenly she sat upright, placing her glass on the maple-stained coffee table. *What if he's hideous? What if he's a beer-bellied old man with a greasy Jheri curl and no teeth?* She'd never considered he may be physically un-appealing. After all, he did say he hoped she wouldn't be disappointed. She needed to pace. She began walking back and forth between the fireplace and coffee table. She had said what he looked like didn't matter, but who was she fooling? Of course it mattered—as much as she knew it mattered to him.

Working herself into a frenzy, Mysti's heart began to pound. As a lawyer she had mastered the art of expressionless feelings in the courtroom. But would she be able to do as well over coffee? Just as she felt panic seize her throat, the phone rang.

She moved to the green-and-black granite bar separating the family room from the kitchen to pick up the cordless handset. Looking at the caller ID she saw that it was her sister Lyric.

"Hello."

"Hello, sister dearest. How are you?" Lyric's voice dripped with sarcasm.

"I'm well, and you? How are the kids?"

"All is well. They're having a great winter vacation. We just returned from a ski trip to Aspen this afternoon. You know we do that annually."

Mysti rolled her eyes. "Yes. I'm aware that you go on a ski trip every year between Christmas and New Year's."

"You really should get out more. I thought you were going to take a vacation. At least that's what Mother told me. Or were you just trying to save face? Do you really have plans?" Mysti cringed at the sound of pity in her older sister's voice.

"I actually decided I needed to get some rest since I did make partner and my new duties will be quite taxing over the next few months." Mysti wanted to get off the phone as soon as she possibly could. "What can I do for you, Lyric?"

"We're having an intimate gathering at our home on New Year's Day, and I wanted to invite you. You're welcome to bring a date, but based on our conversation over Christmas dinner, I thought if you decided to come alone Alex could have one of his associates at the investment firm come to round things out quite nicely."

"Lyric, that's very nice of you and Alex to think of me, however, I already have plans. And even if I didn't I don't need any pity dates. Will Alex be inviting Shaniqua, as well? I'm sure that would make for interesting party conversation."

Sounds of exasperation seeped through the holes of the earpiece on the phone. "You know you don't have to be such a witch. I'm just trying to be nice to you. It was Mother's idea that we invite you. She didn't want you sitting at home alone on a holiday. I should have known better than to try to be nice to your uppity behind. And besides, that affair is long over, and I won't let you keep bringing it up."

"Lyric, I tell you what. I'll worry about my social life and you worry about your husband's." Mysti hit the talk button, ending the call. Lyric's condescending attitude had long been a source of aggravation, but tonight she just wasn't having it.

She knew she shouldn't have been so mean-spirited bringing up the one affair that had brought public humiliation to her sister and almost destroyed her brother-in-law's career, when his around-the-way girlfriend decided she wanted a house in the suburbs with the picket fence and all the trimmings and she thought Alex and Lyric's palatial estate would do quite nicely. But Lyric had brought it on herself with her usual, my-life-is-better-than-yours-and-I-need-to-have-pity-on-you attitude.

Lyric had succeeded, however, to distract Mysti from her panic attack, which now paled in comparison to the fury she felt toward her sister.

Mysti went to the refrigerator and refilled her wine-glass and returned to the family room where she sat on the couch taking deep breaths to relax. How had she let Lyric get her so worked up? She should be concentrating on having two dates on New Year's Eve, less than twelve hours apart.

Diverting her energy elsewhere helped clear her vision and expectations of her date with Stephan. They'd become friends, and as he'd stated, no matter what the outcome she wanted to maintain that. RaMona had a bevy of male friends, and she seemed to always be happy. Her ability to not get involved was to be envied.

Pulling another book from her extensive library of African-American literature, Mysti's mind began to question her decision not to take a vacation. After much personal debate, she decided staying at home, reading, making wedding plans with RaMona, and just enjoying her beautiful home would serve her well.

Lyric had made her second-guess that decision. How did she look to others? Was she a social failure? Did she even care what others thought? On the downhill slope to forty should she be more concerned about marriage and starting a family? For a little less than a month she had taken charge of her personal life with half-decent results. She wondered if she was messing things up with her insistence to see Stephan. She shook her head to clear thoughts that were making her second-guess her midday rendezvous. Laughing to herself she settled in with the novel. She bet some of Carl Weber's *Baby Momma Drama* would help her forget her woes.

Mysti woke as a chill had seeped into her bones. The clock above the fireplace, where the mahogany log had long since burned to ashes, told her it was nearly dawn. She'd fallen asleep reading, dreaming of old, toothless men chasing her with Jheri curl juice flying everywhere. She had to laugh at her own silly thoughts, which had brought on such subconscious visions. "Well, I guess the worst of it is over."

Chapter Twenty-one

Mysti was a bundle of nerve endings as she maneuvered the Mustang through the heavy mid-morning traffic. Where in the world were all of these people going? Stephan had sent her an e-mail in the wee hours of the morning, explaining he was unable to sleep in anticipation of their meeting. Mysti replied, never letting him know she, too, had been up since before dawn.

She had been unable to sleep once she turned off the lights and fireplace and headed to bed just before dawn. She'd tossed and turned for hours before she decided she'd simply get up and head for the fitness center. At least there she could work out her anxieties. In her head she'd cancelled the date at least five times, each with a more lavish excuse than the one before.

With her resolve intact and her doubts under control Mysti was on her way to meet her. BlacKnight. Despite wanting to speak with Keith, guilt had won the best of her, and she decided to wait until their date later in the evening. But what if Stephan swept her off her feet? Would her first real New Year's Eve date in a month of Sundays be ruined? She felt panic seeping in through the vents of the car. Her thoughts so consumed her that she passed the La Tijera exit.

"Gurl, get a hold of yourself. What is wrong with you?" She quickly backtracked and three minutes before the appointed meeting time, pulled into the crowded parking lot of the center owned by Magic Johnson. This had become the hotspot of African-Americans making multi-million-dollar deals over a latte or groupies wishing to star gaze. Friday's and Starbucks were the places to be seen.

I'll be the good-looking brotha with a pink carnation in my left hand. Mysti's steps quickened as she prided herself on being punctual and even sixty seconds was late. Stopping at the door to check her full-length image reflected in the door, she smiled, took a deep breath, and opened the door.

At first glance, to her disappointment she didn't see anyone holding a pink carnation in either hand, good-looking or otherwise. He was late . . . strike one. She made her way around the partition and found a seat. She'd wait fifteen minutes, not a second longer. She positioned herself so she could see the front door and those who approached. She wanted to have as much advantage as possible.

She heard a door open behind her and out of reflex she turned to observe. She saw the carnation first. There was something very familiar about the hand holding it. Her eyes moved from his hand to his face and to her absolute astonishment the face of the man who held the pink carnation in his left hand belonged to Keith.

Her eyes moved so quickly that her mind became confused. She couldn't comprehend why he was there and with her pink carnation no less. As she stood he looked up as he left the rest room and their eyes met. Confusion blanketed his face. Looking at her from head to toe, a hint of recognition sparkled in his eyes.

Stepping to her quickly he said, "I guess this must be for you."

Still in a haze of bewilderment Mysti stuttered, "Wh-what are you doing here?"

Taking her hand, Keith Stephan Douglas bent to kiss it. "You must be Ellie."

Shrinking into the chair she couldn't speak. She opened her mouth several times but no words came forth. She stared from the carnation to Keith's face and back again. "How long have you known it was me?"

Laughing, he sat across from her. "May I get you some coffee? You look like you could use a drink."

I don't want a drink. I want an explanation," Mysti managed to say after a long moment. "Please answer my question. How long have you known it was me?"

"I actually didn't know for sure until I saw you coming across the parking lot, though everything about Ellie was familiar and very comfortable. I was so torn talking to you—I mean MystiqueOne on the computer—because of how I felt about you. About a week or so into our chatting you said something in the IM that made me think of Mysti and then I wanted her to be you."

"So you've been playing me this whole time?" Tears began to form puddles in her eyes.

"Please don't think that. But remember you were caught up with Stephan as well. I only knew that the woman on the other side of that computer screen was very special. Special enough to make me jeopardize what I have with one of the most intriguing women I've ever met."

"Oh my God! I've felt the same way. Guilt would eat

me alive every time we'd chat online for hours. You, Keith, had become so important to me, yet I couldn't let go of what might be with Stephan." Mysti sat back staring out of the window. "I think I'll take that drink now."

"I'll be right back. Don't move a muscle."

Mysti stared after Keith or Stephan—or was it Keith Stephan?—as he moved toward the counter. He ordered two coffees and returned to the table within a minute. "They'll bring them over."

"Keith, I don't know what to feel here. I want to be angry, but how can I be? I deceived you the same way you deceived me. Would it be hypocritical to be angry?"

"As I saw you walk across the parking lot I was a bundle of emotion. Anger was my first response, but as I thought of it I realized this was bigger than either of us. In a split second my life since I've known you flashed before me. You had actually been in touch with Stephan before you met Keith."

"That's true. I'd started the ad thing just before the party."

"So you see, neither of us could have ever guessed that love was just a click away, and we surely can't act as if this is by chance."

Words of Love

Pat Simmons

ACKNOWLEDGMENTS

WORDS OF LOVE would not be possible without the support of the following people:

Genelle Faulkner, a long-time friend who read the story front to cover in one sitting, laughing at the right time and thoroughly convinced she knew my characters.

Dana Lane, a good friend who kept asking me when would it be finished.

Terry Cancila, co-worker and friend who supported my ups and downs.

Parry "EbonySatin" Brown, who said yes to the blind dating anthology.

Portia Cannon, everything a good agent should be . . . and more.

And finally, my family and friends who rejoiced with me when it was published.

"May God bless those who bless me."

Chapter One

A love letter.

Not the corny roses-are-red, violets-are-blue stuff, but the passionate words of a man confessing the hidden secrets of his soul, revealing unspoken weaknesses, uncompromising desires, and subtle strengths. A man who had surrendered to love.

Carmel French closed her eyes, wrinkling her nose as she inhaled the lingering smell of roses emitting from the scented stationery. She giggled. To this day, she still couldn't believe how it all happened. When she casually mentioned to her radio listeners about going on a blind date, she surely didn't think she would fall in love with a man whom she had never seen.

Today, her life would change. She was nervous, excited, and in love.

It all began about seven months ago in mid-October . . .

Carmel's radio show dominated the St. Louis airwaves from six to eight every morning on WPLS. The

twenty-six-year-old media personality was single and trying to convince herself she was satisfied.

Okay, people, let's talk about some good stuff this morning,
Carmel silently pleaded as she sipped her pineapple
juice, adjusted the large headset on her ears, reposi-
tioned the microphone inches above her mouth, and
waited for the countdown to her show.

Carmel swayed her shoulders as she hummed along
with her theme music, which was blaring from the overhead speakers in the studio. She frowned at her techni-
cal board operator and senior engineer, Glen LaCroix,
who sat in the control room behind a glass wall, looking
bored to death.

"Heeeeeeey, it's Monday, and it's open line on 'Don't
Get French with Me,' comin' at ya in three, two, and
one," she said in a bubbly voice.

Just as Carmel's energy kicked into high gear, Glen
yawned. Pitiful. Her show was the first of four Glen engineered daily, and he looked as if he'd already worked
a twenty-four-hour shift and wouldn't stay awake a
minute longer.

"Welcome, St. Louis," she purred into the microphone. "Give me a call at 314-555-0400, and tell me
what's on your mind." Carmel braced herself for any
unexpected topics, since her calls weren't screened.
She had no inkling whether the comments would be
frivolous or serious.

Male listeners had developed a fantasy about the
woman whose voice was described by many as sultry.
One time, she was teased she could turn a simple hello
into five-minute pillow talk. Whatever helped her ratings and paid the bills. The show's popularity meant
only one thing to Carmel—job security.

Carmel taunted Glen with a wide grin as all seven

phone lines lit up as expected. Glen's mouth stretched in a thin line across his face in irritation. More work for him, and he was not happy—too bad. She knew he preferred shows where the hosts were so boring, the phones hardly rang. Glen should've been a Maytag repairman.

"Good morning, Patrick. What's on your mind?"

"Besides you—"

Carmel rolled her eyes. "Patrick, you're five seconds away from hearing a dial tone, my brotha."

Patrick chuckled. "No harm, Frenchie, no harm. I called to talk about materialistic relationships."

Please! She didn't want to waste two hours of morning drive time talking that, after he had the nerve to try and hit on her. That was the problem with open line. Almost any topic could be discussed, but if people became unruly, they fell prey to Carmel's infamous line, "Don't get French with me," before hearing a disconnect tone.

Saying Carmel could relate to the topic was an understatement since her notoriety brought unrealistic expectations to personal relationships like former boyfriend, Victor Coleman, who often complained their relationship was less stimulating than her talk shows, or Greg Knight who boasted to friends he was dating the radio sex kitten. Before him was Calvin Kane. The brotha was fine, but he was just using her to increase personal contacts within the radio industry.

Whoever said that a woman could have it all lied. She had yet to become that woman, considering she was living a double life. Carmel was nothing like the image she portrayed on the radio. She longed for a deep, meaningful, and committed relationship.

Patrick continued, "A few weeks ago I lost my job after a company takeover, buyout, merger, or whatever you want to call it."

"In other words, you've been downsized," Carmel chided. *Serves you right, you flirt.*

"You've got it! The money and benefits were good. My lady, Sheila, and I had a solid thing, or so I thought. When I tried to plead with her to be patient while I planned a career cha—"

Carmel slowly interrupted so listeners wouldn't have to hear his life story for the next hour, "Sorry about your job loss, brotha. Was Sheila supportive?"

"Yeah. Up until the day I was gainfully unemployed," he snapped. "She told me it was time to move on and some other things I can't repeat on the air. I was devastated; I thought we were soul mates."

Carmel held in her laugh. Now the jerk was trying to play the wounded lover. "Are you sure it was because of your job loss and not because she got tired of your flirtatious ways?"

"Frenchie, I loved Sheila. I really did," he defended in a grief-stricken tone.

Shaking her head as if the caller could see her, Carmel sighed. "Well, Pat, we're all in search of that one special person. I've had my share of superficial relationships. People profess one thing, but they're after something else. Many people are seeking what they can get out of it, and I'm not just talking about intimacy. It happens in business dealings, between friends, and within families. Nothing comes from the heart anymore, it seems."

"Frenchie, I've learned my lesson. Believe me."

"I hope so," Carmel responded as she disconnected his call.

Glen eagerly signaled for a break. Carmel glared. Time to air that goofy car dealership commercial he had recorded.

"You're listening to 'Don't Get French with Me' on

WPLS. I want to hear from you when I come back. There's got to be some love out there!"

During Carmel's two-minute commercial break, she twisted her lips. What a waste of good air space. With so many strong topics out there, why dominate the show with a subject people could discuss with their mother, a therapist, or stranger at the bus stop? She had to maintain her professionalism and sincerity. It was Monday, and she assumed these people had pent-up frustrations left over from the weekend.

Glen tapped on the glass partition, signaling five seconds.

Carmel punched the second line. "We're back. Let's welcome Gina to the show."

"Frenchie, I don't know why the brothas are complaining. The guy before the break, Patrick, and other men are only after one thing in a relationship—physical gratification they call intimacy. I think women are tired of being used, and now we're looking out for ourselves so, when the breakup occurs, we can walk away with compensation for a broken heart."

"Hmm, games people play. Just roll the dice and you might get love or a once-scorned companion. C'mon, somebody out there has to have a true love story. Make me want to use this box of tissue."

For the next hour, Carmel's show was inundated with calls about busted, shaky, and unfulfilling relationships. Women described themselves as bitter and broken. Men characterized their former girlfriends as gold diggers.

Finally a sixty-five-year-old retired bus driver phoned in, describing the perfect love affair and marriage with his wife of forty years.

"Okay, I'm out of time. Go out on a blind date,"

Carmel suggested. "Close your eyes, open your heart, and you might find the love of your life. Until next time, peace." Carmel stood, removed her headset, and bowed to Glen, her customary thank-you. Carmel walked out of the studio exhausted and with a headache.

Rice Taylor, a twenty-eight-year-old senior sales rep for a pharmaceutical company was disappointed at the conclusion of Frenchie's show. He had caught the last thirty minutes of the program.

Normally, Rice never listened to talk radio, preferring smooth jazz, but that woman's voice demanded his attention, as did the comments from his ex-girlfriend, Regina "Gina" Larson.

"How dare she call a radio station and publicly justify her actions," he said, huffing.

Rice almost ran into the back of a Cadillac, from the shock of hearing her annoying high-pitched voice again after so many months.

Luckily he saw through her before he got deeper into their six-month liaison. Physical—ha! That was a two-way street. Gina had only been interested in receiving lavish gifts from every destination in which his plane touched down while he was away on business. He spoiled her with expensive dinners at exclusive restaurants and supported her financially when she quit her job.

Rice's nostrils flared. He did not want to think about Regina Larson anymore—ever.

Rice squirmed in his leather seat to shake any lingering memories of Gina. His mind fast-forwarded to more pleasant thoughts, the host, Frenchie, who exhibited such a great sense of humor and intellect. He bit his bottom lip, laughing. *The sistah did a great job holding con-*

versations with the craziest callers. Frenchie definitely kept the flow balanced between male and female comments. It seemed she even saw through Gina's shallowness.

Rice took a deep breath and smiled. Frenchie's voice was intoxicating, unique, and very, very sensuous. He would never forget how her huskiness lowered to a whisper right before the commercial breaks.

Humph, humph, humph.

He bet she was drop-dead gorgeous. Suddenly Rice envied the man who dominated Frenchie's thoughts and shared her special moments.

Rice smirked. One thing for certain, he would never subject himself to a blind date. His eyes were wide-open with Gina, and she still fooled him. When women learned he was a senior sales rep earning a good income, they stopped focusing on him and saw the dollar signs. The next woman he chose had better have a chisel handy to break the ice around his heart.

He slid an Urban Knights CD into the player, smiling, almost chuckling, as he thought about some of the stupid relationship situations couples inflicted upon each other. Rice steered his Dodge Durango through morning traffic en route to Lambert Airport, shaking his head.

Rice would give anything to hear Frenchie's voice and show again, but it wouldn't happen anytime soon, with scheduled morning meetings the next couple of weeks in New York, Boston, Philly, and Baltimore.

Frenchie. Did she earn that nickname because of her sassiness or because of an alluring appearance?

Either way, the sistah earned his respect. "Ah, and to think I was complaining about running late this morning. Well, thanks to Frenchie, it looks like I'm going to have a great day!"

When Rice pulled into the Park and Ride garage, his silly fantasy about the radio personality vanished. If he had time, he would drop her a note.

"I love Fridays," Carmel mumbled, stretching her tired body as she slid out of bed. She was glad she didn't make any big plans for the weekend. She welcomed doing nothing. Okay, to be honest, she would rather have someone to do something with and go someplace for something exciting, but the next best thing for loneliness was self-pampering.

Carmel danced across her femininely decorated bedroom, which showcased a large glass-and-oak vanity table filled with perfumes, powders, and an assortment of nail polishes. Various size floral hatboxes stacked in two corners and tied with white satin bows created identical pyramids. Carmel sighed her pleasure as bright red polished toes sunk into plush lilac carpet on her way to the bathroom.

"Maybe I'll take a bike ride through Forest Park after work today," she mumbled while massaging cool cucumber moisturizing cream on her face, staring into a wall-to-sink mirror in a wheat-and-lilac bathroom. Next, she dressed in all black, from her leather ankle boots to her turtleneck and skirt, to make her look thinner and taller. Other women would probably call the attire sexy and dangerous. She could identify with neither.

Carmel arrived at the station an hour later in an extremely good mood. *Who needs a man?*

Glen cued her with a nod, as her theme music faded. "Heeeey, it's Friday. You're waking up to 'Don't Get French with Me' in three, two, one."

*   *   *

Two hours later, Carmel was almost giddy as her show ended. Payday and the end of another workweek. Smiling, she greeted Esther Truman, program director and her best friend, who seemed to walk the halls like it was a runway—short steps, head high, and the right amount of sway to the hips. "Hey, girlfriend."

"Hey, yourself. Great show on black economic empowerment. You're hot, girl. Just sizzlin'," Esther hissed like a snake before grinning. "Oh, by the way, pick up a couple of pieces of mail on your way out, and have a great weekend."

"Thanks, Es. I'm indulging for the next two days. First, a full-body massage at the spa, a new hairstyle, shopping, and then I'm pigging out on everything high in fat, sodium, and carbohydrates."

Esther laughed at Carmel's sly smile. "Okay, don't come wobbling in here on Monday, whining about how you have to go on another diet because your clothes shrunk."

Carmel hugged her friend, dismissing her comment. She added a wink to her silly smile before walking away. Carmel admired Esther, who had been recently promoted to management and used a no-nonsense approach to solve personnel disagreements. Esther knew how to listen, and when it was time for her to be heard.

Esther was seven years older than Carmel, stood a few inches shorter, and weighed at least twenty pounds more than Carmel. She was the type of white girl who was always in sync with the black community and its issues. She had so many black friends, at times Carmel forgot she wasn't a "sistah."

Carmel swooped the mail off the desk in one smooth

motion as she sauntered to the elevator. She examined the three envelopes as she rode down to the lobby. One letter was handwritten—fan mail. She opened that first, hoping it wasn't a complaint.

Dear Frenchie,

Monday was the first time I ever listened to your show. You made my day. Boy, you're good! Your conversation is lively, but I also heard your gentleness. I agree with your thoughts about relationships. If we could love what's in a person's heart rather than material things, economic status, appearances, and education, then maybe love will find us.

You suggested a blind date. What a challenge! I'm laughing just thinking about some disasters my friends have experienced from them. I regret I may not have a chance to listen again any time soon because of my work schedule, but I cherish the thought of knowing there's somebody else out there who's trying to find the deeper things in life.

Sincerely,

Rice Taylor

Your one time fan

Carmel folded the letter with an audible sigh. "How sweet, and he didn't try to hit on me either." When the elevator doors opened, she stepped out with a smile. "Yep, it's going to be a great weekend."

Chapter Two

A month later . . .

What had possessed Rice to reply to Carmel French's reply? Shock, maybe. Why did she take the time to write him back at all? Rice grinned from ear to ear. It really didn't matter anymore. He was becoming obsessed with Carmel French, not the radio personality, but the woman. He wondered if this was considered blind dating.

> *Rice,*
>
> *Your letters are like a bowl of double-dipped chocolate ice cream on a hot summer night. Believe it or not, you inspire me. I feel that I can really get what I want in a relationship. Sometimes, I think us ladies don't know what we want or expect from a man. Rice, be honest with me. Are women the only ones who want to feel special? Don't men want more than a hot meal, a clean house, and physical pleasure on demand? Your letters are an*

insight into a man's heart. I don't want just a man. I want his heart.

Can't wait for our next heart-to-heart.
Carmel

Rice relaxed in his seat in the business section as he stared out the airplane's window, surrendering his mind to float effortlessly with the clouds. In the past, Rice became agitated with multiple business flights during the week. But now, thanks to his pen pal, he welcomed the trips, which allowed him more time to daydream about Carmel and write her about things he hadn't shared with another woman.

A jet soaring in the distance drew his attention. Suddenly, he wondered if he and Carmel had ever crossed paths from a distance, held a conversation, or made eye contact. "When did your words overpower me like mediating soft whispers? When did your sultry voice fade away?"

"I don't know, most people describe my voice as raspy, but if you think it's sexy—" The elderly black woman sitting next to Rice batted her lids. "I've never been picked up on a plane before."

Rice blushed from embarrassment. "Sorry, I guess I was thinking out loud."

She reached over and patted his hand. "Ah, young love. When you find the right woman," she advised, squinting through her thick glasses, "you'll find your heart uttering all of its secrets."

Rice frowned. "Oh, I'm not in love; I haven't even met her yet."

The passenger adjusted her glasses and peered at Rice, giving him a once-over before turning back around in her seat. "Then, you're one sick puppy."

Rice resisted laughing at the woman's comments and

reached into his pocket for Carmel's last letter. When he re-read it, he was dumbfounded. Something wasn't right. Carmel had always been chatty on paper, often-times writing two to three pages. That's why he was stunned. He recalled his last letter.

> *Dear Carmel,*
>
> *I'm flying to New York again, and of course, I was thinking about you, wondering if you're okay. Are you smiling? Is your day going well? I know we've discussed so many things over the past weeks. I guess you can say we've been comparing notes. Can I get personal? What makes a woman stay in love with her man? Think about it and share your thoughts with me in your next letter. May your days be as lovely as you and your thoughts be filled with the passion of life.*
> *Rice*
> *Your number one fan*

Up to this letter, Rice knew they had been com-pletely truthful with each other. That was the basis for their continued correspondence. Now, Carmel's hon-esty disturbed him.

> *Dear Rice,*
>
> *I've never been in love.*
> *Until next time, may God bless you with the woman of your dreams.*
> *Carmel*

Two lines, few words, but Carmel was saying so much. She was holding back something. What was she not saying? Rice closed his eyes. A *whole lot, that's for sure.* Carmel had never been in love? Unbelievable. Why? She was so open and passionate.

* * *

"Okay, sistah. I can understand pen pals from around the world, but around the neighborhood is a bit much. He's even thrown in a few postmarked letters from the east coast," Esther scolded as she marched to Carmel's desk like a military soldier performing a drill. "Come clean. What's going on with you and this guy?" she asked, shoving a stack of letters in Carmel's face.

Carmel snickered as she sniffed the pink roses Rice had sent a few days ago. Every Monday, fresh roses arrived, and on Fridays, a mixed floral arrangement came for her to take home. Rice was pampering her from a piece of paper. Carmel vaguely heard Esther's tirade. She was too happy, flattered, and preoccupied after reading all of Rice's letters from the previous week.

> *Carmel,*
>
> *Let me treat you like a queen from afar for now, but our day is coming. Personally, I don't think special women get enough flowers. Some receive them for the wrong reasons like after a big fight or a guilt trip on their man's part, but I want you to be surrounded by beauty because that's the way I see you. So that's my reason for the flowers today and every time in the future.*
> *May you have the sweetest day,*
> *Rice*

Carmel burst into laughter. Rice made her feel wonderful every day. "Es, what's wrong with ya, girl? The brotha and I are just exchanging the written word," Carmel defended, smiling innocently.

Esther placed a clenched fist on her hip. "Yeah. You and Mr. *W-R-I-T-E* have been exchanging a lot more than ink. You've been sniffing correction fluid?" Esther

accusingly pointed her red-hot polished fingernail.
"This week alone he's sent—including that stack I've
just given you—about nine letters! Girl, this ain't the
post office." Esther twisted her mouth. "What's gotten
into you? What has this guy been slipping in these envelopes?"

Carmel chuckled at Esther's ranting like an overbear-
ing mother. "Jealous, are ya? I'm really enjoying this,"
Carmel confessed, grinning like a child.

Esther gripped her spiked hair as if she was about to
yank it out. "Please tell me you aren't serious."

"Re-group, Es. His name is Rice Taylor, and we're just
friends."

"Friends?" Esther yelled. "Frenchie, who ya kiddin'?
This is me, white sistah-girlfriend." Esther arched her
eyebrow. "I hope he hasn't been sending drugs through
the mail. What's going on in that hyperactive mind of
yours?"

Carmel rolled her eyes. "Es, this isn't a terrorist plot.
These letters are filled with words that are funny, sensitive, and thought-provoking. This is not an intimate
relationship."

Esther retreated to a nearby chair and collapsed, giving Carmel an I-don't-believe-that's-all look. "Let me
bring you into the new millennium. Ever heard of
e-mail?" Esther slowly folded her hands. "You're planning on getting involved with this Rice-a-Roni brother,
aren't you?"

"His name is Rice! I enjoy his sweet thoughts without
any commitments." Carmel closed her eyes and giggled. She covered her mouth with her hands and leaned
forward. "We've made up this game called Find Me. Every
day, we search the crowd, trying to find each other.
Since we agreed earlier not to disclose any of our physical descriptions, we're supposed to imagine what the

other looks like from the words we've expressed in our letters. For instance, sometimes I'll write, I saw you today, reading the newspaper at Starbucks. Your expression was serious as you wiggled your thick mustache against your nut-brown skin," Carmel whispered in a daydreamy voice, forgetting Esther was present.

Esther shook her head. "Well, that's worth staying up all night and reading again. I think both of you need to enroll at Forest Park Community College in Love 101. I'm surprised he hasn't contacted Miss Cleo for the answers. Just be careful, Frenchie. Please."

Carmel carefully modulated her voice to sound unaffected. "It's my parade. Don't you even think about drizzling on it. I think Rice is searching his heart and making me look into mine."

"He just better not hurt my girl. That's all I've got to say." Esther stood and strutted away.

Carmel rested her chin in her palm. Esther just didn't understand. Rice wasn't a threat on paper. It's the ones who smile in your face who could deceive you.

Later that evening, locked away in her bedroom listening to some smooth jazz Rice had recommended, Carmel leisurely read through the stack of fresh new letters. His words were so inspiring. "Rice, I wish I could hear your voice," she said, groaning. Was it a deep, rich baritone that would mesmerize her as he spoke the very words he wrote?

Carmel closed her eyes and drifted to sleep.

Three weeks later . . .

"So, Frenchie, how is lover boy?" Esther curiously looked at Carmel, while scanning the station's mail.

"Well, he must be moving up in your book. No more

Rice-a-Roni? He's wonderful," Carmel replied, walking into the break room, wearing a smug smile, pleased with the first hour discussion on the future of historically black colleges and universities.

"Well, actually, I was thinking Rice Krispies." Esther released a body-shaking laugh, which turned her face red, and fanned herself from the sudden exertion. "Okay, okay, girlfriend. I admit, Mr. San Francisco treat has been sounding more interesting lately. So when is the big day?" Esther asked.

Carmel remained quiet, ignoring Esther's silly jokes. Rice had been asking the same thing. "Es, I talk the talk, but girl, I can't even begin to take baby steps on this walk. I don't know if I can do this."

"Trust me, you can. And, I want to be there too."

Carmel ignored Esther and began pacing around tables and chairs. "Can you believe our attraction is growing? Our letters have become romantic, sometimes mysterious, but always honest."

"I don't know anything about Rice-a-Roni being romantic on paper, but the man is definitely a mystery."

Carmel stopped and stared out the window, amused by the antics of two blue jays chasing each other on tree branches. "Wouldn't it be something if Rice was incredibly irresistible and devastatingly handsome?"

"Yeah, that would be something," Esther said sarcastically before throwing up her hands. "Carmel French, you're starting to lose it. Hello. Let me burst your bubble. This brotha could also be a loser. I bet he knows exactly what you look like. The sooner you set a date to meet him, the sooner you can dump him!"

Carmel sauntered out of the break room, smiling as she headed back to the studio, yelling back, "I don't

know. He could turn out to be the sexiest man alive."
But what if he isn't?

"And I bet the suspense is killing you." Esther's voice
boomed down the corridor like a bullhorn. "It's definitely killing me!"

Chapter Three

Carmel,
*I saw you today. I watched you from a distance as
you scanned the shelves at Borders Books. You didn't notice me at first, but slowly you must have felt my presence. When our eyes met, I was instantly drawn to your
luscious lashes. Your skin was the color of cinnamon,
your hair swept off your neck held by a gold clip, and
your height was perfect, standing over five feet. Just perfect. Carmel, if that had been you, I know you would've
run into my arms instead of asking someone to call security because I looked suspicious and was possibly
stalking a customer. This Find Me game is going to get
me hurt or arrested. I'm missing you.*
Rice
More than a fan

Reluctantly, Rice sealed the letter to mail on his way
out the door in a few hours. It was two weeks before
Christmas, and for the past two months of exchanging

letters with Carmel, Rice felt he was dying a slow death. If he forced her into a meeting before she was ready, he could lose her. If he held out any longer, he would lose his mind.

Rice dressed in a chocolate-brown pinstriped Ralph Lauren suit, cream shirt, brown silk socks, and coffee-colored snakeskin shoes as he left for the annual 100 Black Men's banquet, held at the Marriott Hotel in downtown St. Louis. He would've given anything to have Carmel with him instead of being around a bunch of men. Every brotha who attended was either well connected professionally, socially, or just wannabes.

Guest speaker Tavis Smiley, former host and executive producer of *BET Tonight* and radio personality, entertained the audience with his witty sense of humor and political insight. Rice was caught up in Tavis' spell until he spotted his old friend, Allan Martin, the station manager for WPLS. *Interesting*.

During a brief intermission, the urge to find out more about the woman who had begun to consume his thoughts caused Rice to seek out Carmel's boss. "Hey, Allan, what's up, man?"

They exchanged a handshake, a measured hug, and a back pat.

"Rice, how ya been, man? Still traveling and making all the money?"

Rice chuckled. He knew Allan earned at least $60,000 more than his $80,000 yearly salary. "Yeah, right. You're the one running the show. How many more stations has Clear Channel purchased?"

The station manager shrugged as he rubbed his clean-shaven head, frowning as he curled his lips. "A few." He was an imposing, rugged-looking, dark-skinned man with a full black beard sprinkled with light-gray strands, oddly complementing wild and thick eyebrows.

A black tailored suit fit his six-foot, seven-inch muscular frame with little room to spare. His gray, collarless silk shirt appeared newly purchased or just professionally pressed.

Women, attached and single, considered the bachelor very attractive and an excellent financial catch. Still, Allan's physical and intellectual attributes could intimidate strangers.

Rice cleared his throat, debating how to approach the subject of wanting information about Carmel. His palms were sweating, his heart was racing as it slammed against his chest, and suddenly his throat became dry.

Rice searched the room, hoping none of his friends would see him make a fool out of himself as he jammed his hands in his pants pockets, gathering courage. "Look, man. You've got a female host . . ." His voice faded.

He swallowed hard as Allan crossed his arms, displaying an amused expression, waiting.

"Well, I was wondering if you can help a brotha out with introductions."

Did his voice just crack? "I have twelve on-air personalities, Rice. So, be more specific, brotha."

"You're probably going to think I'm an idiot."

Allan's chest lifted in a slight chuckle as he waved his hand, dismissing the thought. "Try me."

"I know this is going to sound strange or maybe even prehistoric, but—"

Allan clenched his teeth, snarling, clearly becoming impatient. "Just tell me." He glanced at his watch.

"Well, Carmel French and I . . . we've been corresponding for a few months by mail. We've never met face to face . . . ah, I'm ready to become more than a pen pal."

"Rice, to be honest with you," Allan paused, furrowing his bushy brows in a frown, searching his mind for a noncommittal response. "A blind date would have been easier. I'm not comfortable getting in the middle of what you and Carmel have or don't have going on." He held up his finger. "But, I will say, she's extremely talented, exceptionally bright, and possesses an unmatched sense of humor. She should be taken very seriously." He grinned, showing perfectly even, bright white teeth. "I don't want one of my frat brothers messin' with her head and crushing her heart," he warned.

Rice shook his head, denying he was up to mischief. All he wanted was a hint at what she looked like. He opened his mouth, stuttering.

Allan continued, meticulously massaging his beard. "The best I can do is invite you to our annual Christmas party. That's one event Carmel always attends and truly enjoys. I'm willing to make an introduction. After that," he said, folding his arms, "let's just say, you're on your own."

Rice nodded, relieved that soon he and Carmel would meet. "I'll be there." His imagination was exhausted as he attempted to see Carmel through the words in her letters. Enough was enough.

The following Monday, Allan Martin sat behind his desk, thinking about his conversation with Rice. "Ha!" He had intensely watched Rice slyly ask about Carmel. He had to fold arms across his chest to hold in his laughter. Without guessing, he knew Rice was talking about Carmel, whose sultry voice could lull any man to sleep.

As Carmel's boss, he also knew she was a private person, despite the bold and quick wit she demonstrated on the radio. Every male who listened to his station wanted to know, "Does she look as good as she sounds?"

He usually gave a brief physical description and dropped the subject. But, it was something about Rice's tormented expression that indicated a more personal interest. Allan laughed again.

He drummed his finger on his lips, thinking, as he scanned the stack of resumes, audition tapes, and other mail scattered across his desk. What was going on that Rice and Carmel hadn't met? This was going to be interesting.

Carmel was nothing like the showgirls Rice had dated in the past. She possessed a sweet innocence about her that was hidden behind the microphone.

Allan pressed the intercom, alerting the control room. "Glen, ask Carmel to come to my office after her show."

Glen's monotonous voice suddenly became perky. "She's in trouble, ain't she? I knew slave reparation was too controversial for her show!"

"Glen?"

"Huh?"

"Japanese-Americans and Jews were compensated, so should African-Americans. Through open dialogue people will have an opportunity to hear both sides of the argument. Now, just have Carmel come to my office." He disconnected and waited.

Carmel walked through his door, wearing a red turtleneck sweater, skin-tight jeans, and red leather boots with two-inch heels. The red cap she wore hid the mystery of her hairdo.

"Allen, you wanted to see me? Did you have a problem with the show?" Carmel bowed her head, smiling. "The phone lines jammed as racial lines were clearly divided today. I've never heard so many angry people."

He waved her in. "Nah, heated dialogue is good, even though you had to hang up on more than one irate caller."

Carmel sat down in a brown leather seat facing his massive, intimidating desk and crossed her legs.

Allan watched Carmel's reaction when he mentioned Rice's name and his invitation to the holiday party.

"I'm not going!" Carmel blurted as she leaped out of her seat.

"Carmel, you haven't missed the Christmas party in four years."

Carmel was clearly lost in her own world as she paced the plush tan carpet. If Allan's vibes were correct, Carmel looked scared.

Maybe Rice was stalking her.

"If Rice and I meet, then it's over."

"I'm confused. What's over?"

Carmel didn't make eye contact as she explained. "My escape. Our fantasy. The special something that has developed between us."

"Oh, boy. What is going on here?"

Suddenly, Carmel spun around and raced back to his desk with a panic-filled look. "Allan . . ." Her voice was suddenly laced with a sexy undertone.

He was amused.

She knew her charm only worked on listeners who couldn't see her. Carmel's magic spell had no power over him.

He leaned forward, speaking in his own husky voice. "Yes?" he whispered teasingly.

"Tell me something about Rice," Carmel pleaded. "The shade of his brown skin, the color of his eyes, height, weight, and social security number." She grinned. "Just kidding."

Allan placed his elbow on his desk and propped his fist under his beard-covered chin. "Who says he's brown?" He curled his lips, tickled by Carmel's antics.

Carmel chewed on her bottom lip. "Okay, so he's not the shade of pecan." She paused, closed her eyes, and inhaled deeply. "Okay, okay. Just tell me how the brotha smells. I love musky cologne on men. Of course, whatever you say will remain strictly confidential. Is he nice-looking?"

Allan pushed back from his desk. "That's it! I'm not sniffing behind any man." He waved his hand. "Don't you have a promo or something to record?" He shook his head, humored by Rice's and Carmel's tactics in trying to pry information out of him, but he wasn't having it.

"You're not going to tell me anything, are you?"

"If you came to the Christmas party, you could see, touch, and sniff for yourself."

"Oh, I want to go," Carmel mumbled as she walked to the studio.

The station's party was two days away, and Carmel hadn't slept since Allan informed her Rice was invited. She felt childish for acting so silly over meeting a man. *Just go and get it over with,* a brave voice within her challenged.

Carmel pouted. This was her favorite time of year. She would sorely miss the camaraderie with her colleagues and their families. Carmel ignored the clicking heels approaching as she pounded the wall.

"Hmmm, writing to imaginary boyfriends, arguing with invisible people, and now you're boxing—the true signs of a woman in need of therapy," Esther taunted Carmel.

"Would you stop sneaking up on me?" Carmel said, snarling.

"What's wrong with this picture?" Esther drew an

imaginary square in the air. "You're supposed to be ecstatic about seeing the man you dream about all day and whose letters you read every night."

"I do want to meet Rice, but I feel like the lion in *The Wizard of Oz*. I've got no courage." Carmel avoided Esther's eyes.

Esther jammed a fist on her hip. "Frenchie, please. You don't need any courage to dump the chump."

Carmel slumped against the wall.

Esther scanned Carmel's attire. "Frenchie, have you been getting enough rest? You've got dark circles under your puffy eyes—I've shown you myself how to apply makeup."

Carmel glanced at the digital clock overhead. She had five minutes. "Not now, Es."

"Oh, no, you don't." Esther pointed her finger. "Have you looked at yourself lately? You usually take the time to artistically curl your hair every morning, and your clothes—Whew!—Black and orange only match on Halloween."

"I just haven't been in the mood."

"Why are you allowing yourself to go through these changes?" Esther reached out and fingered Carmel's scarf. "And, red definitely doesn't enhance your outfit."

"I can't concentrate lately."

Esther twisted her lips. "I don't know. Maybe Rice is starting to brainwash me, too, but honey, you sure you don't want to go? I could pretend I'm you while you check out your knight in writing hardware."

"Es, you're so corny."

"Well, if he's all that, I'll dump my husband and marry him."

They hugged and laughed.

Carmel wiped away a tear. "And it's *knight in shining armor*, girl. I'm not ready to lose this wonderful friendship with him." Carmel heard her theme music. "Gotta go." She raced inside the studio, collapsed in the chair behind the microphone, and assessed her attire. Her feelings about Rice were as mixed as her clothes.

Today, Carmel felt the way Glen looked—like he didn't want to be there. She took a series of deep breaths. As Glen cued Carmel three seconds, she perked up. *Time to put on a show.* "Heeeey, it's Friday, and that means open line. It's the end of the workweek, close to the holidays, and maybe your payday. Talk to me in three, two, one."

Carmel punched the first line and welcomed a female listener. "Good morning, Gina."

"Hi, Frenchie, I called a few months ago about being materialistic. "

"Yes, I remember."

"Well, the spirit of Christmas has made me re-think some things that I've done in the past. I'm going to turn my life around and get back my man who I hurt the most with my selfish ways.

"What a wonderful way to close out the year. I wish you much success and all the happiness."

Less than an hour later, Carmel was exhausted as she pulled off her headset. The show went smoothly, with callers commenting about what they planned to do for others this Christmas instead of focusing on themselves. She did her customary bow to Glen and strolled out of the studio.

Carmel walked to the front lobby, with Esther on her heels. At the same time a tall, white FedEx deliveryman appeared in the station doorway, struggling with a large package.

He gave Carmel's attire a strange look and then blushed when he caught her eyes. He nodded. "Ladies," the man said, placing the box on the receptionist's desk.

Esther signed his clipboard and read the receiver's

name. "Either Rice-a-Roni is using larger paper, or it's a laptop bringing you two into the new millennium."

Abruptly, Carmel grabbed the box with a fierce possessiveness. "And, see, all this time I thought you were my girl. Stop calling him that! His name is Rice Anthony Taylor. You're close to being at the top of my list of ex-friends."

"Yeah? Hmmm. Well, his initials even spell *rat*. Be careful, girl. Okay, sorry." Esther feigned innocence at Carmel's glaring. "Now, open the box. I'm nosy, and you know it."

Carmel gradually ripped the packing tape and found a meticulously wrapped gift. She met Esther's questioning eyes as they noticed a sealed envelope taped to the present.

"Skip the letter, girl. Go for the present!" Esther urged, grinning as she clasped her hands. "Hurry up because I'm not going anywhere until you do."

"Don't rush me, Es!" Carmel stomped her purple suede boot as she tore open the envelope. "I sense this letter is very special even without the gift." Carmel slid into the chair behind the desk of the receptionist, who always seemed to be in the bathroom or getting another cup of coffee. "They have the power to mellow my mood," Carmel said with a dreamy expression. *I shut everything else out so my heart can feel Rice's words, my ears can hear my name on his lips, and my eyes can see his handsome face.*

Esther squinted. "You feeling all that from his letters, huh?" She sucked her teeth and without shame boldly peeked over Carmel's shoulder and read Rice's letter aloud.

"Frenchie, open the gift. You want me to do it?"

"Es!" Carmel gasped before smiling as she followed Rice's instruction, pulling out a bracelet covered with tiny birthstones. Next was a lead crystal 5x7 picture frame with a magazine photo of an attractive black couple.

Esther whistled. "Wow." She folded her arms. "Okay, so Rice Krispie has good taste."

Carmel ignored Esther's silly remark and stared at a rhinestone-covered key-shaped brooch. "Rice, what does this mean?" Carmel whispered as a tear fell.

Esther grabbed a tissue off the desk and sniffed. "These are so beautiful."

Carmel looked at Esther as if to say, "You still here?"

"They're also private, so if you don't mind, I'm going to read my letter at home." Carmel grabbed her black-and-brown leopard swing coat and put her arms through the sleeves. "Good-bye, Es. Have fun at the party this weekend," she said with a sorrowful smile.

"I still wish you were coming." She pulled back and shook her head at Carmel's clothes. "Girl, please go home and color-coordinate your life, your man, and your wardrobe."

Saturday night, an hour before the company Christmas party, reality set in. "I can't believe I'm really not going for the first time ever." Rice Taylor had complicated her life, on paper. She laid her gifts across the bed and stretched on top of the comforter to re-read Rice's letter for probably the third time that day.

Merry Christmas, baby,

Carmel closed her eyes, absorbing his endearment. *Hmm . . . That's the first time he's ever called me that.*

I still want to be a part of your holidays since you've decided against going to the party tonight. The picture frame is for us to imagine our future together. Carmel, listen to your heart. It knows how we feel about each other. The bracelet is for you to wrap around your wrist, since I can't wrap my arms around you.

Tears filled Carmel's eyes. "Who needs a good romance novel when I've got Rice's words that reach out and grab me?"

Finally, Carmel, I want you to know that only you hold the key to unlocking the dreams of my heart. The rhinestone pin represents the way you have covered my heart with warm words and bright promises. Baby . . .

Carmel's heart pounded faster at the sight of his endearing word again. Rice's words had the power to possess her body and soul. She could almost hear his voice whisper in her ears.

Hmm, now that's a thought. She smiled, wondering if his voice was strong, deep, and sexy. Would it soften whenever he said *baby?* She gritted her teeth and screamed out her frustration. "Ahhh!" Deep down, Carmel wanted to see him bad.

I do respect your decision to wait for now, but I want more, so much more for us. I pray you'll feel the same way eventually. Again, Merry Christmas, sweetheart. Here's my phone number, 314-555-5081, in case you want to talk . . . about us.
I'm Yours,
Rice

Tears trickled down her cheeks. With blurred vision Carmel closed his letter and placed it over her heart. "I'm addicted to you, Rice Taylor," she confessed.

Chapter Four

One day after New Year . . .

"**S**pecial delivery for a Mr. Rice Taylor." A goofy-looking, gum-popping deliveryman looked Rice up and down. "You him, man?" he asked impatiently.

Rice was about to slam his door, when he noticed the flowers. He blushed as he reached for them with one hand and dug into his pocket for a tip with the other.

The older teenager nodded after stuffing the bills in his pocket and jumping off the snow-packed steps.

Rice grinned. "Maybe I didn't strike out after all." He glided to the kitchen in a two-step, where he ripped opened a large purple envelope. Suddenly, he smelled his sausage burning. Rice rushed to the stove and turned off the burner before he hurried to the table, sat down, and read Carmel's card. Breakfast could wait.

For five long days, Carmel hadn't written him back or used the phone number he gave her. Rice had begun to second-guess himself, believing all Carmel wanted was friendship.

Hi Sweetie,

Rice's chest puffed out. "She loves me. She called me *sweetie.*" *Okay, but it's the first time she didn't call me* Rice. *It's a start.*

> *Sorry, it's taken me so long to gather my thoughts. Rice, you're a special man. I'm blessed to have you dominate my thoughts, dreams, and yes, my life. I'm constantly wondering if you're everything I've dreamed. I just don't know if I'm ready for us to meet.*
> *Anyway, each flower you see, I handpicked for the arrangement because the bright and soft colors remind me of how your words make me feel—alive and happy. Your emotions saturate my mind each day. As our relationship changes, I admit I want more, too. I want you to hold me when you call me* baby. *I long to hear your voice, but my feelings aren't stronger than my fear of losing what we have. I know I'm not making sense. Don't try to figure me out. No man has yet. I can't even figure myself out. I need a little more time.*
> *I'm yours, too,*
> *Carmel*

Rice closed his eyes, whispering, "Carmel, sweetheart, this has to stop. We're falling in love on paper. I'm setting a date."

My Love,
> *I agree that we do have a good thing going. We've both opened up and shared some private things about ourselves. The best Christmas present I could've had*

would've been wrapping you in my arms, looking in
your eyes, and bringing in the New Year with you. It's
time, baby. Will you allow me to pick a date? I can't hold
out any longer. Let's not continue to deny ourselves each
other. I need more than paper and a pen when I'm thinking about you. I need to touch you. I need to understand
your moods and see you when you're happy or sad, my
paper doll. I want you to hear me say, I love you.
I'm yours,
Rice

P.S. Carmel, I'm your friend first and I can give you
more friendship than any person alive because I love
you. That will not change. I know you love me. I can
feel it, sweetheart. Oh, I'm imagining you smell as sweet
as your flowers.

Chapter Five

"How seductive can pretty paper be?" Carmel grinned excitedly. "Rice, you are about to find out." The avid shopper in Carmel couldn't resist the after-Christmas leftovers and the end-of-the-year clear-outs, but when she strolled into Papyrus, a stationery store in the mall, ignoring shoe and clothing sales, Carmel went crazy, snatching brown marble paper with satin bows and ribbons, textured pink paper with raffia ties, and scented, water-stained purple paper.

Later that night, Carmel tossed in her bed, restless. Why did it seem so easy for Rice to disclose his feelings without knowing if she would be physically attractive? She sat up in bed and turned on the light. Her stomach was twisting just like her heart. She grabbed her scented stationery and started scribbling.

Dear Rice,
  You're my love, too. Yes, it's time. Okay, past time. But why do I feel like I'm losing here? Stupid question.

Don't answer that. I can do this. I can, Rice, but I'm
scared. Can we be as happy physically as we have been
on paper? Don't answer that. I'm falling apart. I need
more time.
Yours,
Carmel

A few days later, Rice surprised Carmel with a letter
written on mint-scented green water-stained parchment. She smiled until Rice insisted on Valentine's Day
for their very first rendezvous, less than six weeks away.

Sweetheart,
   I'm craving your voice, your touch, and your smell,
like an addict. I want to put a stamp on my forehead
and deliver myself to your station. I am beyond ready,
but you asked for time. You have thirty-eight days until I
sweep you off your feet. Our first date will be everything
it should be for two people in love—special and roman-
tic. Carmel, I'm going for the gold. You are the prize I
seek, not as a trophy, but as a best friend, special com-
panion, and I'll whisper the rest when I see you.
Rice

Carmel inhaled the peppermint fragrance of the stationery. Her vision was blurred, her heart heavy, and
her mind scared to death. "Whoa. Am I ready to accept
my fate?" Lately, she was asking herself more questions
than she had answers.

Carmel's nerves were frayed. She couldn't eat, sleep,
or concentrate. She should've been happy that a sensitive man was in love with her just for her. "I need a di-
version." She called her older brother and sister, twins
Hershel and Hershey to confirm their upcoming birthday party.

Maybe some family bonding would ease her mind. Besides Es, no other person knew of her love-letter affair. Allan never asked anymore about the situation with Rice, but she could feel his eyes watching her at work. Did he know she was making a big mistake, or would she eventually find happiness?

Hershey, a former runway model, very tall—almost six feet—with glowing medium-brown, flawless skin possessed multicultural features, with her slanted hazel eyes, long, slender nose, short Halle Berry haircut, not to mention an outgoing personality.

Hershel's dark skin complemented his hazel eyes. He stood six foot, five inches, with an athletic body. Both siblings grabbed attention with their bright, photogenic smiles, outstanding looks, and sex appeal. They were gorgeous, but Carmel could only claim her low, soft voice as her best asset, which helped with a radio career. She looked nothing like them, in skin color, height, or weight.

In the weeks that followed, Rice held nothing back in his letters, which became more personal and romantic, penned on different colors and types of stationery, plus each mentioned a "Find Me" scene. Rice was becoming so intense; it was almost giving Carmel a haunting feeling.

I saw you today, sweetheart. I was riding up the escalator at Nordstrom. The harmonious sounds of the piano player soothed my mind. I was caught up daydreaming when I passed by the women's shoe department. I smiled when I thought about how you mentioned you enjoyed shopping for shoes. It seems like you, the color of mocha, were under the music's same hypnotic spell.

You were very tall with shapely long legs. I just froze in the aisle and watched how you gently guided your feet

into low heels, no heels, and high heels. I envied the
shoes and the salesman being so close to you. My heart
dropped when you winked and waved me over. I remem-
bered swallowing and walking toward you. I almost
knelt down and slipped a pair of shoes on your feet until
a deep voice spoke behind, calling you Janice, sweetheart.
Needless to say, I turned like a military soldier in the op-
posite direction. Whew! I told you this game might get me
hurt. Carmel, put your man out of his misery.

I'm counting the days, hours, and minutes until I see
your lovely face. But, I'm worried about you, Carmel.
For the next month, I want you to focus on yourself and
enjoy shopping, movies, or parties until we meet. Maybe,
we'll find each other at one of those places.
Love,
Rice

Days later, Carmel planned to enjoy herself as her
siblings celebrated their twenty-eighth birthday. The
French twins resided in the posh middle to upper-class
area of West County in Creve Coeur. Replicas of old-
fashioned gaslights lined the streets, saluting Rolls
Royces, Benzes, and BMWs that paraded the neighborhood, taking their owners to nearby eateries, exclusive
shopping, and secluded homes. Populated with less
than twenty percent minorities, few blacks could afford
the exorbitant home prices, without being an entrepre-
neur or possessing an upper-management position.

Hershey had recently purchased a two-level condo
ten minutes away from Hershel's split-level townhouse,
and both were at least ten miles away outside St. Louis's
city limits. But Carmel preferred the city, opting for a
small one-bedroom apartment in the pricey Central
West End, minutes from downtown and even closer to
her job.

Before Carmel could ring the doorbell, Hershey opened the thick maple door and embraced her baby sister in a bear hug, almost lifting Carmel off her feet. "Hey, girl, what's up?" Hershey displayed a dazzling smile.

Carmel sniffed Hershey's expensive, sweet perfume. She always felt inferior around Hershey. Regardless of how well Carmel dressed, Hershey always did it better and with flair.

"C'mon. I thought you would never get here. I don't want to be late for my own birthday party. You'll see some old and new faces, but there'll be plenty of men for both of us." Hershey's waxed eyebrow rose, mischief gleaming in her eyes, as she slipped into a white leather jacket with its reddish-brown fox collar.

The only man I want to see is Rice Taylor, and God knows, I could barely keep myself composed if I saw him. Carmel cringed. She didn't want to be bothered with any other man. She should've stayed home and talked to Rice— correction, written him. "Doesn't matter, Hershey. I'm very content with the man I have at the moment," Carmel replied softly.

"Really?" Hershey reached over and finger-combed Carmel's curls, always trying to improve what she felt was out of place. "I can't wait to hear about him on the ride over to Hersh's place."

After they left the house, Carmel strapped on her seat belt and took a deep breath. "Hershey, he's so deep, he could write a love song with Babyface."

"Ooh, a man who knows how to express himself. I love it. Okay, so what does he look like—decent, fine, or gorgeous?"

Carmel braced herself. *Here I go.* "Funny you should ask. Remember when you told me that looks aren't everything?"

"Yeah, and I should know. Some of the best-looking models can't hold a conversation."

"Well, I've never met him. I mean I don't know how he looks. We've been writing back and forth for months."

Hershey squinted. "You're kiddin', right? When did you become desperate?"

Carmel felt deflated. *Oh well, forget the family support.*

Hershey fanned her recently manicured finger at Carmel. "That doesn't sound good. You remember Marie?"

"What about Marie?"

"Well, the same thing happened to her. She fell in love with a guy she had been writing to for months. I can't remember the details on how she came about writing the loser but, girl, it turned out to be a nightmare."

Carmel swallowed and sat straighter in her seat. "What happened?"

Hershey sucked her teeth. "Brotha turned out to be an inmate at the state prison in Jefferson City. He had seen her picture in the paper, when she got her job promotion, and instantly fell in love with her."

Oh no. Carmel held her breath. *She was a pen pal of a convicted felon.* But Rice was too gentle and sensitive to be a criminal. Carmel began to chew the lipstick off her bottom lip. He did write her a lot. Was it a sign that he had too much time on his hands? Her mind drifted until she heard Hershey's voice.

"So, girl, you better nip that in the bud."

Carmel closed her eyes. *Rice, a convict?* It was going to be a long weekend. But she was almost convinced Rice was the right man. She had to believe in what they had. "Hershey . . . I'm in love."

"What!" Hershey stopped at a green light, causing tires to screech behind her. "Not with an invisible man?

Are you crazy? You are my sister, right?" Silence filled
the car before Hershey cleared her throat. "Girl, put
the paper man away and go for the flesh-and-blood
man who can touch, talk, and kiss you."

Kissing. Carmel blushed like she had tasted one of
Rice's kisses. Their letter writing had made her bold.
Never had she told a man how she liked to be kissed!

Rice insisted a passionate kiss couldn't be controlled.
"*Kisses will replace our words of love, sweetheart,*" he had said.

Suddenly, she wondered if Rice's kisses would be
strong and intoxicating.

Hershey nudged Carmel's leg for attention. "Car, all
men aren't looking for a model type to love." Her sister's voice softened as she reached for Carmel's hand.
"I wonder what your pen pal is hiding."

Carmel gripped the door handle. "It's not him. It's
me. He's been trying to see me since Christmas, but I'm
chicken. We've set a date . . . no, Rice has picked Valentine's weekend."

"That's a few weeks away. Maybe some smart brotha
will change your mind tonight at the party."

Carmel hoped not, unless it was Rice Taylor himself.
Carmel couldn't believe the number of cars that packed
the cul-de-sac. Carmel smiled at the orange cones
Hershel had placed in his driveway to reserve a space
for his sisters. Carmel smirked, wondering what road
her brother had picked them up from.

"Well, don't sit in the car. We're here." Hershey jumped
out and walked to Hershel's door like she was on a runway. Suddenly, Carmel wished Rice was a guest at the
party.

Hershel opened his door, a crowd standing behind
him. Some faces Carmel recognized, others she hadn't
seen before greeting them as they walked in the foyer.
Carmel watched a very tall, dark-skinned, and very

handsome brotha check out Hershey in her body-fitting black leather pants, black sweater, and black boots. He didn't look at Carmel with the same appreciation.

Hershel engulfed Carmel in a tight hug. "Hey, shortie. You're looking a little tired, but good." He smacked a juicy kiss against her cheek.

Carmel smiled at her brother, who looked extremely suave tonight dressed in a denim shirt and jeans. "You think you invited enough people?" she asked teasingly.

Hershel looked around. "Nah," he said, grinning. "I could've crammed in another fifty. But it's my birthday. Hershey and me felt like doing it up."

Some guests cheered, while others chuckled. Hershel introduced his sisters to the crowd congregating in the T-shaped foyer.

Carmel quickly forgot names and faces as she strolled toward his kitchen for a soda. *Wouldn't it be something if Rice were here?*

Carmel strolled downstairs to the lower level, where she suspected an even bigger party was going on. The enormous three-room area was designed with entertaining in mind, equipped with a surround-sound home theater and half a dozen tall marble tables with matching bar stools. A sliding door leading to a patio was cracked to cool the heated air of so many bodies.

Several laid-back guests gathered around the pool table, contemplating their next strategic shot. More high-strung visitors bragged on their ability, as they guided darts to hit the bull's-eye on a large, colorful dartboard.

Suddenly, a heated dispute between two rowdy couples seated at a makeshift card table drew Carmel's attention. She chuckled at their intense argument before laughter erupted.

In the midst of the activity, without warning, Carmel sensed someone following her movements, as if she was the highlight of the party. *Could Rice be here? Don't be silly. Of all places, Rice doesn't even know the twins.*

Carmel banished the ridiculous thoughts as non-sense, despite the tumbling jabs in her stomach warning her something was about to happen. She moved to an empty bar stool and waited for a new round of darts. She turned as Hershel caused a break in activity as he treaded down the stairs, lugging a stack of pizza boxes, an aroma following like the Pied Piper's spell.

"Hi," a deep voice whispered close to Carmel's ear.

Carmel's heart raced as she gripped the table. Afraid to move, she held her breath. Slowly she turned and met the softest brown eyes she had ever seen. *Whew!* She almost slumped to the floor. Were these the same warm eyes following her? He wasn't as tall as Hershel, but the brotha was definitely inches taller than her. He looked very nice, casually dressed in a cocoa-colored Oxford shirt and jeans.

"I'm also waiting for a turn. Would you like to play a round against me?" His smile was so mesmerizing Carmel could only nod. He grabbed a stool and scooted close to her. "I'm Anthony."

Carmel didn't realize she had been staring, until she heard him clear his throat and gave her a wide smile, stretching his thick mustache. Carmel blushed from embarrassment, lowering her head. "Sorry, I'm Carmel."

Anthony curled his lips. "I don't have a problem forgoing a dart game if you want us to stare at each other all night; plus I love the sound of your voice."

Carmel took a deep breath and inhaled his spicy cologne.

"Carmel is a beautiful name."

She gulped down the choked air in her throat. "So is Anthony."

Anthony lifted a brow. "Really? Hmmm." He chuckled. "Nobody ever said that to me before except my mother who named me. But, that's my middle name. My first name is a bit unusual, so I don't use it."

With Carmel's curiosity piqued, she smiled and leaned closer. "Tell me."

Anthony chuckled and winked. "It begins with an *R*. That's all I'll divulge." He looked around the room. "Say, can I get you a drink?"

"No, thank you. I don't drink."

Anthony tilted his head. "Oh, is it a religious thing or something else?"

"No, it's because drunk drivers kill about three hundred people every week of every year."

Anthony frowned. "Whoa. That seems a bit excessive. Are you sure?"

Carmel glanced across the room and met Hershey's eyes as her sister nodded in approval of Anthony. The guy who was admiring Hershey in the foyer was clinging to her side for now, until Hershey decided to dump him. Carmel squinted at Hershey before turning back to Anthony. "I'm a talk show host and it's my job to know the latest news and information. Mothers Against Drunk Drivers just released its figures a few weeks ago."

"I'm impressed. I'll have to start listening when I'm not traveling with my job." Anthony paused, smoothing his silky mustache. "Hey, wait a minute, you're not Carmel French, aka Frenchie, the sassy sister on the radio, are you?" He then proceeded to scrutinize her face, from the silly auburn wig she was wearing that Hershey had raved about, insisting the color enhanced Carmel's skin, to her bulky sweater and then her maybe-a-little-too-tight jeans—the extra weight from eating too many scoops of ice cream while reading Rice's letters.

"Yeah, that's me," she mumbled apologetically, wondering if Anthony was really impressed by her appearance, or depressed.

He pointed his finger in the air. "You know, I did catch the tail end of your show months ago when you challenged listeners to try the blind date thing. Remember that show?"

"How could I forget?" She chuckled. "My life has never been the same."

"Hmmm," Anthony responded as if a great revelation hit, but he wasn't sharing.

After a few moments of awkward silence, the mood changed. For the rest of the night, they observed each other. Carmel was feeling good vibes. She noticed he smiled a lot, forming an unusual indentation right below his right eye—a dimple.

Anthony seemed relaxed in his surroundings. They competed with other couples in darts, high-fiving themselves every time they won and childishly pouting together when they lost. Carmel wondered more than once if Anthony was her Rice Anthony? If it were Rice, wouldn't he identify himself once he found out who she was? Unless he was disappointed with what he saw.

After the guests concluded a second round of singing "Happy Birthday," Carmel gathered her coat to leave.

Anthony linked his fingers through hers. "I would like to see you again."

Carmel froze. All night Anthony said the right words, acted like he had been her escort to the twins' party, and made her laugh so much, her cheeks ached. Carmel stared again into magical brown eyes, deciding what to do. If he were Rice, she would see him again. If not, then Rice would have a hefty price to pay for making her miss out on a handsome and interested brotha. Was this a test of love?

Anthony squeezed her hand. "You've talked to me all

night, now you're speechless?" he teased, offering an enticing smile and his one-of-a-kind dimple. "Carmel," his voice called softly, "I really enjoyed tonight. I don't want our great time to end here. Say you'll see me again."

"Maybe, you will see me again," Carmel said confidently, inwardly scared that she was passing up a good man. Giving Anthony a seductive smile, Carmel walked away on shaky legs and a pounding headache from her too-tight wig. *Rice, you better not be playing with my head!*

Chapter Six

The Find Me game was starting to affect Rice even when he didn't want to play. His secret desires had actually brought Carmel to his front door. He rubbed his tired eyes. *Now I'm hallucinating.*

When Rice steered the SW into his driveway, there was a gorgeous woman waiting for him. *It can't be.* But it was—Gina Larson. Rice snarled. What did she want? Gina had the nerve to show her face at his house and then dress in that dark-brown designer suede outfit he bought her for a birthday gift. The form-fitting pants and the short faux-fur-and-brown suede jacket still looked good on her.

Enticing, yes. Beautiful, no doubt about it. Cunning, deceitful, and shallow; all of the above, and then some. Rice methodically turned off the ignition, retrieved his briefcase, and opened the driver's side door. Cautiously approaching his porch and the woman who played on his emotions, he nodded. "Gina, why are you here?"

Gina's professionally applied makeup demanded she

be noticed. Her face brightened with a smile meant to please. "To say I'm sorry."

Rice purposely stared into Gina's hazel eyes, which tightly held its secrets and kept the windows to her heart closed. Eyes that, at one time, had him enthralled. He had felt lucky to be in the presence of such a rare beauty. But not any more. Beauty can be bought, applied surgically, or blossom from within. He desired the latter.

"Hmmm. Yeah, okay. I accept. Good-bye."

He moved to step around her, but Gina blocked his front door with her entire body. She waved an envelope as she defiantly relaxed against Rice's screen door. "You wouldn't take my calls. You left me no choice but to come. I wrote you a long letter, Rice."

"What could you possibly say?" He folded his arms and waited impatiently, occasionally peering down the street, looking at nothing, but searching for a distraction. "Gina, I'm glad you saved the stamp, but you could've also saved the trip. You can't, don't, and won't push my buttons any more." Gina's seductive expression registered the shock. The moment was comedic.

"Rice," Gina whined, "I poured out my heart. I searched my soul. I confessed my faults to you in this love letter."

Rice was tired, irritable, and just wanted to relax and write Carmel. "Gina, what we had ended months ago. So again, I ask, why are you really here, today—now wait a minute. Valentine's Day is coming. Expecting more sweet treats?"

"I deserved that. Especially after the stunt I tried to pull—it was stupid and childish. I know it went against the brotherly bond thing of trying to date brothers. I realize that now, but when I saw you at the Esquire Theatre last week alone, I was also there by myself, suffering through my loneliness. I thought—or rather hoped—we could salvage . . . there, it's all in my letter." She pressed the envelope to his chest.

"I only read love letters from one woman, and you could never be her. She is everything you're not, including faithful. Your letter isn't going to change how I feel about her or you, Gina. "

Gina lowered her lashes. The gesture had always weakened Rice to her demands. "If you just read it, I know it will."

"Not this time. I'm already too deeply in love with my lady."

Body language, a silent but active form of expressing sadness, anger, or seduction.

A few weeks later, three sistahs at the corner table by the window were giving free lessons, and Rice felt he was sitting at the head of the class. A tall woman whose skin looked honey-dipped kept puckering her fire engine-red lips. Rice thought she was sucking food from between her teeth. The chocolate-skinned woman on her right winked endlessly, and Rice figured a lash was stuck in her eye, but the other woman, who was extremely pretty, posed seductively with an enticing smile that lifted her cheeks to her eyes. Their antics had caught the attention of several willing patrons.

Rice chuckled. *Must be the suit.* But he was more concerned with the blizzardlike snow dropping outside New York's Marriott Hotel. Rice sat, bored at their flirtatious game, and smiled as he fantasized about Carmel. He felt confident she looked better than the three of them.

Restless in the crowded hotel dining lounge, Rice picked at his steak and salad. The soft music drifting in the background did nothing to soothe savage travelers.

A group of stranded business airline passengers huddled around a television monitor attentively listening to the forecast, wondering when LaGuardia would reopen for air traffic.

Rice returned to his suite and phoned his parents' house.

"Mom, just letting you know I'm stuck in New York, maybe for an extra night."

Sharon Taylor gasped. "Oh, that's too bad. I just made a big peach cobbler."

"Thanks for making me homesick, Mom. I'm so ready to get back to St. Louis."

"I hate it when you travel so much and alone."

"Well, three women tried to pick me up a while back in the hotel restaurant. Does that make you feel better?"

"You were wearing that blue pinstriped Christian Dior suit, weren't you?"

"Yep."

Sharon snorted. "Them little wenches smelled money."

Rice shook his head. "I don't know 'bout that, Mom, but at times they were so aggressive, I thought I was at a sleaze bar. It would have been hilarious if it wasn't such a big turn-off," he said disgustedly.

"Well, Rice, you are almost wealthy, making near a hundred thousand a year, you're still cute as a button, like the day I brought you home from the hospital, and need I remind you, you're single and very available."

"Not really."

"You've met someone?"

Suddenly Rice heard the phone shuffling as his older brother, Winston, came on the line. His questions were rapid and nonstop, causing Rice's mind to recall Carmel's last letter.

Rice,

Last night I met you, R. Anthony. Your seductive brown eyes and slow smile captivated me all evening. Rice, were you playing with me last night? If yes, you're in big trouble. If not, you still could be in big trouble— competition. I desperately wanted him to be you.
Carmel

Rice stared out his hotel suite window. He replayed the words of Carmel's letter again in his mind. Should he be worried? When he suggested a harmless game of Find Me, he really didn't expect Carmel to find someone else. He had crushed her letter in his fist. "I must have been crazy to let this go on this long."

"What has gone on this long?" Winston queried.

Rice ignored the interruption. He was still rattled by that letter. His meeting in New York went well, his southern region sales team was producing impressive figures, with the introduction of new drugs Glivec and Cozaar for stroke and cardiac patients, but he couldn't focus. He was close to forgoing their special date and showing up at her job. But, after he calmed himself down, Rice was able to shake the feeling of anger. He responded with words of love, passion, hope, and laced his thoughts with extra sweetness.

Sweetheart,

There is no other woman my heart craves. I believe you, Carmel French, were made just for me. Although our relationship has been based on the written word, it has withstood four months of us soul searching, purging the undesirable things and nourishing the adorable can't-get-enough-of traits we both seek. It's a relationship I faithfully honor, baby. We've shared secrets of the heart, our eyes have searched for the images we've created, and

*soon sweet kisses will erase all the loneliness we endured
apart. No, Carmel, if I were at the same party with you,
you would've known it. Our hearts would've beat as
one. So close your eyes and count the final ten days and
baby, I'll be there.*
Rice,
Your genuine love

What Rice didn't mention to Carmel was that he saw
and had dodged his ex-girlfriend at a party the same
weekend. Funny how they both went to parties, but different ones. It was just their luck.

Flames suddenly roared in the fireplace, jolting Rice
to his conversation with Winston. He dismissed thoughts
about Gina, and smiled, forgetting he had started the
fire logs. Immediately, his thoughts drifted involuntarily
to Carmel and her interesting relaxation techniques—
fireplace therapy.

Dear Rice,
   *Most people don't like the cold weather, but I enjoy the
brisk winds, chilly temperatures, and heavy snow. I'm in
awe at the warmth from sitting in front of the fireplace.
the glowing embers gently ease my stress away as I relax
and begin to pamper my mind and body. Usually, I soak
my feet before giving myself a pedicure. Then, I apply a
generous amount of a cleansing mask to my face. The
heat of the fire helps open my pores and mind. Afterward,
I apply a cold milky facial conditioner that helps rejuve-
nate my skin.*
   *Rice, I know some people call a fire romantic. I call it
my quiet-time therapy. I really get into it. I have my soft
instrumental music playing in the background. No television or phone is competing for my attention, just my
mind meditating about all the blessings in my life. It is*

*an activity I don't rush. Plus, this is my time with God
to work out my problems. So when you see a nice warm
fire, think of me.*

Done. It was such a simple request from his baby.
What he wouldn't give to be with Carmel at this very
moment. He stared back into the fire, imagining them
both sitting on the floor. He would probably massage
her soft feet. Maybe he would even paint her toenails.
Yeah, he would watch the pleasure his massage would
bring to her face. He missed her! This emotion was so
strange. He hadn't even met her, but he could feel her
desires, passions, and even her fears.

He loved Carmel senseless, if that was possible. And
to think, like every other red-blooded man, he had been
drawn to women based solely on looks. How stupid! As
if a gorgeous woman validated his manhood. Most had
told him his looks didn't matter. They just wanted a decent, caring man. He guessed they thought that would
pacify him. What women saw were the dollars, the car,
and the clothes. Rice discovered his past girlfriends'
looks and hearts were a mixed bag of lies. They proved
to be heartless, when it came to possessions.

Rice had accepted months ago that Carmel might
not be a looker but was someone who filled him, but he
would bring his paper doll to life! She had to be beautiful, he thought, because her qualities would find a way
to radiate. Carmel's passion ignited a fire within him
that could not be extinguished. He was still wrestling
with the doubt, but love had overpowered him. Plus,
Rice could wish a little.

"Hey, bro. You must either be 'sleep, bored with talking to me, or in love," his older brother commented.

Rice couldn't believe he had zoned out while on the
phone. "Hey, sorry, Winston, man. Just thinking."

"Humph. I'm glad you're paying for this call because you have been thinking and moaning for about ten minutes. Who is she?"

Rice smiled. "Well, I can't say it's written all over my face."

"No, but I hear it in your voice. Just make sure you keep your wallet closed this time, until you find out where she's coming from. And, watch out for Gina. Whew! I ran into her, and brother, she's asking about you."

"That sistah was crazy."

"Tell me. Gina tried to hit on me while you two were dating, saying we were more compatible." Both laughed. "You know, it was because I was the better-looking brother."

Rice threw his head back, laughing. "Oh, I thought it was because you were pulling in six figures."

"I'm sure she factored that in."

Suddenly Rice heard the ruffling sound of the phone receiver. His mother's voice returned to the phone. "Rice, you haven't told me about a new girlfriend."

"Well, we've been writing each other several times a week; sometimes I write more than once a day. Mom, I'm convinced I'm in love with her. There, it's out. I've said it. I don't know what she looks like—"

"What made you decide to pursue this young lady in this manner?"

"Never one for long stories, were you?"

"You got it. It's almost my bed time, so get to the point." Sharon yawned without trying to hide her fatigue.

"Mom, I think our relationship has been honest from the very first letter. We had nothing to lose by sharing the truth about ourselves. We've become addicted to each other. Our first date is Valentine's weekend."

"Rice, a lot of couples have found happiness after a blind date experience. Nothing is wrong with that. Just remember, you've invested your feelings, so what you see is also what you get."

"Great, Mom. Remind me never to talk to you again about a woman," Rice mumbled.

"I sure hope you two don't have ugly kids."

Chapter Seven

Thursday, February 13, Carmel woke up anxious like it was Friday the thirteenth and her heart would be ripped into shreds in one day. But then her eyes focused on and stared at Rice's phone numbers—cell, beeper, and home—a morning routine she had involuntarily developed since Christmas. Somehow, just knowing his numbers caused her to relax. Several times Carmel had dialed them, only to realize that she had been dreaming. Today, the urge to hear Rice's voice had been overwhelming.

Tomorrow they would celebrate Valentine's Day face to face. Carmel had been stressing herself. She ignored her feelings of anxiety as she dressed for work.

Since meeting Anthony, he had called and sent flowers to the station. The attention was nice, but Rice denied being R. Anthony, so Carmel promptly put an end to their communication, refusing his calls and giving Esther his floral deliveries. Too bad because Anthony was very attractive. Depending on Rice, her blood pres-

sure could return to normal after Friday. Shame on her.
Where was her faith? Hiding.

Carmel moved like a zombie entering the radio station. Her goal was to make it through two shows, skip
the rest of the day, and head back home.

A few guests commented she didn't sound like her
usual energetic self, so Carmel had to refocus.

"Welcome back to 'Don't Get French with Me.' I'm
Frenchie, and this hour I'm interested in your thoughts
about the recent rash of police shootings of unarmed
black youths. I need you to talk to me—unless you're
driving, then keep both hands on the wheel." Carmel
looked up to see Glen rolling his eyes. She lowered her
voice to a pillow-talk tone. "If you're just waking up," she
purred before clearing her throat and shouting into the
microphone. "Get up! You're already late for whatever."

Carmel giggled as Glen adjusted the audio level on
the control board and rubbed his ears.

Fifty minutes later, Esther opened the door and stuck
her head in the studio as Carmel's theme music ended
her show. "How police shootings translated to home
schooling totally confused me, but as usual, you kept
the phone lines jammed."

"Thanks. It was the sixth police shooting in south
St. Louis in weeks. It's been front-page news. Everybody
had an opinion."

"Keep the shows hot, girlfriend. Tomorrow's the big
date, huh?"

Carmel nodded. She grabbed her notes before the
next host, a plump retired electrician, hurriedly stormed
into the studio for his show on home repairs.

Later that night, Carmel climbed in bed, vaguely remembering the day's conversations or events. "I really
need to talk to you, Rice," she whispered.

She could hear Es saying, "Get a grip, girl!"

Nothing could take her mind off Rice Taylor. Carmel switched the television on and off with the remote. Then she picked up a book on the table, and fingered through pages she didn't remember reading before unconsciously dialing Rice's home number, which she had memorized.

Carmel's heart pounded against her chest as she gripped the phone, listening for a connection. A sudden cold sweat made her shiver. Carmel bit a recently manicured nail as the first ring started. She hung up and collapsed back into her pillow, gnawing on her bottom lip. *What if he had picked up? What would he sound like? Would she be disappointed if his voice wasn't deep?* She sat up in the bed with a renewed bravado, punched redial, and disconnected. *Chicken!* An internal battle ensued within Carmel as she dialed twice again and disconnected when the ringing began. Carmel slammed the cordless on her nightstand. "This is crazy," she mumbled, reaching to turn off her bed lamp. *I'll just talk to Rice in my dreams.*

Rice was simmering tomato sauce for his spaghetti dinner, when his phone rang. It stopped after the third ring. He shrugged. *Probably just a wrong number.*

Within ten minutes, his phone chimed three more times. *What in the world is going on?* He stormed into his bedroom and checked the caller ID—C French. Rice folded his arms with a smile. His baby. She was probably nervous. Rice momentarily forgot about his growling stomach. He relaxed in a chair next to the phone and waited. "Don't be scared, sweetheart," he whispered, coaching the phone like a pet. "Call one more time, baby, and I'll pick it up faster than an Internet connection." He laughed, staring at the phone, willing for it to ring.

Seconds turned to minutes, and finally an hour had passed. Rice concluded Carmel wasn't calling back. He sat down to eat but couldn't taste his dinner. He contemplated calling her. "I've got your number now." He grinned with excitement.

Finally, Rice was resigned to the fact that he would just have to wait until the next day.

Later that night, he stepped out of the shower and checked his caller ID—no more calls. He was too excited to be disappointed. As Rice prepared for bed, he wore a smile, thinking about their love, relationship, and future. He glanced across the room at the stack of letters Carmel had written him—almost thirty to date. "That's a lot of love between us," he whispered, leaning back against his cherrywood sleigh bed headboard. He closed his eyes, remembering one particular letter he'd sent her.

> *Sweetheart,*
>
> *I miss you crazy, and I love you deeply. I had to write you again today. Are you willing to believe in our love and in me? Will you say yes to marrying me—sight unseen? If you just fainted, then pick yourself up and sit down. Yes, I am proposing. This is how strongly I feel about you—about us.*

Carmel's response surprised him.

> *Rice,*
>
> *If you were really everything that I hope for and I pray you are, then I'd be a fool to say anything but yes.*

*One condition, as long as it's not this Valentine's Day. I
love you with all my being but I'm still scared.*
Carmel

Rice opened his eyes and stared at the ceiling. The
next day, regardless of how his woman looked, he
would get on bended knee and ask her to be his wife.
He didn't care about the outer beauty. He was in love.
"Okay, I do care a little, but I'm not asking for much."
Rice, feeling at peace, turned off the light and drifted
to sleep.

Carmel leaped out of bed after a catfight with her
cover, punching her pillows. and body-slamming her
limbs against the mattress. Sleep was impossible. She
needed to get a grip on her emotions. "This is crazy!"
She eyed the cordless phone like it was a piece of candy.
Her lids fluttered as she inhaled. Carmel delicately
touched the phone pad like she was playing Rice's number on a keyboard. She didn't hear the phone ring.

"Hello?"

Carmel's lids popped open as she sucked in air. She
climbed in the bed and melted under the sheets. *Whoa,
he sounds so good. Say something, girl,* her mind commanded,
but she couldn't. *Speak,* her mouth shouted! Carmel
couldn't utter a whisper. She was paralyzed.

"Hello?" Rice repeated almost chuckling. "Hi, baby.
I'm glad you called back."

Rice must have had his hand on the receiver, ready
to see what idiot had been calling his house and playing
on the phone.

Carmel's eyes watered as she tried to find her voice.
Finally, she whispered, "Oh, Rice . . . I'm sorry about

calling earlier and hanging up. I was so scared. I'm a fake, a big chicken."

Rice's soothing voice interrupted her babbling. "But you're my chicken, and I love you."

His words, his voice, and his patience helped Carmel relax. "Rice, I love you, too, but I don't know if I can do this tomorrow."

"Sweetheart, we're both scared," Rice replied in a re-assuring tone. "God knows you've been a sweet torture to me. I'm praying I'm everything you want because you're what I desire."

"But, Rice—"

"Your looks can't change what my heart feels."

Carmel lay quietly, listening. The richness of Rice's voice soothed her, his rhythmic breathing hypnotized her, and his unwavering confidence in their love strengthened her, but Carmel still had her doubts. "Rice, what if my hair is shorter than what you like?"

"I'll buy you a weave," he teased.

"Funny, mister non-materialistic man. What if I'm not the size of a model and overweight?"

"I'll put you on a diet and promise to exercise with you."

Carmel mimicked an offending gasp. "Rice!" But, she could sense the love behind his words.

"Just kidding, sweetheart."

"What if my skin is a darker chocolate than what you want?"

"I'll find out what Michael Jackson used and get you a year's supply."

They both laughed.

"Look, Carmel, I want the woman who authored the words, the lady who controlled my heartbeat with the stroke of a pen, and the diva who slips into my mind when I'm lonely, driving, or trying to concentrate on something else. I'm all yours, baby, if you want me."

Carmel closed her eyes to capture the sudden tears. "I love you," she whispered, thinking his voice was the best therapy.

"And I love you, too," he murmured back.

The phone line was silent, but neither was asleep.

Rice added, "Yeah, baby."

"I hear what I've been missing."

"I've longed for you, all of you—your enchanting smile, your revealing expressions, and only God knows what else."

Carmel stared at the ceiling as tears escaped. "How can you be so sure, when I'm petrified? I could have teeth missing."

"You aren't getting out of our date tomorrow, Miss French." He laughed. "Besides, braces and bridges work wonders."

"I think you are a wonderful man."

Silence.

"Rice?"

"If you believe that, Carmel, then agree to be my wife."

"Mmm," Carmel moaned. She smiled as she gripped the phone. *How romantic.* Rice was bold enough to propose in a letter and over the phone, but somehow, looking into his eyes and watching his lips move would still probably overwhelm her the next day. "You sound so good, just like the letters you've written me."

"Toying with the man who loves you, huh? Well, I feel you."

"Rice, don't tease me. How can you feel me, when you haven't even met me?"

"I've met you, sweetheart. In my mind, my dreams, and my heart. Don't think for one minute that I'm not in tune with your love, desires, and fears. I understand your confusion, but just remember, this man loves you."

Carmel questioned him about certain letters for hours, often asking him to repeat his thoughts. Time was forgotten until she heard him stifle a yawn.

"It's late, sweetheart. I plan to smother you with a lot of love this weekend, so get ready to be emotionally overpowered and spiritually conquered. See you in the morning, okay?"

"Okay, Rice Anthony Taylor."

"Night, baby."

Chapter Eight

Rice parked his Durango in front of the building housing WPLS. He exited his vehicle with a bounce in his step. Today was a good day to fall in love. *This is it.* Rice had dressed meticulously, experimented with a new cologne, and began his day on his knees, giving God thanks, mixed with moments of pleading for a happy ending. *What could go wrong?* Rice's confidence guided his footsteps as he departed the elevator, stepping onto the thirteenth floor. Rice flexed his arm muscles, feeling powerful and very anxious to meet the woman who had seized control over his emotions.

His readied smile faded, and the sparkle in his eyes dimmed as a heavy-set white woman stood in front of the receptionist's desk, staring him down like a security guard. *Why?* Clearly, she wasn't impressed with his attire. He knew he should have worn his Christian Dior suit. Her eyes twinkled with mischief, like she was sizing him up for battle. Now his mind was starting to play tricks. He knew Carmel wasn't white, although they had never divulged any physical characteristics, but anything was possible.

Rice paused in his steps. Should he take the subtle hints and race down thirteen flights of stairs, leaving a trail of red roses? Suddenly, he realized he was already on an unlucky floor.

Without a smile, in a nonchalant voice, the woman spoke. "Are you lost? May I help you?"

Add a gray wig and some glasses and the woman could easily pass as a wicked step-godmother.

Rice gave the woman a bright smile as he pulled flowers from behind his back. "I'm here to see Miss Carmel French, please."

The chilling laugh emitting from her throat vibrated throughout the small lobby area. "Ya kidding right? Whom might you be, young man?"

Rice cleared his throat so he wouldn't stutter. "Rice Taylor."

"So . . . you're the one keeping the United States Postal Service in business," she said, looking him up and down. She sucked her front teeth. "I told her she could do better. I hope she won't be disappointed."

Rice was speechless as he watched the haughty woman talk without smiling or pleasantries. She definitely didn't know what the word *friendly* meant.

Allan walked out of his office, and Rice relaxed. Hopefully Allan overheard their conversation and would put this rude woman in her place.

Allan offered Rice a grin and a handshake. "Esther, be nice. Hey, Rice, the big day, huh? You ready for the unexpected?" he asked cautiously. "Just remember Carmel is a sweet and together sistah. Hurt her, and I'll take it as a personal assault on my business. I'm not about to lose my best talent over any nonsense." Allan winked slyly at Esther.

"Carmel has been a nervous wreck for weeks, dressing without fashion coordination, and I could tell she even lost some weight, not that she was fat!" Allan said apologetically and shrugged.

"Well, at least her clothes are matching today," Esther interjected.

Rice nodded. What had he gotten himself into? The short walk down the hall with Allan seemed endless. Rice's uneasiness dissipated as Carmel's sultry voice vibrated through the airwaves. This was it. Carmel was his woman, he kept reminding himself. The on-air sign blinked above a closed door that separated him from Carmel.

Allan ushered Rice into an adjacent room, instead of opening the studio door to Carmel. "It's a little crowded, but you'll find a seat beside those mini-disc racks," Allan said, pointing to a chair behind a grinning engineer and next to a large window overlooking historic mansions and a large park in midtown. "You'll be able to see Carmel better."

Rice was tempted to peek. "Thanks, Allan. I can wait a few minutes longer." *We will do this together.* He closed his eyes, stroking his chin, grinning as Carmel's voice lulled, excited, and soothed him simultaneously.

"It's Valentine's Day on Friday's edition of 'Don't Get French with Me.' I hope today will be very special for you."

Rice could hear the humor in Carmel's voice, her words flowing with ease. She sounded lively, although he suspected she was on the edge of her seat, afraid to begin a new chapter of life with him.

* * *

Carmel exaggerated a long exhale. "I must say, I'm impressed with the men out there, showing their ladies love through poems, songs, and other expressions." She sensed Rice was probably on the other side of the glass because she started experiencing major premature hot flashes. Carmel fanned herself to slow down her racing heart.

Minutes earlier, Carmel saw Allan and a shadow of a man enter the control room. Glen had purposely turned off the lights! She couldn't make out any of the man's features, except she knew that he wasn't short.

Glen's usual laid-back, bored-to-death, and un-friendly expression was suspiciously different. He sat grinning. Glen hadn't shown his extremely large teeth since one of Carmel's guests fell out of a chair while on air. She rolled her eyes. Could someone let her in on the joke? Did Rice look that disgusting? If the sparkle in Glen's eyes didn't fade soon, Carmel would probably throw up.

She ignored his amusement and focused on another call. "Finally, I have a woman on the air. Gina, wel-come."

Rice's mellow mood immediately vanished as he sat erect in his chair. Gina? Had she been calling Carmel's show all along? Was this some type of a joke? He gritted his teeth in fear and anger. *Please don't let Carmel be in ca-hoots with Gina,* he pleaded.

"Frenchie, I'm really enjoying the men on your show this morning, girl. They make me miss what I had, but I'm surprised your man hasn't phoned in. What about your honey?"

Carmel swallowed. "Well, Gina, I've got thirty sec-onds before my next break. What about my man?"

Carmel hoped she was wearing extra-strength deodorant because she was beginning to sweat like she was in the middle of a morning cardio workout.

"Frenchie, I was kinda interested in hearing about that special someone in your life."

Never at a loss for words, Carmel was dumbfounded. The caller's request had her hands shaking. What could she say? What if it didn't work out between them?

"Gina?" Carmel said, her voice cracking. "What did you want to know?" Carmel replied with anything but confidence.

"I've never heard you talk about your man. Give us some juicy details. Describe him and the romantic things he does."

Carmel huffed. She straightened her shoulders. There go her show's high ratings. If she didn't say something soon, Allan would barge through the studio door for an explanation for the dead air. She looked up at the studio clock. Five seconds had passed. She was busted. She closed her eyes to describe the man she felt in her heart.

That's it! Rice leaped to his feet, squeezing the plastic-wrapped red roses. *What was Gina up to?* He hadn't determined if he was more annoyed or angry with Gina's call. Rice wondered if she had learned about Rice's interest in Carmel and planned to humiliate Carmel on air. *Well that's not going to happen.*

A few long strides brought him face to face with the studio door. He forced it open and froze. He blinked and commanded his lungs to inhale and exhale. God had indeed answered his prayers.

Carmel French seemed to glow like a fuzzy vision. Rice captured the first sight of his angelic mirage and stored the image deep inside his mind for recall. Carmel's shoulder-length hair streaked with different hues of brown, amazingly blended with her creamy caramel skin coloring. Rice's eyes traveled downward from her off-white turtleneck sweater to her matching wool pants. He guessed she stood about five-and-a-half feet, without the cream leather boots she was wearing. She was too shapely to be a model, but she could definitely be the mold for a Coca-Cola bottle.

Tears formed in Carmel's eyes. "Rice?" she asked in a soft whisper away from the microphone. Restrained by her headset, Carmel remained seated but opened her arms. Carmel was mesmerized by Rice's six-foot-plus height, his muscular build outlined in a black turtleneck enhancing his soft tan complexion. Silky, thick, dark eyebrows matched a black goatee that framed his full lips. She never saw this man in her dreams.

"Yes." Rice nodded as he slowly approached, staring into her brown eyes protected by thick, black lashes. He knelt down as if he was worshipping her presence, gathering Carmel's shaky body in his arms.

Carmel closed her eyes at the same moment Glen faded up a Luther Vandross love song, momentarily taking her off the air. She sniffed and slowly smiled. Carmel reached out and stroked his high cheekbones, whispering, "I can't believe this is you and you're really here with me." She dropped her hands on his shoulders and hugged his neck.

The love song ended too soon as Glen pounded on the glass, frantically giving Carmel hand signals.

She motioned for Rice to be seated next to her.

Rice reached for Carmel's right hand, mouthing, "You okay?"

His concerned look made Carmel want to start crying again. When she nodded, Rice caressed her fingers and offered an encouraging wink.

Carmel took a deep breath as Glen cued her. She

had completely forgotten about her last caller. "Welcome back to Valentine's Day. Sorry for the interruption, but my honey just surprised me with a guest appearance, and to answer Gina's question, I'd be more than happy to describe him, and then he can tell you what he has planned for us this weekend." She turned and touched his cheek. "Rice has the most expressive baby brown eyes." She scanned his chest. "He has an athletic build but a gentle heart to match his tender touch." She squeezed his hand before reaching up and tracing his lips. Carmel giggled. "His kisses are indescribable." She lifted her brow and mouthed, *I hope.*

"*Humph!* Sounds like you've found a winner, Frenchie." Gina sighed heavily. "I need me one of those."

Rice adjusted the microphone in front of him, and Glen opened his mike. "Gina, this is Rice Taylor. Remember me? You had me and didn't appreciate what I had to offer, so stop your whining and lying."

Carmel frowned, perplexed. "You dated her?" she mouthed.

Rice scooted his chair closer. "She's the past, quickly becoming a present pest. But you're my future," he whispered in her ear.

Carmel couldn't fault Rice for past mistakes. She had dated a few herself, so she hit disconnect and spoke her mind. "Gina, I don't feel sorry for you. Rice is an exceptional man, not only in looks, but also in his heart. The reason why I fell in love with him was his faith in our relationship that held us together. Thank you, baby." Carmel cleared her throat, returning her voice back to a strong, businesslike tone.

"Okay, enough of that. I need to regroup and catch up on my sponsors. We'll take more of your calls on the other side of this break."

When the overhead on-air light blinked off, Carmel

snatched off her headset. Tears wet both their cheeks as they stood to hug each other.

"Hi again, baby," Rice whispered over and over as they rocked in a tight embrace. He sniffed the banana scent of her hair before he took her face in both his hands.

Silently their eyes and smiles communicated a happiness, suddenly interrupted by Glen banging on the studio glass frantically, signaling thirty seconds. Carmel motioned for Rice to sit back down beside her. She handed him a headset.

Carmel mouthed, "I'm sorry I doubted. I really do love you."

Rice laid his hand over his chest. "I know." His lips stretched into a warm smile.

When the on-air light flashed on, Glen surprisingly cued Rice instead of Carmel. She was tongue-tied.

"I'm Rice Taylor and Happy Valentine's Day on WPLS. I've stopped by to tell my special lady and sweetheart how much I love her . . ." Rice spoke in a deep, rich voice, ignoring Carmel's startled expression as the phone lines lit up. Taking her hand he said, ". . . and to ask her to have enough faith in me to be my wife." His coarse finger touched her lips. "Baby, please."

Carmel's eyes misted from Rice's romantic gesture. She inhaled each of his words, memorized his expression, and became hypnotized with his pleading eyes. Carmel realized she loved hearing him speak in a deep, husky whisper and she had missed so much, delaying a face-to-face date. Music and Glen's voice danced circles around her head. Vaguely, Carmel heard herself faintly answer, "Yes."

"This is Glen LaCroix, Frenchie's engineer. As you can imagine a live daytime soap is unfolding. Let's take a music break, and Frenchie will return in a moment."

Esther barged into the control room screaming, clearly flustered. "Glen, I'm glad you're on top of this show. The past hour has been emotional. Perfect for Valentine's Day."

Glen grinned. "Yeah . . . it's the goofiest show I've engineered in six years. I knew something was going down, when I spoke to Carmel earlier. She couldn't seem to focus. Now I know why. I don't know whose getting a bigger kick out of today's show, the listeners or management."

"By the looks of the blinking lights on the phone board, our listeners are eating this up," Esther said.

"The only problem is, that Gina woman keeps calling back, demanding to speak with Frenchie," Glen told her.

"Hmmm, I hear firecrackers poppin'. Well, by all means, put her through," was Esther's reply.

Glen smirked. "Certainly. I can always nap with the next host. I can only take so much excitement in one day." Glen banged on the window.

During the break, Rice's smoothing words mellowed her. "We're back with only a few minutes left. I hope your Valentine's Day will be just as special as Rice is making mine." Carmel looked into Rice's dark brown eyes and noticed his long, beautiful lashes, definitely too long for a man. Good-looking didn't describe him.

She almost fainted, when Rice kissed the inside of her hand. Carmel attempted to shift back into her professional mode, but she couldn't. She was ready to begin her dating adventure.

Glen signaled to take line two.

Carmel did as Glen instructed, without looking at the name on her computer. "Let's wrap up today's show with your thoughts."

"Frenchie," Gina said in a monotone voice, "I can't

believe you've hooked Rice Taylor. I guess you're as materialistic as the rest of us."

Rice frowned and reached for the microphone, but Carmel held up her hand and smiled. "Gina, don't get French with me." Then she disconnected.

Chapter Nine

"**Y**our eyelashes are driving me to distraction and to the point of insanity. *Umph, umph, umph.* And you say my name so possessively, like you named me. It's so loving and caressing." Rice released a throaty chuckle, his eyes slowly roaming across her face.

Carmel blushed as she stood to retrieve her coat from the rack. Her shyness complemented her beauty.

Rice was glued to his seat, staring at Carmel's movements like he was in a trance. He smiled contentedly while massaging his goatee. Carmel was breathtaking. "I could watch and talk to you all day." As Carmel reached for her coat, Rice quickly stood and followed her sweet perfume trail across the room. Rice lifted Carmel's coat off the rack as he pulled her closer, wrapping her inside, before twirling her around into a hug.

Carmel reached out and stroked his hair-covered chin. "The way our relationship began and developed is still mindboggling. You fascinate me."

"And you make me happy."

"Thank you for believing."

"It was my pleasure." Rice winked and took her hand. "C'mon, let's make our dreams come true. By the way, you didn't sound too confident when you answered a very important question. You know I'm going to keep asking you until you shout 'Yes.' "

"I know."

"As long as you know, sweetheart."

On the way out of the station, Carmel introduced Rice to her co-workers and finally Esther, who was dangling the phone in her air. "Gina's holding for you, Frenchie."

"She's already been disconnected."

They all roared with laughter.

Rice coached Carmel into the elevator. When the doors closed, Carmel pushed the lobby button and became quiet, not facing him.

Rice immediately sensed her withdrawal. This was it. They were finally alone. "Sweetheart, you've just hugged, talked, and touched me emotionally, now you won't look at me?" He leaned against the wall and opened his arms. "Come here, baby. My paper doll."

Carmel walked into Rice's arms and collapsed into tears.

Rice held her tightly, her body shook with sobs, brushing soft kisses against her eyes. "Why are you crying? I love you," he said, puzzled.

The elevator doors opened, and an elderly couple eyed them suspiciously. The gray-haired, pin-curled woman tapped her cane and leaned into her companion with concern. "George, maybe we should call the police."

George nodded as Granny pressed her fingers against her lips.

"Get your hands off her!" She lifted her cane for battle. "Honey, are you okay?"

"Step back from that woman, young man," George threatened feebly.

Carmel looked away from Rice and then covered her face in embarrassment. "I'm fine, really." She grabbed Rice's hand. "I'm so happy. He just asked me to marry him."

The old woman sighed so heavily, Rice and Carmel thought she was about to faint. "George, they're in love. You are going to say yes, aren't you, honey? Oh, I remember my wedding day to George here almost sixty years ago." She turned to her husband and smiled before lifting a wrinkled finger and wagging it. "See, George, you worry too much. I knew everything was okay." She patted the couple's hands and scuffled into the elevator.

Rice threw his head back and released a rich, deep laugh and his eyes became watery. He stopped long enough to compose himself and pull Carmel into his arms. Slowly he brought her knuckles to his lips for a kiss before his mouth moved to her top lip and then nipped at the bottom one. He tried to touch every part of her mouth. Their kiss was thorough, very thorough, but too short because of lack of privacy. "I guess we better go to lunch before we create another scene."

When Carmel slowly opened her eyes, she giggled, rubbing her fingers along his lips, removing Burnt Almond lipstick and juices from their kiss.

Rice responded by kissing each of Carmel's fingers.

Outside, snow flurries drifted around them. Carmel

snuggled closer while Rice helped her into his Durango.
They would come back later and get Carmel's car.

She reached out and held his chin, steadily looking
into his eyes. "If I wasn't already in love, then I would
want to fall in love with you."

"Will you write that down and mail those words to
me in a letter?" Rice grinned. "My serenade ain't over. I
plan for us to fall so deeply in love with each other this
weekend, words won't be necessary."

Chapter Ten

Rice memorized Carmel's expressions, as she sipped raspberry lemonade. Carmel moaned her pleasure at the scrumptious meal, licking ketchup from her fingers. The cozy atmosphere of the lunch crowd at the Pasta House in the Central West End seemed to mellow the mood. Rice engaged Carmel with questions for which he already knew the answers, just to hear her voice.

But it was when Rice began to recite lines from past letters that Carmel glowed. "Remember this one? ' 'Sweetheart, there is no other woman my heart craves. I believe you, Carmel French, were made just for me. Although our relationship has been based on the written word, it has withstood four months of us soul searching. It's a relationship I faithfully honor, baby. We've shared secrets of the heart and soon sweet kisses will erase all the loneliness we endured apart. So close your eyes and count the days and, baby, I'll be there.' "

"I remember."

"And I did promise you sweet kisses."

"Hmmm. I like the sampling so far."

Rice's heart swelled with contentment as Carmel became more comfortable with teasing him unmercifully about some of his letters:

"Dear Carmel, I'm flying to New York again, and of course, I was thinking about you. Wondering if you're okay. Are you smiling? Is your day going well? I know we've discussed so many things over the past weeks. I guess you can say we've been comparing notes. Can I get personal? What makes a woman stay in love with her man? May your days be as lovely as you and your thoughts be filled with the passion of life." Carmel paused. "Okay, I want the truth and nothing but the truth." She reached out and caressed his cheek with the back of her hand. "Were you trying to hit on me?"

Rice smirked his embarrassment and kissed her wrist. "Honestly, I don't think my mind knew what my heart was doing. On the surface, no, but my soul was connecting with yours and didn't want to let go." Rice bit his bottom lip and nodded toward her. "Your turn. Tell me you weren't trying to flirt with me with: 'Rice, your letters are like a bowl of double-dipped chocolate ice cream on a hot summer night. Believe it or not, you inspire me.' "

Carmel snickered. "Whew! I can't believe I wrote something like that."

"I'm glad you did."

With their meals eaten, they relished each other with hand caresses, squeezes, and smiles.

"I've got a surprise for you."

Carmel twisted her lip and arched an eyebrow. "Really? Don't you think us making a love connection is surprise enough? I mean, do we dare repeat our story? Who's going to believe we did something like this?"

"There is so much I want to smother you with. I feel like you're my new Lego set at Christmas, and I want to discover all the ways we work." Rice swallowed the last bite of his chicken broccoli pasta. He pulled money from his wallet and helped Carmel stand.

After making sure she was bundled against the cold outdoor weather, Rice drove them to Generations Photography, a small loft studio near downtown, known for its unique style. Photographer and long-time family friend, Greg Newsome had assured Rice he would be impressed.

"Rice, I don't want to start complaining, but it's getting colder and we're suppose to get more snow. Couldn't we wait for a warmer day to take pictures?"

Rice had quickly developed a habit of stroking Carmel's narrow nose when he talked to her. "You are my fantasy, woman. Indulge me." When Carmel closed her eyes slightly nodding, Rice couldn't resist placing soft kisses on her thick lashes. "I love you so much."

How many times had he said those words that day? Now that he'd looked into her eyes, he couldn't help himself.

Minutes later inside the building, Carmel's eyes sparkled as they walked into the room set up for their session. Greg had frozen a video shot of a bright moon illuminating a clear night sky against a large wall-size screen. "It's beautiful." Carmel gasped, turned in Rice's arms and offered him a tight hug.

"So are you," Rice whispered against her hair.

When Carmel stared into his eyes and swallowed, Rice knew blindly that they had gained each other's heart, trust, and love. He closed his eyes, absorbing Carmel's embrace, just as Greg's camera flashed.

Rice felt subdued as he rubbed foreheads with Carmel. Her thick lashes still captivated him. Behind her voice of seduction radiated a special woman who sheltered a hidden virtuous side. They memorized the other's features, completely shutting out Greg's flashes.

Carmel snaked her arms up Rice's chest, around his neck. "What would you've done if I was disgustingly ugly?" she asked sincerely.

"Accepted my fate. You already possessed my heart."

Carmel's fingers played in the waves in Rice's hair. "Do I still possess your heart?"

Rice blinked as Greg clicked. "Yes."

An hour later, Greg presented them with video proofs. Carmel softly sighed as Rice alternated between scanning the portraits and her face. Finally, he leaned closer, tickling her ear with his breath. "Do you realize we know everything about each other?"

Carmel giggled. "Yes."

"I'm in love with you, Carmel French."

Greg cleared his throat.

"Oh, sorry." Rice grinned. "I want instant proofs of all the shots, and we'll take the Valentine special Love Story deluxe package." Rice held Carmel's stare, but continued talking to Greg.

Greg chuckled as he filled out their contract, shaking his head. "You two didn't need me to capture what you have." He examined one pose. "Anybody on the street could see you two glowing."

"But I needed to see my woman's face in my dreams, since I didn't know what she looked like until a few hours ago."

"Huh?"

Rice and Carmel recounted their story to an astounded Greg.

Greg rubbed his chin, thinking. "Amazing. I don't

believe it. You two act like you've known each other for years. Frenchie, I would be interested in hearing about any other ideas you've got for getting a good woman."

Rice wrapped his arm around Carmel's shoulder, smirking. "Sorry, I've got the last one. I feel so complete. I'm blessed with her sweetness."

Carmel bowed her head in embarrassment.

"Maybe I need to send this cute auditor I've been checking out a love letter. If it can work for you, then there's hope for me."

"Who would have thought it would have turned out like this?" Rice turned to Carmel. "Ready for your next surprise?"

Carmel nodded with a dreamy look of worship in her eyes. "You are everything to me."

Rice blinked rapidly. Her words held so much power over him. He cleared his throat, so he wouldn't fall apart emotionally in front of Greg. He knew the dinner he had planned the next evening would bring tears to her eyes.

Later that night, the mood was light and carefree, as they enjoyed a romantic comedy, *Love the One You're With,* performed at the Black Repertory Theater. Rice wanted to shower Carmel with a love where they could laugh together, talk with each other, and feel completely content.

What a difference a day made. The previous day, Carmel woke feeling exhausted after tossing and turning most of the night. She had feared falling in love with a disgusting, unattractive, and deceiving man. But the day ended as if they had been dating for months, enjoying a stage play with local performer, Denise Thimes, who was hilarious in her role as a rejected lover. She wondered if Rice was hinting she could have rejected him.

It wasn't going to happen. Rice was more than she could have ever imagined.

Bright sunshine kissed Carmel awake around noon Saturday morning. She lay in bed with her arms folded behind her head, gazing at the smiling couple inside the crystal frame Rice had sent her for Christmas. Rice was barely touching her cheek, when Greg had snapped the pose. Carmel blew a seductive kiss at Rice.

The phone rang as she was climbing out of bed. She answered with a smile, knowing it would be Rice.

"Good morning, sweetheart."

"Mmm, now that's something your letters can't do."

"What?"

"Wake me up. Usually, I dream about your words all night and fight with myself about waking up."

"I know."

They spoke for a few more minutes before he said he'd see her later.

Around one in the afternoon, Rice sent a letter to Carmel via telegram. He suggested attending an early-morning church service the next day in celebration of God bringing them together, followed by meeting each other's family after a Sunday morning brunch. "I will be thanking God for a long time."

Carmel smiled. Most of the men she knew had to be dragged to church and then nailed to their seats. God, was this man for real? Or had she been in a fantasy-induced dream for the past four months? Rice was perfect and definitely refreshing!

An hour later, a different mail service brought another letter from Rice.

Baby,
    Other men can only wish you would appear in their dreams, but somehow I was the lucky one to have you re-

visit mine every night—my dream come true. I'll make
you happy. I promise.
Love,
Rice

At exactly three, the second man returned and
handed Rice's third letter to Carmel.

Sweetest Valentine,
    How would you describe our love? If you're speechless,
then let me. Unpretentious; unique; a bomb waiting to
explode; a gentle, caressing breeze; a sweet piece of candy
with an everlasting flavor just like gooey caramel. I'll
whisper more tonight.

Throughout the day a letter arrived every hour as
Carmel pampered herself for their special dinner. She
wore different shades of makeup and a very feminine
dress, and she changed her usual perfume for a sweet-
musk scent. Rice's patience the night before tempted
her to be more flirtatious this evening.

Carmel was disappointed, when the doorbell didn't
ring at four. She was dumbfounded, trying to predict
what Rice Taylor was conjuring up next.

Ten minutes later, after pacing the floor, Carmel
heard the motor of a van speed past her apartment,
then the shrieking sound of brakes skidding on slick
pavement. When she peeked out the window to investi-
gate, a van was cautiously backing up to her building.

Carmel met him with an open door, before he could
knock.

"Sorry, madam, for the late delivery." The courier
huffed as he looked down at his package. "It says deliver
by four sharp, but I wasn't familiar with the neighborhood. Sorry." He shrugged with an apologetic grin.

Carmel sighed with relief and offered a tense smile. "That's okay," she said sweetly. What she wanted to do was strangle the young boy for increasing her anxiety level. She ripped the letter open before she closed the front door.

My Lady,
   I can't wait to see your eyes, smell your perfume, touch your lips, and hold you close. Miss me? Well, I've been missing you since I said goodnight yesterday.
Your man,
Rice

At five, Carmel peeped out her door, looking for Rice's next letter. She met the carrier before he pressed the doorbell, startling him. She stunned him further as she held out her palm ceremoniously, expecting her package.

Carmel,
   No words can describe how happy I am at this moment. The more I think about you, the more I desire to see your smile, hear the words you write, and lose myself in the hypnotic powers of your thick lashes, girl. See you in an hour, sweetheart.
Love you,
Rice

Carmel couldn't stand it any longer. Rice's short love notes were creating havoc on her senses, more so than when she had no idea what he looked like. Carmel had made up her mind to express herself in a letter just as the doorbell chimed. Instead, Carmel sprayed behind her ears and raced to the door. She wanted to bring Rice to his knees in a playful seduction. But Rice was one step ahead of her, because when she opened her door, that's how she found him—on his knee.

Unbelievable. He's the perfect charmer. Carmel had never met a man so sincere and yet intense with his feelings. This was definitely a good sign.

Rice pulled out every conceivable romantic tactic he knew, had read from dating books, or had heard from happy couples. There was no limit. After he rang Carmel's doorbell, it just felt right greeting her on his knee, to demonstrate how much he cherished her, presenting a dozen long-stemmed chocolate roses, to create the ultimate effect of romance.

But when Carmel opened the door, her subtle seduction began. She turned the tables on him. Rice thought he had stopped breathing, staring. Carmel was more beautiful than when he first saw her. Her loveliness had arrested his senses. "I love you," he whispered in adoration.

"And I love you, Mr. Taylor." Carmel bent and initiated a well-planned kiss that commanded him to stand and take the assault like a man. Breathless, Carmel reluctantly released his lips, still pecking kisses on his mouth.

"If you want food for dinner, I suggest you lock your door. If you want me, then keep doing what you're doing, woman, and it's on!"

Carmel's lips teased his with one more peck, before turning and closing her door.

Outside, the snow-covered ground glistened and icicle-covered tree branches twinkled as the bright moonlight danced on the earth. Rice had stretched a long piece of red nylon fabric from the building's front door to his vehicle, elegantly creating a privileged red-carpet entrance designed for the rich and famous. He knew the reception was well received, when he heard Carmel gasp.

"Rice, did you do this?"

Rice's heart pounded against his chest in excitement. He wasn't sure if Carmel would appreciate his corny romantic idea to create a magical night. "My intent was to make you feel special."

Carmel shook her head in disbelief. "I do." Her eyes were still wide in shock. "Oh, my goodness. Rice, you are incredible."

Soft jazz floated inside Rice's SUV, mixing with his musk cologne, intensifying their enchanting date. Carmel inhaled and relaxed as she turned in her seat, folded her arms, and gazed at Rice in amazement. There was nothing simple about this man or his love. Carmel's heart swelled with fulfillment.

When Carmel opened her eyes, she memorized Rice's movements as he concentrated on his driving. His eyes sparkled when he stole glances in Carmel's direction. Rice was well groomed, very attentive, and extremely handsome. How could Gina or any woman allow him to walk out of her life? The thought caused a slow smile.

Thank you, ladies. "Rice?"

Grabbing Carmel's hand, Rice guided her fingers to his mouth before softly brushing his lips against it. "Yeah, baby."

"Are you going to tell me where you're taking me?" She squeezed his hand. Carmel heard a deep laugh rumbling in Rice's throat. She smiled at the rich sound.

"Nope." He reached over and stroked her cheek. "What happened to all that patience you had the past months?"

"I lost it," Carmel stated flatly, twisting her lips. "It was torture not seeing you, especially after I realized how much you really loved me." Was it Carmel's imagination, or were his eyes really smiling at her, as if saying, "I know."

"Sweetheart?" His expression changed.

Carmel became concerned. "Hmmm?"

"About us getting married . . ."

Panic hit her like a brick. She could have gone through the roof of his Durango. Had Rice changed his mind? Carmel's vision blurred. She entwined her fingers and forced out a whisper. "You don't want to marry me?" Tears spilled over.

"Huh?" Rice checked his rearview mirror, turned on his signal, and parked his vehicle on the shoulder of the highway. Activating his flashers, Rice shut off the engine and tenderly pulled Carmel's face to his. He gave her a loving look before taking a deep breath.

"Baby, listen to me." His finger guided her chin closer to his mouth. "I love you. I want to marry you now, right now, woman. But I'm leaving the date—whether it's next week or next year—up to you. I just don't want you to feel rushed, pressured, or obligated, although you told the whole world on the air that you would marry me, barely, but I heard a yes."

When Rice pouted, it gave his face an unusual innocent look. Carmel felt the tension leave her body.

"In all fairness, I just want you to be completely ready to receive what your man has for you, because I'm not going to let you go, understand?"

Carmel nodded, absorbing his words. At that moment, she did understand that this man really loved her and wasn't taking her love for granted. She hiccupped between dwindling tears.

Rice gently massaged Carmel's neck until her sniffing subsided then resumed driving on Highway 367, crossing the Missouri River into Alton, Illinois.

Ten minutes later, he arrived in Grafton and Pere Marquette Lodge.

The earlier snow had created a picturesque winter wonderland, with scattered cabins and the lodge, reminding Carmel of a Christmas village. "Ooh, this is pretty."

"No, baby, *you're* pretty."

Carmel blushed from his stare and compliment. As they trotted carefully in the wet snow to the main building, Carmel peered through the large ceiling-to-floor window at roaring flames dancing in a massive stone-and-brick fireplace centered in a huge lounging area. "Rice, this is so beautiful. Every moment with you becomes a fairy tale."

Rice brushed the softest kiss behind Carmel's ear as he took off her coat and led her to an oversized black sofa and two matching love seats positioned in front of the fire. The room was enormous; it had four separate reclining areas, three with fireplaces, and massive overhead chandeliers glistening.

Rice snaked his hand lazily around Carmel's waist. "When I heard about the multiple fireplaces, I thought about you, me, and a warm fire. I wanted to make sure we had time to relax before dinner." Rice glanced down at his watch. "But unfortunately we've only got about fifteen minutes to talk, touch, and tantalize our senses with each other until our reservation is ready. C'mon, baby, sit wherever you want."

Carmel crossed her arms. She craved the oversized couch entertained by dancing flames—the perfect setting for snuggling. But the game area a few feet away with a room-size floor-model chessboard, complete with life-size chessmen, fascinated her. She watched the children giggle as they played. "Mmm, nice family atmosphere and cozy."

"Okay, where would you like to sit, my queen?" Rice bowed with a grin.

Carmel pointed to the large sofa and looked up into his hypnotic eyes. "I can't resist the fire and a therapy session with you."

"I can't resist you," Rice whispered against her mouth as he sat down and dragged Carmel with him. He chuckled as she settled against his chest. "This is definitely the right choice."

Rice's mind drifted as he moaned. "I'm utterly satisfied," he admitted. Within minutes, Rice pierced the quietness with the soft humming of "So Amazing," by gospel artist Darwin Hobbs. His smooth baritone voice hypnotized both of them. Rice stopped abruptly. "I hope you're extremely happy."

Carmel answered by staring into his eyes and offering a loving smile, before relaxing deeper in his chest while he continued humming. Yeah, she was very satisfied, too.

Other couples mingled around, engaged in their own intimate conversations as they held hands, stole kisses, and hugged their sweethearts.

Rice whispered as he inhaled Carmel's hair. "I want a woman who loves me despite my faults and insecurities. If my woman has to re-mold me, I only want her loving hands to shape me." He gently stroked the soft-red knit jersey fabric on her arms. "I need a woman who's strong when I'm weak, one who's not afraid to love me from the depths of her soul."

Carmel beamed. She recalled how Rice wrote those very same words a few months ago. "I still can't believe how you have memorized some of our letters. I could spend a lifetime in your arms, enjoying a cozy fire and listening to you."

Rice flexed his muscles in a tighter hug. "Hmmm, a

simple request from my beautiful woman." He planted a soft kiss against her forehead.

After a few minutes, Carmel became so still Rice nudged her, thinking she probably had fallen asleep. When she turned and faced him, he noticed her tears.

As Rice used his thumb to catch them, Carmel kissed the inside of his hand. "I do love you, Rice," she said, looking into his eyes, pleading for him to believe her. "More love than I knew I had inside of me."

"Oh, honey, I knew your love was inside of you a long time ago because you brought it out in me. I just had to be strong enough for both of us while you were trying to accept my love, and baby, you were worth it."

Their dinner reservation echoed over a loud intercom. Rice slowly disentangled their arms, stood, and guided Carmel down a wide, glass-enclosed hallway that overlooked the outdoor wintry scenery. Soft jazz music seductively romanced dinner guests in a large but cozy banquet room. Flickering candlelight welcomed them as assortments of aromas floated to their noses, enticing them to sample.

Rice seated Carmel first before going to the buffet to fill her plate with shrimp scampi, roast, grilled chicken, roasted potatoes, mixed vegetables, and warm bread. "That should hold ya," he said, grinning.

Unchecked time passed as Carmel and Rice sluggishly leaned back in their seats, patting their stomachs. "It's time for a little dessert," Rice teased as a waiter approached with a dozen white heart-shaped teacakes on a crystal platter. Rice acted nonchalant as he quietly waited for Carmel's reaction to his surprise—their names written expertly on each cake in pink icing.

Carmel looked from the dessert to Rice and back again. "Rice?"

"I love you, sweetheart. Here, let me do that." Rice

lifted a miniature cake and teasingly coached Carmel to take a bite. When she obliged him, Rice kissed her manicured fingers after each treat, until the miniature cakes were gone.

"Ready to leave?"

"And realize that I've been dreaming? No," she said, chuckling, applying fresh lipstick before standing.

Carmel cuddled next to Rice, as they left Pere Marquette for the forty-five-minute drive back to St. Louis. "Thank you. This night was perfect, just perfect."

But not as perfect as the kiss they shared when Rice delivered Carmel to her door. Their lips dueled, controlled, and surrendered. After a non-retreating battle, Carmel almost slid to the floor.

Rice braced his arms against the wall to recover from the draining passion. It had overpowered both of them.

"I hope that keeps you warm tonight," Rice whispered as he backed away, winking.

They reluctantly ended their night on the phone three hours later.

Chapter Eleven

Early Sunday morning, Carmel and Rice, hands intertwined, drove leisurely around St. Louis neighborhoods looking for the perfect quaint church to celebrate their newfound love. Something about the tall, gold steeple of God's Blessings Apostolic Church off Interstate 70 near Lambert Airport beckoned to them.

Upon entering the enormous white stone-and-brick structure, Carmel felt somewhat intimidated. The church was a lively contrast from the quiet Catholic masses she attended while growing up. "It has a lot of energy."

A tall African-American male usher who appeared to be in his late teens directed them to thickly cushioned brown seats about ten rows from the back of the church. The auditorium with plush beige carpeting gave the illusion of a large cathedral setting, but in reality the most it could have easily held was about six hundred members.

Rice possessively tugged on Carmel's hand, tenderly

rubbing her fingers, in a reassuring and comforting gesture. "You look pretty in your brown wool-and-fur hat. And that suit, no one else could wear it as classy as you."

"Thank you. I wanted to match your chestnut suit. I wanted us to look like we belonged to each other."

Rice winked his appreciation as they climbed over a couple with two small children.

Minutes later the minister instructed everybody to stand. "It's time for our one minute of praise, saints. Just think about the one special thing the Lord has done for you this week!"

The congregation stood, initiating a vigorous wave of clapping. High-pitched and deep baritone voices shouted together nonstop with praises, like they were cheering at a baseball game.

Rice had a lot to be thankful for, including internal resolution from the bitter breakup with Gina. Otherwise his heart may not have been able to patiently hold out for the jewel standing beside him. God had done all right by him, now it was time for Rice to really get his act together. He didn't want to chance anything going wrong between him and Carmel.

Before complying, Rice sneaked a peek at Carmel, her lids fluttering as she clapped energetically. He almost jumped out of his shoes, startled, when Carmel's voice blended with the others in a shout, "Thank You, Jesus, for bringing Rice into my life!"

At that moment, Rice was humbled, proud, and appreciative that Carmel would consider him as a gift from God. He realized they both had been on the same page. Rice breathed a sigh of relief, not sure how Carmel would respond to the church's lively songs and spirited crowd. Together they would grow emotionally and spiritually.

Gradually the praise died down. Re-linking fingers, Rice and Carmel sat contentedly, listening as the pastor preached on "God Makes No Mistakes in Our Lives."

Rice shoved Carmel's shoulder, tilted his head under her hat, and whispered in her ear, "Do you believe God has brought us together?"

"Yes."

As the sermon ended, Rice stretched his long legs. "Maybe this church is a sign. The minister had a good message, but I really got into the sub-theme, 'Hold on to whatever God gives you.'" Rice enjoyed watching her blush. "Carmel French, you aren't going anywhere. I'm going to see to that."

Carmel squeezed his hand and mouthed, "thank you."

When the pastor blessed the congregation and dismissed them, some members lingered, welcoming the visitors. Others personally invited Rice and Carmel to come back.

The couple left the service laughing, holding hands, and inspired.

"Thank you."

Rice rubbed his thumb over her hand. "For what, sweetheart?"

"For including church in our weekend dating plans. I feel so uplifted. I don't know many men who would take time out for God." Carmel chuckled. "Usually many of them avoid any building resembling a church."

"Guilty. Maybe that's why I got burned with women like Gina, but I have you now and that's all that matters. I'll be indebted to God for life."

"Ready to meet my siblings, the twins?"

Rice deactivated the Durango's alarm. "Sure, why not? After that sermon, I'm ready for anything."

But thirty minutes later, Hershel and Hershey French proved to be a challenge to Rice's newfound happiness.

"You're getting married?" Hershel and Hershey yelled in unison.

"Car, please tell me this isn't the 'paper man'?" Hershey queried with a worried expression.

Hershel frowned. "He delivers paper? Carmel, I will not allow you to support a man who won't get a decent job."

Rice turned to Carmel and mouthed, "What?"

Carmel held up both hands to ward off any more questions. "Okay, let me explain. Purely by coincidence we wrote each other very innocent letters. One note and one reply led to more notes and letters. Finally, without ever seeing what the other looked like, we got hooked and fell in love. The layers of our feelings are so deep. Hershel, Hershey, I am so much in love with this man."

Rice's heart puffed with pride as Carmel's eyes misted. He loved hearing her describe their budding relationship. Rice squeezed her hand gently, nodding his support.

Hershey eyed them suspiciously, twisting her red-painted lips, quietly assessing the emotional damage her sister would have to deal with after the real truth came to surface. "So what if Rice Krispie Treat is about six feet of stunning maleness," she said, shrugging. "I can't say I'm getting good vibes about this." She paused. "As a matter of fact, I would bet the runway he's playing you, Car. What do you really know about him? Are you sure he has never served time?"

"What!" Hershel jumped to his feet, standing erect with fists thrust on his waist. "You sure know how to pick them, baby sister. Of all the men I could fix you up with, you chose a parolee." Hershel paced the floor like he was prosecuting a criminal in the courtroom. "Rice, you're saying you had no idea what my sister looked like, huh? Why do I find that hard to believe considering her picture's in the paper every now and then." Hershel froze and casually folded his arms. "Your game is weak, man, if you expect me to believe something like that."

Mimicking her twin, Hershey folded her arms and tilted her head. "My brother does make an excellent point. Well, Rice, I guess you won't mind if we run a police check on you."

"What!" Carmel cried out furiously.

Rice held up his hand. "Hershel and Hershey, you two don't know me, but Carmel holds all my secrets. I will not let you tear us down." He stood eye-to-eye with Hershel—well almost. "Although what you're asking me is an intrusion of my privacy, I will gladly submit to a police, credit, and physical exam, if that will make you feel better."

"Done. It will," Hershey and Hershel responded together without hesitation.

Rice held Carmel in his arms, to soothe her downcast look. "It's all right, honey. I have nothing to hide."

Carmel turned into his chest and whispered, "Rice, I'm so sorry."

For the next hour, Rice was cross-examined about his education, financial portfolio, and family background. The twins took notes, compared notes, and held conference breaks before mellowing down.

Later, once inside Rice's SW, Carmel mumbled, "Wasn't that fun?" Carmel sighed as Rice reached over and began massaging her fingers. "I hadn't expected such a rebellion."

"Whew! That was a revolution. I won your trust. I will fight them for theirs." Rice tightened his grip. "Shhh, everything will work out. We built this relationship word by word, sentence by sentence, and one letter at a time. We can overcome anything, baby."

When Rice parked in front of his parents' home, he noticed Carmel's intensity as she twirled the hair behind her ears, evidence her confidence was slipping. He also didn't like the frown marring her beautiful face. He rubbed her lips, eyelashes, and cheeks with gentle strokes. The only sound was their soft breathing.

Within minutes, Carmel gave him a smile, confirming that she felt and knew what he was conveying with his fingers.

Rice made introductions as soon as his short, plump mother opened her door. "Hi, Mom." He encircled her in a warm hug. He turned back and winked. "Carmel, my mother, Sharon Taylor."

Carmel smiled as his mother embraced her with genuine warmth. Rice watched as Carmel physically relaxed.

"Rice, she's much prettier than the last one," Sharon commented proudly. "And not as snooty and uptight. It's all about the attitude."

"Mom," Rice whined, "let's not start crying on the doorstep."

Sharon stepped back, held her hands to her chest, and released a hearty laugh. "Sorry, I'm not usually rude and forgetful, just forgetful."

They all laughed.

A booming voice approached from around the corner. Winston Taylor strolled out of the kitchen, clenching a thick double-decker sandwich in one hand. He was known for raiding his parents' house for a snack before heading to his own apartment minutes away to eat again. As Winston approached the foyer, he stopped dead in his tracks. "Whoa, bro, who is this?" Shock, surprise, and amazement played across his face. Winston easily forgot about his food as he leaned against the wall. "Please tell me she has some sisters," he said.

Carmel laughed and turned to Rice. "Is your family prone to drama, too?"

"Who knows?" Rice shook his head. "Meet my older brother, Winston. Winston, my lady, Carmel French."

Carmel shook his hand, squinting, looking for a resemblance.

Rice chuckled. "We really are brothers, despite Winston's dark mahogany skin, slimmer build, and shorter height. The best thing he has going for him is his dazzling three-thousand-dollar smile. Braces do wonders."

"And so do these lips." Winston made a loud smacking sound. "I'm harmless, really. So, this is the woman behind the voice?" He took a bite from his sandwich and started chewing, thinking. "How . . . when . . . where did you two . . . so this is the one . . . hmmm. Really, do you have any sisters as gorgeous as you?"

"I have a sister who *is* gorgeous, but she's more than a challenge."

Winston's laugh was deep and rich, like Rice's. "I'll remember that, when I'm mentally ready for a battle. It's still nice to meet you, Carmel."

Rice's sisters walked into the foyer and barely hugged him, staring at Carmel as he grabbed her hand.

"Carmel French, these are my two sisters, Tellie and Giselle. Ladies, this is the woman I plan to marry, so don't scare her away." Rice pulled Carmel through the hall, ignoring their gasps and Winston gagging on his food.

"You're engaged?" Tellie asked in a whisper.

"To the most sought-after female media personality?" Giselle added, trailing them.

"Ladies, I'm sure we'll hear the whole story. Let

them get comfortable first," Sharon admonished her daughters.

"Tellie, did Rice ever mention to you about having a new girlfriend?" Giselle whispered loudly.

"No, but evidently our brother has been moving on and improving with his taste."

A few hours later, after rehashing the details of their meeting, the Taylors congratulated the happy couple as everyone relaxed in front of a warm fire in the family room. Rice nudged Carmel to snuggle closer as she listened with fascination to his family's childhood stories about him. He would end Carmel's uncontrollable laughing episodes, with quick pecks on her lips. Some of his mother's tales caused him to hide his face in embarrassment, but Carmel restored his pride with soft whispers of love.

"I needed that encouragement and you," he would say, tickling her ears with his breath.

Winston Senior, who had been quietly observing their interaction, cleared his throat. "All right, these lovebirds don't need an audience. Let's give them some privacy. Winston, go home to your empty fridge and think about finding yourself a wife. Tellie, make sure your next boyfriend treats you how Rice responds to Carmel, and Giselle, don't you even think about anything serious until after you graduate from Tennessee State next year."

Rice locked eyes with his dad and nodded his appreciation as his family left the room. He stood and strolled to the fireplace and carefully placed another log on the fire. He gave Carmel a wicked grin, deliberately adjusting the lights to the softest glow.

"Are you trying to seduce me?" Carmel batted her eyes and returned her own grin.

"No, sweetheart. My father taught us to love and respect women, never seduce them. Besides, I'm sure my sisters are somewhere within ear's reach." Rice inserted *Pieces of a Dream* into the CD player before rejoining Carmel on the couch. As Rice held Carmel tight, he sighed. "You know, our beautiful Valentine's weekend is almost over, and I'll be traveling again."

"Will you write me?"

"Don't I always?"

Chapter Twelve

Late Sunday night, Carmel drifted to sleep totally content, but awoke within hours restless and fitful. She lifted her eyes to the clock. "Four in the morning," Carmel huffed as she yanked off the covers. She turned over and quietly lay in bed, looking at the night sky through partially opened blinds. Since Friday, Rice had made her breathless in the day and sleepless at night as she remembered his attention, love, and very handsome looks.

Soon the sun would make its appearance and Rice would be at the airport for his flight to New York, a routine trip to meet with the sales staff, which would take him away for almost a week. He needed a new job. *No, thank God, he's a black man with a good-paying job!*

Falling in love with Rice had become a romantic adventure filled with wonderful surprises. Things really could have turned out disastrously. Carmel sighed as she fingered the rollers in her hair, thinking her man was probably in a deep sleep. She smiled, reminiscing about the men she'd dated in the past, and concluded they weren't deserving of her trust, but with Rice, the trust came naturally.

"Plus, the man is dripping with sexiness. Rice is too fine, genuine, and too confident for his own good, but I ain't complaining," she confessed to her empty room. "How am I going to survive with him away?"

Since sleep had evaded her, Carmel got up and started her morning exercise before scanning the news channel for story ideas for her show. Within minutes she made a detour to the phone.

Rice answered quickly, interrupting the completion of the first ring. "Good morning, sweetheart. Couldn't sleep?" his husky early morning voice whispered into the phone.

Carmel blushed. "No, not after this weekend. I'm addicted to you," she said, breathless. "I'll miss you badly. Sorry to wake you." Carmel heard Rice shifting the phone.

"Come on, baby. Talk to me. I'm just as addicted to you, " he gladly admitted. "Tell me what you're feeling."

They spoke for forty-five minutes, the shortest conversation they had engaged in to date.

As Carmel fingered her bracelet from Rice she glanced at her wristwatch. It was 8:00 A.M., and Rice was probably boarding the plane as Carmel was about to broadcast the last hour of her show.

"Hey, St. Louis. It's Monday, and I'm Frenchie, comin' at ya in three, two, one."

When she looked up at Glen, he shook his head. Carmel twisted her lips in a wicked grin. She couldn't help it that just the thought of Rice Taylor energized her.

"It's a wonderful Monday morning. Before I open the phone lines for your calls, I want to say to my female listeners, I hope your sweetheart made you feel real special this weekend."

"Good morning, Frenchie. This past weekend marked my mother's tenth year being cancer free. So we had a big party for her, and other breast cancer survivors attended."

Carmel released a deep breath. She wasn't expecting such a deep topic following Valentine's Day, but she loved talking about serious issues, especially those affecting the black community disproportionately.

"Jason, what a wonderful day of love! I'm glad she's a survivor because for African-American women, we're often dead before aggressive treatment starts." She paused, reflecting on the disparity. "Although whites and minorities are both afflicted with breast cancer, many blacks are usually diagnosed in later stages, when it's too late for remission. The lack of adequate medical insurance, proper education, and the lack of trust in doctors are factors that cause us to die at a higher rate."

Jason's muffled voice became clearer through his cell phone. "I agree, Frenchie, but let me say this in Doctor Chandra Kem's defense: Although she is an Asian-American doctor, she knew how quickly the disease spread in blacks, and she didn't waste any time with Mom's treatment."

"Thanks, Jason, for setting us up this hour. Women who have survived breast cancer—their treatment and the illness. Let's talk about your personal experience or somebody you love, right after this short break."

During the commercial, Carmel's phone lines lit with female callers. As her music faded, she punched line two. "Regina, welcome to the show."

"Frenchie, this is Gina. I know how sweet Rice can be. How sweet was he to you this weekend?"

Carmel's heart pounded as her body stiffened with anger. How dare this chick call and jeopardize the serious nature of her show with a personal vendetta? "Gina, that's not the topic for discussion this morning."

"Let's make it."

Carmel rolled her eyes. "Let's not. As a matter of fact, don't get French with me." She disconnected and signaled Glen to block her number.

After the show Carmel walked out of the studio heavyhearted about the large number of young women battling cancer, but also irritated Gina had the nerve to act ghetto on her show.

Esther stood waiting for Carmel at the receptionist's desk. "Good show, crazy woman, and sad topic, but you made everybody more aware and put the sister in her place. Rice would be proud," she said, grinning like a proud mother. "Okay, details, girlfriend, details."

Carmel chuckled as Esther smacked her lips like a dog waiting for mealtime. "And if I don't?"

"Well, I guess this letter from Rice-a-Roni remains in my hands."

Carmel tried to yank the envelope, but Esther moved back. "Don't play, Es. You could seriously get hurt by a love-possessed woman over one of his letters." A smile broke through before she continued, "Girl, he was worth every letter I ever wrote!" Carmel stomped her feet as she closed her eyes like she was savoring her favorite treat. "He's kind, sweet, gentle, and patient, but you already knew that." Carmel grinned.

"Stop with the dramatics. Was he just as romantic as his letters?"

Carmel sauntered to one of the three lounge chairs

in the reception area, snickering while Es grew red with frustration. Carmel slowly sat down, crossed her legs, and blew on her nails, emphasizing each gesture. Carmel leaned her head back, closed her eyes, and whispered, "Rice was the perfect gentleman, and he didn't disrespect me or my body this weekend, and the brother is Shemar Moore fine!" she shouted as she opened one eye to see Es patting her chest and fanning her face. "God molded Rice Taylor with a woman's heart in mind."

Es sniffed as she handed Carmel the envelope. "Okay, okay, I'm sold on Mr. San Francisco Treat." She turned and walked back into her office, laughing.

Carmel caressed the pink envelope tied with a rose-colored wired-ribbon. "When?" she wondered as she hurried to her own cubbyhole-size office for privacy.

To my baby,

I know words brought us together, but now there are no words to express my feelings for you and every sweet moment that we shared this weekend. I fell in love with you over and over, woman. Thank you for letting me love you. How did I survive the many months without touching you, kissing you, and looking into those sexy caramel-colored eyes hidden by those thick eyelashes? Baby, you have put me in my place as a prisoner of your love, a place I would fight any man to keep.

You are an incredible woman, my desire, and my gorgeous paper doll who captured my heart one day as I scanned the radio. I would have never, ever thought that listening to talk radio would enrich my life, but it has. You are a feast to my eyes. Right now, I'm remembering your soft whispers and gentle squeezes my hand enjoyed when you conveyed a special moment that was just for us to share. Remember, I love you, and I'll call you as soon

as I return Thursday night. Have a good show today,
baby, and smile often when you think of me.
Hugs, kisses, smiles, and more kisses,
Rice

Carmel refolded the letter, with misty eyes. Rice had
stolen her heart, and she couldn't get it back. She gathered her purse and left. As she stepped into the elevator, an extremely beautiful woman walked off.

"Frenchie?" the stranger asked, her tone indicating
she already knew.

"Yes."

"Humph! Yeah, I recognize the voice."

"And I recognize your attitude, Gina."

Chapter Thirteen

Images of Carmel's contagious smile and her thick, black eyelashes invaded Rice's dreams, acting as an alarm clock every hour on the hour. Several times Rice thought he had heard Carmel's sultry voice or inhaled remnants of her perfume.

Rice shifted his body under the sheets, folding his arms behind his head. He forced his eyes open and tried to focus on the red neon numbers on his bedside clock. His lips twisted into a smirk. "She's probably sleeping like a baby, my baby," he mumbled, stretching his lips across his face. Oh, how his ears craved to hear his name on her lips, but it was too early to wake her.

Reluctantly Rice climbed out of bed. He had to touch her, even if it meant writing her to release feelings that had robbed him of sleep. When his phone rang, Rice relaxed. Carmel French was his morning sunrise.

That was early Monday before Rice left for the airport. They had whispered their feelings over the phone as if they were the only two people awake in the world and didn't want to share their musings with anyone else. He had come to a decision about his job, and later he would share it with his woman.

Now, minutes into Tuesday morning, Rice needed Carmel to begin his sunset. He sat behind a desk in his hotel suite in New York, reviewing marketing concepts to expand new pharmaceutical drugs in larger areas that were discussed in morning seminars, a luncheon, and a late dinner business meeting.

Rice rubbed his eyes and tried again to compute blurred sales figures on his calculator two of his three East Coast groups had submitted earlier, but he was too exhausted. Their performances were improving, but they would still need some restructuring if he expected to see million-dollar sales by the end of the year. But right now, his priority was to invest in his lasting relationship with Carmel.

Enough! Rice's brain screamed from fatigue as he stood and stretched his weary body and massaged his stiff neck. A warm shower, soft bed, and Carmel's lovely voice would lull him to sleep. First, he needed to check his home recorder for any important messages. He closed his eyes, when he recognized Carmel's husky voice. Immediately, his tired body was energized.

"Rice, you are so sweet and thoughtful. You overwhelmed me before last week. Your love saturated me Valentine's weekend, and even now while you're away, you are still incredible. Thank you for the letter that was waiting for me this morning. Now, when I close my eyes, I'll see you.

"I keep asking myself if I'm dreaming. Rice, did you have any idea it would be this wonderful between us? I have so many things to say, a paper and pen won't cut it any more. That's why I called. I'm counting the minutes until we speak tonight. Love you. By the way, I met Gina today. Lovely woman."

"What!" Rice's sedated mind switched to full alert as he gripped the phone in annoyance and uneasiness. "What has Gina done now? Whatever scheme she had concocted had better not upset Carmel," he spat out through clenched teeth.

Rice showered in record time before punching in Carmel's phone number. It was late, but he promised to call her every night while he was away. He settled back in the bed, wondering how long Carmel would make him wait to marry her. He wanted to make love to her so bad, he felt he might suffer a stroke waiting, but he knew she was uncomfortable about sleeping together before marriage.

Carmel told him it was her Catholic upbringing. Rice smiled. He had a Pentecostal upbringing, so he knew better, too, although he had slipped at times. Carmel had brought him back to God, with the church she randomly selected for them to attend, and he would just have to wait.

"Hello? Rice?" Carmel's drowsy voice whispered into the phone.

"Hi, baby. Sorry, it's so late."

"Your calls are always welcome."

Rice smiled at the way Carmel could make him feel privileged. "Say you miss me," Rice demanded softly as he closed his eyes, listening for the response he desperately needed to hear.

"Of course I miss you." Carmel paused. "And I love you too."

"I love you more," he teased.

Carmel strained her voice, "Oh Rice, you're torturing me! Four months is the longest I can hold out to be your wife."

Rice frowned and sat up in his bed. He could hear the tears in her voice, and sniffling. His baby was crying, and he wasn't there to hold her. "Shhh, sweetheart, I can't wait for us to share together forever either."

"I miss you.

"And I, you." Rice inhaled deeply as he soaked in Carmel's desperate need of him and his love. He thought about Carmel mentioning Gina, but that topic would have to wait. Gina was at the bottom of his list. Instead, he shared some good news. "I spoke with my vice president earlier today and requested to be reassigned to the Midwest region. It's less travel, and it's closer to home. The territory doesn't generate the revenues I'm accustomed to, but that will be my new challenge. Everything will work out, sweetheart. I promise. Just hold on a few more weeks until the headquarters can review the transfer papers and name a replacement. Then, baby, I'll cook dinner for you every night."

"I'd like that."

Rice imagined Carmel's smile. "Now, tell me about Gina. When did you see her?"

"She came to the radio station . . . I guess to see the competition . . . to talk; basically she wants you back, and plans to have you."

"She can't have me," Rice reacted sharply.

"That's what I told her, among other things, but she said she poured out her soul to you in a letter revealing the real Gina. The woman she knew you craved."

"I never read it. Only one lady captured my heart in a letter. It's a special thing I won't share with anyone else."

"Thank you."

Chapter Fourteen

If rain, sleet, hail, and snow didn't stop the postal service from delivering mail, then the weather wasn't going to keep Carmel away from surprising Rice later at the airport. Forecasters had predicted two or more inches of snow, gusty winds, and bone-chilling temperatures, but Carmel was adamant about riding the city's light rail public transportation, Metrolink, to the airport so she could ride back with Rice. She had almost gone insane with loneliness while he was away.

She felt adventurous as she approached a woman manning an airport kiosk and watched as the florist expertly intertwined two long-stemmed roses as Carmel had requested. She dressed stylishly in her new brown fur-lined leather jacket over a black turtleneck and suede pants that offset with brown knee-high leather biker boots. A red, black, and brown printed silk scarf laid draped around her neck and tied at the shoulder. She laughed silently at the crazy person she had become, thinking back to the time when she was a bundle of nerves wondering about Rice and wearing anything to work. Carmel had recently washed and set her shoulder-length hair. That night, she wore it down in a soft flip, which bounced as she walked.

Carmel stood outside the security checkpoint, occasionally sniffing the flowers in one hand as she clutched a Mahogany pocket greeting card she had purchased at Afrocentric Books in the other. Carmel couldn't believe the tiny ten pages were filled with one-liners that described how she felt about Rice.

"Those miniature cards are big sellers. It will keep you on Rice's mind while he's gone," the bookstore owner had said with a big grin.

"Thanks. Keep me posted when new ones come in, and don't forget to call me about that new author you want me to interview on my show."

Carmel sucked in her breath to slow her rapid heartbeat. She realized this was the boldest thing she had ever done since meeting Rice. Friends had always advised her against surprising your man because you'll be the one left with a surprise. Since Carmel never wanted to lose control, she didn't chance getting herself ambushed, but what she had with Rice was so different.

She had even purchased his favorite cologne and dabbed a little behind her ears instead of wearing her own perfume. Would Rice notice and like it? Would her feminine scent sweeten the smell? She smiled mischievously. "I've lost my mind."

Carmel checked her watch. She knew his gate and flight number, but because of the new airport security measures she wasn't allowed access to the concourses. She leaned against the wall, waiting, ignoring men's appreciative stares, low whistles, and flirtatious hellos. Usually she shied away from attention, but that night she felt like taunting every man with an eat-your-heart-out-I-belong-to-Rice look. Carmel sighed when she thought about Rice's perfectly formed lips that curled into a smile whenever he said her name.

Carmel inspected her makeup again. It was flawless. Her smile was eager, and her heart pounded offbeat with excitement. "He's going to be so happy to see me . . ." Her happiness faded to shock. "Wait a minute!" She blinked twice and stared at Rice walking intimately down the concourse, holding hands with another woman.

Then, they stopped, embraced before sharing a kiss that wasn't meant for public viewing. It was nasty!

Get a grip, girl, you're imagining that every man looks like Rice.

As the couple reluctantly separated, Carmel craned her neck, watching as the woman walked away fast, disappearing in the crowd.

What was that all about? Her heart dropped to the bottom of her stomach. Her strength began to seep out of her body as she recognized it was indeed the man she loved. Who was that woman? Did they take these trips together all the time? She felt betrayed, used, but most of all, ticked off. How could she have been so stupid to believe in a man whom she met "on paper"?

Rice still hadn't seen her. She walked right up to him and slapped him with the long-stemmed roses. "Liar!" she shouted in a high-pitched voice she didn't recognize.

"Noooo." Carmel shot up in her bed, breathing heavily, shivering in a cold sweat, with her head spinning. She couldn't believe her own voice was shrieking. She rubbed her forehead. "It was just a dream," she murmured over and over.

Carmel looked around her room, disoriented. She got out of bed and walked into her bathroom, patting her forehead with cold water to fully wake up and calm her nerves. The dream was actually indulgently wonderful until she got to the "other woman" part. Carmel hated cheating, lying, no-good men. "Please don't let this be a premonition. I can't handle that."

Rice wouldn't deceive her, would he? Later that night, when she went to the airport, she would find out.

As Carmel strolled through Lambert Airport, the feeling of *déjà vu* surrounded her. It was her dream to a *T,* from the flowers, her clothes, the card, and even the men behaving like they had in her dream. "This is scary. Rice, please don't do this to me," she whispered.

An eerie feeling descended on Carmel as she stood waiting for Rice by the same wall as in her dream. She wondered if fate would twist her happiness after months of her addiction to Rice.

When overhead television monitors flashed Flight 1147 had arrived, Carmel swallowed slowly, for strength, and nervously adjusted her clothes, removing imaginary dirt. Anxious, she began crossing and uncrossing her arms. The real waiting was just beginning.

Finally, through the throngs of travelers pressing toward her, she spotted Rice alone.

Carmel exhaled in relief and sniffed back her tears. She admired his Shemar Moore-handsome looks and confident gait with a physique that drew the attention of several ladies in the terminal, but Rice hadn't seemed to notice or he just ignored them.

Good sign.

As if sensing Carmel's presence, Rice searched the faces, before locking eyes with her in a loving stare. Rice's face softened with a widening smile as his steps increased toward her. Swiftly he approached Carmel as a predator and without saying a word devoured her mouth in a strong, possessive, and short whirlwind kiss.

Tears trickled down Carmel's face anyway as she submitted to his loving assault. *He wants me. He wants just me.*

"I missed you," Rice confided faintly as he gasped for air, caressing her cheeks, eyes, and neck.

Then Carmel noticed Rice's misty eyes. "Miss me again," she softly pleaded.

Rice's lips descended again, but this time the kiss was very thorough, gentle, and soft. Thank God she only had a bad dream. Rice stroked her chin, coaching her to open her eyes. He engulfed her in a protective hug. "I would ask you what you're doing here, but it's obvious you're in love with me." He squeezed her shoulders and kissed her forehead. "I missed you, baby, real bad. I even had a dream that another man was hitting on my woman. I woke up in a cold sweat. I almost called you."

Carmel froze and gave Rice an incredulous look. They were in the same nightmare.

Chapter Fifteen

"I want a small, intimate, and incredibly romantic wedding with you and me reciting our own vows."

Rice stared through the dancing flames flickering on the two candles centered on his dining room table at the woman whose words kept him mesmerized. He laid down his fork, reached across his place setting, and played with Carmel's fingers. "I think that's only appropriate, considering we've expressed our feelings so well on paper," he said, his voice husky with emotions.

Carmel nodded. Her eyes seemed to sparkle with the crystal stemware and china from their dinner of baked salmon, steamed vegetables, creamy spinach, and tortellini. "I still can't believe it. I'm in love with you, Rice Taylor."

"Just keep saying that for the next fifty years, woman." Rice removed his white linen napkin and stood, reaching for Carmel's hand. Rice enjoyed indulging Carmel with home-cooked meals as they planned their nuptials. Dinner always ended with a soft, lingering kiss.

Rice thrived on pampering his woman with faint music and a roaring fire on the remaining chilly winter nights as they communicated their love wordlessly with stares and winks.

"Rice, you're spoiling me," Carmel would always say sweetly before surrendering to his kiss.

But Rice's response would always be a stern, serious look. "Yeah, and there's no room for a compromise."

Their comfortable routine continued until they were married. Carmel started to attend more station-sponsored functions, since Rice was in town to escort her. Esther stopped calling him Rice-a-Roni, instead nicknaming him Hunk-a-Roni, Carmel's preferred Rice Krispie Treat.

Letters, flowers, and gifts still littered Carmel's office at WPLS. Rice surprised Carmel on her birthday, when he called her radio program.

"Welcome back. Let's continue our discussion on stress and depression. Before the break, many of you listed factors in your life you felt were causing stress. Now it's time to look at some solutions."

Glen cued Carmel to take a female caller on line three.

"Tracey, welcome to 'Don't Get French with Me.' Share with the listeners what works for you."

"Frenchie, girl, I'm really into yoga. Not only does it relax my body, but my mind, too. It works for me . . ."

Carmel's mind drifted as her long-winded caller talked about classes and techniques. She noticed Glen signaling that Rice was on line two.

She nodded with a dreamy smile. She loved a man who wasn't shy about publicly showing his affection. Rice's bold approaches made her feel cherished. Since his promotion to vice president of the Midwest region, Rice listened faithfully to every show.

"Thanks, Tracey. I haven't tried yoga yet, but I'll keep that in mind. For me, it's one special man, and he's on the line. Hi, honey."

"Hi, sweetheart. Happy birthday."

"Thank you."

"Can I add a comment to your show?"

"Of course."

"Well, the best way to keep stress away from your lady, brothas, is to take care of her emotionally, financially, and physically. Treat her special and make sure she's always happy. "

"I'm happy."

"I know," Rice agreed before hanging up.

Epilogue

On the night of June 1, in a small white renovated historic chapel surrounded with rows of perfectly planted white tulips, lilies, hyacinths, and dashes of red roses, a small crowd of fifty family members and friends waited for the bride and groom to exchange their vows. Many whispered about the hundreds of white roses and yards of tulle covering the altar, giving it an angelic look.

An hour before their wedding, Rice, handsomely dressed in his black Ralph Lauren tails tuxedo, slipped a pink satin-covered envelope under Carmel's dressing room door and strolled away without knocking. He had penned his last love letter as a single man, carefully stroking each word with gold ink on white water-stained parchment paper.

Carmel smiled when she noticed the dainty pink package on the floor. She scooped up the letter like it was a delicate infant, sniffing the scent of the envelope. She slowly opened the letter by unfolding all four sides. Surprisingly, she released dozens of white rose petals that drifted to her satin pumps. Rice's message contained few words but was worth a fortune to her. The sweetness of his letter competed with the attention of the fragrant flowers.

> *Carmel,*
>   *Words of love are meant to linger long after they're written. I can't wait to show you that I'm indeed the man worthy of your love, trust, and desire. Watch me, baby. I plan to back up my words until I take my final breath.*
>   *I'm closing my eyes and holding my breath until I see you, my bride.*
> *Rice,*
> *Your soon-to-be husband*

The Switch

by Lisa Watson

Dedication

The Switch is dedicated to those who supported me, believed in me, and never let me rest on my laurels. I'd like to acknowledge GOD for bestowing on me my spiritual gift and seeing that I use it.

ACKNOWLEDGMENTS

My undying love and gratitude goes to my father, the late George A. Dodson, Jr. I'll miss you every day for the rest of my life, but I'm "hanging tight!" And my mother, Harriette Y. Dodson, when I try to relay how much I love you and all you've done to make me who I am today, words fail me. Eric J. Watson, you are the Yang to my Yin. You are tireless in your pursuit to care for and nurture your wife and children. I love you. Brandon and Alyssa, your mommy loves you both for your patience, love and dedication to *Veggie Tales* DVDs. Linda, Loreen and David, you three are truly the best siblings ever. Doug, Martijn and Darlene are the perfect compliments for you. The Aunts: Betty, Margaret, Sondra and Adele. Nuff said! The true benchmarks for excellence are my beloved grandparents, Carl & Corona; you both are incredible role models. To my extended family of aunts, uncles and cousins, a world of thanks for showing me how strong and steadfast the love of family can be.

In my journey through life and in pursuit of my goals, I get by with a lot of help from my friends. Christy, Rena, Lisa and Deirdra—After knowing each other for over three decades, we are indeed Girlfriends! Stefania Wheeler, the best friend, Godmother to my children, and editor a woman could ever have. I love you, *Liebchen*! Sebastian, you've given me all the love and laughs I could ever need. *Te Amo*. Tina and Amy, you both have given me more long-distance love and friendship than I could use in a lifetime. To the newest link in my chain of love, Kimberly Weeter, thanks for being there and being you! The Boxford Court Cul de Friends, you guys are the best neighbors I've ever had!

Now to my literary anchors: "The Write Stuff" at WVU, The Long Ridge Writer's Group and my endearing, national and international fans that indulge me at my site, Fictioncove.com. Thank you all for being my sounding board, for letting me practice on you and for chewing me out when I didn't write fast enough! Pat Simmons, I knew I wasn't the only crazy woman around! What can I say, my cup runneth over. Thanks for bringing me along for the ride, for the long hours and showing me that being in the right place, at the right time, is indeed a gift from above. Parry "Ebony Satin" Brown, you've given me the opportunity of a lifetime, the vitality that only you can exude and the dedication to see this through. You are truly the Queen of Marketing and Special Projects, and I'm buying you a tiara the first chance I get! My heartfelt thanks and appreciation to Portia Cannon. You are tireless in your commitment, and you are the best agent I ever borrowed! Carl Weber and the Urban Books family, thank you for the chance to make my dream a reality!

Prologue

Norma Jean Anderson set the piping-hot tray of biscuits on the dinner table. Sitting down, she looked across at her husband and only child, her heart swelling with pride, until her son opened his mouth.

"Mom, this dinner is delicious! None of the women I date can hold a candle to your cooking!"

"Humph." Norma rolled her eyes, pointing a skinny finger in his direction. "I'd bet my favorite church dress none of those high-fashioned 'ho's you dally with have ever been in a kitchen, much less cooked a meal."

Heathcliffe Anderson lowered his glasses, staring reproachfully at his wife. He was a tall, broad man with stark white, curly hair, every bit as handsome as his son. Though he towered over her, he usually gave his petite wife run of the house, steering clear of her machinations, unless she was going overboard. Like now.

"Jeanie!"

She looked at her husband and glared. "What? Don't give me that look, Heathcliffe. You know I'm right."

"Now, darling, I think we should stay out of our son's love life."

Norma usually softened when he used that tone, but this was too important to just drop. "Cliff, our son is thirty-three years old, and it's high time he settled down."

Adrian sighed tiredly. "Starting a bit early this Sunday, aren't you, Mom? Usually you wait until dessert before I get the 'When are you going to settle down and give me grandbabies?' speech."

"You bet I'm going to start up again. Adrian, every woman in my Bible study group has a wallet full of pictures of their grandchildren. What have I got? Nothing! Just credit cards and pictures of you two."

"Gee, thanks," her husband said dryly.

"You know what I mean, Cliff." Norma redirected her efforts toward her insolent son. "Honey, it's time you stop playing around and start looking for a nice woman to marry, settle down, have babies with."

Adrian arched his eyebrow at his mother. Ever since her fiftieth birthday three years ago, she'd stepped up the campaign to get him settled down with any woman breathing and to impregnate her as soon as humanly possible. He would have laughed if she weren't serious. "Look, Mom, I appreciate the concern, but we've beat this dead horse enough, don't you think? I'm not looking for a wife right now; I've just gotten my business off the ground. I need to devote all my energy to making a name for myself."

Norma slammed her fork down on the table then began clearing the dinner dishes. "Oh, Adrian, please," she said derisively, grabbing his plate. "Your business has been off the ground for three years now. You've got one of the most successful real estate companies in Chicago. Besides that, it's making money hand over fist. How many more names do you need?"

She went to seize her husband's plate.

But he refused to relinquish his hold. "Oh no, you don't," he said quickly. "I'm still eating this."

In a huff she walked into the kitchen. Seconds later the two men heard pans banging loudly.

Adrian rubbed his temples in an effort to alleviate the pounding behind his eyes. "Dad, are you going to help me on this?"

His father beamed proudly. "Nope. You're doing just fine, son."

When Norma returned she tried a different approach. "Darling, I wish you'd reconsider. My friend Hazel has a niece who's perfect for you. She's smart, hardworking—"

"Does she have all her teeth, Mom?"

Years of conditioning had made Adrian immune to his mother's charm.

"Because the last 'nice girl' you set me up with didn't! You remember that wonderful woman who was so into the church? I doubt she mentioned the reason she was so dedicated was because she'd been sleeping with the deacon."

Norma put up her hands to halt his tirade. "Okay! I get the point but, honey, this one's different. Just let me do this for you."

"No! And that's final!"

He struggled to regain his composure. He didn't revel in hurting her feelings, but she needed to back off.

After a few moments of awkward silence, Adrian spoke. "Mom, I know you mean well, but I don't need you playing matchmaker." He rose from the table, kissing his mother's cheek. "Now if you'll excuse me, I've got to go. Dinner was great. Mind if I take home the leftovers?"

Norma could tell by the look in her son's eyes that it was time to drop the subject. Nodding, she went back in the kitchen and silently packed food in the disposable Glad plasticware. "Mark my words, my darling boy," she whispered in a voice only she could hear, "when all this is said and done you'll be thanking me for my interference."

Chapter One

"This is all Adrian's fault!" Justin Langley complained into the silence. "Why do I bother trying to keep him from looking bad? He doesn't even appreciate my efforts."

He stopped at a red light and tried to calm himself. His mind vividly recalled the night before and the events that had gotten him into this mess in the first place.

"Hey, the light's flashing on your answering machine," Stanley Bryant observed.

"Must be my flavor of the month," Adrian called to his three friends from the kitchen. "Someone hit play for me."

Dwayne Kendall pressed the message button.

A woman's voice resonated through the room. "Hi, honey. It's Mom. I haven't heard from you since you came over for dinner last week. I hope you're not still upset about our little disagreement."

"What disagreement?" Justin whispered.

Adrian waved his hand in dismissal. "Long story."

"Anyway, darling, I just wanted to let you know that I've arranged a date with you and Sabrina Ridgemont."

Adrian choked on his beer but was shushed by his friends who were paying close attention to Norma Anderson.

"It's set for tomorrow at eight o'clock at Catch 35. I know it's one of your favorite restaurants, so you should have a wonderful time."

A horn blared behind him, effectively snapping Justin out of his reverie. It was a moment before he'd realized the light had turned green. He glanced at his watch and pursed his lips. *If she's there, she'd be waiting almost fifteen minutes by now.* "Why should I care if I'm late?" he shouted at the steering wheel. "It's not like it's my date. If Adrian wants to be a player and dog every girl he comes in contact with, who am I to interfere?"

You're a nice guy, his conscience reminded him.

"You the man! No matter what, you always have my back." Justin mimicked Adrian's tone. *I guess tonight's no exception.*

Catch 35 was close to downtown Chicago's finest theatres. That, combined with its impeccable reputation, guaranteed a constant throng of patrons. Finding a parking space during dinnertime on a Friday night was practically unheard of. Justin didn't even bother trying; instead he left his car with the valet parking attendant. After all, he was only going to be there a few minutes. Silently he hoped the black slacks and sweater he'd worn to work would be adequate. This was Adrian's stomping ground, not his.

Justin paused short of the front door, stepping to the side so he wouldn't be seen. *What the hell am I doing?* he asked himself. *This is crazy. Why should I give a damn if he stands her up? It's not my problem. I'm not the one being a dog.*

Suddenly their earlier conversation surfaced again.

"You aren't going to stand her up, are you?" Justin asked incredulously.

Adrian picked up the remote and aimed it toward the entertainment center. He shrugged, not bothering to look up. "My mother took it upon herself to set this up so she can deal with the fallout. I'm going to show her once and for all that I don't need her interfering in my love life!" Adrian threw the remote on the couch. "Look, man, I'll see you at the gym tomorrow."

Justin blinked to clear the image from his mind. "I guess you don't need me interfering either," he said aloud.

He turned on his heel to go retrieve his car. He'd gotten two steps when he stopped. Justin stifled a curse. Indecisiveness battled with his conscience until, finally, the decision was made. He strode to the door, wrenching it open. Once inside, he shrugged out of his black leather jacket and tossed it over his arm. Taking a calming breath, he approached the hostess' desk and asked to be shown to Adrian's table.

Justin had never been to Catch 35. As they walked, the hostess pointed out a few particulars, like the large Grand Piano Bar that hosted an array of local jazz artists.

One happened to be playing at the moment. The restaurant was decorated in rich peach, green, and blue hues. There were large, almost floor-to-ceiling square windows and opulent lighting fixtures. The effect was dramatic, with a romantic flare.

As they walked through the dimly lit dining room, the hostess mentioned the menu was changed daily, then pointed out the fresh seafood displayed in a large glass cooler near the open kitchen. She stopped at a small, intimate table and invited him to enjoy the evening.

Sabrina had risen when they arrived. She stared at him with interest.

Justin focused on the woman standing before him. She was breathtaking; at least six feet tall, with the shapeliest body he'd ever seen.

When she spoke the name Adrian, he was so mesmerized, he could only stand there gaping at her. Her voice had a silky tone that caressed his ears.

It felt like a full minute before he could find his voice. Clearing his throat, he extended his hand. "Sabrina?"

She smiled, accepting his outstretched hand.

"I'm sorry you've been kept waiting. It couldn't be helped." Justin remained standing until she was seated comfortably in the cozy booth. When he sat down across from her he couldn't help but smile.

"It's no problem. I was a few minutes late myself," she said companionably. "It's been a while since I've been in the city. I'd forgotten how hard it is to find a parking space."

Her sultry voice put him at ease.

"I had the same problem." He grinned. Sabrina immediately returned the gesture.

He tried not to openly stare at her, but it was difficult; she had a dazzling smile, dimples enhancing its warmth. Her straight, shoulder-length, brown hair was streaked with highlights and pulled neatly behind her ears. She wore a black long-sleeved, knee-length dress. It looked like silk and hugged her in all the right places.

Justin swallowed hard then grasped his hands together under the table; they itched with an intensity to punch Adrian the moment he saw him. He cleared his throat. "Sabrina, there's something I—"

"Hello, Ridge. I thought that was you," a voice boomed from above them.

Sabrina and Justin looked up in unison and saw a man standing there. Justin didn't recognize him, but from the ashen look on Sabrina's face, he realized immediately that she did. Justin took a few seconds to assess the stranger. He fit the cliché: tall, dark, and handsome. He looked like a model; Justin disliked him instantly.

"So, how have you been, Ridge? It's been, what . . . three years now?"

Sabrina took a deep breath. She tried not to let him get to her, but it was difficult. He was as annoying as a telemarketer calling at dinnertime. "Actually it's been two," she said flatly. "And the name is Sabrina."

"Oh, right," he said nonchalantly. "You didn't care for that nickname much, did you?" His gaze flickered over Justin then back to Sabrina.

She eyed him pointedly.

His mouth raised on one side in a lazy smile. "Well, aren't you going to introduce me?"

Sabrina remained silent.

After a few discomfitting moments, the stranger extended his hand toward Justin. "I'm Christopher Warren, Sabrina's ex-fiancé." He paused purposefully. "And you are?"

Justin looked at Sabrina's stricken face. He longed to put the arrogant bastard in his place. He stood, firmly grasping Christopher's hand. "I'm the man fortunate enough to have a date with this incredible woman. The name's Anderson . . . Adrian Anderson."

Christopher grasped Justin's hand then pumped it vigorously. He scanned his mental Rolodex to see if Adrian Anderson was anyone of consequence. He came up blank a few moments later and abruptly turned off the charm.

Justin remained standing, keeping constant eye contact with Mr. Arrogant. If he wanted to intimidate Sabrina any further with his little walk down memory lane, he'd have to get through him to do it. Granted, Justin had just claimed to be Sabrina's date and her best friend, but it was for a good cause, he rationalized. He couldn't stand by and let her be humiliated in front of that bozo. Lie or no lie, he wasn't going to let this man play any more head games with her.

Christopher noted Justin's rigid stance, his challenging stare. Brushing an imaginary piece of lint from his suit jacket, he cleared his throat. "Well, don't let me interrupt your intimate evening any further. It's been a pleasure, Mr. Anderson. Sabrina, it was great seeing you again." He winked before walking away.

Justin's eyes followed him back to his table, where he joined an attractive woman, one who was practically spilling out of her too-small dress. He noticed Sabrina had also watched him leave. He heard her expel a slow breath.

"I'm sorry about that. He's the last person I expected to run in to."

Justin returned to his seat. "I'm glad to hear that."

He could see Sabrina was still upset by the encounter. Reaching over, he gently squeezed her hand. Her fingers were cold and trembling. "I take it things didn't end amicably for you two?"

Sabrina blinked to keep the tears at bay. She took a

few ragged breaths. "No, they didn't." She shrugged, forcing a smile. "Anyway, it was a long time ago; it should be water under the bridge by now."

"But it isn't," he surmised.

The waiter arrived at their table, precluding further conversation.

With reluctance Justin released her hand.

Once he'd welcomed them to the restaurant, the waiter proceeded to go over the wine list and the chef's specialties for the evening.

"Would you like me to order our appetizers?"

"That would be nice," Sabrina told him.

"We'd like the fried calamari and steamed Prince Edward Island mussels." Justin looked over the wine list. "We'd also like a bottle of Lamberti Pinot Grigio."

"Excellent choice, sir." The waiter retreated to place their order.

Sabrina thought the pain and humiliation she felt at Christopher's betrayal was ancient history. She was wrong. Seeing him brought it all back, fresh and new, but the genuine concern in Adrian's eyes rallied her spirits. Taking deep breaths she willed the pain to subside. Christopher was no doubt at his table enjoying his dinner. She refused to let him ruin hers.

Justin watched various emotions flitter across her face. "If you want to talk about it, I'm a great listener."

Sabrina waved her hand in dismissal. "How about we just forget Christopher Warren ever stopped by?"

Justin flashed a grin. "Consider him forgotten."

While Justin studied his menu, Sabrina scrutinized him from under her lashes. She'd observed him walk toward her table, silently praying that he was her date. When he halted in front of her table, her breathing stopped. It's not that he was drop-dead gorgeous; no, his was the dangerous type of handsome, the one that grew the longer you were around him.

Suddenly Justin looked up from his menu. "Do you know what you want?"

Startled, Sabrina blinked. "Huh?"

"Have you decided what you're having for dinner?"

"Oh, no, not yet," Sabrina said in a slightly elevated voice. She looked over at his tall, muscular physique, more than evident through the snug-fitting sweater, and nervously took a sip of her water.

Adrian had jet-black, curly hair that was closely cut. His skin tone, somewhere between light- and medium-brown suited him. By far the most intriguing thing about him was his eyes, which held a mystery all their own. They were light-brown, with a hint of green. When he smiled at her, they twinkled mischievously.

"Wow." She sighed audibly.

Justin looked up in confusion. "Excuse me?"

Sabrina was mortified. She hadn't realized she'd said the word aloud. *Oh God, no, I didn't just salivate out loud. Where is a black hole when you need one?* Sabrina groaned inwardly. "I said *now*," she rushed out, "as in, what were you going to say before Christopher interrupted us?"

Clearing his throat, Justin looked down at the table. Now that the chance to clear the air had arrived, he wasn't that eager to set the record straight. So far Adrian was doing rather well on this blind date. He wasn't convinced Justin would fare as well if he switched places. Having the sparkle in Sabrina's eyes suddenly fade or the smile on her lips slip away wasn't a risk he was willing to take, not yet. He desperately wanted to get to know her, if that meant posing as Adrian for a while.

"Adrian?"

Justin snapped out of his reverie. "Hmmm?"

"Was there something you wanted to tell me?"

"Oh, I . . . it was . . . nothing important."

"Are you sure?"

"Positive." Justin picked up his menu. "So, let's see what the big buzz is about this place."

"That's a good one," Sabrina said, laughing. "From what I've heard, you should be telling me what the house specialties are."

Justin could've kicked himself for the slip. "Too true," he said quickly. "Well I'm partial to salmon, but I have been known to get adventurous from time to time."

Sabrina eyed him coyly. "Oh, really? Sounds intriguing, Mr. Anderson."

Their server arrived with the appetizers and wine. Deftly opening the bottle, he covered the neck with a white linen napkin before giving the cork to Justin. The waiter poured out a small sample then handed him the glass.

Swirling the dark liquid a few times, Justin leaned over and held the glass to Sabrina's lips.

She smiled and slowly sipped the wine. After a few seconds she swallowed and nodded to the waiter, who quickly poured generous portions into both glasses, set the bottle between them, and left.

They kept up light conversation while they ate their appetizers. Often Justin would look up to catch Sabrina putting a mussel or calamari into her mouth. When she'd take a bite, her eyes closed, a look of pure bliss on her face. Just watching her eat left him captivated. He could only stare in amazement. At times his fork paused in mid-air, his breathing would halt and resume only after she'd swallowed. "You must love seafood."

"I can't help it. I'm a native Washingtonian, so I guess it's hereditary. My father taught me how to eat Maryland blue crabs by the time I was three. There's no doubt that seafood is in my blood." She took another bite before scrunching her nose at him playfully.

He had to fight the overwhelming urge to reach over and kiss the tip of that nose. *Good Lord, she is beautiful. That seafood is damned lucky.*

Ten minutes later they were still pondering their dinner selections when Sabrina lowered her menu to gaze at him. The moment their eyes locked, their surroundings faded into the background. Each assessed the other with a frankness that left the air around them heavy with tension.

Justin was the first to recover. Sitting back, he crossed his arms in front of his chest, eyeing her pointedly. "So, Sabrina, do you see anything you like?"

Sabrina's eyes twinkled, followed by a slow smile across her face. She didn't know if he was purposefully using a double entendre. She decided to find out. Leaning back against the plush cushion, Sabrina gazed at him like a well-placed caress. She knew by the darkening of his hazel eyes the similarity wasn't lost on him. He'd reacted exactly as intended. It was bold and uncharacteristic of her, but she reveled in her newfound bravado. When she spoke, her voice had a softer, deeper timbre than before. "There are many things in this restaurant that catch my eye."

Undaunted, Justin leaned in so close, Sabrina's pupils dilated. "Is that so?" he said in a voice that caressed her right back. "Then I'd say we're in total agreement." Raising his wineglass he toasted her.

Chapter Two

The real Adrian looked at his watch for the fourth time. He grimaced. "What the hell is keeping Justin? He didn't phone any of you to say he'd be late?"

Dwayne and Stanley shook their heads in the negative. The four men had been friends since elementary school; Adrian was the prima donna, Justin the keeper of the peace, Dwayne was the wise guy, and Stanley, AKA Stan the Answer Man, always had the plan to get them in or out of trouble. While they were inseparable, Adrian considered Justin to be his best friend. Justin felt the same, but had known Stan the longest, usually deferring to him for the more serious issues.

Adrian hit the basketball against the back wall in frustration. "Well, this is just great. We can't get a game going with three players."

"What about Malcolm?" Dwayne replied. "He arrived a few minutes ago."

"Malcolm Douglas?" Adrian snorted. "You're kidding, right? Dwayne, if I wanted my grandfather to play, I would've asked him. You know Malcolm has two left feet and neither one of them work!"

"How about some lay-ups?" Stan suggested.

Adrian grabbed his gym bag. "Forget this. I'm out. If Justin's tired ass gets here, kick it for me!" Adrian stomped off the court while Stan grabbed a nearby ball.

At six foot, four and 230 pounds, Stan had no trouble hitting a fade-away shot. His dark baldhead glistened with sweat as he charged the hoop repeatedly, hitting with staggering accuracy every time. He played around a few minutes before noticing Dwayne sitting on a nearby bench. "Hey, what happened to you? Are we going to shoot some hoops or what?"

Nodding, Dwayne hit his washboard stomach. "Yeah, sure. I've got time to kill before I have to pick Tracey up from work. I might as well be maintaining this awesome body by showing you how it's done."

Stan rolled his eyes then passed the ball. "Spare me the Bowflex commercial, will you?"

"It works, man. You really need to try it. You know, once you're over two-fifty, it's harder getting the weight off."

Stan snorted. "Who you calling fat?"

"If the tire fits, wear it." Dwayne whipped by him, slam-dunking the ball for effect.

"You know, I never understood why you don't get another car. That way you won't have to worry about picking Tracey up all the time."

Dwayne was dribbling the ball but stopped suddenly. "Oh, are you offering to pay the car note?"

Stan couldn't shake his head fast enough. "Man, please."

"Then shut your no-wife-having butt up and shoot!"

* * *

"Would you care for dessert?" Justin asked Sabrina. "The chocolate terrine is sinful." At least he hoped it was.

"Where would I put it?" She clutched her stomach. "Dinner was delicious, Adrian. I've never had seared Chilean sea bass before. Thanks for suggesting it. I'm glad we came here, despite our earlier interruption."

"I'm glad we did too," Justin replied, feeling a pang of guilt at deceiving her. He'd started out intending to save her from further discomfort by her ex-fiancé. Along the way, his good intentions took a sharp turn down "selfish lane." Adrian's abominable behavior set off a course of events from which Justin was having a hard time wanting to extricate himself. He'd been attracted to the woman across from him the moment he stopped in front of her table. She intrigued him like no other woman he'd ever met. He was hard pressed to tell her he wasn't the man she thought he was.

When Justin looked up there was surprise on Sabrina's face. "What?" he inquired.

"I must admit to having reservations when my aunt suggested I meet you. Now that I have, I don't think I'll be doubting her matchmaking abilities again."

"'Again'?" he sputtered playfully. "Oh, so you're just going to make a habit of going out on blind dates?"

Sabrina took a sip of her wine and set it down slowly. She studied him for a moment. "Well, that depends."

Those three spoken words altered the atmosphere around them. The air was laced with innuendo so thick it was palpable. Suddenly the thought of Sabrina out with another man was unsettling. When his mind conjured up an image of her with the real Adrian, Justin's stomach tightened. He didn't like the feeling one bit. With a concentrated effort, Justin forced himself back to the conversation at hand.

"It depends, huh?" He studied her. "On what?"

Sabrina looked at him from under her lashes and smiled seductively. "On what happens after this one."

Justin was speechless. How could he tell her that this date wasn't even supposed to happen? Or worse still, that he was enjoying himself immensely and was hard-pressed to end it.

When the bill came, Justin and Sabrina reached for it simultaneously. He batted her hand away, refusing her repeated attempts to split the bill. For him, money definitely was an object, but he'd enjoyed himself too much to worry about how much dinner would set him back.

Justin placed the customer copy of the bill in his wallet and reached for her arm. "Ready?"

Nodding, Sabrina retrieved her bag.

Putting his hand lightly at her elbow, Justin escorted her out of the restaurant. "Where are you parked?" he asked, hoping to prolong the evening.

"Around the corner. I was able to find a space that's not too far."

"I'll walk with you."

"You don't have to," Sabrina said quickly.

Justin linked his fingers through hers. "Yes, I do."

The unexpected touch made her quiver inside.

They strolled down the sidewalk in relative silence, each in thought. Smiling, Sabrina hugged her coat tighter. Even in the cold, she enjoyed walking in downtown Chicago. She loved the way it looked at night, especially Michigan Avenue. The Magnificent Mile, as it was called, was shopper's paradise, resplendent with white lights draped throughout the trees and horse-drawn carriages. It offered a romantic interlude among the large horde of cars and foot traffic.

Justin leaned toward her. "You're smiling," he whispered in her ear. "What are you thinking about?" His warm breath made her skin tingle.

How wonderful your hand feels intertwined with mine. "The Magnificent Mile," she said aloud.

His booming laugh filled the air. "Uh-oh, are you one of those women who moonlights as a professional shopper?"

"Me?" She laughed aloud. "Hardly. I just love the way it looks at night. I'm not much for large crowds or traffic. Both are synonymous with Michigan Avenue."

"True."

Sabrina stopped in front of a black Ford Explorer. "I'm right here," she said softly.

"So you are."

Justin reached out and slowly raised her hand to his lips. They connected for a brief moment before he reluctantly released her hand. "I, uh, I had a really great time, Sabrina. It was a pleasure meeting you."

"Likewise, Adrian." Her voice shook slightly. "Thank you for dinner and thank you for the date. It was a pleasant surprise." Sabrina hesitated a moment before getting into her truck and starting the engine.

Justin stood there staring at her, for want of something better to do.

Sabrina rolled the window down, and he immediately stepped closer to her door. She tentatively handed him a business card. "I know you didn't ask for my number, but . . . I just thought I'd give it to you anyway. Just in case," Sabrina said awkwardly.

He took the card and studied it closely. He stared at it a few seconds before finding his voice. "I'm glad you did. Thank you."

"You're welcome. Well, good night, Adrian."

"Good night, Sabrina. Drive safely."

"I will." Sabrina rolled up her window and waved good-bye before cautiously pulling into traffic.

Justin watched until her vehicle faded from view. He looked down at the crisp, white card in his hand; her name and the title *Recruiter* were etched boldly on the expensive stock paper. He flipped the card over in his fingers, pondering his sanity.

Pulling his cell phone out of his jacket pocket, he turned it back on. After a few seconds the small icon for messages flashed on the screen. Justin grimaced. At least one of those would be from Adrian—he'd be expecting the reason Justin had stood them up. "What in the hell have I just done?" He breathed raggedly. Shaking his head, he shoved his phone into his pocket before walking back to the restaurant to retrieve his car.

Chapter Three

Opening the door to his Lincoln Park apartment, Justin flipped on the light and dived for the phone. "Hello!" he said breathlessly.

It was the real Adrian firing off a barrage of questions. "Man, what the hell happened to you? Why didn't you call me back? Don't tell me you didn't get my messages."

Justin's face contorted at hearing Adrian's voice. "Sorry, man. I got tied up. I had to take care of something."

Adrian expelled a loud breath into the phone. "What could've been more important than our game?" he demanded indignantly.

Seconds ticked by with painful sluggishness while Justin searched for the right words to describe the situation. His right eyebrow furrowed in concentration and his leg tapped rapidly against the wood floor, as he struggled for an answer.

"Justin!" Adrian shouted into the phone. "Are we talking via satellite or what? Answer the question!" Adrian's impatience was tangible; he wasn't going to drop the subject.

Annoyed, Justin wondered why he put up with his friend's tirade. Silently, he berated himself for answering the phone at all. "I had to work late."

" 'Work late'? It took you two minutes to tell me you had to work late? Come on, J. That was lame. You'll have to do better than that."

"I was at work and—"

"You met this girl, right?" Adrian's tone perked up—nosiness got the better of him.

"Yes. No!" Justin stammered.

"Which is it?" Adrian chuckled. "Look, if you don't want to tell me about her yet that's cool, but I expect a full report soon."

"No, really, it's not what you think."

"Sure, it isn't." Adrian hung up.

"Great." Justin replaced the receiver on its cradle with a loud slam. He threw his keys in the ceramic bowl on the coffee table and collapsed onto the couch. Cradling his head in both hands, he expelled a loud breath. "Well, that went smooth." Sitting up, Justin suddenly looked around the room as if the answer to his dilemma was spray painted across the walls.

Justin loved his apartment; it was as comfortable as Adrian's was sleek. It was right off Lake Shore Drive in an old six-floor, vintage-style building with an impressive rotunda-style entry. It was on a residential street lined with trees, and his balcony had an impressive view of Lake Michigan. It was small, only nine hundred square feet, but it had charm. Two bedrooms were separated by a living room/dining room combination. It had one bathroom and a small but well-outfitted kitchen.

Whenever Justin was troubled, he went out on the balcony to think. Now was no different. Walking outside Justin leaned over the wooden deck beam, his elbows supporting his weight.

The night was cold, clear, and peaceful. His apartment was on the top floor, affording him a picturesque view of lights flickering from nearby buildings and the lake. He closed his eyes and rubbed his throbbing temples. *What the hell have you done?*

He went over the events of the night. What started out as a kind deed had blown into a full-scale bad idea.

Justin hadn't meant to say he was Adrian, but seeing that jerk Warren, combined with Sabrina's distress, caused him to act without thinking about the ramifications. Protecting Sabrina from further discomfort was foremost in his mind when he'd assumed his friend's identity. He couldn't put into words how he felt watching her interact with her ex-fiancé. It wasn't a pleasant feeling, though it was strong enough to keep him from blurting out his real name. He'd tell her eventually, just not in front of Christopher Warren. Deep inside him was a startling need to protect her from further hurt.

When he felt the familiar pull of attraction, Justin knew the consequences of his reckless actions were about to escalate.

He laughed aloud at the irony. He was there to break a date for Adrian and before he'd batted an eyelash, he was hooked. The chemistry was definitely there.

Sabrina was intelligent, witty, and incredibly sexy. He was certain she'd never get involved with a liar; though he'd met her only a few hours ago, he could tell she was an honest, decent person.

Pulling the business card from his pocket, Justin flipped it over. Her home number was on the back, beckoning to him. His inner voice rang in his ear. *Tell the truth.*

It was simple; he'd call her up, explain he'd pretended to be Adrian so she wouldn't feel awkward in front of her ex-fiancé.

He looked at his watch. It was late, but not too late for something this important. Who knows? Maybe she'd see the humorous side of this fiasco—maybe even go out on a date with him being himself.

Who am I kidding? She'll be pissed. Adrian will, too, when he finds out.

Angrily, Justin shoved the card back in his pocket. The next day was time enough to deal with reality. At the moment, he wanted to take a hot shower and live in the fantasy. Dousing the lights Justin headed to the bathroom with purposeful strides.

Stripping off his clothes, he laid them across the toilet seat. Turning the shower spray on full blast he hummed a tune while waiting for the water to heat up. Eventually steam swirled around the bathroom, engulfing the mirror.

He eased into the shower. His smooth, light-brown skin took on a red hue as hot water pelted his body. He breathed slowly until his taut muscles and nerves began to relax. Leaning his head against the cool tiled wall, he sighed loudly.

Suddenly, Sabrina materialized before his eyes. Her flawless espresso skin, dimples, combined with her luscious smile drove him to distraction. She wore a tight, red halter dress.

"Turn around," he said thickly.

When she did, he noticed her dress pitched daringly low. Sabrina looked at him over her shoulder, enticing him, beckoning him.

He moved toward her, halting when she shook her head. He stood riveted to his spot.

She turned around, walking slowly to him, her eyes never breaking contact with his. Stopping mere inches from him, she held out her arms.

Suddenly, Justin was in front of her, touching her, rubbing his hands over her shoulders.

She tipped her head back and laughed.

It was a sexy, throaty laugh that caused his stomach to tighten. Pure need coursed through his veins, pulling at his groin, making his mouth dry.

He pulled Sabrina to him, desperate to claim her mouth. When their lips finally touched, he almost died from the sheer pleasure that flooded his system. Justin moaned audibly. The sound wrenched him from his dream, catapulting him back to reality.

Opening his eyes he blinked in confusion. The breath burst from his lungs in rapid succession. The way his body trembled with arousal at seeing her, tasting her, astounded him.

"Sabrina," he whispered, "what are you doing to me?" He stood there listening, as if he expected her to answer him. "Get a grip, man," he admonished.

Clenching his teeth he flipped the cold-water lever all the way to the right. After a few seconds Justin stepped out of the frigid spray to dry off. He hung his towel on the bar, grabbed his clothes, and headed to the bedroom.

Because space was minimal, Justin turned his master bedroom into his office and exercise room. Though small, the second bedroom had enough space for his queen-size bed. Matching nightstands held gray ceramic lamps, his cordless phone base and alarm clock. He'd recently painted the stark white walls a soft, light gray, giving the small room a masculine feel. The bed had an enormous navy blue goose down comforter, a present from his parents. At first he'd laughed at the girly present. All his laughter and bantering ceased when he tried it. It was the most comfortable thing he'd ever slept under.

Walking to the closet, he threw his clothes in the pile reserved for dry cleaning. He retrieved a pair of cotton pajama bottoms from his dresser and pulled them on. Turning the lamp out he sank beneath the covers. In his current state of anxiety, Justin thought sleep would elude him. He was wrong. He was sound asleep seconds after his head hit the pillow.

Chapter Four

Sabrina's alarm blasted the silence. Her arm snaked from under the covers to smack the off button before she'd even opened her eyes. Turning over on her back, Sabrina blinked a few times while stretching languidly. Smiling, she looked up at her pale peach ceiling. Her evening with Adrian had been an unexpected success. Even Christopher's sudden appearance, mingled with his boorish behavior, hadn't dampened the evening. Adrian was warm, polite, and she'd definitely enjoyed his conversation. That he was tall, gorgeous, and beyond sexy only heightened the instant attraction she'd felt.

Gorgeous? Her mind interceded. *When had Adrian turned from handsome to gorgeous?*

Their short walk to her car confirmed that he was at least six foot, two; his broad shoulders and large frame complemented his height. He obviously worked out because she hadn't noticed any excess weight on him. On the contrary, his body looked firm in all the right places. His hair made her want to run her fingers through it.

His face was devoid of facial hair, giving him a boyish quality that captivated Sabrina, until she'd noticed the brilliance of his smile. He had the type of looks she usually steered clear of. Her history with Christopher had made that realization a painful lesson for her. She closed her eyes, allowing recollection to proceed.

Years ago, Christopher was everything she thought she'd ever want or need. He was witty, charming, such a loving man. He'd done more than sweep her off her feet; he'd tackled her. Tall, incredibly handsome, successful, and ambitious, Christopher had made her feel like a queen. She was wary of his intentions at first, but despite herself, she was drawn to him. They had a whirlwind romance that had led to an extravagant engagement, with plans for an even bigger wedding. A wedding that never happened. It was a month before their marriage was supposed to take place, when she'd discovered the true nature of the beast.

What started as one of his typical business trips had turned into the second most disastrous moment in her life. Sabrina arrived at the Ritz-Carlton hotel in downtown Chicago to meet her best friend, Lauren, for afternoon tea. It was her first time at the illustrious hotel. She was in quiet awe at the hotel's opulent splendor. They enjoyed the posh treatment by the hotel staff; the windows in the Greenhouse Café afforded an incredible view of the city.

Sabrina had just bitten into a scone covered with fresh clotted cream, when her calm, relaxed demeanor came screeching to a halt. Walking into the crowded café was her fiancé, Christopher, with a well-dressed woman Sabrina had never seen before. Her eyes followed their procession to a table some distance from hers, but still in plain sight. She watched in silent, disgust-filled misery, as Christopher and his unidentified beauty ripped her heart out of her well-dressed body, shredding it carelessly over the highly polished tiled floor.

For anyone observing, they looked like a couple in love that would soon be utilizing one of the plush hotel suites. Bile rose to her throat, and her palms grew clammy.

Abruptly she excused herself, barely making it into the immaculate bathroom stall, where she lost the few bites of scone she'd eaten, along with the Earl Grey tea. Tears threatened to engulf her when she'd returned to her table, but she refused to make a scene in public.

Lauren had seen the trouser snake with his date moments after Sabrina had. When her friend returned to the table, Lauren silently signaled the server to bring their check. Sabrina blinked furiously to keep the tears in place. It was during that time her eyes wandered again to his table.

Seconds later it was a laughing Christopher who looked up, unexpectedly locking gazes with Sabrina. Recognition instantly registered on his features; his smile wavered then slid abruptly off his face. Time slowed, finally screeching to a halt as they conversed with each other in utter silence from across the crowded room—accusation, admission, acceptance, and dismissal.

Lauren settled their bill. Afterward she gently suggested they leave.

Numb, Sabrina nodded then stood on legs that valiantly supported her without buckling. Being betrayed by Christopher was a pill that took months to swallow. It made her wary of men, or finding a truthful, lasting relationship.

*   *   *

"Stop this," Sabrina said loudly. Eager to end the stroll down disaster alley, she threw the wheat-colored, damask comforter aside with flourish. Striding over to the window, she pulled back the floral curtains. Instantly sunlight flooded the room, bathing it in warmth. Grabbing her robe, she went into the bathroom to shower.

Chapter Five

The employees at the McMillan Group dressed in business casual, unless they had clients or prospective hires coming in for meetings. Sabrina's schedule was clear that day, so she chose a pair of navy blue slacks, a yellow cardigan with a short-sleeve white blouse. Navy blue flats and gold hoop earrings, plus a matching chain, topped off her outfit. Sabrina sailed into Suite 1147, practically singing a hello to Janice Carmichael, the receptionist and the world's oldest busybody.

At sixty-two, Janice was twice divorced, a widow, and having a fling with a man ten years her junior. To top it off, she had a body to rival Tina Turner's.

When Sabrina stopped at her desk, Janice pulled down the glasses already perched dangerously low on the bridge of her nose. "Miss Ridgemont, what's going on with you?"

Sabrina scanned her messages. "What do you mean?"

"Either you just won the lottery, or you finally met the most handsome man in Oak Brook."

"Excuse me?"

"You know the one. He works down on the fifth floor in Legal. I tell you, if I were twenty years younger . . ."

Sabrina laughed. "Don't you mean *thirty*?"

"Hah! That boy doesn't know what he's missing. As my mother used to say, 'It ain't over till it's over.' Ooh, the things I could do to him," the woman said dreamily.

Sabrina cringed at the image that popped into her mind. "Okay, Janice, that really was too much information." Turning on her heel, Sabrina prayed she'd be able to escape before her co-worker went into interrogation mode. She'd made it three feet before the energetic woman leaned over the desk to call after her.

"Wait. You can't leave before I hear the juice! Come on, girl, you can tell me. You know I can keep a secret!"

Sabrina almost bit her tongue to keep from laughing. It was well known around the office that if you wanted to keep your business your own, you didn't tell Janice a word, much less a sentence. The look Sabrina gave must have spoken volumes because the receptionist rolled her eyes then sat down to answer the phone.

Hanging her coat on the knob behind her office door, Sabrina put her purse in the bottom desk drawer and sat down. She thought of the elderly woman again. "Keep a secret indeed," she said aloud. "Now that was a good one."

Flipping on her computer, she leaned back in her chair while it booted up, to read her phone messages. There was one marked urgent from her aunt Hazel, causing Sabrina immediate concern. Had something happened to her aunt or dad? Sabrina hit the second speed dial number on her phone. Her aunt answered on the second ring. Without preamble, Sabrina asked what was wrong.

"Nothing, sweetheart." Nothing for her father's sister

was definitely something. Hazel couldn't go a day without being brought up to speed on her latest project—her niece's love life.

Sabrina sat deeper into her chair. "Nothing, huh? Then why did you leave a message saying it was urgent?" She sat up abruptly. "Is Dad okay?"

"Of course he is, honey. I just wanted to find out how your date went. I called you last night and left a voice message on your phone. Didn't you get it?"

"What? The only thing you wanted to ask was how my date went? Why am I not surprised?"

"Now don't go using that tone with me, missy," Hazel said indignantly. "If you would've dished the dirt last night, I wouldn't be calling you at work this morning."

Shaking her head, Sabrina smiled into the phone. The woman would never cease her meddling. Frowning, she looked down at her watch. "I'm sorry, Hazel, I've got to go now. I've got a meeting in ten minutes, and I can't be late. I'll call you tonight when I get home, I promise."

"You mean I have to wait all day to find out?" Hazel was as relentless as a pit bull, when she wanted information.

"I'm afraid so," her niece said, laughing. "Say hello to Dad for me." She hung up.

Without warning the door to Sabrina's office burst open, and a tall, shapely redhead walked in, dramatically plopping herself in the chair across from her desk.

"Well?" the woman demanded. "Don't make me ask how it went."

"Lauren, don't you have something better to do?"

"Sabrina!" Her friend gave her a come-clean-or-I'll-clobber-you look.

"Okay, okay," she acquiesced. "It was great."

Screaming softly, Lauren spun around in her chair.

"I told you it would work out. Now come on, we've got a meeting to go to."

She followed Sabrina out the office and down the hall. "Did Richard mention he wants us to attend that job fair at UIUC in three weeks?"

Sabrina nodded, flipping through her day planner. "When will the information packets be back from the printer?"

"They're due Thursday. The cool pens with our logo on them arrived yesterday. I tell you, if I was a college senior, I'd come work for us."

They were almost to the conference room, when Lauren whispered into Sabrina's ear, "So, Miss Secretive, is he cute?"

Justin stared blankly at the screen. He'd gone over the same line of computer code for the last five minutes. He was ready to pitch his monitor out the window. The only thing he could concentrate on was the business card burning a hole in his pocket. *This is ridiculous.* He reached inside his back pocket and eyed the telephone number Sabrina had written in bold, elegant strokes. Even her handwriting was attractive. Picking up the receiver, he pursed his lips in concentration. This was a mistake, a huge one, yet he couldn't help himself. He'd been thinking about her all day. It was starting to affect his work, not to mention his peace of mind.

A loud, screeching sound broke through his daydream. He'd been holding the phone so long the dial tone stopped working. Pressing the hook button again he dialed her number. The phone rang three times before she picked up.

"The McMillan Group, Sabrina Ridgemont speaking."

"Hi, Sabrina. This is Adrian." Justin grimaced at how strange the name felt on his lips.

Sabrina's stomach did flip-flops at the sound of the deep, familiar voice. Startled, she sat back in her chair so suddenly, it almost fell over backward. She grabbed the desk to steady herself. The action left her winded, giving her voice a breathless edge. "Hi, Adrian. How are you?" She squeezed her eyes shut, groaning inwardly. *Great, with that voice you should be lounging on a divan somewhere with a drink in your hand.*

Justin closed his eyes. *Lousy. I'm a liar, and I can't get you off my mind,* he thought. "Just fine, and you?"

At that moment, if the power in her office had gone out, the smile on Sabrina's face would've lit up the room. "I've been great. I was starting to think you weren't going to call." *Okay, now you sound pressed,* she scolded herself.

"To be honest, you've been on my mind so much, I couldn't help but call."

There was a note in his voice that made her tingle. "Really? And why was that?" she asked in a calm voice that camouflaged her feelings.

"So that I can get some work done, of course." He laughed.

She giggled. "I suppose it's a great deal of work running a real estate company. Do you have a large office?"

His mind raced for an appropriate answer. "Uh, not really. There are only three people in the office besides me: my partner Christy, our receptionist Donna, and our newest associate, Diego. Our office is downtown . . ." *What are you doing?* a voice screamed inside his head. He was desperate to know her, but continuing this charade would ultimately come back to haunt him.

"That must be exciting."

"Yes, it is." *Change the subject.* He disregarded his inner voice. "So, I noticed you're a recruiter. What exactly do you do?"

"I work for a consulting firm in Oak Brook. The majority of our new hires are college recruits, so I spend a great deal of time on campus at job fairs. I hate monotony, so it's great getting out meeting new people."

"I can tell you like it."

She smiled into the phone. "You're right, I do."

Leaning back in his chair, Justin focused on her voice, letting its huskiness caress him. He closed his eyes and imagined his real name rolling off her lips. Before he knew it, he'd asked her out on a date.

"What did you have in mind?" Sabrina asked, swirling around in her chair.

Justin's chair snapped forward with a loud pop. *You asked her out on a date? Are you an idiot?* Frantically his mind raced. There had to be someplace they could go without running into Adrian. "Uh, how about I pick you up? Then we can decide."

"I live in Naperville. You don't mind coming out to the suburbs, do you?"

Perfect. No Adrian. "That sounds great. I'll call you before I leave work, so we can finalize the details."

Sabrina spun around in her chair. "Okay."

After they'd hung up, she dialed her aunt to give her the good news.

"Great, honey. I'll be sure to tell your father all about your plans."

Sabrina looked skeptical. "I'm sure he'll be glued to his La-Z-Boy, waiting for an update."

"How did you know?" Her aunt teased.

Sabrina was certain he'd give his sister the usual hard time for butting in, though it would fall on deaf ears; Hazel was an incorrigible romantic.

"So, where is he taking you tonight?"

"We haven't decided yet."

"Well, honey, wherever it is, he won't stand a chance," Hazel said delightedly.

Smiling wickedly, Sabrina hung up. *That's what I'm counting on.*

Chapter Six

Justin parked his car and switched off the engine. He was a few minutes early, thankful that he'd left work before five o'clock. He had friends who lived in the western suburbs so the rush of commuter traffic was anticipated.

Sabrina's house was on a quiet cul-de-sac with five other homes. From the looks of it, cost her quite a bit. Small lanterns illuminated the walkway and beautifully landscaped entrance. The front door had a large, intricate glass front that was flanked by matching sidelights.

It was March, still a few weeks of winter left. To prove the point a sudden gust of wind caused Justin to retreat deeper into his yellow-and-black parka. Though cold, his pulse raced in anticipation of seeing Sabrina again, which warmed him.

He pressed firmly on the doorbell. A cheerful melody, not the usual two-toned doorbell, chimed. Justin smiled. He knew the small touch was indicative of Sabrina's personality.

The door opened, bringing a warm gush of air to caress his chilled skin. The fragrant aroma of raspberries wafted over him.

"Hi there." Sabrina stood aside to let him enter. "Welcome to 'Casa del Ridgemont.'"

Justin laughed while unzipping his coat. "Thank you. I see you love those popular scents all the women rave about. Some type of raspberries, right?"

Sabrina hung his coat in the hall closet. Turning she put her hand to her forehead in a mock damsel-in-distress stance. "You caught me. I just can't resist smelling like a basket of fresh fruit," she admitted with an impish grin.

He smiled knowingly. "You sound just like my sister." He followed Sabrina into the living room and sat down. When he leaned back against the cushions he noticed a puzzled look on her face.

"Your sister? I'm certain Aunt Hazel told me you were an only child."

Justin cleared his throat. "Uh, I am—I . . . was referring to a friend of the family, Shelley. She and I grew up together, so she's kind of like a sister to me."

Justin could've kicked himself over his slip-up. If his sister could see the mess he'd made of everything she'd read him the riot act. What made it worse was that he deserved it.

"Oh," Sabrina replied. "Well, I'm sure I'll meet her eventually. Or am I being presumptuous?"

Reaching over, he touched her thigh. Her skin tingled through her jeans. "No, Sabrina, you're not off base. I'd love for you to meet her soon." *You're playing with fire.*

"Are you sure? You hesitated there for a moment. I don't want you to think I'm pushing." Sabrina found it difficult to concentrate when he intermittently rubbed her leg.

Justin mistook the look in her eyes for worry, not knowing that it was really full-blown panic—his touch was wreaking havoc on her system. Moving his hand to her shoulder he squeezed lightly. "Don't sweat it, Sabrina. I was just deep in thought."

When she turned to look at him, her hair brushed over his fingers.

Justin twirled a lock; it felt soft and silky against his fingers. He wondered how it would feel draped over his chest. The image of Sabrina in all her natural splendor was too great to deny. His body tightened in reaction causing him to shift uncomfortably. "Truthfully, I was thinking about you," Justin said with considerable effort. "And how incredible you look right now."

Sabrina noticed the desire coating his already mellow voice. His eyes darkened to the color of melted caramel, and she dragged her upper teeth over her lower lip.

Justin caught her reaction. He almost moaned aloud. He longed to pull her tremulous lip in between his, to taste her luscious mouth until her body quaked with need.

"Wow, you do know all the right things to say, don't you?" Sabrina said anxiously.

When Justin smiled, his right eye twitched. *You don't know the half of it.* He decided to switch to a safer topic, one that didn't leave him wanting to lay her against the plush cushions of her couch, one that didn't make him want to devour her with deliberate precision. He shifted slightly. His jeans were becoming tighter by the minute. "It's not hard," he said after finding his errant voice. "You're easy to compliment. Speaking of compliments, your home is incredible."

"Are you speaking from a professional opinion, Mr. Anderson?" Sabrina joked, hoping to ease the sexual tension.

"It's a fact, Ms. Ridgemont. It is wonderful; I'm sure you knew that."

Sabrina looked around. She couldn't help beaming with pride. "There are times when I wondered about the sanity of buying it, since I'm not married nor do I have kids. Still, I wouldn't live anywhere else. It suits me just fine."

You suit me just fine. He stood cautiously, extending his hand to her. "So, ready for dinner?"

Sabrina looked slightly embarrassed. "I hope you don't mind, I've taken the liberty of cooking for us. I thought it would make it easier to talk, get to know each other."

Justin looked at the beige chenille couch. Visions of the two of them in a passionate embrace reappeared. *Damn.* He swallowed painfully. "No, not at all. It's a great idea."

"Great! Just let me warn you, I'm an excellent cook, so follow me and prepare to be dazzled!" Sabrina boasted.

Just watching her walk made his jaw clench. "I'm already dazzled."

Sabrina heard him and almost tripped over the grin on her face.

Justin offered to light the candles in the dining room while Sabrina put the final touches on their meal.

While flipping though her *Midwest Living* magazines, Sabrina found a recipe for lamb with porcini mushrooms and herbs with a white bean ragout. A salad of mixed field greens with caramelized pecans and mandarin oranges complemented the main course. *Does that go with lamb? Well, it will tonight,* Sabrina thought.

Luckily she had a cheesecake on hand, so dessert was covered. After pulling out a bottle of Merlot, her gourmet meal was ready to be served.

Presentation was everything, so she'd used her best serving dishes and china.

Justin helped her carry everything into the dining room.

On her last trip from the kitchen, she flipped on the built-in stereo system. Soft jazz drifted through the air, making Sabrina smile. She took her seat across from Adrian. When he winked at her, the gesture warmed her insides, causing her to sigh softly. It couldn't get much better than this.

Justin moaned with pleasure after taking his first forkful of food. "Lady, you've outdone yourself. Everything looks and tastes incredible!"

Sabrina beamed with pleasure. "Thank you."

Companionable silence filled the room while they ate.

After a few minutes Sabrina looked across the table at Justin cutting a piece of lamb. She was able to observe him without being caught ogling. Just looking at him caused her thoughts to stray in a romantic direction. She was attracted to him on every level: intellectually, physically, emotionally, and considering how long they'd known each other, the realization was disconcerting.

"So tell me more about yourself. Aunt Hazel gave me some background, but nothing too personal. What do you like to do for fun, besides eat at elegant restaurants?"

Justin placed his fork on his plate before speaking. "Well, I have a few close friends I hang out with when I'm not working."

"Which isn't too often, right?"

"True," Justin agreed. "We do the typical guy stuff: play basketball, golf, work out at the gym."

"Any ex-girlfriends with detachment issues?"

Justin chuckled. "None worth mentioning. When I first started my company, there wasn't time for serious relationships. I dated, but only occasionally."

Sabrina held her breath. "And now?"

His gaze pinned her with its intensity. Reaching over he ran a finger over the back of her hand. Hunger was evident in Justin's light-brown eyes. "Now, I'd say I'm open to something more."

The air around them was charged with electricity. Sabrina studied the gold damask tablecloth with avid curiosity, negating the fact that she saw it every day. She found it difficult to concentrate when he stroked her hand like that. How could she, when every nerve ending that had lain dormant since her breakup with Christopher screamed out to be acknowledged?

When they finally did make eye contact, it was hard for either to look away. Justin cleared his throat and shifted in his chair while Sabrina folded and refolded her white linen napkin.

"So, what about you? I've already had the displeasure of meeting Warren. Anyone else still out there pining?"

Sabrina's unladylike snort filled the air, causing Justin to laugh heartily. "Christopher isn't one to pine, at least not over anything but money. No, I've gone out occasionally, but he was the most serious relationship I've had and look how that turned out." Silently she berated herself for letting the past affect her.

Justin reached over and tilted her chin with his finger. When they made eye contact, he smiled. "Just thinking about how much of an idiot any man would be to break your heart makes me—" He stopped suddenly, his jaw flexing, in an effort to control his emotions. "Warren's a fool!" he said harshly.

She returned his smile. "I won't argue there." Sabrina's eyes clouded over. "Anyway, after my mother got sick, I all but dropped out of the dating scene. She tried to get me to go out, meet people, but I couldn't. I didn't want to waste precious time."

Justin's fingers covered hers. "I'm sorry, Brina. I can only imagine what a terrible time that must've been."

It was strangely comforting hearing him use the nickname her family and friends provided her. She tried to concentrate on their current conversation. "Finding out about Christopher's infidelity and losing my mother all in the same year?" Sabrina laughed in a voice devoid of joy. "It was definitely my idea of hell on Earth. I got over it. The jilted part, that is." The pain etched in her features would have been visible to a blind man. It was apparent she wasn't over the loss of her mother or the man that she thought held her future.

Sabrina tried to wipe away the tears without being noticed.

Justin noticed. "Sabrina, if you want to—"

"I don't," she interrupted harshly then immediately softened her voice. "Besides, these aren't the typical topics people discuss on second dates or over dinner."

"Hey, I'm not complaining."

The understanding and concern in his gaze startled Sabrina. At a loss for words, both went back to eating. It was a few moments before either spoke again.

Sabrina decided a lighter topic was in order. Justin listened intently, stroking her hand as she talked about herself and the rest of her family.

"Your family sounds really nice. They obviously love you a great deal."

She nodded vigorously. "Enough to think I'm wilting on the vine by my lack of companion prospects."

"So they are a little overzealous," Justin countered; "I'm sure they mean well."

"'Overzealous'?" Sabrina choked on her wine. "My aunt filled out an application for a dating service for me. Luckily my dad found out what she was up to. He made her tell me what she'd done before men began showing up on my doorstep!"

Justin looked incredulous. "Okay, now your aunt sounds just plain weird to me," he said, laughing. "No wonder she's Norma Jean's best friend."

Sabrina looked puzzled. "Your mother lets you call her by her first name?"

"Are you kidding?"

"Then why . . ."

"Oh, sometimes I use her first name when I'm teasing her. I'm crazy but not that crazy."

The wine Justin consumed was making him relaxed, but he was careful to have only one serving. He studied Sabrina over the rim of his glass. He could never tire of looking at her. She was attracted to him, that was obvious, but as Adrian, not himself. He wondered how well he'd fare against the fancy sports car, half-a-million dollar condo, and the self-assured persona that was Adrian. He cringed just thinking about his prospects. *Tell her the truth. Tell her soon, before you get in too deep.*

Justin sat his glass hastily on the table then licked his lips with determination. "Sabrina?"

Startled, she looked up from her plate. "Yes?"

His mouth opened to tell her all, but the confession died in his throat. After a few painful seconds he stood and extended his hand. "Dance with me." He pulled her toward the living room.

"What?" Sabrina choked.

"You heard me—dance with me."

"Here? But I . . ."

"Right here, right now," Justin pleaded. He grasped her hand and spun her around before settling her against him.

Her body trembled the instant they connected. The intimate touch pulsed heat through her in all the right places.

Lord, if he could affect her like this from just a touch, what would happen if they took it to the next level?

Fireworks. Sabrina sighed, her skin quivering at the prospect.

A soft, romantic ballad drifted from the stereo system in the kitchen. The song's poignant words blended seamlessly with the sensual strains of acoustic guitar. It was an enchanted moment. The sway of their bodies melded with the music, charging the air with electricity.

Pulling her closer, Justin inhaled her scent. She felt incredible in his arms. He never wanted this moment to end. "My God, Brina, you're so beautiful."

As if on cue, both tilted their heads closer—Justin lowered his, and Sabrina raised hers. Their lips met cautiously at first then with more persistence.

Sabrina was drowning in sensations that had been quiescent for years. They were slowly re-awakening, making her giddy from the rush. It was impossible to recall the last time she'd been mesmerized by a mere kiss.

Justin felt her timid response and increased the pressure, coaxing her mouth open so that his tongue could explore her fully. When it did, time stopped. The music, their surroundings, all ceased to exist. The only thing that mattered was the raw heat generating between them. Justin's hand slid farther down Sabrina's back to caress her.

Her arms tightened around his neck, pulling him closer. How they made it to the couch was a mystery to Sabrina. She vaguely remembered feeling pressure at the back of her knees, then being gently lowered onto the soft cushions.

Justin's body was stretched out against hers; he was kissing her senseless.

The black skirt she wore, with its precarious slit, inched higher by the minute. Sabrina felt his right hand move beneath her disheveled silk blouse and rest just under her breast; she tensed in anticipation.

She ran a shaky hand over his hair then down his neck. She reveled in the way his body molded perfectly to hers.

Too long, Sabrina's mind screamed. It had been too long since she'd let a man in or allowed him emotional access. Adrian was breaking down her defenses, not that she was offering much resistance.

"Brina," Justin whispered raggedly.

She heard the want as clearly as if he'd shouted it aloud. The need was there, resounding in that one word. She felt it imploring her, serenading her to let go.

Suddenly alarm bells resounded in her head, a barrage of questions overloading her system. How much did she really know about this man? Other than the fact that he was a terrific kisser, wanted her, and overwhelmed her like no man had before. *It's too fast!* She panicked.

Sabrina put her hands on his chest, pushing slightly. "Adrian, wait."

When he didn't acknowledge, she tried again. "Adrian, please, we've got to stop," she said weakly.

The instant Justin heard her moan, "Adrian," he froze. The haze of desire immediately cleared, leaving him dazed, confused, and frustrated beyond recognition. Hearing his best friend's name on her lips, instead of his, was the wet blanket needed to douse the flames of passion that were raging uncontrolled.

Justin pulled away as if he'd been branded. He looked at Sabrina in confusion; saw her tousled clothes, swollen lips, and passion-soaked eyes. He swallowed painfully.

"I'm sorry, Adrian, but I—"

"Don't!" he interrupted with more force than he'd intended.

Surprise at his tone was evident in Sabrina's expression.

"I mean," he lowered his voice, praying it didn't sound as harsh, "it isn't necessary to explain. We both got kind of carried away in the moment." Suddenly it was too much. He had to get out of there. Each minute he stayed was making him guiltier.

Ashamed at his duplicitous behavior, Justin took a few deep breaths, straightening his attire. He avoided her eyes. "Listen, Sabrina, I think I'd better go. The dinner was great, and the dancing, incredible."

"You don't have to leave, Adrian."

He flinched. "Yes, I do. I'll call you later, okay?" Without waiting for an answer, Justin practically ran to the foyer.

Sabrina could only follow him; her body was numb, her mind reeling in bewilderment. Something wasn't right. She sensed it, though unclear what had caused Adrian's drastic mood swing. Sabrina deftly pulled his coat from the closet and handed it to him.

Justin shrugged it on, kissing her hastily on the lips. He was careful to avoid eye contact. "I'll see you later."

"Good night," she called after him. Closing the door Sabrina fell back against it. Tears threatened to consume her. She ran a shaky hand through her hair. Quietly, she wondered what the hell had just happened. It felt like she was going insane a little piece at a time. She closed her eyes in a desperate attempt to re-group her senses. Touching her quivering lips she wondered at how her safe, manless life had been turned upside down in such a brief period. The longer she was in Adrian's presence, the shorter her grip on her neat, orderly feelings became.

Cutting off the hall light, she went back into the kitchen. She breathed a sigh of relief that there wasn't much to clean up or put away. Sabrina always cleaned up while she cooked so not to be faced with a huge mess at the end of the evening.

It didn't take her long to put the food away or clean the counters. Turning off the lights, she armed the alarm system before climbing the wide staircase to the second floor.

Sabrina looked toward the bathroom. With a sigh she flopped down on her bed instead. Usually she enjoyed her nightly regimen of preparing for bed: tonight she just wasn't feeling it. She lay down on top of the bed covers. Wearily, she put a hand over her eyes.

Being with Adrian was sheer pleasure; whether he was whispering in her ear, laughing at something she'd said, or sharing her meals, she enjoyed every moment with him. It was scaring her to death! His abrupt departure left her feeling confused and exposed. She'd wondered if his sudden mood change was due to her halting their impromptu make-out session. She didn't want to think he was only interested in a physical relationship, but how could she be sure? It wasn't like they'd been dating for months and she knew where his head was. Were they even dating at all?

Everything about their association thus far was foreign to her—being attracted to someone from the moment their eyes met, the overload on her senses from just being around them, and the pure need were unlike anything she'd experienced before. Her relationship with Christopher had taken years to develop, yet it had ended with him being unfaithful and breaking her heart. With Adrian, everything felt like she was flying by the seat of her pants. It was scary, yet exciting. "So this is what a whirlwind feels like," she said in amazement.

Chapter Seven

If working out is supposed to be good for the soul, why don't I feel better? Justin heaved the barbell up into another arm curl. His muscles strained from the unrelenting weight of numerous repetitions. Justin hoped the pain of working out would take his mind off his callous behavior at Sabrina's house. He'd taken off without warning or an explanation.

That had been two days ago. He hadn't spoken more than ten words to her since. Justin's mind was reeling from trying to figure out how to extricate himself from the mess he'd created. The lies were growing by the day. He knew the longer he put off confessing the truth, the more his gut would wrench and his conscience would nag him. Sabrina was all he'd ever hoped to find in a woman. He wanted her with a searing need that leveled him. She was beautiful, intelligent, sexy as hell, yet he was blowing the one chance God had given him at true happiness. *Man, you're an idiot . . .*

The doorbell sounded, interrupting his solo pity

party. Putting the heavy weight down on the mat with a resounding thud, Justin grabbed a towel and wrapped it around his neck. Pulling the door open, he moaned aloud at the man on the other side, "Stan, what the hell do you want?"

Stan arched an eyebrow. "Real smooth, Langley."

Justin stepped aside, letting his friend enter. Without waiting he headed back to his office/exercise room. Sitting back on the bench, Justin picked up a smaller dumbbell and began working his triceps.

Stan leaned against the doorjamb, watching the troubled man with interest. They had been next-door neighbors growing up, so they were much closer than Justin and Adrian. It's not that Adrian wasn't a great friend; he just tended to be self-involved at times.

"Must be serious," Stan noted.

"What?" Justin huffed out.

"Whatever's on your mind that's got you so out of sorts."

"Don't have a clue what that could be."

"Uh-huh, if you say so, man." Stan pulled up the computer chair by Justin's desk. He twirled around in circles.

After a few moments of silence Stan turned to Justin with interest. "So, you talk to Adrian lately?"

"Nope. Why?"

"He's got a new lady friend. Met her at a conference or something."

"Adrian's got a girlfriend?" Justin looked up in surprise.

"You don't get out much, do you?"

"I've been tied up lately."

"Really? By whom?" Stan grinned wickedly.

Justin grabbed his towel. He wiped the sweat from

his face before draping it across his leg. "You were saying?"

"Turns out, she lives here, right here in the Windy City. How's that for *convenient?*" Stan chuckled.

"That's great," Justin said in a distracted voice.

"I'll say. I forgot her name, but Adrian says she's so fine she'd stop time in a watch shop. I suppose it's lucky for him that he did stand up that blind date."

Justin looked up, frowning sharply. "Drop it, Stan."

Stan was oblivious to Justin's flexed muscles or smoldering anger. "I'm just saying, some friend of his mother's couldn't possibly hold a candle to—"

Justin practically snarled as he jumped up and hauled Stan to his feet. He pulled him up so that they were face to face. "Shut your face, Stan. You don't know what the hell you're talking about!" Justin roared. "Sabrina didn't deserve to be stood up like that! Adrian is a rude, selfish bastard who can't see past his Palm Pilot." Justin shoved Stan away from him, ran a hand over his face, and shook his head.

"Sabrina? Justin, what's up with you? And don't bother denying it. You just took my head off for something Adrian did. Mind telling me why?"

"Yes," Justin said sourly.

Stan was undaunted. "Tough. Spill it, Langley—now." Sitting, Stan turned the chair so his feet could rest on the desk nearby.

Justin sat down heavily on the bench he'd just vacated. He took a deep, troubled breath and began. "It all started . . ."

Chapter Eight

Moving her right hand over the mouse, Lauren clicked then dragged the card over to the long row on the screen. She smiled like a Cheshire cat when the rows of black and red playing cards danced across the computer screen. "I won!" She loved playing computer solitaire.

"Lauren, are you listening?" Sabrina asked loudly.

"Listening to what—you breathing into the phone? If so, yes, Brina, I'm listening to you not saying anything."

"You're not funny."

"Neither is your sighing every six seconds. It's obvious you're upset about something. The question is, What's got your panties in a bunch?" Lauren clicked New Game and settled further into her chair. "Or should I say who?"

Sabrina sputtered. "And what makes you think this is about a man?"

"Sabrina, what are you eating?"

Sabrinas spoon stopped in mid-air. She looked down guiltily. "Breyers Cookies 'n Cream. Why?"

Lauren shook her head at the phone. " 'Nuff said. Now, stop playing hard to get and tell me what Adrian's done that's got you so out of sorts. You're eating ice cream straight out of the carton with a soupspoon. If that's not a dead giveaway, I don't know what is."

Twenty minutes later, Sabrina sat sideways in the chenille-covered armchair, her foot hanging against the side. A fire blazed in the family room hearth, giving the room a soft, amber glow.

"So what you're saying is I shouldn't take this personally? Lauren, the man almost broke the sound barrier leaving my house the other night. You think that shouldn't faze me?"

"Sweetie, all I'm saying is that you tend to overthink things. If I were you, I'd just relax and wait to hear from him. From what you've told me, it's obvious Adrian likes you. He isn't blind, Sabrina; I'm sure he knows just how incredible a woman you are. Hell, if I were a man I'd take a go at you," Lauren said, chuckling.

"You would, too." Sabrina laughed. "Thank you for the vote of confidence. Now, what do you mean I 'overthink' things? Are you calling me paranoid?"

The doorbell rang, interrupting her next retort. She looked at the antique grandfather clock sitting on the fireplace mantel. It was nine forty-five. *Maybe it's Adrian,* she thought expectantly.

"I've gotta run, Lauren. I'll call you later," she said without waiting for an answer.

Walking quickly to the door she flipped on the front light and peered through the glass. She was equally divided between surprise and exasperation as she slowly opened the door.

"Why, Christopher? What an unexpected displeasure!

What could possibly have brought you to my door at all, much less this late hour?" she said dryly.

"Hello, Ridge. I know you weren't expecting me, but may I come in?"

Sabrina leaned against the doorjamb and shook her head. "What could you possibly say that I'd want to hear?"

"If you'd let me come in out of the bitter cold, I could tell you," he implored.

Sabrina rolled her eyes. Her tone was clip when she spoke. "Fine, Chris, you've got five minutes, then it's happy trails." She stood aside, giving him a wide berth as he entered. She didn't bother asking for his coat.

Christopher arched an eyebrow but remained silent. Removing the heavy garment, he draped it over his shoulder while looking at Sabrina questioningly.

Sabrina rolled her eyes and walked into the living room. It was the closest room to the front door, and she wanted him gone. She didn't wait to see if he followed her. Sitting down, she glanced at the gold-and-silver watch on her wrist. "The clock's ticking, Christopher. So what was so important you couldn't drop me an e-mail?"

The air was thick with tension, but Christopher ignored the hostility permeating the room. He slowly looked around, his eyes finally resting on the woman sitting rigidly before him. "You've done some decorating. It looks nice," he said conversationally, as if nothing untoward had ever transpired between them.

"I think so, too. You've got four minutes."

Christopher laid his coat over the arm of the couch and sat down next to her.

She didn't hesitate to move farther away from him.

"I didn't stop by to upset you, Sabrina," he began.

"Sure, you didn't."

"Seeing you at the restaurant . . . well, it caused some old feelings to resurface."

Sabrina looked at him in stunned silence. This was a dead subject for her. Her feelings where he was concerned were as useless as the piles of ash coating the inner recesses of her fireplace. She put up her hand to stop him. "Christopher, I don't think this—"

"Please, just let me finish."

She sighed loudly.

"Things ended rather abruptly between us . . ."

Sabrina glared at him in disbelief as she stood. She was far too annoyed by his audacity to remain sedentary. "'Abruptly'?" she scoffed. "You were cheating on me, Christopher! For how long is irrelevant because, frankly, one minute would've been too long."

Christopher stood and closed the distance between them. He raised a hand to touch her but refrained. He wasn't sure if she'd accept its presence or smack it away. "It wasn't my intention to cause you additional pain. I just came by to tell you that I feel remorse over what I did." Christopher took a deep breath and lightly touched her arm. When she didn't shrug it off, he continued, "I've said I'm sorry countless times but—"

"It was just lip service."

"Justin, are you insane?" Stan yelled. "What were you thinking?"

Justin paced a few times then sat down heavily on the exercise bench. Shaking his head, he put his elbows on his knees. "I wasn't thinking, obviously," Justin said with exasperation. "I just didn't think it was cool for him to stand her up like that."

"So, you show up and before you've ordered an appetizer, you've posed as your best friend, lied to the date he stood up, and fallen in love with her?" Stan joined Justin on the bench. "Have I covered all the highlights of the evening?"

Justin laughed. It wasn't a happy sound. "You forgot her ex-fiancé's unplanned arrival. I wouldn't have said I was Adrian if that pompous ass hadn't shown up," Justin said miserably.

Stan punched him on the arm. "Well, you've put your foot in it big time, Langley, not to mention acting like a retard when you saw her last. So, how are you ever going to fix this daytime drama?"

Justin was pensive for a few moments before shaking his head. "I don't know, Stan. I really acted like a jerk the other night, and I haven't done much to fix it. I've got to think of something—and fast—before things get any worse."

"Why?"

Justin looked over at his friend and frowned. "Because, I love her." The words clung heavily to the silence drifting through the room. He'd finally said what had been in his heart since the second their eyes met and she'd smiled.

"Justin, are you sure? I mean, it's only been a few days, right?"

Justin stood, pacing the room like a caged animal. "Of course, I'm sure! I know it may sound crazy, I know it's too soon, but I am in love with her." He ran a hand tiredly over his eyes. "It's all I can do to get through an hour of the day and not think about her or want to call her. I can't begin to track the hours of sleep I've lost just fantasizing about her. She's in my mind, my gut, and my heart," he said in amazement. "I don't know what I'm going to do about it."

"So, uh, what kind of fantasies?"

"Stan!" Justin said with annoyance.

"Okay, okay," Stan replied, watching his friend wear a hole in the floorboards. On the fourth trip by, Stan reached for his arm to stop him. "Man, give it a rest. You're making me dizzy," he complained.

"Stan, this is serious. I've got to find a way out of this mess."

His friend was contemplative for a moment. "Here's a thought: Have you tried telling her how you feel, that you're in love with her?"

Justin glanced at his friend as though he'd taken leave of his senses. "You've got to be kidding! How well do you think she'd take that news, on the heels of my confessing I'm not really Adrian Anderson, that I've been lying to her the whole time?"

Stan opened his mouth to answer.

Justin put his hand in the air to stop him. "I'll tell you how she's going to react. She'll be hurt, pissed, and she'll drop me faster than—"

"Than an auto insurance company after one too many accidents?"

"This isn't funny," Justin said tersely.

"I know it's not. I'm sorry, man. You've got yourself into one helluva mess. Question is, how are you going to come out of this without your girl or Adrian beating you within an inch of your life?"

Justin left the office and headed to the kitchen.

Stan automatically followed.

"Remind me not to have you try to cheer me up again," Justin said dryly. He pulled bottled water from the refrigerator and slammed the door. Twisting the cap off he flicked his wrist; it sailed effortlessly into the trashcan.

"I'm not trying to make this worse."

Justin leaned against the counter. "I know."

"Do you think she's in love with you?"

Justin was introspective before answering. "I'm certain she has feelings for me."

"Well, unless you want to be in love alone, you've got to get off the dime and tell her the truth, Langley."

Justin stared into his water bottle as if it were a crystal ball. *If only it were.* Justin sighed.

After a few minutes he looked over at his friend. "I'm going to tell her."

"Great!" Stan cheered. "I'll call you tomorrow to see how everything went." Getting up, Stan headed for the door.

Justin called after him. "What do you mean, call you tomorrow?"

"Dude, you aren't going to sit around sulking all night, are you? Go tell her how you feel. Stop sitting on the sidelines and get into the game."

Justin pondered his friend's advice. "I'm going to go over there tonight, tell her everything. I only pray she'll forgive me," he called over his shoulder on the way to the bathroom to shower.

"Great plan, Langley," Stan called after him. "I hope, for your sake, it works."

Forty-five minutes later Justin walked up the sidewalk to Sabrina's house. He looked at the flowers he'd purchased for her. Stan's words echoed in his head. Somehow he'd find the right words to explain the bizarre circumstances that surrounded his impersonation of Adrian. He walked up the steps. *Good luck, man. You're going to need it,* he told himself.

Justin raised his hand to press the doorbell. When he looked through the glass door, he saw Sabrina and she wasn't alone. He peered closely. Sabrina had her back to him, but he could clearly see the man standing in front of her. "Warren," he said between clenched teeth. Justin's jaw ticked as he watched the two in intimate conversation. Warren's hands were on Sabrina's shoulders, his fingers resting on her hair.

Justin straightened and backed up unsteadily. Anger mixed with confusion coursed through him, as did a growing urge to put a hole through Sabrina's elaborate front door. At the moment it was closer to him than Christopher Warren. *Fool,* instantly came to Justin's mind. He'd obviously stumbled upon a tête-à-tête between past lovers.

Looks like I was about to bare my soul for nothing. Justin shook his head at his stupidity. *You should've known things weren't over by her reaction to him at the restaurant,* his conscience chided.

He looked down at the bouquet of flowers in his hand and back to the scene in Sabrina's living room. He uttered a single curse before lobbing the fragrant bunch over his shoulder. He didn't wait to see where it landed but strode angrily back to his car. He got in, slammed the door shut, and started the engine in one fluid motion. With a violent pull he put the car in reverse and backed up. He looked at the house one final time before roaring off in a screech of tires and smoke.

Christopher released her shoulders. "I know I should've told you this sooner. I'm not altogether sure why I didn't."

"I'll tell you why—because then you would've had to admit you did something wrong. Well, spare me the confessions of a guilty man." She moved away from him. "I'm not here to assuage your conscience for destroying my whole world years ago. You were my future, Christopher. Do you have any idea how much I loved you? How much I looked forward to our life together?" Sabrina didn't give him a chance to speak. "No, as usual you were clueless about my feelings. I realized that afternoon at the hotel that you didn't really know or give a damn about me!" She said acidly.

"That's not true, Ridge." He touched her shoulder.

This time she smacked his hand off. "I loved you then."

Sabrina laughed bitterly. "Love isn't a marriage of convenience, Christopher. It isn't starting a union that's tainted with lies and deceit."

"I know that now," he said quietly.

She looked at him closely. He was still incredibly handsome and persuasive, but she felt nothing. No spark, no pull, just an empty promise etched on a painful memory. There were no tears threatening to overcome her. She'd used up her quota on him a long time ago. "Time's up, Christopher. You said what you came to say, now I'd appreciate it if you'd leave." Sabrina walked toward the foyer and stood by the door, waiting for him.

Grabbing his coat, Christopher sighed heavily. He stopped in front of the door and studied her.

Sabrina returned his frank gaze and refused to drop it.

"I guess this is truly good-bye then?"

Sabrina opened the door without breaking eye contact. "We said good-bye years ago at the Ritz-Carlton."

Christopher nodded and left.

Following him out, Sabrina stood on the front porch. Wearily, she closed her eyes and inhaled the crisp night air. Its chill revitalized her frayed nerves and tumultuous emotions.

Sabrina turned to go into the house, but a streak of color caught her eye. Red roses were scattered over the bushes. Sabrina leaned over to pick up the remnants of the tattered bouquet. She inhaled the flowers, still fragrant despite their trauma.

Fear, then realization gripped her. Looking at her door she trembled. She shook her head in denial while tears pooled in her eyes, her heart constricted painfully in her chest.

Looking out into the night she knew it was too late. He'd already gone.

"Oh God," she whispered. "Adrian." Sabrina bolted into the family room and grabbed the cordless telephone off the coffee table. Her newly manicured nails clicked loudly on the keypad as she dialed the cell phone number Adrian had given her, then impatiently waited for the line to connect.

"Come on, pick up," she whispered tearfully. "You couldn't have left that long ago."

The phone rang four times before voice mail kicked in and an automated message informed her that the caller she'd reached wasn't available.

She sighed in frustration but left a message anyway. "Adrian, this is Sabrina. I need you to call me as soon as possible. It's important," she stressed and hung up. Sabrina felt the familiar lurch of her stomach, assessed the undercurrent of panic she felt and knew her carefully structured relationship-free world would never be the same again. She raised trembling fingers to her mouth. "I love him," she whispered.

Sitting down heavily on the stone hearth, she stared unseeingly into the blazing fire. The brilliant amber and yellow flames hungrily devoured the strategically placed logs. The intriguing sight was lost on Sabrina. *When did this happen? It's too soon! Does he feel this too?* Her brain rambled. She shivered, despite the warmth enveloping her.

Slowly, hesitantly, she became comfortable with her newfound feelings. Eventually, she admitted to herself that loving Adrian was as welcome as it was unexpected. Finding a man who made her feel so many variations and contradictions left her awestruck. She loved him, yet she was scared. She trusted him, yet still wondered why they affected each other with an intensity that left her wary, as if the other boot would be dropping any moment. She hadn't been looking for love, but it had certainly sought her out and knocked her over. Nervously she looked at her watch to see how long it had been since she left her last message. She was up and walking in one flowing movement.

Grabbing the telephone she dialed the number again. "Please answer," she pleaded. When she heard the same monotonous message she hung up. Her heart tightened in her chest. Sabrina knew without a doubt that she had to get this sorted out. She needed him in her life, wanted him with a desire so powerful it made her breath catch in her throat—the silly smiles that came across her face at the most inopportune times, the way her stomach flipped over when the telephone rang, and the incredible way she felt just thinking about him or hearing his voice.

With a heavy heart Sabrina walked over to the window and stared desolately into the night. "Christopher, if you've ruined this for me, I swear you'll regret it," she vowed passionately.

Justin's phone rang shrilly in the cabin of his car. The neon green back light flashed the number across the screen. *Sabrina*. Tensing, Justin gripped the steering wheel harder, ignoring the call. He'd fallen in face first; now there was no way he'd be able to back out intact.

Loving Sabrina was twisting his insides into tight, complex knots. He didn't know how to unravel them without causing collateral damage. He'd swallowed a bitter pill that night—jealousy. Seeing her so cozy with the man who had intentionally ripped her heart to shreds made him want to shake some sense into her. It also made him want to claim her for his own, to kiss her until she was so intoxicated by the love and passion they shared, she'd be hard-pressed to remember anyone or anything but him.

Unfortunately we can't always get what we want. Or whom we want, his inner voice reminded him.

A solitary beep interrupted the silence a few moments later. It was the telephone's indicator that a voice mail message had been left. Another one. When the telephone rang a third time, Justin swore violently then pulled off the road. He jammed his finger on the button with a green telephone on it. Curtly he answered.

"Adrian? I'm glad I reached you; I've been trying to get a hold of you. I left two messages and—"

The muscle in his jaw clenched before he interrupted her. "I know."

"We need to talk. Not on the phone, in person. I know you aren't too far away. Would you mind coming back to the house?"

The harsh laugh that emanated from the line made the hair on the back of Sabrina's neck stand.

"Fine. I'll be there shortly. Try to have your company gone before I get there," he ground out.

Sabrina didn't bother with a reply. He was already angry enough. Hanging up, she crossed her arms around her middle and waited.

Twenty minutes later the doorbell sounded. Sabrina set her coffee mug down and went to answer it. Swinging the ornate door open she stepped aside.

Justin didn't bother with pleasantries. He strode past her and into the family room.

Sabrina noticed his quick glance toward the living room. She didn't comment.

Justin didn't bother taking off his coat. He stopped in the middle of the floor before turning around to face her. "Okay, I'm here. What did you need to say that couldn't be done over the phone?"

"It's not what you think," Sabrina said without preamble.

Justin laughed unkindly. "Is that right? Well, tell me, Sabrina, what should I think? I show up on your doorstep, flowers in hand, to apologize for my behavior the last time we were together, and lo and behold, I find the prior administration here in what appeared to be a pretty intimate embrace. Now, you expect me to believe he hasn't taken up his duties again? That one plus one doesn't equal me out in the cold?"

Sabrina bristled at his accusation. "Well, it appears you've got this whole thing figured out, don't you, Adrian? But in regards to Christopher, there's just one flaw in your logic—every word that just came out of your mouth!" Sabrina strode up and got in his face. When she spoke, it was in a tone as frigid as dry ice. "First off, Christopher wasn't here on my invitation. He showed up on my doorstep *uninvited,*" she stressed. "He came here of his own accord, to apologize for the disaster that was our life together. Why? I don't have a clue, but that was all it was. You just happened to show up when I was upset and Christopher was trying to comfort me. I didn't let him. If you would've—oh I don't know, rang the doorbell or stuck around a few minutes longer, you would have seen the 'prior administration' leaving."

Justin's eyes widened, but the words wouldn't come.

Sabrina was too worked up by the heated exchange to end it there. Placing her hands on her hips, she eyed him pointedly. "Better yet, you should've just come in, then you both could've gone straight to the testosterone contest—kicking each other's asses and whoever was left standing won. Well, Mr. Anderson? What have you got to say for yourself? Whatever it is, I'll have to listen pretty closely. I'm sure you'll have difficulty talking with that size twelve shoe in your mouth!"

Justin swallowed painfully. He looked at Sabrina and sighed. "It would appear I've acted like a complete jerk tonight and that I owe you a rather hefty apology." Justin took a deep breath. "I'm sorry, Brina. I came over here with a purpose. When I saw Warren here, well, everything kind of unraveled."

Sabrina looked at him and sighed heavily. "Isn't it obvious how I feel about you? I didn't downplay how over my relationship with Christopher I am. It's done, finished, and I've laid those demons to rest. Finally! I don't want to be with him. I want to be with you, which you'd notice, if you'd stop acting like a caveman," Sabrina said, smirking.

The air around them lightened, and the anger between them began to dissipate.

Justin reached down and lightly caressed Sabrina's cheek before twisting a lock of her hair around his finger. "What can I say? I'm told men do extremely crazy things when they're in love," he said quietly.

If he heard her heart slamming loudly in her chest, he didn't mention it. Sabrina glowed with the pure pleasure his declaration caused. She looked up at him, powerless to stop the moisture forming in her eyes. "Well, it's a good thing I love you too," she said poignantly, "or there would be hell to pay."

Justin's hazel eyes darkened. The warmth and intensity they generated took Sabrina's breath away. Her breath caught in her throat at the sudden desire that coursed between them.

Justin leaned toward her; his deep voice caressed her ear. "So, you love me."

"Don't get cocky," Sabrina teased and wrapped her arms around his neck. "I can always change my mind."

Justin's hands ran down the length of her back, pulling her closer to dip his head into the crook of her neck. He firmly planted a kiss there; his lips lingered at feeling her pulse.

The tender kiss sparked a hunger in Sabrina that she couldn't deny. Urgently, she pulled his head up to meet hers. Their lips met in a searing kiss that was fueled by their heated battle moments before, and newly declared love.

Justin felt the spark the moment their lips met. The warmth rushing through his body told him his feelings for Sabrina weren't insignificant. He wanted to know every square inch of her body, to revel in the depths of her soul. The realization was profound. It shook him to his core. He loved this woman with a force that left him humbled. He wanted desperately to make love to her, to lose himself in the velvety softness of her body so completely they'd have trouble telling where one ended and the other began. But that level of intimacy required trust, complete trust and absolute honesty. Justin knew he couldn't make love to Sabrina until he'd achieved it. She deserved nothing less.

Sabrina sensed the change before he'd verbalized it. When he'd released her lips, she looked into his face and saw resolution in his eyes. "Sweetheart, what's the matter?"

Justin smiled down at her. God, he truly did love this woman. "Nothing—everything."

Sabrina opened her mouth to speak, but Justin smoothed a fingertip over her swollen lips. She kissed his finger.

"What you do to me, Brina." Justin shuddered. "The things you make me feel, they're overwhelming."

"You think I'm feeling any less?" she said incredulously. "Do you know how long it's been since I've felt this strong, this . . ." Sabrina's voice broke, and she looked away.

Justin turned her face back toward him to kiss the tip of her nose. "Believe me, sweetheart, I want nothing more than to take you upstairs and love you till we both pass out," he said fiercely.

Instinctively she knew he wouldn't. "But, you can't."

"No, I can, I just won't," he clarified. "I want to be completely honest with you, Brina. I love you, and I want to clear the air between us before we go any farther."

Sabrina didn't begin to understand what was holding him back, but the look on his face told her that something was keeping him from opening up. "Adrian, you can tell me anything. Whatever it is, we'll get through it together."

Justin took hold of her hands and brought each one to his lips. He held them against his face and closed his eyes. At that moment, he wished time would stop and that it was his name lovingly sliding off her lips. "Tomorrow," he said with a strength he didn't feel. "We'll meet at Catch 35 for dinner." *Where it all started,* he thought to himself.

Chapter Nine

Dwayne rolled his eyes and shifted the awkward weight in his hands. The suitcases he carried were slipping precariously out of his grasp. *How could anyone use this much stuff and be gone only three days?* he grumbled inwardly. "Adrian, get a move on. These things are heavy!"

"Will you hang on a minute?" Adrian barked, flipping another key out of the way. "Besides, I'm carrying stuff, too, you know."

Dwayne rolled his eyes a second time. "Oops, almost forgot about that enormous briefcase of yours."

Adrian was concentrating on his task and didn't bother to look up when he spoke. "Where are Justin and Stan anyway? Couldn't one of them have picked me up from the airport?"

"Stan volunteered for some coach thing with his nephew's Boy Scout troop, and Justin said something about having plans tonight."

Smiling smugly, Adrian waved the correct key as he

slid it into the lock and turned. "See, all that belly-aching for nothing." Adrian gallantly stepped aside to let his friend enter.

Dwayne struggled in, moaning under the weight of his burden. "Easy for you to say, fly boy. You aren't the one toting the heavy Gucci bags. Next time hire one of those fancy limousine services."

"Point taken. Anything is better than listening to you drone on. Hey, watch it!" he yelled when Dwayne ceremoniously dumped his designer luggage on the floor.

"You damned right, I'm watching it—watching it hit the floor. Say good-bye to your little bags," Dwayne said in an exaggerated Cuban accent.

Adrian laughed aloud at the reference to Tony Montana in the movie *Scarface*—the movie on every man's top ten list of all-time favorites. "Al Pacino is the man!" Hitting the blinking button on his answering machine, he kicked off his expensive leather shoes.

The first message was his associate, Christy, reminding him of a dinner meeting that night. Grimacing, he pulled a small leather date book out of his jacket. "Damn. Forgot about that."

"No rest for the rich," Dwayne replied.

The second message had him groaning aloud. "Hi, honey. It's me." His mother's voice echoed around the room. "Now, Adrian, don't you dare hit the erase or whatever button it is."

"That's my cue, man. I'm out." Dwayne grinned, quickly bolting for the door. "If Tracey complains later about my stamina, I'll tell her to blame you and your bags."

Adrian hit the pause button on the machine. "Thanks a lot!" he called after his friend. He sat down and finished going through his huge pile of mail. Adrian loved getting away for extended weekends, whether it was skiing in Colorado, going on a Jet Ski in the Caribbean, or eighteen holes in Florida. Competition was in his blood, not to mention enjoying whatever lady was holding his attention at the time.

This trip it was all about Jennifer Simpson, a gorgeous, tax attorney, whose business he'd been dying to mix with pleasure. From the moment he'd met her, he'd been unable to think about any other woman. She intrigued him, challenged him, and most importantly, he couldn't wait to get between the sheets with her. He had no doubt she'd make it hurt in all the splendidly wrong places. He'd waited longer to get her package unwrapped than any other woman he'd dated, but he was making a great deal of progress, and in the end it would be worth it. If this weekend was any indication of how much she was attracted to him, he'd have her unraveling at his feet within the next week or two.

Adrian moaned aloud and closed his eyes to recall their delectable weekend in Palm Coast. His naughty daydream was interrupted, when he remembered his mother's message. Rolling his eyes, he walked over to start her message again.

"And just think how I felt when I had to hear about this budding romance with Sabrina from Hazel," she admonished. "Really, Adrian, why I have to be the last person to find out you've hit it off with Hazel's niece is beyond me. So, I think it's high time you both came over for dinner with your father and me."

"Huh?" Adrian raised an eyebrow, went over and stopped the message. He hit rewind a few seconds then the play button. He listened intently to make sure he'd heard what he thought he did. Erasing the rest of the message, Adrian picked up his cordless phone and immediately dialed his mother's number.

His parents had splurged and added caller ID to their phone. His mother picked up on the first ring.

"Well, saints preserve us. You finally decided to call your mother!"

"Mom," Adrian interrupted before she got on a roll, "what's up with that message about me and Sabrina Ridgemont? What the heck are you talking about?"

"Why are you being so secretive?" Norma continued in a voice laced with censure. "You knew I'd find out about it eventually, even if you didn't find it important enough to mention it to me first."

Adrian took a deep breath. "Mom, I didn't go on the date you set up with Hazel's niece. I stood her up to prove a point to you."

She started sputtering.

"I don't need you knee-deep in my love life."

"Well, the cheese has fallen off somebody's cracker, and it sure as heck isn't mine!" she replied loudly. "Hazel's been talking to her niece almost daily, keeping tabs on what's going on with you two."

Shaking his head, Adrian ran a hand over his eyes. "Hello? Weren't you listening? There is no Sabrina and I. There isn't a Sabrina at all. I'm dating someone named Shelby Simpson. I have been for a few weeks now."

"Mmm-hmm," his mother said suspiciously. "Well, you hold on a minute."

Adrian heard a click and then silence, which gave him the time he needed to calm down. His mother truly was relentless when she got stuck on something. Another click sounded in his ear.

"I'm back," Jeanie announced, "and I've got Hazel on the line."

"Oh joy," Adrian said dryly. "And when did you get three-way calling?"

"Never mind that. It's time we cleared up a few things."

* * *

Twenty minutes later Adrian was sitting on the side of his bed, waiting for the three Advil he'd taken to kick in. He'd played round-robin with his mother and Hazel so long, he'd developed a splitting headache. More insane than them trying to convince him he wasn't telling the truth was this crazy woman, Sabrina. She'd obviously been devastated he'd blown her off and felt the need to lie to her family about it. "Thank God, I spared myself that drama," Adrian said as he lay back on the bed. "I've already done the mental patient thing, and I'm hardly trying to go back there."

Taking another sip of water, Justin glanced at his watch. Sabrina hadn't gotten there yet, and secretly he'd been glad to arrive first. The moment of truth was upon him. He needed some time to compose himself.

"This is it, man. After tonight you'll either be the happiest or the most devastated man on earth." He laughed nervously.

Sabrina's voice interrupted his solo conversation. "Talking to yourself again?"

"Hey, baby," Justin said, immediately getting up and kissing her cheek. "I hear it's normal to talk to yourself, as long as you don't answer back." Justin sat down across from Sabrina, trying to appear at ease. "Would you like a drink? Maybe a bottle of wine?"

Sabrina smiled. "Sounds nice."

Justin signaled the waiter over and ordered a bottle of Merlot.

"My aunt drinks so much of that stuff, we call her Aunt Merlot." Sabrina laughed.

Justin smiled and ran his sweaty palms over his black

slacks. *God, this is hard. How can I confess what's sure to run a knife through my heart?*

Like you have any choice, his conscience replied.

Five minutes later the wine had been uncorked, the glasses filled, and the wine was breathing carefully in an ice bucket nearby.

Sabrina eyed Adrian thoughtfully. She reached over and held out her hand.

When he laid his hand in hers, she felt the slight tremble and quirked an eyebrow. "All right, Adrian, you've stalled long enough. Tell me what's got you wound so tight you're about to shatter into little pieces."

"You," Justin said quietly. "It's always been about you."

"Me?" Sabrina replied with surprise.

Justin took a deep breath and released it for what seemed like an eternity. "You know how things start out with the best of intentions, but then something happens that throws everything out of kilter?"

"Yeah, I guess so," Sabrina replied in a tone she prayed disguised her confusion.

"Well, you happened." He stared past her for a few seconds. "I started out trying to do the right thing. I wanted to protect you from more hurt, but I'm sure I've done more harm than I'd ever bargained for."

Sabrina shifted uncomfortably. "Adrian, you're scaring me. What's all this about?"

"A name," Justin whispered. "One name has thrown my life into chaos, and it's time you knew the truth."

Justin leaned in and Sabrina instinctively followed. They were both oblivious to their surroundings, until a man cleared his throat above them.

"We're not ready to order yet," Justin immediately replied.

"Well, it's a good thing I'm not here to take your order," the man said, chuckling.

The familiar voice effectively siphoned all the air from Justin's chest. He closed his eyes and knew the bell had finally tolled. Retribution for his crimes would be neither swift nor painless. With finality, he slid his fingers from Sabrina's grasp and looked into his best friend's face.

"So this is the reason you've fallen off the face of the earth." The real Adrian chuckled.

Sabrina looked at the man above her with interest and then back to Adrian. The look he wore made her gasp. There was something so desolate in his face, something that tugged painfully at her heart.

Justin looked up at his friend, braced himself for the death blow. "What are you doing here?"

"I just wrapped up a dinner meeting and happened to see you over here."

The silence that proceeded was earsplitting.

"Adrian?" she said with concern.

"Oh, so you know my name, but I don't know yours? Justin, what's up with that? You're so far gone, you can't even introduce your lady to your boys?"

Sabrina looked up in confusion. "Your name's Adrian too?"

"'Too?' Not *too*, period," he replied. "I'm Adrian Anderson." He eyed his friend in confusion. "Hello, Justin? Jump in anytime."

"Why do you keep calling him Justin? Is that your middle name?" Sabrina demanded. Slowly, dread crept into her body, invading her bloodstream, conquering her senses as it moved swiftly and decisively toward its final destination—her heart. She looked confused until realization dawned clear and painful. "Your name is Justin?"

He nodded. "Justin Langley," he said hoarsely.

Sabrina blinked quickly and shook her head. "I don't want to hear this. I'm outta here." Sabrina stood.

Justin grasped her arm, impeding her flight from the table. "Sabrina, wait!"

"'Sabrina'?" Adrian looked startled. "As in Ridgemont?"

When she nodded distractedly he looked at Justin and finally got the clear picture.

Adrian arched an eyebrow. When he spoke, his tone was filled with censure. "I'll have to deduct points for originality."

Justin ignored his friend and focused only on Sabrina. "I lied!" he finally admitted.

The declaration was too much. Sabrina snatched her arm out of his grasp and slapped him across the face. In the stunned silence that followed she fled.

Justin's cheek throbbed, but he ignored it and called after her. When she didn't stop, he dug into his pocket, pulled out his wallet and threw forty dollars onto the table. He ran after her, followed by a bewildered Adrian. "Sabrina, wait!" Justin pleaded running in front of her.

"For what?" She tried to push him out of the way. "So you can try to give me some weak explanation for why you've been lying to me this whole time? What reason could you possibly have for impersonating your best friend? Is this how you two get your kicks? The old bait and switch?"

Adrian held up his hands in protest. "Whoa, we? Honey, I'm a guest to this party. I'm as floored by all this as you."

"No, this wasn't a bait and switch," Justin stressed. "Adrian had nothing to do with it. When I got here that first night I was planning to tell you the truth, Sabrina, but then that jerk Warren showed up. I could see how upset you were, and when he asked me my name, what was I supposed to say? That I was Justin Langley, and your intended date, Adrian Anderson, was an ass and decided to stand you up?"

"I resent that, Justin," Adrian interrupted.

You would, Justin thought. Justin looked over and pinned his friend with a deadly glare. "Stay out of this."

Sabrina held up her hand and cut him off. "Spare me the sad, pathetic details. I've had enough of this *Jerry Springer* episode," she said tearfully. "I trusted you, and you broke that trust. I gave you my heart, and you stomped all over it. You could've told me the truth the moment you sat down at my table."

"You're right, I should have, but I thought you'd blow me off without so much as a backward glance. I felt . . . I felt the sparks between us from the moment I laid eyes on you. I didn't think you'd give me a chance if I was myself."

"That was my call to make, not yours! You had countless times to tell me the truth and you didn't."

"And for countless times I wanted to," Justin confessed. "This ate me up inside, Brina. I fell for you. Hard. I wanted to come clean, but I couldn't risk losing you." He threw up his hands. "I'm just a software developer. I'm not rich. I don't own my own company, don't have a fancy condo, or a fifty-thousand-dollar car—"

"Actually, it was sixty-four," Adrian corrected.

"Shut up!" Justin and Sabrina said in unison.

Justin turned Sabrina to face him. "You mean the world to me, Sabrina. I wanted you to love me for me—"

Angrily she pulled away. "Don't you see? I never knew the real you. You were living a lie this whole time." Sabrina wiped the tears from her face.

"My feelings for you were real—are real."

"Like I'm supposed to believe that? You can't even tell me the truth about your real name. You're that insecure you had to switch places with an arrogant, stuck-up playboy who makes it a habit of standing women up without having the guts to be straight with them?" She glared at Justin then eyed Adrian with contempt.

Undaunted, Adrian glowered back. "Hey, you don't know me like that. Have you forgotten I'm a victim here, too? I got my identity stolen and dogged out by somebody I thought was my boy. Do you know what I had to go through to convince my mother you and I weren't picking out china patterns?" He shuddered at the recollection.

"Oh, poor you." Sabrina threw her hands up in dismissal, encompassing both of them. "You know what? You both deserve each other." Sabrina laughed bitterly. "I'm sorry, Justin." She said his name as if it were a curse. "I want off this crazy-go-round. You aren't the man I thought you were." She looked at Adrian and shuddered. "And meeting the man I thought you were, it's painfully obvious I got the better end of the deal. I suppose I should thank you for having the decency not to . . ." her voice broke.

He knew instantly she was referring to their not making love. "I couldn't," Justin said, quietly understanding her torment. "Not before I told you everything."

She leaned in closer. "Well, now you have, so do us both a favor and stay the hell away from me!" she yelled and slapped him again, so hard this time that her palm burned.

The second one was far worse than the first. Justin's cheek was on fire, and his ears rang as he watched Sabrina run down the sidewalk, away from the restaurant and him. He was about to run after her, when Adrian stopped him. "Let her go, man. Nothing you can say at this point is going to help."

Justin rubbed his cheek and watched her retreating form until she disappeared from sight. His face throbbed agonizingly, but it was nothing compared to the anguish felt deep in his soul or the chasm caused by his imploding heart. The gulf was indeed wide, and it was too much to bear. Self-preservation kicked in; anger surfaced in an effort to keep him from being overwhelmed by his grief. Justin turned sharply toward Adrian. "This whole fiasco is your fault!" he said with contempt.

"My fault?" Adrian raised an eyebrow. "I held a gun to your head and made you lie like a cheap rug?" he countered. "Man, all I have to say is I hope it was good because it looks like you've gotten your last free pass into the cookie jar."

Instantly, Justin's fist connected sharply with Adrian's perfectly chiseled face. The force of the blow knocked Adrian backward. He tasted blood in his mouth before he'd even hit the ground.

"Oh, this is priceless!" He yelled up at Justin. "You say you're me in order to keep a girl, and I'm the one who gets punched in the face?"

Justin flexed his hand and looked distastefully at his friend. "You're a real piece of work, Adrian Anderson. I can't imagine what I was thinking to ever say I was you. If you didn't have a love-'em-and-leave-'em attitude about every woman you've ever met, we wouldn't be in this predicament! You're thoughtless, selfish, and treat women like they were put on earth just to entertain and fawn over you!" He took a breath and continued his tirade. "It sickens me, when I think of how many times I've covered for you and made excuses when you dogged some woman out. How many has it been, Adrian? How many beautiful, intelligent, incredible women have you tossed aside once they've bored you? Like you're some male paragon who should be fought over and worshipped. News flash, pretty boy—you don't deserve them, any of them, and I pray for the day a woman gives you your just desserts and love kicks you square in your ass!" he said dismissively and walked away.

Adrian stared after him so long, a parking attendant ran over and knelt beside him. "Sir, are you all right? Do you need me to call an ambulance?"

Adrian shook his head, spit blood out of his mouth, and slowly rolled over and up onto his feet. He stood there a few moments until he trusted his legs to support his body weight, before heading toward his car.

"You sure you're going to be okay?" the man called after him.

"Of course," he said with bravado. "I'm not the one who just got his heart ripped out of his chest and served back to him in a chafing dish." *Love is indeed a fickle thing. Give me lust any day.* Adrian smiled, despite the pain in his jaw.

Chapter Ten

Stan pressed the buzzer a fourth time and didn't let go for one full minute. "Justin, I know you're in there!" he called through the door. "Open up!"

When there was no reply and the door remained unopened, Stan reached into his pocket and pulled out the key Justin had given him for emergencies. He inserted it into the lock and turned. Gingerly he opened the door and poked his head around the corner. What he saw made his eyes widen and his nose scrunch up. Stan walked through the living room. It was a laborious effort—the obstacles in his way too numerous to count; dirty dishes, newspapers, clothes, shoes, and books became the new carpet lying brazenly over the once visible hardwood floors.

Stan surveyed the battle zone that was once called a kitchen. It was obvious this room had born the brunt of the war, its interior sagging heavily under dishes, eating utensils and cookware that had fought valiantly, but had succumbed to a force more powerful and determined.

As he continued down the hallway, Stan breathed deeply in an effort to prepare him for what he'd find in the bedroom. *It can't be any worse,* he surmised.

He opened the door and staggered backward. "It's worse," he said, groaning. The room was thrown into darkness that belittled the afternoon hour and sunshine outdoors. Cautiously, Stan walked toward the general vicinity of the windows. His hands swept the air in front of him to avoid unforeseen collisions.

"Man, it smells like someone crawled up in here and died," he whispered then cursed loudly when his leg came in contact with an immovable object. "Oh, don't worry about me, I'm fine," he said tersely when there was no reply from the bed that he knew contained Justin.

Staggering around because of his sore leg, he continued on course. When he found the windows, the relief was so great he almost cheered. He grabbed a handful of material and ceremoniously pulled the heavy curtains open. The room was instantly flooded with daylight, and Stan wished for a moment he'd kept the damn things closed. Walking over to the bed he looked down at its contents. He decided sitting on it was out of the question, so he remained standing. "Justin? Are you awake?"

"Go away," Justin replied hoarsely.

"Ah, he doth speak," Stan said lightly. "If you think I'm leaving after slogging through that hell on earth out there, you can think again."

"Stan, I want to be alone."

"You have been. For too long now. It's time you got out of this bed and not just to go buy food to support your recluse habit. It's time to get back to work and life. You wasting away in here isn't going to fix your relationship with Sabrina."

Justin laughed harshly and pulled the blanket over his head. "What relationship? There isn't one. She won't return my calls, the letters I sent have *return to sender* written all over them, and in case you haven't noticed, there's a gaping hole in the middle of my chest that once contained my heart," he choked out.

"Really?" Stan replied neutrally. "There's so much grime and dried food on that shirt of yours I couldn't tell."

Justin opened his eyes and had to blink rapidly in an attempt to adjust them to the overwhelming light. "For God's sake, close those things," Justin roared. "The light's too bright!"

"What are you, a damn gremlin?" Stan yelled back. "Get up, Justin. Time to get back to being a real person. I'll give you one minute. If you don't get your stank, disheveled butt out of that bed, I'll get you up."

Justin sat up and glared at his friend. "Oh yeah? You and what army?"

Stan eyed him a moment before putting his fingers in his mouth and whistling loudly.

A few seconds later, footsteps resounded on the floorboards, and two figures appeared at the door.

"What the heck is this?" Justin demanded.

Stan pointed at the door with a jerk of his thumb. "Army." He smiled wickedly.

Dwayne and Adrian came in and stood next to Stan.

Justin looked from left to right and pierced Stan with a venomous look. "I wouldn't advise it."

"Consider this an intervention," Dwayne replied, undaunted by Justin's foul mood.

"So, are you getting up, or do we tip the mattress over and dump your raggedy ass on the floor?" Adrian inquired.

Justin looked directly at him. "I thought you weren't talking to me anymore."

"Your words not mine, Justin. I may not have liked what you did; you may have been justified in assassinating my character and attempting to punch my lights out, but you could've told me what was up from day one. We're supposed to be boys, aren't we? Since when can't we be straight with each other? I could've helped you out, made sure it worked. I mean, if you're going to walk around being me, at least get it right," Adrian mocked. "I'd never wear that crap you had on the night you put me on the concrete. Makes me cringe just thinking about it."

Justin blinked a few times and stared at Adrian.

Adrian held his gaze, but after a few moments a smile crept slowly across his face. "Don't make me get all mushy, Langley. We've been friends since the fourth grade. I think it's going to take a lot more than you telling me off and doing a bad job of being me to end this friendship. We're boys, man. That stuff runs deep." Adrian extended his hand, and after a moment Justin grabbed it. Adrian pulled him up and hugged him. They clapped each other on the back loudly.

"I'm sorry, man," Justin said gruffly, fighting back his emotions.

"Apology accepted," Adrian said distractedly as he checked his shirt for any stains that might have been transferred during the hug. "Do it again and you'll be the one on the concrete, ruining your Armani suit," Adrian remarked gruffly after giving his shirt a final once-over.

"You gonna cry?" Dwayne teased.

"Shut up!" Adrian said, glaring.

Stan the Answer Man took over. "Okay, now that the

group hug is over, I think it's time Justin hit the shower. Lord knows, it's going to take an hour just to get him clean. Dwayne, find someplace for us to go for dinner and make reservations for—" Stan looked at his watch and back to Justin. "Seven. Adrian, call the cleaning service you use and have them come over first thing in the morning. Tell them it's a pigsty, so bring reinforcements. I'll see if I can find something for Robinson Crusoe here to wear."

Justin walked slowly toward the door and turned around at the threshold. He looked at his three best friends and was overwhelmed with gratitude. *At least I've got my friends to help me get over losing you, Sabrina, because, God knows, I can't do it alone.* Justin sighed inwardly.

Chapter Eleven

"**S**o, you ready to talk about it?" Lauren's voice pitched. Her head snapped back from the impact of Sabrina's left jab on the padded cushion she was holding.

Sabrina alternated between gasps of breath and jabs. "Nothing to talk about."

"Uh-huh," Lauren said lowering the pads.

Sabrina frowned and walked over to an elliptical machine. She rapidly keyed in her stats then selected a program. Slowly she moved her legs to start the machine's forward momentum.

Lauren sighed, grabbed the machine next to Sabrina, and followed suit. "Going on another recruiting trip this weekend?"

"No—why?" Sabrina huffed.

"Just wondering. You've been traveling a lot lately."

"That's my job," Sabrina said, panting.

"I know. It's just that you've been volunteering for a lot of out-of-town job fairs, in addition to your scheduled ones. I was just wondering if there's a method to your madness."

Sabrina looked away. "I don't know what you mean."

"Well, then let me spell it out for you—You're running away from dealing with Adrian turned Justin."

Sabrina scoffed. "That's ridiculous. I'm more than over that freak show."

Lauren looked skeptically at her best friend. "Right, then you haven't lost six pounds without even trying? You don't have bags under your eyes that wouldn't be allowed as carry-on luggage at the airport, and you don't stare off into space every time someone isn't having a conversation with you that requires your input?"

Sabrina stopped pedaling. "Been thinking about this much?" Sabrina said dryly. "Look, Lauren, I'm fine. I'm not sitting around pining for that no-good, lying sack of—" Sabrina halted. "Oh, just forget it! He's not worth the air I'm using up talking about him." She stomped into the locker room. Sabrina, intent on opening her locker to get the toiletries needed for her shower, didn't hear Lauren approach.

"There are a few places left in the world where air is free," her friend replied from behind her.

Sabrina sat down heavily on the bench by her locker. "Yeah, but repairing my heart isn't. It's cost me a lot, Lauren—time, effort, and more tissues than I can count. I'm over it. I just want to move on with my life."

"Have you forgotten that I'm your best friend, Brina? If you were over it, just mentioning the man's name wouldn't cause your right eye to twitch. You think I don't know how much you loved Justin?"

Sabrina laughed harshly. "Don't you mean Adrian?"

"Sweetie, I'm not condoning what he did."

"Glad to hear it."

"Still, I can't help wondering what's behind this

adamant stand you've taken not to forgive him. You loved him, Brina. Don't even try denying it. What's more, he was in love with you. Are you really willing to throw all that away because he tried to protect and impress you?"

Sabrina looked at her friend incredulously. "Lauren, he impersonated his best friend. He lied to both of us. I don't care if he thought he was trying to keep me from being embarrassed in front of Christopher! He had every opportunity to tell me the truth. There were numerous chances for him to come clean. He could've done it when Christopher left, the next day, a week later; anything would have been better than waiting until I—"

"Fell in love with him?"

Sabrina grabbed her towel and toiletry bag. "What he did was unforgivable. Besides, I fell in and out of love once before, and I can do it again."

Lauren watched her friend head for the shower. She looked around and, confident she was alone, grabbed her cell phone and dialed a number.

"Hazel? It's Lauren. No, she didn't budge. Listen, we need to put plan B into action. Did you speak with Adrian? Great, I'll call you tonight, and we'll finalize our plans." She hung up and replaced the phone in her locker.

"Well, Brina, the subtle approach didn't work, so I guess it's time for more drastic measures."

Chapter Twelve

Sabrina set the hot dinner plate gingerly on the place mat at the kitchen table. Sitting down, she pulled the napkin ring from around the napkin, placing it to the left of her water glass. After she'd blessed the food, she began eating. After a few bites she looked at her plate in disgust; her meal was as tasteless as the water floating carelessly in her glass. She took a sip of her water to assist her reluctant dinner in its quest to find her stomach.

After a while the blaring silence was more than Sabrina could bear. Getting up she turned the stereo to her favorite jazz station. "See," Sabrina said aloud, "a perfectly enjoyable evening. Just me, myself, and I."

A few minutes later a Kevin Toney song came on. She eyed the traitorous wall unit, as the familiar song floated through the air. Her mind reluctantly recalled a night months ago when she was in Justin's arms and they were swaying provocatively to the sensuous music surrounding them. Her body had ached for him that night, with a force that left her trembling with need. He'd held her in arms which were powerful, yet she felt completely safe. *And loved.*

"Stop it!" Abruptly she strode over and shut the music off with a resounding click. Suddenly Sabrina was taken by an overwhelming urge. Suppressing it didn't help; its pull was strong and unrelenting. As if in a trance, she walked purposefully to the hall table. Sifting through her mail, she found the letter buried under a few promotional flyers and retrieved it. Turning, she flipped the light switch off then climbed the stairs.

Lying down across the bed, Sabrina eyed the letter resolutely. She turned it over repeatedly, running her fingers over its smooth surface before finally breaking the seal. Bold ink and fluid words sprang from the thick, ecru-colored paper. Taking a deep, cleansing breath, she set the written words in motion.

Sabrina,

I beg you not to rip this letter up before you've read what's been on my mind since that night so long ago. I know you don't want to hear "I'm sorry." Truthfully, those two words would buckle under the weight of remorse I'm feeling at this very moment and every moment since you walked away. I'm terrified at how empty I am inside, how I destroyed what was between us. I lied to you, damaged your trust in me, because of my own selfishness and insecurity. I've lost the one thing in this life that's priceless to me—you.

Sabrina had to put the letter aside because she couldn't see any longer. Tears blurred her vision and flowed unreservedly down her face onto the bed linens. Her heart ached with such force she thought it would rupture. Confusion struggled against determination within her. Could she forgive his deception? "Is it even possible?" she cried aloud.

"Why can't we just beat Justin up and put him in the hospital? That's bound to cause Sabrina to realize she loves him and can't live without him."

Stan cracked his friend over the head with the nearest thing he could find—a *TV Guide* magazine. "Dwayne, have you lost your mind?"

"What? It's worked before," Dwayne said stubbornly.

"Where? *The Young and the Restless?* Everyone knows that would never work; besides, everybody feels sorry for people when they're in the hospital. This has to be real, not that Florence Nightingale stuff."

Hazel waved her hands in dismissal. "Enough from the peanut gallery. Lauren, have all the plans been made?"

"Everything is done, Hazel," Lauren assured her. "We're on for seven-thirty. The owner is a friend of mine, so we have as long as we need."

Hazel loved when a good plan was put into action, especially one of hers. Looking at her co-conspirators she nodded approvingly. "Excellent! Adrian, you're on," Hazel said, handing him the phone.

Adrian dialed Justin and worked him for points. Two minutes later the call was complete. He winked at Hazel.

Her robust chest moved spasmodically as she laughed. "Good Lord," she said in awe, "you are your mother's son."

"I learned from the best," Adrian said, smiling. "Justin will be there as planned."

"You're sure he bought it?" Lauren asked.

He arched an eyebrow. "Of course. He thinks I'm tied up showing a multimillion-dollar house in Burr Ridge. He's agreed to meet a client of mine who's relocating, Sasha Mazur, and keep her company until I get there."

"And Brina thinks I twisted my ankle in spinning class," Lauren chimed in. "I asked her to fill in and take our potential hire, Sasha Mazur, out for dinner and then to the airport."

Hazel looked at her watch. "We don't have much time, so places, everybody. This has to work. Two very stubborn and in-love people are counting on us to show them that they'd be better off together than apart."

A look of concern briefly crossed Lauren's face. "I sure hope they see it that way."

Justin arrived at the restaurant five minutes early and was immediately shown to a private room in the back. Looking around he made a mental note of how much this dinner would set Adrian back. *Who am I kidding?* he thought to himself. *This dinner wouldn't put a nick in Adrian's wallet, much less a dent.* Taking a seat, he ordered an iced tea from the waiter. Justin really wasn't in the mood to play the host, especially not to some snobby, rich woman. But things had been going well; his friendship with Adrian was back on track, and they were as tight as they used to be. If only his love life would follow suit.

He still hadn't heard anything from Sabrina. She hadn't sent his last letter back, which had given him hope. That had been more than a week ago. Each day that passed since had plunged his optimism deeper into despair. His mind insisted he should let her go, but his heart refused to follow suit. He was swirling his iced tea around, deep in thought, when he heard the door open behind him.

Suddenly he wasn't in the mood to entertain some

stranger. He'd explain that Adrian was delayed but would be arriving shortly, and then he was out of there. Pleased with his plan, he took another sip of tea and stood when he saw a shadow above the table. He looked up and promptly choked on the liquid sliding down his throat.

It took a few seconds of the waiter patting him rapidly on the back before he was able to breathe again.

All the while Sabrina was standing, pale faced, in front of him. "What are you doing here?" she croaked, when she'd found her voice.

"Meeting a client of Adrian's," Justin rasped out. "What are you doing here?"

"I'm here meeting a potential hire. Obviously they've sent me to the wrong table. If you'll excuse me, I'll go find out where Ms. Mazur's table is."

Justin's next words stopped her cold. "Mazur? Sasha Mazur?"

"Yes," Sabrina said with surprise. "How do you know her?"

"I don't. I'm meeting her for dinner, and I'm supposed to keep her occupied until Adrian gets here."

"I'll bet," Sabrina said distrustfully.

"What's with the tone?" Justin asked.

"Oh, nothing. I see you two are up to the old bait-and-switch thing again. I guess it's Adrian's turn this time," she said frostily.

"Of course not," Justin said indignantly. "Look, something's going on, but I had nothing to do with it. We're both supposedly here to meet the same person—you don't find that a bit odd?"

"Oh, come off it. It's not like I have that much experience being able to trust you." Sabrina laughed bitterly.

Justin took a deep breath and tried to remain calm. "Brina, I've tried numerous times and ways to show you how bad I feel about deceiving you."

"I'm not interested in anything you have to show me. Give my regrets to Ms. Mazur for being the next unlucky victim," Sabrina said frostily and strode off. She gave the door a firm tug. She tried again, but the door didn't budge.

"Trying to perfect your exit?" Justin said testily.

"Hardly," Sabrina barked. "It would appear the door is locked."

"Easy, Brina, I just asked. You don't have to bite my head off."

"If it were up to me, you wouldn't have a head, and stop calling me Brina. That's a name reserved for my close friends and loved ones." She turned and looked at him pointedly. "Neither of those apply to you anymore." Sabrina tried the door again to no avail. She banged on it in frustration. She'd been set up, again, and she held Justin fully responsible. Turning around, Sabrina leaned against the door in exasperation. "So, how long are we in here for?"

Justin shrugged and leaned against a nearby settee. "How the heck should I know? I'm not the one who locked us in here."

"Well . . . can you hear anything? Are they talking?" Hazel asked impatiently.

"Not right now," Lauren whispered. "At least the banging's stopped. That's got to be a good sign, right?"

"Unless she's slashed him with her butter knife," Dwayne interjected.

"Dwayne!" everyone whispered loudly.

"What? I'm just trying to ease the tension."

"How about easing your butt into the nearest chair and keeping quiet before they hear us out here," Stan barked.

Justin's eyes roamed over Sabrina's figure. There were only slight differences in her appearance since the last time he'd seen her. He noticed she'd lost some weight and there were slight smudges underneath her eyes, but other than that, she looked the same. *Incredible.* He sensed her animosity toward him, realized it was justified, but it still hurt. "Would you like some iced tea?" Justin pointed to his table. "The waiter left the pitcher."

Sabrina didn't bother looking up. "No, thank you."

Justin sighed. "Sabrina, I had nothing to do with this. You've got to believe me. It's obviously one of our friends playing a trick on us."

Sabrina wrapped her arms protectively around herself, shivering slightly. "Why would they do that? They should know by now how we feel about each other."

"I know how I feel about you. My feelings haven't changed."

"Well, poor you," she shot back.

"You don't know the half of it," he said without thinking. "Looking at you now makes the pain more unbearable. It was better when you were just an image in my head—a splendidly vivid, desirable memory that didn't walk, breathe, and hate me beyond redemption."

"I don't hate you." The words hung in the air between them. Sabrina wished she hadn't said them, but it was too late for regrets.

"You don't?"

She shook her head.

"But you don't trust me," he stated flatly.

"How can you expect me to? You lied to me, Justin. I don't think I can ever get over that." Her voice trembled.

"Well, can you get around it?" Justin pleaded softly. He walked closer to her but didn't sit down. He longed to erase the damage he'd done but knew that feat was impossible.

"What's that supposed to mean?" Sabrina replied warily.

Justin knelt beside her. He didn't attempt to touch her, even though the ache inside him begged him to. "It means I can't undo the disaster I've made of this relationship but, Sabrina, I beg you to give me a chance to make things right between us. I've been living in hell since you left me. I deserve to—I know that. I'm the one who screwed this up. I am desperate for you to give me another try, to trust me to take care of your heart and not break it this time. Please, just consider it?" His voice broke under the heaviness of his heart.

Tears streamed down Sabrina's face. She tried, but words wouldn't come. They couldn't come.

Justin stood and blinked away the moistness that pooled around his eyes. He interpreted her action to mean no. He'd lost. Again.

Dejectedly Justin walked over to the door and pounded on it. "Open up!" he yelled threateningly. "The experiment is over. It failed. Let us out of here before I break this door down!"

After a few moments of excruciating silence the door opened. Justin wasn't surprised as their five jailers filed in one by one. There was an elderly lady bringing up the rear, who he assumed was the warden and Sabrina's aunt Hazel.

Hazel stated the obvious. "So, you two kids talked?"

"Oh yeah, we talked," Justin replied sadly. "Toward the end I did most of the talking and Br—Sabrina listened. I suppose that's more than my behavior warranted." He sighed. Walking on legs that supported him valiantly, he passed the crowd of people.

As he went by, Adrian put a hand on his shoulder and stopped him. "I'm sorry, man, really."

Justin saw genuine concern in his friend's face and smiled. "Thanks, man," he replied and walked out of the room.

Chapter Thirteen

Sabrina heard the doorbell ring and groaned. Frantically she dabbed her tear-soaked eyes with the back of her terry-cloth bathrobe. Rolling off the couch, she took her time walking to the door. She quirked an eyebrow and pulled the door open. "Dad, what are you doing here?"

Charles Ridgemont stepped into the foyer. "Hazel is driving me crazy."

Sabrina took his coat and hung it in the hall closet. "That doesn't surprise me. For two siblings who live together, you two get along like cats and dogs. Can I get you anything?" Sabrina asked, wrapping her arm around her father's middle.

"We get along just fine, as long as Hazel isn't being a busybody. Which, now that I think about it, is all the time, so I guess I should move out, huh?" Her father sighed.

Sabrina looked up at her father with amusement. He

tried but couldn't keep the smile out of his rich, brown eyes.

"You two are hopeless." Sabrina laughed. "Come on, I'll make you a toddy."

Her father's toddy turned out to be a large cup of coffee-blended hot chocolate with a large dollop of whipped cream on top. She carefully slid the tall, black ceramic cup in front of her father. He looked like a kid getting a big, unexpected bowl of ice cream. Sabrina sat across from him at the Corian-topped island and swirled her whipped cream around with a teaspoon.

"Hazel told me what happened," he said between sips.

"I figured she would." Sabrina blew her coffee-cocoa mixture. "I suppose she needed another ally to aid her noble cause."

"Sweetheart, you know I'm not here to try to pressure you into anything. I just wanted to see how you're doing."

"I'm fine, Daddy." Sabrina smiled reassuringly.

"I can see that," her father said, running a finger under her swollen, bloodshot eyes. "I know why you're not being straight with your family and friends; question is, why you're lying to yourself."

Sabrina reared back so suddenly she almost toppled off her stool.

"Sweetheart, do you think this is what your mother wanted for you? To be held up in your big, fancy, professionally landscaped house in your bathrobe, crying your eyes out and being miserable?"

"Daddy, I can't go through what I did with Christopher. It was too much," she whispered.

Her father squeezed her hand in his. "I know it was, baby. That was a tragic time for you, losing your mother and the breakup with an idiot who didn't deserve the slack you cut him."

"Daddy, no need to open this up again," Sabrina said before he went off on a tangent. "I'll never have what you and Mom did."

"Of course you won't, if you close yourself off to keep from getting hurt."

"More hurt. The operative word is *more*." Sabrina went to the sink and looked out the window. Her reflection stared back at her. "I've thrown myself out there twice, and look what happened. I'm a magnet for men who will only end up breaking my heart. Honestly, Dad, I'm all cried out."

Charles turned and observed his daughter knowingly. "Sabrina, don't let your fear paralyze you. You think your mother and I didn't have our ups and downs? We did. Like every married couple we had our doubts and fears. There was a time when we even contemplated divorce," her father admitted.

Sabrina spun around with wide eyes. "What?" she said in shock. "Why didn't you ever tell me?"

He shrugged. "Because some troubles can only be worked out between the two people involved. Besides, we got past it, so there wasn't a need to worry our daughter."

"So you're saying I should have forgiven him?"

"What? No! That bastard got what he deserved!" her father said angrily. "He was lucky I didn't shoot him."

"Dad, you have a pellet gun," Sabrina reminded him gently.

He took a sip of coffee and looked indignant. "That's because your mother refused to let me keep a real one in the house. But don't fool yourself, young lady, a well-placed pellet can bring a man to his knees."

Sabrina giggled and took her seat across from him.

"Anyway, the point I was trying to make, sweetheart,

is that nothing is guaranteed to run smoothly all the time. There are ups and downs in any relationship. You and Justin will have to work this out between the two of you. Granted, I haven't met the young man." Her father eyed her reproachfully. "But from what Hazel tells me, he's a good one, when he isn't impersonating people," her father added with a smile. He stood and hugged her.

Sabrina returned the hug and walked him to the door.

He pulled his coat from the closet and put it on. "All I'm saying is, be true to your heart, Brina. It's the most precious commodity you have. It's important you keep others from breaking it," he cautioned. "But most importantly, you have to make sure you don't break it yourself. Fear is a powerful weapon when wielded correctly."

Sabrina nodded and kissed her father good-bye. "You're such a sage, man."

"The way your mother used to tell it, she taught me everything I know." He chuckled. "Thanks for the toddy, honey. You know your aunt never fails to get the proportions wrong. Between you and me, I think she does it on purpose."

He was almost out the door, when Sabrina grabbed his arm. "Dad? What if it's too late? I let him go twice. What if he doesn't want me back?" she asked shakily.

"Oh honey, don't you know how special you are? Everyone can see it. It's time you did too. You're worth any hurdle that young man has to cross to win your heart. Give yourself the credit you deserve, Sabrina." He rubbed a finger against her cheek and winked.

"I love you, Daddy," she whispered.

"And I, you, sweetheart."

Sabrina shut her door and leaned heavily against it.

Taking a deep breath, she closed her eyes. *Mom, is love ever simple?* She used to ask her mother that all the time.

Instantly she heard her mother's voice as clearly as her own. *"Brina, darling, love is many things, but simple, it ain't!"*

Chapter Fourteen

Justin leaned against the rails of his balcony and stared bleakly into the night. He longed to call his sister, Shelley, to get advice, but he couldn't. His family would have a conniption when they found out about the chaos his life had become, the secret he'd kept from them. Someday he'd tell them everything, but it was too soon. He couldn't take the looks of sympathy he'd get from his mother and sister.

Ominous clouds gathered in the pitch-black sky, and the air smelled heavy with rain.

"Great, just what I need, a storm to rival my crappy mood," Justin said sardonically.

He was just about to go in, when he heard a woman's voice below him.

"Excuse me, sir, could I trouble you for a ladder?"

Puzzled, Justin leaned farther over the balcony and stared at the woman below. He gasped and blinked several times to make sure he wasn't hallucinating. "Sabrina?" he said unbelievingly.

"Well, it would be if you'd answer your door. I've been knocking on it for a few minutes now."

Justin stupidly looked at the door in question then back over the balcony. "Where? How? I didn't know you knew where I lived."

"Aunt Hazel was nice enough to give me Adrian's number, and he was more than happy to give me your address."

A clap of thunder, combined with a sudden gust of wind, announced the impending storm.

"Um, I'm getting a crook in my neck talking this way; plus, I think it's about to rain. If you aren't sending down that ladder, would you mind opening your door?"

Justin jumped as if he'd been hit by lightning. "Oh! I'll go open the door now. Come on up!" he said, rushing into the house.

Shutting the balcony door, Justin spun around in a complete circle, making sure everything was relatively decent. He ran to the bathroom to check his appearance. Cupping his hand, he breathed loudly into it. Grimacing, he wrenched open his medicine cabinet and grabbed the Listerine bottle. He combed his hair while swishing the fiery liquid around his mouth. "Uh!" He almost screamed after he'd spit the liquid gratefully down the drain. He hated Listerine.

This time he heard the door when Sabrina knocked. He gave himself a final once-over, tucking his T-shirt inside his jeans while he walked. Opening the front door, he just stood there. It was Sabrina, in all her splendid beauty. *Invite her in,* he chided himself. "Hi," he said.

"Hi yourself," Sabrina replied.

He stood aside awkwardly as she walked in. He'd forgotten to move out of the way, so she had to turn sideways to get by him. When her side connected with his stomach, he nearly stopped breathing. He did remember to take her coat before inviting her to sit.

"Can I get you anything?" he inquired politely.

Yes. You in a delectable gift basket marked FOREVER, she thought to herself. "No, thanks. I'm fine."

You're way past fine, his mind screamed. "I'm sorry I didn't hear the door last time you knocked. I was out on the balcony."

Sabrina noted the short distance between both doors. "Deep in thought?"

"Something like that." Justin sat down a considerable distance from her. After passing several seconds in silence, he cleared his throat nervously. "Don't take this the wrong way, Sabrina, but what are you doing here?"

Looking down at her hands Sabrina prayed she'd get everything out before she lost her nerve, wrote happiness off as unlikely, then bolted from his house. Taking a deep breath, Sabrina squared her shoulders and looked at him. "Things ended rather badly the last time we were together."

"That was twenty-four hours ago. To be honest, I didn't think I'd ever see you again, much less this soon. You told me you couldn't forgive me. I figured by your silence there wasn't anything left to be said." His jaw clenched, remembering the second time his heart had been ripped out of his chest.

"I know," Sabrina said softly. "I was feeling overwhelmed earlier. I wasn't ready to sort out the jumbled emotions running through me."

His pulse raced wildly when he looked at her. He didn't think he could survive another frontal attack. Flexing his hands in an effort to calm himself, he prayed his voice sounded casual as he repeated the words she'd used before. "And now?"

Although he was sitting some distance away, he was

close enough for Sabrina to smell the unique blend of Cool Mint Listerine and men's cologne.

That's got to be a good sign, right? I mean, he wouldn't go through all that trouble unless he was still interested. The possibility had a heady effect on her. She stood to put some space between them while she calmed herself. "You've got a great apartment, Justin. I love the view." She opened the door and all but ran onto his balcony. "Wow, you can see the lake from here," she called over her shoulder. She shrieked in surprise because he was right behind her.

"Sorry, Brina, I didn't mean to scare you," he said in that mellow voice that drove her crazy.

Brina. He called me Brina. Her heart soared. "You don't scare me," she said breathlessly.

Justin thought getting the answer to his question was worth the risk of possible mortal danger. He leaned in closer and caressed her with his voice and his nearness. "What do I do to you?"

She swallowed with difficulty because her throat was as dry as sandpaper. His close proximity was fanning flames that had been simmering under the surface, longing to be enlarged into a full-scale inferno. Her hand came up to her chest. "Well, right now you're making it pretty difficult for me to breathe," she said slowly.

Justin had to ball his hands into fists to keep from touching her. Even now, after everything, her nearness could still undo him. "I've got a lot of experience with that. From the moment we met, I've had more joy than I've ever known and more torment and pain than I ever thought I could bear. Sabrina, I need to know what you've decided," he pleaded. "Can you trust me to take care of your heart?"

The tears pooling in Sabrina's eyes blinded her. When she finally remembered how to blink, they slid in a torrent down her face. "You didn't promise not to break it this time," she choked.

"You're right," he said, nodding. "I can't guarantee not to break it, Brina, though I can promise to keep the knocks and dings to a minimum." He smiled warmly.

"Fair enough." Sabrina's eyes sparkled through the tears. "There's a lot we'll have to work through," she said seriously.

Justin wiped the tears from her cheeks. "I know."

She closed her eyes and had to concentrate on not leaning into his touch. "It's going to take a while to get to know each other again, you know, without all the drama."

"Absolutely."

Sabrina noted the muscle flexing in his jaw, the restrained desire turning his hazel eyes into smoldering embers and the barely controlled need emanating from his incredible body. The combination was too exhilarating for her to ignore. She felt the heat rising within her, her body responding to a subliminal plea from his. To deny the love that flowed between them would take more strength than her body, heart or soul possessed. Sabrina decided it was time to follow her heart. Looking into his eyes she showed him what he needed to see, the love that she'd held carefully in check, until now.

Justin eyed her lips with avid fascination. When his gaze reached her eyes, he sucked in a harsh breath at the love displayed there.

"Can't we just skip to the part where you're kissing me?" she implored.

Justin sagged with relief and was overcome with emotion at seeing her compliance, her love, and, unbelievably, her trust. Pulling her into his arms, he kissed her like he'd been searching his whole life just for her and had finally found the object of his desire. "I love you, Sabrina Ridgemont," he whispered solemnly.

"And I love you, Justin Langley." She wrapped her arms around his neck and kissed him.

As their lips connected, the surroundings slowly faded into oblivion. The storm clouds that had been threatening the sky above traveled slowly by, as if reluctant to intrude upon the couple below and their idyllic moment.

Epilogue

Justin grinned as the cork broke free from the champagne bottle with a resounding pop. The crowd of family and friends cheered as he poured the effervescent liquid into a flute glass and handed it to Sabrina. She accepted it, waiting patiently, while he poured himself a goblet then passed the bottle to the nearby waiter.

Once all the flutes were filled, Justin cleared his throat, wrapped his free hand around Sabrina's waist, and began, "To my gorgeous, intelligent, adorable wife. This past year has given me more happiness and wedded bliss than I ever imagined was possible. Our beginning started out a little shaky, but never doubt how I feel about you. I love you with everything I am, Brina, and I look forward to the rest of my life with you by my side."

"Here, here," everyone around them said in unison, as they all toasted the happy couple.

Beaming proudly, Justin's mother, Harriette Langley, a portly woman, raised her glass. "I know I'm looking forward to some grandchildren." She laughed robustly.

"Mom, we're trying as hard as we can." Justin winked as Sabrina blushed.

His father, George, an equally stout man, leaned over to his son and said in a voice for his ears only, "You owe me twenty bucks."

Justin nodded prior to taking a sip from his glass.

Adrian came over to Justin and elbowed his best friend in the ribs. "I'm glad you got married, but you realize you've taken my mother to a whole new level of desperation?"

"I heard that, Adrian," Norma Jean said loudly from across the room.

Adrian gave her his best smile. "I'll bet you did, Mother."

Justin's sister, Shelley, came up and wrapped her lithe body around Adrian. She and Justin hadn't inherited their parents' tendency to gain weight and not let go of it.

Adrian smiled down affectionately at his "little sister." "Hey, squirt."

"Where's Jennifer, Adrian?" she inquired. "I thought for sure you'd bring her to the party."

"I don't think Adrian was ready to risk a full-out war to get him married," Sabrina said to her sister-in-law, while kissing the best man on the cheek.

"I think not," Adrian said, laughing. "The last thing I need is my mom, your mom, and Sabrina's aunt swooping down on Jenny, filling her head with all sorts of craziness. Things are just starting to head in the right direction. Personally, I'd like to keep it that way."

"That means he hasn't knocked the ball out of the park yet," Stan said, joining the small group.

"I'll have you know we're mixing business with pleasure quite nicely, thank you." Adrian eyed Stan pointedly.

"Uh-huh, that means he's still in pursuit mode," Dwayne added from across the room.

"Dwayne," Adrian said sweetly, "don't you have to pick Tracey up from work?"

Dwayne gasped then looked at his watch. "You're right. I'll catch up with you guys later. Sabrina, thanks for the invite and congrats!" Dwayne said, running out the front door.

Sabrina leaned up and kissed her husband on the lips. "Excuse me, I'm off to see what the ladies in question are up to."

Adrian called after her, "No good, that's what!"

"Oh, don't get all cranky just because your days are numbered," Justin teased.

Adrian didn't find it amusing. "Ha! In your dreams, Langley. The day I get all whipped over a woman is the day I'll tattoo your name on my butt!" He scoffed, taking a healthy drink of his champagne.

Justin opened his jacket to retrieve a small notebook. Taking out a pen he scribbled a few lines and put it back.

"What was that?" Stan asked curiously.

"Oh nothing. I'm just writing the date, time, and promise that Adrian just made. That way when he falls in love and loses what little sense he has over her, I'll remind him of the foot he stuck in his mouth."

Sabrina passed her father and father-in-law on the way to the kitchen. "Having a nice time, gentlemen?"

"We'll be having an even better time when you get those waiters to stop serving all those girly sandwiches and get to the real food!" Justin's father told her.

"I'll see what I can do, George." Sabrina kissed them both on the cheek.

When she reached the kitchen, it was to find the four ladies in question hunched over her dining table like they were in a football huddle. She stood just inside the door, watching the ladies with interest. "Just what's going on in here? Aunt Hazel, I'd have thought you and Jeanie had learned your lesson by now. I see you've recruited Lauren and Justin's mother for your campaign."

"Hey, I'm just along for the ride," Lauren replied.

"Child, the only lesson we've learned is that we need to take a more indirect approach next time," Adrian's mother concluded.

"We could use reverse psychology," Harriette chimed in. "I read somewhere that—"

"Mother!" Shelley gasped from the doorway.

Sabrina decided to leave the love brokers to their task. Craving a few minutes of solitude, she slipped quietly out of the house onto the patio. The air was crisp but not cold enough that she required a coat. Wrapping her arms around her waist, she closed her eyes and inhaled the chilled air.

So much had changed in the last year—she'd married the man of her dreams, was welcomed with open arms into his family, and had gained an extended circle of friends. She was surrounded by love and basked in its warmth. The only element missing from this joyous, wedded bliss was her mother, but Sabrina knew her mom was watching over her and would be pleased with Justin.

"What's my beautiful wife doing out here all alone?" Justin asked, sliding his arms around her middle.

She leaned back against him. "Waiting for you."

Justin kissed her softly on the neck. "Good answer, Mrs. Langley."

Sabrina turned in his arms and wrapped hers around his neck. "Enjoying your anniversary party, Mr. Langley?"

"I'll be enjoying it a whole lot better tonight." He grinned wickedly.

Sabrina kissed him longingly. "I do love how you think."

"Somehow, I don't think you married me just for my mind." Justin smiled down at his wife.

Sabrina leaned up and whispered into her husband's ear. "Somehow, I think you're right."

THE JUDAS
KILLER

by
Jon Sharpe

Ⓢ
A SIGNET BOOK
NEW AMERICAN LIBRARY
TIMES MIRROR

NAL BOOKS ARE AVAILABLE AT QUANTITY DISCOUNTS
WHEN USED TO PROMOTE PRODUCTS OR SERVICES.
FOR INFORMATION PLEASE WRITE TO PREMIUM MARKETING DIVISION,
THE NEW AMERICAN LIBRARY, INC., 1633 BROADWAY,
NEW YORK, NEW YORK 10019.

SIGNET TRADEMARK REG. U.S. PAT. OFF. AND FOREIGN COUNTRIES
REGISTERED TRADEMARK—MARCA REGISTRADA
HECHO EN CHICAGO, U.S.A.

SIGNET, SIGNET CLASSIC, MENTOR, PLUME, MERIDIAN and NAL BOOKS are published by The New American Library, Inc., 1633 Broadway, New York, New York 10019

First Printing, August, 1983

1 2 3 4 5 6 7 8 9

PRINTED IN THE UNITED STATES OF AMERICA